THE PROFESSOR,

A Tale

THE PROFESSOR,

A Tale.

BY

CURRER BELL

(Charlotte Brontë)

IN TWO VOLUMES.

VOL. I.

GYAN

Published by

GYAN

Gyan Publishing House
5, Ansari Road
Daryaganj, New Delhi-110002
Phone: 011-47034999, 9811692060
E-mail: books@gyanbooks.com

Distribution Network
gyanbooks.com
India, USA, Canada, UK, Australia

ISBN: 978-81-212-0651-8 (Set)
978-81-212-0657-0 (HB)
First Published, 1857

2nd Impression 2024

Printed at: Gyan Press, Delhi.

THE PROFESSOR, A TALE (VOL. I.)
Author: CURRER BELL (CHARLOTTE BRONTË)

THE PROFESSOR;

A Tale.

THE PROFESSOR,

A Tale.

BY

CURRER BELL,

AUTHOR OF "JANE EYRE," "SHIRLEY," "VILLETTE," &C.

IN TWO VOLUMES.

VOL. I.

LONDON:
SMITH, ELDER & CO., 65, CORNHILL.

1857.

PREFACE.

THIS little book was written before either "Jane Eyre" or "Shirley," and yet no indulgence can be solicited for it on the plea of a first attempt. A first attempt it certainly was not, as the pen which wrote it had been previously worn a good deal in a practice of some years. I had not indeed published anything before I commenced "The Professor," but in many a crude effort, destroyed almost as soon as composed, I had got over any such taste as I might once have had for ornamented and redundant composition, and come to prefer what was plain and homely. At the same time I had adopted a set of principles on the subject of incident, &c., such as would be generally approved in theory, but the result of which, when carried out into practice, often procures for an author more surprise than pleasure.

I said to myself that my hero should work his way through life as I had seen real living men work theirs—that he should never get a shilling he had not earned—that no sudden turns should lift him in a moment to wealth and high station; that whatever small competency he might gain, should be won by the sweat of his brow; that, before he could find so much as an arbour to sit down in, he should master at least half the ascent of "the Hill of Difficulty;" that he should not even marry a beautiful girl or a lady of rank. As Adam's son he should share Adam's doom, and drain throughout life a mixed and moderate cup of enjoyment.

In the sequel, however, I found that publishers in general scarcely approved of this system, but would have liked something more imaginative and poetical—something more consonant with a highly wrought fancy, with a taste for pathos, with sentiments more tender, elevated, unworldly. Indeed until an author has tried to dispose of a manuscript of this kind, he can never know what stores of romance and sensibility lie hidden in breasts he would not have suspected of casketing such treasures. Men in business are usually thought to prefer the real; on trial the idea will be often found fallacious: a passionate preference for the wild, wonderful, and thrilling—the strange, startling, and harrowing—agitates divers souls that show a calm and sober surface.

Such being the case, the reader will comprehend that to have reached him in the form of a printed book, this brief narrative must have gone through some struggles—which indeed it has. And after all, its worst struggle and strongest ordeal is yet to come; but it takes comfort—subdues fear—leans on the staff of a moderate expectation—and mutters under its breath, while lifting its eye to that of the public,

"He that is low need fear no fall."

CURRER BELL.

The foregoing preface was written by my wife with a view to the publication of "The Professor," shortly after the appearance of "Shirley." Being dissuaded from her intention, the authoress made some use of the materials in a subsequent work—"Villette." As, however, these two stories are in most respects unlike, it has been represented to me that I ought not to withhold "The Professor" from the public. I have therefore consented to its publication.

A. B. NICHOLLS.

Haworth Parsonage,
September 22nd, 1856.

THE PROFESSOR.

CHAPTER I.

INTRODUCTORY.

THE other day, in looking over my papers, I found in my desk the following copy of a letter, sent by me a year since to an old school acquaintance:—

"DEAR CHARLES,

"I think when you and I were at Eton together, we were neither of us what could be called popular characters: you were a sarcastic, observant, shrewd, cold-blooded creature; my own portrait I will not attempt to draw, but I cannot recollect that it was a strikingly attractive one—can you? What animal magnetism drew thee and me together I know not; certainly I never experienced anything of the Pylades and Orestes sentiment for you, and I have reason to believe that you, on your part, were equally free from all romantic regard to me. Still, out of school hours, we walked and talked continually together; when the theme of conversation was our companions or our masters we understood each other, and when I recurred to some sentiment of affection, some vague love of an excellent or beautiful object, whether in animate or inanimate nature, your sardonic coldness did not move me. I felt myself superior to that check *then* as I do *now*.

"It is a long time since I wrote to you, and a still longer time since I saw you. Chancing to take up a newspaper of your county the other day, my eye fell upon your name. I began to think of old times; to run over the events which have transpired since we separated; and I sat down and commenced this letter. What you have been doing I know not; but you shall hear, if you choose to listen, how the world has wagged with me.

"First, after leaving Eton, I had an interview with my maternal uncles, Lord Tynedale and the Hon. John Seacombe. They asked me if I would enter the Church, and my uncle the nobleman offered me the living of Seacombe, which is in his gift, if I would; then my other uncle, Mr. Seacombe, hinted that when I became rector of Seacombe-cum-Scaife, I might perhaps be allowed to take, as mistress of my house and head of my parish, one of my six cousins, his daughters, all of whom I greatly dislike.

"I declined both the Church and matrimony. A good clergyman is a good thing, but I should have made a very bad one. As to the wife—oh how like a night-mare is the thought of being bound for life to one of my cousins! No doubt they are accomplished and pretty; but not an accomplishment, not a charm of theirs, touches a chord in my bosom. To think of passing the winter evenings by the parlour fire-side of Seacombe Rectory alone with one of them — for instance, the large and well-modelled statue, Sarah — no; I should be a bad husband, under such circumstances, as well as a bad clergyman.

"When I had declined my uncles' offers they asked me 'what I intended to do.' I said I should reflect. They reminded me that I had no fortune, and no expectation of any, and, after a considerable pause, Lord Tynedale demanded sternly, 'Whether I had thoughts of following my father's steps and engaging in trade?' Now, I had had no thoughts of the sort. I do not think that my turn of mind qualifies me to make a good tradesman; my taste, my ambition does not lie that way; but such was the scorn expressed in Lord Tynedale's countenance as he pronounced the word *trade*—such the contemptuous sarcasm of his tone—that I was instantly decided. My father was but a name to me, yet that name I did not like to hear mentioned with a sneer to my very face. I answered then, with haste and warmth, 'I cannot do better than follow in my father's steps; yes, I will be a tradesman.' My uncles did not remonstrate; they and I parted with mutual disgust. In reviewing this transaction I find that I was quite right to shake off the burden of Tynedale's patronage, but a fool to offer my shoulders instantly for the reception of another burden—one which might be more intolerable, and which certainly was yet untried.

"I wrote instantly to Edward—you know Edward—my only brother, ten years my senior, married to a rich millowner's daughter, and now possessor of the mill and business which was my father's before he failed. You are aware that my father—once reckoned a Crœsus of wealth—became bankrupt a short time previous to his death, and that my mother lived in destitution for some six months after him, unhelped by her aristocratical brothers, whom she had mortally offended by her union with Crimsworth, the ——shire manufacturer. At the end of the six months she brought me into the world, and then herself left it without, I should think, much regret, as it contained little hope or comfort for her.

"My father's relations took charge of Edward, as they did of me, till I was nine years old. At that period it chanced that the representation of an important borough in our county fell vacant; Mr. Seacombe stood for it. My uncle, Crimsworth, an astute, mercantile man, took the opportunity of writing a fierce letter to the candidate, stating that if he and Lord Tynedale did not consent to do something towards the support of their sister's orphan children he would expose their relentless and malignant conduct towards that sister, and do his best to turn the circumstances against Mr. Seacombe's election. That gentleman and Lord T. knew well enough that the Crimsworths were an unscrupulous and determined race; they knew also that they had influence in the borough of X——; and, making a virtue of necessity, they consented to defray the expenses of my education. I was sent to Eton, where I remained ten years, during which space of time Edward and I never met. He, when he grew up, entered into trade, and pursued his calling with such diligence, ability, and success, that now, in his thirtieth year, he was fast making a fortune. Of this I was apprised by the occasional short letters I received from him, some three or four times a year; which said letters never concluded without some expression of determined enmity against the house of Seacombe, and some reproach to me for living, as he said, on the bounty of that house. At first, while still in boyhood, I could not understand why, as I had no parents, I should not be indebted to my uncles Tynedale and Seacombe for my education; but as I grew up, and heard by degrees of the persevering hostility, the hatred till death evinced by them against my father—of the sufferings of my mother—of all the wrongs, in short, of our house—then did I conceive shame of the dependence in which I lived, and form a resolution no more to take bread from hands which had refused to minister to the necessities of my dying mother. It was by these feelings I was influenced when I refused the Rectory of Seacombe, and the union with one of my patrician cousins.

"An irreparable breach thus being effected between my uncles and myself, I wrote to Edward; told him what had occurred, and informed him of my intention to follow his steps and be a tradesman. I asked, moreover, if he could give me employment. His answer expressed no approbation of my conduct, but he said I might come down to ——shire, if I liked, and he would 'see what could be done in the way of furnishing me with work.' I repressed all—even *mental* comment on his note—packed my trunk and carpet-bag, and started for the North directly.

"After two days' travelling (railroads were not then in existence) I arrived, one wet October afternoon, in the town of X——. I had always understood that Edward lived in this town, but on inquiry I found that it was only Mr. Crimsworth's mill and warehouse which were situated in the smoky atmosphere of Bigben Close; his *residence* lay four miles out, in the country.

"It was late in the evening when I alighted at the gates of the habitation designated to me as my brother's. As I advanced up the avenue, I could see through the shades of twilight, and the dark gloomy mists which deepened those shades, that the house was large, and the grounds surrounding it sufficiently spacious. I paused a moment on the lawn in front, and leaning my back against a tall tree which rose in the centre, I gazed with interest on the exterior of Crimsworth Hall.

"'Edward is rich,' thought I to myself. 'I believed him to be doing well—but I did not know he was master of a mansion like this.' Cutting short all marvelling, speculation, conjecture, &c., I advanced to the front door and rang. A man-servant opened it—I announced myself—he relieved me of my wet cloak and carpet-bag, and ushered me into a room furnished as a library, where there was a bright fire, and candles burning on the table; he informed me that his master was not yet returned from X—— market, but that he would certainly be at home in the course of half an hour.

"Being left to myself, I took the stuffed easy chair, covered with red morocco, which stood by the fireside, and while my eyes watched the flames dart from the glowing coals, and the cinders fall at intervals on the hearth, my mind busied itself in conjectures concerning the meeting about to take place. Amidst much that was doubtful in the subject of these conjectures, there was one thing tolerably certain—I was in no danger of encountering severe disappointment; from this, the moderation of my expectations guaranteed me. I anticipated no overflowings of fraternal tenderness; Edward's letters had always been such as to prevent the engendering or harbouring of delusions of this sort. Still, as I sat awaiting his arrival, I felt eager—very eager—I cannot tell you why; my hand, so utterly a stranger to the grasp of a kindred hand, clenched itself to repress the tremor with which impatience would fain have shaken it.

"I thought of my uncles; and as I was engaged in wondering whether Edward's indifference would equal the cold disdain I had always experienced from them, I heard the avenue gates open: wheels approached the house; Mr. Crimsworth was arrived; and after the lapse of some minutes, and a brief dialogue between himself and his servant in the hall, his tread drew near the library door—that tread alone announced the master of the house.

"I still retained some confused recollection of Edward as he was ten years ago—a tall, wiry, raw youth; *now*, as I rose from my seat and turned towards the library door, I saw a fine-looking and powerful man, light-complexioned, well-made, and of athletic proportions; the first glance made me aware of an air of promptitude and sharpness, shown as well in his movements as in his port, his eye, and the general expression of his face. He greeted me with brevity, and, in the moment of shaking hands, scanned me from head to foot; he took his seat in the morocco-covered arm-chair, and motioned me to another seat.

"'I expected you would have called at the counting-house in the Close,' said he; and his voice, I noticed, had an abrupt accent, probably habitual to him; he spoke also with a guttural northern tone, which sounded harsh in my ears, accustomed to the silvery utterance of the South.

"'The landlord of the inn, where the coach stopped, directed me here,' said I. 'I doubted at first the accuracy of his information, not being aware that you had such a residence as this.'

"'Oh, it is all right!' he replied, 'only I was kept half an hour behind time, waiting for you—that is all. I thought you must be coming by the eight o'clock coach.'

"I expressed regret that he had had to wait; he made no answer, but stirred the fire, as if to cover a movement of impatience; then he scanned me again.

"I felt an inward satisfaction that I had not, in the first moment of meeting, betrayed any warmth, any enthusiasm; that I had saluted this man with a quiet and steady phlegm.

"'Have you quite broken with Tynedale and Seacombe?' he asked hastily.

"'I do not think I shall have any further communication with them; my refusal of their proposals will, I fancy, operate as a barrier against all future intercourse.'

"'Why,' said he, 'I may as well remind you

at the very outset of our connection, that "no man can serve two masters." Acquaintance with Lord Tynedale will be incompatible with assistance from me.' There was a kind of gratuitous menace in his eye as he looked at me in finishing this observation.

"Feeling no disposition to reply to him, I contented myself with an inward speculation on the differences which exist in the constitution of men's minds. I do not know what inference Mr. Crimsworth drew from my silence—whether he considered it a symptom of contumacity or an evidence of my being cowed by his peremptory manner. After a long and hard stare at me, he rose sharply from his seat.

"'To-morrow,' said he, 'I shall call your attention to some other points; but now it is supper time, and Mrs. Crimsworth is probably waiting; will you come?'

"He strode from the room, and I followed. In crossing the hall, I wondered what Mrs. Crimsworth might be. 'Is she,' thought I, 'as alien to what I like as Tynedale, Seacombe, the Misses Seacombe—as the affectionate relative now striding before me? or is she better than these? Shall I, in conversing with her, feel free to show something of my real nature; or ——' Further conjectures were arrested by my entrance into the dining-room.

"A lamp, burning under a shade of ground-glass, showed a handsome apartment, wainscoted with oak; supper was laid on the table; by the fire-place, standing as if waiting our entrance, appeared a lady; she was young, tall, and well shaped; her dress was handsome and fashionable: so much my first glance sufficed to ascertain. A gay salutation passed between her and Mr. Crimsworth; she chid him, half playfully, half poutingly, for being late; her voice (I always take voices into the account in judging of character) was lively—it indicated, I thought, good animal spirits. Mr. Crimsworth soon checked her animated scolding with a kiss—a kiss that still told of the bridegroom (they had not yet been married a year); she took her seat at the supper-table in first-rate spirits. Perceiving me, she begged my pardon for not noticing me before, and then shook hands with me, as ladies do when a flow of good-humour disposes them to be cheerful to all, even the most indifferent of their acquaintance. It was now further obvious to me that she had a good complexion and features sufficiently marked but agreeable; her hair was red—quite red. She and Edward talked much, always in a vein of playful contention; she was vexed, or pretended to be vexed, that he had that day driven a vicious horse in the gig, and he made light of her fears. Sometimes she appealed to me.

"'Now, Mr. William, isn't it absurd in Edward to talk so? He says he will drive Jack, and no other horse, and the brute has thrown him twice already.'

"She spoke with a kind of lisp, not disagreeable,

but childish. I soon saw also that there was a more than girlish—a somewhat infantine expression in her by no means small features; this lisp and expression were, I have no doubt, a charm in Edward's eyes, and would be so to those of most men, but they were not to mine. I sought her eye, desirous to read there the intelligence which I could not discern in her face or hear in her conversation; it was merry, rather small; by turns I saw vivacity, vanity, coquetry, look out through its irid, but I watched in vain for a glimpse of soul. I am no Oriental; white necks, carmine lips and cheeks, clusters of bright curls, do not suffice for me without that Promethean spark which will live after the roses and lilies are faded, the burnished hair grown grey. In sunshine, in prosperity, the flowers are very well; but how many wet days are there in life—November seasons of disaster, when a man's hearth and home would be cold indeed, without the clear, cheering gleam of intellect.

"Having perused the fair page of Mrs. Crimsworth's face, a deep, involuntary sigh announced my disappointment; she took it as a homage to her beauty, and Edward, who was evidently proud of his rich and handsome young wife, threw on me a glance—half ridicule, half ire.

"I turned from them both, and gazing wearily round the room, I saw two pictures set in the oak panelling—one on each side the mantel-piece. Ceasing to take part in the bantering conversation that flowed on between Mr. and Mrs. Crimsworth, I bent my thoughts to the examination of these pictures. They were portraits—a lady and a gentleman, both costumed in the fashion of twenty years ago. The gentleman was in the shade. I could not see him well. The lady had the benefit of a full beam from the softly shaded lamp. I presently recognised her; I had seen this picture before, in childhood; it was my mother; that and the companion picture being the only heir-looms saved out of the sale of my father's property.

"The face, I remembered, had pleased me as a boy, but *then* I did not understand it; *now* I knew how rare that class of face is in the world, and I appreciated keenly its thoughtful, yet gentle expression. The serious grey eye possessed for me a strong charm, as did certain lines in the features indicative of most true and tender feeling. I was sorry it was only a picture.

"I soon left Mr. and Mrs. Crimsworth to themselves; a servant conducted me to my bed-room; in closing my chamber-door, I shut out all intruders—you, Charles, as well as the rest.

"Good bye for the present,

"WILLIAM CRIMSWORTH."

To this letter I never got an answer; before my old friend received it, he had accepted a Government appointment in one of the colonies, and was already on his way to the scene of his official labours. What has become of him since, I know not.

The leisure time I have at command, and which I intended to employ for his private benefit, I shall now dedicate to that of the public at large. My narrative is not exciting, and above all, not marvellous; but it may interest some individuals, who, having toiled in the same vocation as myself, will find in my experience frequent reflections of their own. The above letter will serve as introduction. I now proceed.

CHAPTER II.

A FINE October morning succeeded to the foggn evening that had witnessed my first introductioy to Crimsworth Hall. I was early up and walking in the large park-like meadow surrounding the house. The autumn sun, rising over the ——shire hills, disclosed a pleasant country; woods brown and mellow varied the fields from which the harvest had been lately carried; a river, gliding between the woods, caught on its surface the somewhat cold gleam of the October sun and sky; at frequent intervals along the banks of the river, tall, cylindrical chimneys, almost like slender, round towers, indicated the factories which the trees half concealed; here and there mansions, similar to Crimsworth Hall, occupied agreeable sites on the hill-side; the country wore, on the whole, a cheerful, active, fertile look. Steam, trade, machinery had long banished from it all romance and seclusion. At a distance of five miles, a valley, opening between the low hills, held in its cups the great town of X——. A dense, permanent vapour brooded over this locality—there lay Edward's "Concern."

I forced my eye to scrutinize this prospect, I forced my mind to dwell on it for a time, and when I found that it communicated no pleasurable emotion to my heart—that it stirred in me none of the hopes a man ought to feel, when he sees laid before him the scene of his life's career—I said to myself, "William, you are a rebel against circumstances; you are a fool, and know not what you want; you have chosen trade and you shall be a tradesman. Look!" I continued mentally—"Look at the sooty smoke in that hollow, and know that there is your post! There you cannot dream, you cannot speculate and theorize—there you shall out and work!"

Thus self-schooled, I returned to the house. My brother was in the breakfast-room. I met him collectedly—I could not meet him cheerfully; he was standing on the rug, his back to the fire—how much did I read in the expression of his eye as my glance encountered his, when I advanced to bid him good morning; how much that was contradictory to my nature! He said "Good morning" abruptly and nodded, and then he snatched, rather than took, a newspaper from the table, and began to read it with the air of a master who seizes a pretext to escape the bore of conversing with an underling. It was well I had taken a resolution to endure for a time, or his manner would have gone far to render insupportable the disgust I had just been endeavouring to subdue. I looked at him: I measured his robust frame and powerful proportions; I saw my own reflection in the mirror over the mantel-piece; I amused myself with comparing the two pictures. In face I resembled him, though I was not so handsome; my features were less regular; I had a darker eye, and a broader brow—in form I was greatly inferior—thinner, slighter, not so tall. As an animal, Edward excelled me far; should he prove as paramount in mind as in person I must be his slave—for I must expect from him no lion-like generosity to one weaker than himself; his cold, avaricious eye, his stern, forbidding manner told me he would not spare. Had I then force of mind to cope with him? I did not know; I had never been tried.

Mrs. Crimsworth's entrance diverted my thoughts for a moment. She looked well, dressed in white, her face and her attire shining in morning and bridal freshness. I addressed her with the degree of ease her last night's careless gaiety seemed to warrant, but she replied with coolness and restraint: her husband had tutored her; she was not to be too familiar with his clerk.

As soon as breakfast was over Mr. Crimsworth intimated to me that they were bringing the gig round to the door, and that in five minutes he should expect me to be ready to go down with him to X——. I did not keep him waiting; we were soon dashing at a rapid rate along the road. The horse he drove was the same vicious animal about which Mrs. Crimsworth had expressed her fears the night before. Once or twice Jack seemed disposed to turn restive, but a vigorous and determined application of the whip from the ruthless hand of his master soon compelled him to submission, and Edward's dilated nostril expressed his triumph in the result of the contest; he scarcely spoke to me during the whole of the brief drive, only opening his lips at intervals to damn his horse.

X—— was all stir and bustle when we entered it; we left the clean streets where there were dwelling-houses and shops, churches, and public buildings; we left all these, and turned down to a region of mills and warehouses; thence we passed through two massive gates into a great paved yard, and we were in Bigben Close, and the mill was before us, vomiting soot from its long chimney, and quivering through its thick brick walls with the commotion of its iron bowels. Workpeople were passing to and fro; a waggon was being laden with pieces. Mr. Crimsworth looked from side to side, and seemed at one glance to comprehend all that was going on; he alighted, and leaving his horse and gig to the care of a man who hastened to take the reins from his hand, he bid me follow him to the counting-house. We entered it; a very different place from the parlours of Crimsworth Hall—a place for business, with a bare, planked floor, a safe, two high desks and stools, and some chairs. A person was seated at one of the desks, who took off his square cap when Mr. Crimsworth entered, and in an instant was again absorbed in his occupation of writing or calculating—I know not which.

Mr. Crimsworth, having removed his mackintosh, sat down by the fire. I remained standing near the hearth; he said presently—

"Steighton, you may leave the room; I have some business to transact with this gentleman. Come back when you hear the bell."

The individual at the desk rose and departed, closing the door as he went out. Mr. Crimsworth stirred the fire, then folded his arms, and sat a moment thinking, his lips compressed, his brow knit. I had nothing to do but to watch him—how well his features were cut! what a handsome man he was! Whence, then, came that air of contraction—that narrow and hard aspect on his forehead, in all his lineaments?

Turning to me he began abruptly:—

"You are come down to ——shire to learn to be a tradesman?"

"Yes, I am."

"Have you made up your mind on the point? Let me know that at once."

"Yes."

"Well, I am not bound to help you, but I have a place here vacant, if you are qualified for it. I will take you on trial. What can you do? Do you know anything besides that useless trash of college learning—Greek, Latin, and so forth?"

"I have studied mathematics."

"Stuff! I dare say you have."

"I can read and write French and German."

"Hum!" He reflected a moment, then opening a drawer in a desk near him took out a letter, and gave it to me.

"Can you read that?" he asked.

It was a German commercial letter; I translated it; I could not tell whether he was gratified or not—his countenance remained fixed.

"It is well," he said, after a pause, "that you are acquainted with something useful, something that may enable you to earn your board and lodging: since you know French and German, I will take you as second clerk to manage the foreign correspondence of the house. I shall give you a good salary—90*l.* a year—and now," he continued, raising his voice, "hear once for all what I have to say about our relationship, and all that sort of humbug! I must have no nonsense on that point; it would never suit me. I shall excuse you nothing on the plea of being my brother; if I find you stupid, negligent, dissipated, idle, or possessed of any faults detrimental to the interests of the house, I shall dismiss you as I would any other clerk. Ninety pounds a year are good wages, and I expect to have the full value of my money out of you; remember, too, that things are on a practical footing in my establishment—business-like habits, feelings, and ideas, suit me best. Do you understand?"

"Partly," I replied. "I suppose you mean that I am to do my work for my wages; not to expect favour from you, and not to depend on you for any help but what I earn; that suits me exactly, and on these terms I will consent to be your clerk."

I turned on my heel, and walked to the window; this time I did not consult his face to learn his opinion: what it was I do not know, nor did I then care. After a silence of some minutes he recommenced:—

"You perhaps expect to be accommodated with apartments at Crimsworth Hall, and to go and come with me in the gig. I wish you, however, to be aware that such an arrangement would be quite inconvenient to me. I like to have the seat in my gig at liberty for any gentleman whom for business reasons I may wish to take down to the hall for a night or so. You will seek out lodgings in X——."

Quitting the window, I walked back to the hearth.

"Of course I shall seek out lodgings in

X——," I answered. "It would not suit me either to lodge at Crimsworth Hall."

My tone was quiet. I always speak quietly. Yet Mr. Crimsworth's blue eye became incensed; he took his revenge rather oddly. Turning to me he said bluntly—

"You are poor enough, I suppose; how do you expect to live till your quarter's salary becomes due?"

"I shall get on," said I.

"How do you expect to live?" he repeated in a louder voice.

"As I can, Mr. Crimsworth."

"Get into debt at your peril! that's all," he answered. "For aught I know you may have extravagant aristocratic habits; if you have, drop them; I tolerate nothing of the sort here, and I will never give you a shilling extra, whatever liabilities you may incur—mind that."

"Yes, Mr. Crimsworth, you will find I have a good memory."

I said no more. I did not think the time was come for much parley. I had an instinctive feeling that it would be folly to let one's temper effervesce often with such a man as Edward. I said to myself, "I will place my cup under this continual dropping; it shall stand there still and steady; when full, it will run over of itself—meantime patience. Two things are certain. I am capable of performing the work Mr. Crimsworth has set me; I can earn my wages conscientiously, and those wages are sufficient to enable me to live. As to the fact of my brother assuming towards me the bearing of a proud, harsh master, the fault is his, not mine; and shall his injustice, his bad feeling, turn me at once aside from the path I have chosen? No; at least, ere I deviate, I will advance far enough to see whither my career tends. As yet I am only pressing in at the entrance—a strait gate enough; it ought to have a good terminus." While I thus reasoned, Mr. Crimsworth rang a bell; his first clerk, the individual dismissed previously to our conference, re-entered.

"Mr. Steighton," said he, "show Mr. William the letters from Voss, Brothers, and give him English copies of the answers: he will translate them."

Mr. Steighton, a man of about thirty-five, with a face at once sly and heavy, hastened to execute this order; he laid the letters on the desk, and I was soon seated at it, and engaged in rendering the English answers into German. A sentiment of keen pleasure accompanied this first effort to earn my own living—a sentiment neither poisoned nor weakened by the presence of the taskmaster, who stood and watched me for some time as I wrote. I thought he was trying to read my character, but I felt as secure against his scrutiny as if I had had on a casque with the visor down—or rather I showed him my countenance with the confidence that one would show an unlearned man a letter written in Greek; he might see lines, and trace characters, but he could make nothing of them; my nature was not his nature, and its signs were to him like the words of an unknown tongue. Ere long he turned away abruptly, as if baffled, and left the counting-house; he returned to it but twice in the course of that day; each time he mixed and swallowed a glass of brandy and water, the materials for making which he extracted from a cupboard on one side of the fireplace; having glanced at my translations—he could read both French and German—he went out again in silence.

CHAPTER III.

I SERVED Edward as his second clerk faithfully, punctually, diligently. What was given me to do I had the power and the determination to do well. Mr. Crimsworth watched sharply for defects, but found none; he set Timothy Steighton, his favourite and head man, to watch also. Tim was baffled; I was as exact as himself, and quicker. Mr. Crimsworth made inquiries as to how I lived, whether I got into debt—no, my accounts with my landlady were always straight. I had hired small lodgings, which I contrived to pay for out of a slender fund—the accumulated savings of my Eton pocket-money; for as it had ever been abhorrent to my nature to ask pecuniary assistance, I had early acquired habits of self-denying economy; husbanding my monthly allowance with anxious care, in order to obviate the danger of being forced, in some moment of future exigency, to beg additional aid. I remember many called me miser at the time, and I used to couple the reproach with this consolation—better to be misunderstood now than repulsed hereafter. At this day I had my reward; I had had it before, when on parting with my irritated uncles one of them threw down on the table before me a £5 note, which I was able to leave there, saying that my travelling expenses were already provided for. Mr. Crimsworth employed Tim to find out whether my landlady had any complaint to make on the score of my morals; she answered that she believed I was a very religious man, and asked Tim, in her turn, if he thought I had any intention of going into the Church some day; for, she said, she had had young curates to lodge in her house who were nothing equal to me for steadiness and quietness.

Tim was "a religious man" himself; indeed, he was "a joined Methodist," which did not (be it understood) prevent him from being at the same time an engrained rascal, and he came away much posed at hearing this account of my piety. Having imparted it to Mr. Crimsworth, that gentleman, who himself frequented no place of worship, and owned no God but Mammon, turned the information into a weapon of attack against the equability of my temper. He commenced a series of covert sneers, of which I did not at first perceive the drift, till my landlady happened to relate the conversation she had had with Mr. Steighton; this enlightened me; afterwards I came to the counting-house prepared, and managed to receive the millowner's blasphemous sarcasms, when next levelled at me, on a buckler of impenetrable indifference. Ere long he tired of wasting his ammunition on a statue, but he did not throw away the shafts—he only kept them quiet in his quiver.

Once during my clerkship I had an invitation to Crimsworth Hall; it was on the occasion of a large party given in honour of the master's birthday; he had always been accustomed to invite his clerks on similar anniversaries, and could not well pass me over; I was, however, kept strictly in the background. Mrs. Crimsworth, elegantly dressed in satin and lace, blooming in youth and health, vouchsafed me no more notice than was expressed by a distant move; Crimsworth, of course, never spoke to me; I was introduced to none of the band of young ladies, who, enveloped in silvery clouds of white gauze and muslin, sat in array against me on the opposite side of a long and large room; in fact I was fairly isolated, and could but contemplate the shining ones from afar, and when weary of such a dazzling scene, turn for a change to the consideration of the carpet pattern. Mr. Crimsworth, standing on the rug, his elbow supported by the marble mantel-piece, and about him a group of very pretty girls, with whom he conversed gaily—Mr. Crimsworth, thus placed, glanced at me; I looked weary, solitary, kept down like some desolate tutor or governess; he was satisfied.

Dancing began; I should have liked well enough to be introduced to some pleasing and intelligent girl, and to have freedom and opportunity to show that I could both feel and communicate the pleasure of social intercourse—that I was not, in short, a block, or a piece of furniture, but an acting, thinking, sentient man. Many smiling faces and graceful figures glided past me, but the smiles were lavished on other eyes, the figures sustained by other hands than mine. I turned away tantalized, left the dancers, and wandered into the oak-panelled dining-room. No fibre of sympathy united me to any living thing in this house; I looked for and found my mother's picture. I took a wax taper from a stand, and held it up. I gazed long, earnestly;

my heart grew to the image. My mother, I perceived, had bequeathed to me much of her features and countenance—her forehead, her eyes, her complexion. No regular beauty pleases egotistical human beings so much as a softened and refined likeness of themselves; for this reason, fathers regard with complacency the lineaments of their daughters' faces, where frequently their own similitude is found flatteringly associated with softness of hue and delicacy of outline. I was just wondering how that picture, to me so interesting, would strike an impartial spectator, when a voice close behind me pronounced the words—

"Humph! there 's some sense in that face."

I turned; at my elbow stood a tall man, young, though probably five or six years older than I—in other respects of an appearance the opposite to common-place; though just now, as I am not disposed to paint his portrait in detail, the reader must be content with the silhouette I have just thrown off; it was all I myself saw of him for the moment: I did not investigate the colour of his eyebrows, nor of his eyes either; I saw his stature, and the outline of his shape; I saw, too, his fastidious-looking *retroussé* nose; these observations, few in number, and general in character (the last excepted), sufficed, for they enabled me to recognise him.

"Good evening, Mr. Hunsden," muttered I with a bow, and then, like a shy noodle as I was, I began moving away—and why? Simply because Mr. Hunsden was a manufacturer and a millowner, and I was only a clerk, and my instinct propelled me from my superior. I had frequently seen Hunsden in Bigben Close, where he came almost weekly to transact business with Mr. Crimsworth, but I had never spoken to him, nor he to me, and I owed him a sort of involuntary grudge, because he had more than once been the tacit witness of insults offered by Edward to me. I had the conviction that he could only regard me as a poor-spirited slave, wherefore I now went about to shun his presence and eschew his conversation.

"Where are you going?" asked he, as I edged off sideways. I had already noticed that Mr. Hunsden indulged in abrupt forms of speech, and I perversely said to myself—

"He thinks he may speak as he likes to a poor clerk; but my mood is not perhaps so supple as he deems it, and his rough freedom pleases me not at all."

I made some slight reply, rather indifferent than courteous; and continued to move away. He coolly planted himself in my path.

"Stay here awhile," said he: "it is so hot in the dancing room; besides you don't dance; you have not had a partner to-night."

He was right, and as he spoke neither his look, tone, nor manner, displeased me; my *amour-propre* was propitiated; he had not addressed me out of condescension, but because, having repaired to the cool dining room for refreshment, he now wanted some one to talk to, by way of temporary amusement. I hate to be condescended to, but I like well enough to oblige: I stayed.

"That is a good picture," he continued, recurring to the portrait.

"Do you consider the face pretty?" I asked.

"Pretty! no—how can it be pretty with sunk eyes and hollow cheeks? but it is peculiar; it seems to think. You could have a talk with that woman, if she were alive, on other subjects than dress, visiting, and compliments."

I agreed with him—but did not say so. He went on.

"Not that I admire a head of that sort; it wants character and force; there 's too much of the sen-si-tive (so he articulated it, curling his lip at the same time) in that mouth; besides there is Aristocrat written on the brow and defined in the figure; I hate your aristocrats."

"You think then, Mr. Hunsden, that patrician

descent may be read in a distinctive cast of form and features?"

"Patrician descent be hanged! Who doubts that your lordlings may have their 'distinctive cast of form and features' as much as we ——shire tradesmen have ours? But which is the best? Not theirs assuredly. As to their women, it is a little different: they cultivate beauty from childhood upwards, and may by care and training attain to a certain degree of excellence in that point, just like the oriental odalisques. Yet even this superiority is doubtful. Compare the figure in that frame with Mrs. Edward Crimsworth—which is the finer animal?"

I replied quietly: "Compare yourself and Mr. Edward Crimsworth, Mr. Hunsden."

"Oh, Crimsworth is better filled up than I am, I know; besides he has a straight nose, arched eyebrows, and all that; but these advantages—if they are advantages—he did not inherit from his mother, the patrician, but from his father, old Crimsworth, who, *my* father says, was as veritable a ——shire blue-dyer as ever put indigo in a vat; yet withal the handsomest man in the three Ridings. It is you, William, who are the aristocrat of your family, and you are not as fine a fellow as your plebeian brother by a long chalk."

There was something in Mr. Hunsden's point-blank mode of speech which rather pleased me than otherwise, because it set me at my ease. I continued the conversation with a degree of interest.

"How do you happen to know that I am Mr. Crimsworth's brother? I thought you and everybody else looked upon me only in the light of a poor clerk."

"Well, and so we do; and what are you but a poor clerk? You do Crimsworth's work, and he gives you wages—shabby wages they are, too."

I was silent. Hunsden's language now bordered on the impertinent, still his manner did not offend me in the least—it only piqued my curiosity; I wanted him to go on, which he did in a little while.

"This world is an absurd one," said he.

"Why so, Mr. Hunsden?"

"I wonder you should ask: you are yourself a strong proof of the absurdity I allude to."

I was determined he should explain himself of his own accord, without my pressing him so to do—so I resumed my silence.

"Is it your intention to become a tradesman?" he inquired presently.

"It was my serious intention three months ago."

"Humph! the more fool you—you look like a tradesman! What a practical business-like face you have!"

"My face is as the Lord made it, Mr. Hunsden."

"The Lord never made either your face or head for X——. What good can your bumps of ideality, comparison, self-esteem, conscientiousness, do you here? But if you like Bigben Close, stay there; it 's your own affair, not mine."

"Perhaps I have no choice."

"Well I care nought about it—it will make little difference to me what you do or where you go; but I'm cool now—I want to dance again; and I see such a fine girl sitting in the corner of the sofa there by her mamma; see if I don't get her for a partner in a jiffy! There 's Waddy—Sam Waddy making up to her; won't I cut him out?"

And Mr. Hunsden strode away. I watched him through the open folding-doors; he outstripped Waddy, applied for the hand of the fine girl, and led her off triumphant. She was a tall, well-made, full-formed, dashingly-dressed young woman, much in the style of Mrs. E. Crimsworth; Hunsden whirled her through the waltz with spirit; he kept at her side during the remainder of the evening, and I read in her animated and gratified countenance that he succeeded in making himself perfectly agreeable. The mamma too (a stout person in a turban—Mrs Lupton by name) looked well pleased; prophetic visions probably flattered her inward eye. The Hunsdens were of an old stem; and scornful as Yorke (such was my late interlocutor's name) professed to be of the advantages of birth, in his secret heart he well knew and fully appreciated the distinction his ancient, if not high lineage conferred on him in a mushroom-place like X——, concerning whose inhabitants it was proverbially said, that not one in a thousand knew his own grandfather. Moreover the Hunsdens, once rich, were still independent; and report affirmed that Yorke bade fair, by his success in business, to restore to pristine prosperity the partially decayed fortunes of his house. These circumstances considered, Mrs. Lupton's broad face might well wear a smile of complacency as she contemplated the heir of Hunsden Wood occupied in paying assiduous court to her darling Sarah Martha. I, however, whose observations being less anxious, were likely to be more accurate, soon saw that the grounds for maternal self-congratulation were slight indeed; the gentleman appeared to me much more desirous of making, than susceptible of receiving an impression. I know not what it was in Mr. Hunsden that, as I watched him (I had nothing better to do), suggested to me, every now and then, the idea of a foreigner. In form and features he might be pronounced English, though even there one caught a dash of something Gallic; but he had no English shyness: he had learnt somewhere, somehow, the art of setting himself quite at his ease, and of allowing no insular timidity to intervene as a barrier between him and his convenience, or pleasure. Refinement he did not affect, yet vulgar he could not be called; he was not odd—

no quiz—yet he resembled no one else I had ever seen before; his general bearing intimated complete, sovereign satisfaction with himself, yet, at times, an indescribable shade passed like an eclipse over his countenance, and seemed to me like the sign of a sudden and strong inward doubt of himself, his words and actions—an energetic discontent at his life or his social position, his future prospects or his mental attainments—I know not which; perhaps after all it might only be a bilious caprice.

CHAPTER IV.

No man likes to acknowledge that he has made a mistake in the choice of his profession, and every man, worthy of the name, will row long against wind and tide before he allows himself to cry out "I am baffled!" and submits to be floated passively back to land. From the first week of my residence in X—— I felt my occupation irksome. The thing itself—the work of copying and translating business-letters—was a dry and tedious task enough, but had that been all, I should long have borne with the nuisance; I am not of an impatient nature, and influenced by the double desire of getting my living and justifying to myself and others the resolution I had taken to become a tradesman,

I should have endured in silence the rust and cramp of my best faculties; I should not have whispered, even inwardly, that I longed for liberty; I should have pent in every sigh by which my heart might have ventured to intimate its distress under the closeness, smoke, monotony and joyless tumult of Bigben Close, and its panting desire for freer and fresher scenes; I should have set up the image of Duty, the fetish of Perseverance, in my small bed-room at Mrs. King's lodgings, and they two should have been my household gods, from which my darling, my cherished-in-secret, Imagination, the tender and the mighty, should never, either by softness or strength, have severed me. But this was not all; the antipathy which had sprung up between myself and my employer striking deeper root and spreading denser shade daily, excluded me from every glimpse of the sunshine of life; and I began to feel like a plant growing in humid darkness out of the slimy walls of a well.

Antipathy is the only word which can express the feeling Edward Crimsworth had for me—a feeling, in a great measure, involuntary, and which was liable to be excited by every, the most trifling movement, look, or word of mine. My southern accent annoyed him; the degree of education evinced in my language irritated him; my punctuality, industry, and accuracy, fixed his dislike, and gave it the high flavour and poignant relish of envy; he feared that I too should one day make a successful tradesman. Had I been in anything inferior to him, he would not have hated me so thoroughly, but I knew all that he knew, and, what was worse, he suspected that I kept the padlock of silence on mental wealth in which he was no sharer. If he could have once placed me in a ridiculous or mortifying position, he would have forgiven me much, but I was guarded by three faculties—Caution, Tact, Observation; and prowling and prying as was Edward's malignity, it could never baffle the lynx-eyes of these, my natural sentinels. Day by day did his malice watch my tact, hoping it would sleep, and prepared to steal snake-like on its slumber, but tact, if it be genuine, never sleeps.

I had received my first quarter's wages and was returning to my lodgings, possessed heart and soul with the pleasant feeling that the master who had paid me grudged every penny of that hard-earned pittance—(I had long ceased to regard Mr. Crimsworth as my brother—he was a hard, grinding master; he wished to be an inexorable tyrant: that was all). Thoughts, not varied but strong, occupied my mind; two voices spoke within me; again and again they uttered the same monotonous phrases. One said: "William, your life is intolerable." The other: "What can you do to alter it?" I walked fast, for it was a cold, frosty night in January; as I approached my lodgings, I turned from a general view of my affairs to the particular speculation as to whether my fire would be out; looking towards the window of my sitting-room, I saw no cheering red gleam.

"That slut of a servant has neglected it as usual," said I, "and I shall see nothing but pale ashes if I go in; it is a fine starlight night—I will walk a little farther."

It *was* a fine night, and the streets were dry and even clean for X——; there was a crescent curve of moonlight to be seen by the parish church tower, and hundreds of stars shone keenly bright in all quarters of the sky.

Unconsciously I steered my course towards the country; I had got into Grove-street and began to feel the pleasure of seeing dim trees at the extremity, round a suburban house, when a person leaning over the iron gate of one of the small gardens which front the neat dwelling-houses in this street, addressed me as I was hurrying with quick stride past.

"What the deuce is the hurry? Just so must

Lot have left Sodom, when he expected fire to pour down upon it, out of burning brass clouds."

I stopped short, and looked towards the speaker. I smelt the fragrance, and saw the red spark of a cigar; the dusk outline of a man, too, bent towards me over the wicket.

"You see I am meditating in the field at eventide," continued this shade. "God knows it 's cool work! especially as instead of Rebecca on a camel's hump, with bracelets on her arms and a ring in her nose, Fate sends me only a counting-house clerk, in a grey tweed wrapper."

The voice was familiar to me—its second utterance enabled me to seize the speaker's identity.

"Mr. Hunsden! good evening."

"Good evening, indeed! yes, but you would have passed me without recognition if I had not been so civil as to speak first."

"I did not know you."

"A famous excuse! You ought to have known me; I knew you, though you were going ahead like a steam-engine. Are the police after you?"

"It would n't be worth their while; I 'm not of consequence enough to attract them."

"Alas, poor shepherd! Alack and well-a-day! What a theme for regret, and how down in the mouth you must be, judging from the sound of your voice! But since you 're not running from the police, from whom are you running? the devil?"

"On the contrary, I am going post to him."

"That is well—you 're just in luck: this is Tuesday evening; there are scores of market gigs and carts returning to Dinneford to-night; and he, or some of his, have a seat in all regularly; so, if you 'll step in and sit half-an-hour in my bachelor's parlour, you may catch him as he passes without much trouble. I think though you'd better let him alone to-night, he 'll have so many customers to serve; Tuesday is his busy day in X—— and Dinneford; come in, at all events."

He swung the wicket open as he spoke.

"Do you really wish me to go in?" I asked.

"As you please—I 'm alone; your company for an hour or two would be agreeable to me; but, if you don't choose to favour me so far, I 'll not press the point. I hate to bore any one."

It suited me to accept the invitation as it suited Hunsden to give it. I passed through the gate, and followed him to the front door, which he opened; thence we traversed a passage, and entered his parlour; the door being shut, he pointed me to an arm-chair by the hearth; I sat down, and glanced round me.

It was a comfortable room, at once snug and handsome; the bright grate was filled with a genuine ——shire fire, red, clear, and generous, no penurious south-of-England embers happed in the corner of a grate. On the table a shaded lamp diffused around a soft, pleasant, and equal light;

the furniture was almost luxurious for a young bachelor, comprising a couch and two very easy chairs; bookshelves filled the recesses on each side of the mantel-piece; they were well-furnished, and arranged with perfect order. The neatness of the room suited my taste; I hate irregular and slovenly habits. From what I saw, I concluded that Hunsden's ideas on that point corresponded with my own. While he removed from the centre-table to the side-board a few pamphlets and periodicals, I ran my eye along the shelves of the book-case nearest me. French and German works predominated, the old French dramatists, sundry modern authors, Thiers, Villemain, Paul de Kock, George Sand, Eugene Sue; in German—Goëthe, Schiller, Zschokke, Jean Paul Richter; in English there were works on Political Economy. I examined no further, for Mr. Hunsden himself recalled my attention.

"You shall have something," said he, "for you ought to feel disposed for refreshment after walking nobody knows how far on such a Canadian night as this; but it shall not be brandy and water, and it shall not be a bottle of port, nor ditto of sherry. I keep no such poison. I have Rhein-wein for my own drinking, and you may choose between that and coffee."

Here again Hunsden suited me: if there was one generally received practice I abhorred more than another, it was the habitual imbibing of spirits and strong wines. I had, however, no fancy for his acid German nectar, but I liked coffee, so I responded—

"Give me some coffee, Mr. Hunsden."

I perceived my answer pleased him; he had doubtless expected to see a chilling effect produced by his steady announcement that he would give me neither wine nor spirits; he just shot one searching glance at my face to ascertain whether my cordiality was genuine or a mere feint of politeness. I smiled, because I quite understood him; and, while I honoured his conscientious firmness, I was amused at his mistrust; he seemed satisfied, rang the bell, and ordered coffee, which was presently brought; for himself, a bunch of grapes and half a pint of something sour sufficed. My coffee was excellent; I told him so, and expressed the shuddering pity with which his anchorite fare inspired me. He did not answer, and I scarcely think heard my remark. At that moment one of those momentary eclipses I before alluded to had come over his face, extinguishing his smile, and replacing, by an abstracted and alienated look, the customarily shrewd, bantering glance of his eye. I employed the interval of silence in a rapid scrutiny of his physiognomy. I had never observed him closely before; and, as my sight is very short, I had gathered only a vague, general idea of his appearance; I was surprised now, on examination, to perceive how small, and even feminine, were his lineaments; his tall figure, long and dark locks, his voice and general bearing, had impressed me with the notion of something powerful and massive; not at all—my own features were cast in a harsher and squarer mould than his. I discerned that there would be contrasts between his inward and outward man; contentions, too; for I suspected his soul had more of will and ambition than his body had of fibre and muscle. Perhaps, in these incompatibilities of the "physique" with the "morale," lay the secret of that fitful gloom; he *would* but *could* not, and the athletic mind scowled scorn on its more fragile companion. As to his good looks, I should have liked to have a woman's opinion on that subject; it seemed to me that his face might produce the same effect on a lady that a very piquant and interesting, though scarcely pretty, female face would on a man. I have mentioned his dark locks—they were brushed sideways above a white and sufficiently expansive forehead; his cheek had a rather hectic freshness; his features might have done well on canvas, but indifferently in marble: they were plastic;

character had set a stamp upon each; expression re-cast them at her pleasure, and strange metamorphoses she wrought, giving him now the mien of a morose bull, and anon that of an arch and mischievous girl; more frequently, the two semblances were blent, and a queer, composite countenance they made.

Starting from his silent fit, he began:—

"William! what a fool you are to live in those dismal lodgings of Mrs. King's, when you might take rooms here in Grove Street, and have a garden like me!"

"I should be too far from the mill."

"What of that? It would do you good to walk there and back two or three times a day; besides, are you such a fossil that you never wish to see a flower or a green leaf?"

"I am no fossil."

"What are you then? You sit at that desk in Crimsworth's counting-house day by day and week by week, scraping with a pen on paper, just like an automaton; you never get up; you never say you are tired; you never ask for a holiday; you never take change or relaxation; you give way to no excess of an evening; you neither keep wild company, nor indulge in strong drink."

"Do you, Mr. Hunsden?"

"Don't think to pose me with short questions; your case and mine are diametrically different, and it is nonsense attempting to draw a parallel. I say, that when a man endures patiently what ought to be unendurable, he is a fossil."

"Whence do you acquire the knowledge of my patience?"

"Why, man, do you suppose you are a mystery? The other night you seemed surprised at my knowing to what family you belonged; now you find subject for wonderment in my calling you patient. What do you think I do with my eyes and ears? I've been in your counting-house more than once when Crimsworth has treated you like a dog; called for a book, for instance, and when you gave him the wrong one, or what he chose to consider the wrong one, flung it back almost in your face; desired you to shut or open the door as if you had been his flunkey; to say nothing of your position at the party about a month ago, where you had neither place nor partner, but hovered about like a poor, shabby hanger-on; and how patient you were under each and all of these circumstances!"

"Well, Mr. Hunsden, what then?"

"I can hardly tell you what then; the conclusion to be drawn as to your character depends upon the nature of the motives which guide your conduct; if you are patient because you expect to make something eventually out of Crimsworth, notwithstanding his tyranny, or perhaps by means of it, you are what the world calls an interested and mercenary, but may be a very wise fellow; if you are patient because you think it a duty to meet insult with submission, you are an essential sap, and in no shape the man for my money; if you are patient because your nature is phlegmatic, flat, inexcitable, and that you cannot get up to the pitch of resistance, why, God made you to be crushed; and lie down by all means, and lie flat, and let Juggernaut ride well over you."

Mr. Hunsden's eloquence was not, it will be perceived, of the smooth and oily order. As he spoke, he pleased me ill. I seemed to recognise in him one of those characters who, sensitive enough themselves, are selfishly relentless towards the sensitiveness of others. Moreover, though he was neither like Crimsworth nor Lord Tynedale, yet he was acrid, and, I suspected, overbearing in his way: there was a tone of despotism in the urgency of the very reproaches by which he aimed at goading the oppressed into rebellion against the oppressor. Looking at him still more fixedly than I had yet done, I saw written in his eye and mien a resolution to arrogate to himself a freedom so unlimited, that it might often trench on the just liberty of his neighbours. I rapidly ran over these thoughts, and then I laughed a low and involuntary laugh, moved thereto by a slight, inward revelation of the inconsistency of man. It was as I thought: Hunsden had expected me to take with calm his incorrect and offensive surmises, his bitter and haughty taunts; and himself was chafed by a laugh, scarce louder than a whisper.

His brow darkened, his thin nostril dilated a little.

"Yes," he began, "I told you that you were an aristocrat, and who but an aristocrat would laugh such a laugh as that, and look such a look? A laugh frigidly jeering; a look lazily mutinous; gentlemanlike irony, patrician resentment. What a nobleman you would have made, William Crimsworth! You are cut out for one; pity Fortune has baulked Nature! Look at the features, figure, even to the hands—distinction all over—ugly distinction! Now, if you 'd only an estate and a mansion, and a park, and a title, how you could play the exclusive, maintain the rights of your class, train your tenantry in habits of respect to the peerage, oppose at every step the advancing power of the people, support your rotten order, and be ready for its sake to wade knee-deep in churls' blood; as it is, you 've no power; you can do nothing; you 're wrecked and stranded on the shores of commerce; forced into collision with practical men, with whom you cannot cope, for *you 'll never be a tradesman.*"

The first part of Hunsden's speech moved me not at all, or, if it did, it was only to wonder at the perversion into which prejudice had twisted his judgment of my character; the concluding sentence, however, not only moved, but shook me; the blow it gave was a severe one, because Truth wielded the weapon. If I smiled now, it was only in disdain of myself.

Hunsden saw his advantage; he followed it up.

"You 'll make nothing by trade," continued he;

"nothing more than the crust of dry bread and the draught of fair water on which you now live; your only chance of getting a competency lies in marrying a rich widow, or running away with an heiress."

"I leave such shifts to be put in practice by those who devise them," said I, rising.

"And even that is hopeless," he went on coolly. "What widow would have you? Much less, what heiress? You 're not bold and venturesome enough for the one, nor handsome and fascinating enough for the other. You think perhaps you look intelligent and polished; carry your intellect and refinement to market, and tell me in a private note what price is bid for them."

Mr. Hunsden had taken his tone for the night; the string he struck was out of tune, he would finger no other. Averse to discord, of which I had enough every day and all day long, I concluded, at last, that silence and solitude were preferable to jarring converse; I bade him good-night.

"What! Are you going, lad? Well, good-night: you 'll find the door." And he sat still in front of the fire, while I left the room and the house. I had got a good way on my return to my lodgings before I found out that I was walking very fast, and breathing very hard, and that my nails were almost stuck into the palms of my clenched hands, and that my teeth were set fast; on making this discovery, I relaxed both my pace, fists, and jaws, but I could not so soon cause the regrets rushing rapidly through my mind to slacken their tide. Why did I make myself a tradesman? Why did I enter Hunsden's house this evening? Why, at dawn to-morrow, must I repair to Crimsworth's mill? All that night did I ask myself these questions, and all that night fiercely demanded of my soul an answer. I got no sleep; my head burned, my feet froze; at last the factory bells rang, and I sprang from my bed with other slaves.

CHAPTER V.

THERE is a climax to every thing, to every state of feeling as well as to every position in life. I turned this truism over in my mind as, in the frosty dawn of a January morning, I hurried down the steep and now icy street which descended from Mrs. King's to the Close. The factory work-people had preceded me by nearly an hour, and the mill was all lighted up and in full operation when I reached it. I repaired to my post in the counting-house as usual; the fire there, but just lit, as yet only smoked; Steighton was not yet arrived. I shut the door and sat down at the desk; my hands, recently washed in half-frozen water, were still numb; I could not write till they had regained vitality, so I went on thinking, and still the theme of my thoughts was "the climax." Self-dissatisfaction troubled exceedingly the current of my meditations.

"Come, William Crimsworth," said my conscience, or whatever it is that within ourselves takes ourselves to task—"Come, get a clear notion of what you would have, or what you would not have. You talk of a climax; pray has your endurance reached its climax? It is not four months old. What a fine resolute fellow you imagined yourself to be when you told Tynedale you would tread in your father's steps, and a pretty treading you are likely to make of it! How well you like X——! Just at this moment how redolent of pleasant associations are its streets, its shops, its warehouses, its factories! How the prospect of this day cheers you! Letter-copying till noon, solitary dinner at your lodgings, letter-copying till evening, solitude; for you neither find pleasure in Brown's, nor Smith's, nor

Nicholl's, nor Eccle's company; and as to Hunsden, you fancied there was pleasure to be derived from his society—he! he! how did you like the taste you had of him last night? was it sweet? Yet he is a talented, an original-minded man, and even he does not like you; your self-respect defies you to like him; he has always seen you to disadvantage; he always will see you to disadvantage; your positions are unequal, and were they on the same level your minds could not assimilate; never hope, then, to gather the honey of friendship out of that thorn-guarded plant. Hollo, Crimsworth! where are your thoughts tending? You leave the recollection of Hunsden as a bee would a rock, as a bird a desert; and your aspirations spread eager wings towards a land of visions where, now in advancing day-light, —in X—— daylight—you dare to dream of congeniality, repose, union. Those three you will never meet in this world; they are angels. The souls of just men made perfect may encounter them in heaven, but your soul will never be made perfect. Eight o'clock strikes! your hands are thawed, get to work!"

"Work? why should I work?" said I sullenly: "I cannot please though I toil like a slave." "Work, work!" reiterated the inward voice. "I may work, it will do no good," I growled; but nevertheless I drew out a packet of letters and commenced my task—task thankless and bitter as that of the Israelite crawling over the sun-baked fields of Egypt in search of straw and stubble wherewith to accomplish his tale of bricks.

About ten o'clock I heard Mr. Crimsworth's gig turn into the yard, and in a minute or two he entered the counting-house. It was his custom to glance his eye at Steighton and myself, to hang up his Mackintosh, stand a minute with his back to the fire, and then walk out. To-day he did not deviate from his usual habits; the only difference was that when he looked at me, his brow, instead of being merely hard, was surly; his eye, instead of being cold, was fierce. He studied me a minute or two longer than usual, but went out in silence.

Twelve o'clock arrived; the bell rang for a suspension of labour; the work-people went off to their dinners; Steighton, too, departed, desiring me to lock the counting-house door, and take the key with me. I was tying up a bundle of papers, and putting them in their place, preparatory to closing my desk, when Crimsworth re-appeared at the door, and entering closed it behind him.

"You'll stay here a minute," said he in a deep brutal voice, while his nostrils distended and his eye shot a spark of sinister fire.

Alone with Edward I remembered our relationship, and remembering that, forgot the difference of position; I put away deference and careful forms of speech; I answered with simple brevity.

"It is time to go home," I said, turning the key in my desk.

"You'll stay here!" he reiterated. "And take your hand off that key! leave it in the lock!"

"Why?" asked I. "What cause is there for changing my usual plans?"

"Do as I order," was the answer, "and no questions! You are my servant, obey me! What have you been about ——?" he was going on in the same breath, when an abrupt pause announced that rage had for the moment got the better of articulation.

"You may look, if you wish to know," I replied. "There is the open desk, there are the papers."

"Confound your insolence! What have you been about?"

"Your work, and have done it well."

"Hypocrite and twaddler! Smooth-faced, snivelling greasehorn!" (this last term is, I believe, purely ——shire, and alludes to the horn of black rancid whale-oil, usually to be seen suspended to cart-wheels, and employed for greasing the same.)

"Come, Edward Crimsworth, enough of this. It is time you and I wound up accounts. I have now given your service three months' trial, and I find it the most nauseous slavery under the sun. Seek another clerk. I stay no longer."

"What! do you dare to give me notice? Stop at least for your wages." He took down the heavy gig whip hanging beside his Mackintosh.

I permitted myself to laugh with a degree of scorn I took no pains to temper or hide. His fury boiled up, and when he had sworn half-a-dozen vulgar, impious oaths, without, however, venturing to lift the whip, he continued.

"I've found you out and know you thoroughly; you mean, whining lickspittle! What have you been saying all over X—— about me? Answer me that!"

"You? I have neither inclination nor temptation to talk about you."

"You lie! It is your practice to talk about me; it is your constant habit to make public complaint of the treatment you receive at my hands. You have gone and told it far and near that I give you low wages and knock you about like a dog. I wish you were a dog! I 'd set-to this minute and never stir from the spot till I'd cut every strip of flesh from your bones with this whip."

He flourished his tool. The end of the lash just touched my forehead. A warm excited thrill ran through my veins, my blood seemed to give a bound, and then raced fast and hot along its channels. I got up nimbly, came round to where he stood and faced him.

"Down with your whip!" said I, "and explain this instant what you mean."

"Sirrah! to whom are you speaking?"

"To you. There is no one else present, I think. You say I have been calumniating you — complaining of your low wages and bad treatment. Give your grounds for these assertions."

Crimsworth had no dignity, and when I sternly

demanded an explanation, he gave one in a loud, scolding voice.

"Grounds! you shall have them; and turn to the light that I may see your brazen face blush black, when you hear yourself proved to be a liar and a hypocrite. At a public meeting in the Town-hall yesterday, I had the pleasure of hearing myself insulted by the speaker opposed to me in the question under discussion, by allusions to my private affairs; by cant about monsters without natural affection, family despots, and such trash; and when I rose to answer, I was met by a shout from the filthy mob, where the mention of your name enabled me at once to detect the quarter in which this base attack had originated. When I looked round, I saw that treacherous villain, Hunsden, acting as fugleman. I detected you in close conversation with Hunsden at my house a month ago, and I know that you were at Hunsden's rooms last night. Deny it if you dare."

"Oh, I shall not deny it! And if Hunsden hounded on the people to hiss you, he did quite right. You deserve popular execration; for a worse man, a harder master, a more brutal brother than you are has seldom existed."

"Sirrah! sirrah!" reiterated Crimsworth; and to complete his apostrophe, he cracked the whip straight over my head.

A minute sufficed to wrest it from him, break it in two pieces, and throw it under the grate. He made a headlong rush at me which I evaded, and said—

"Touch me and I'll have you up before the nearest magistrate."

Men like Crimsworth, if firmly and calmly resisted, always abate something of their exorbitant insolence; he had no mind to be brought before a magistrate, and I suppose he saw I meant what I said. After an odd and long stare at me, at once bull-like and amazed, he seemed to bethink himself that, after all, his money gave him sufficient superiority over a beggar like me, and that he had in his hands a surer and more dignified mode of revenge than the somewhat hazardous one of personal chastisement.

"Take your hat," said he. "Take what belongs to you, and go out at that door; get away to your parish, you pauper: beg, steal, starve, get transported, do what you like; but at your peril venture again into my sight! If ever I hear of your setting foot on an inch of ground belonging to me, I'll hire a man to ane you."

"It is not likely you'll have the chance; once off your premises, what temptation can I have to return to them? I leave a prison, I leave a tyrant; I leave what is worse than the worst that can lie before me, so no fear of my coming back."

"Go, or I'll make you!" exclaimed Crimsworth.

I walked deliberately to my desk, took out such of its contents as were my own property, put them in my pocket, locked the desk, and placed the key on the top.

"What are you abstracting from that desk?" demanded the millowner. "Leave all behind in its place, or I'll send for a policeman to search you."

"Look sharp about it, then," said I, and I took down my hat, drew on my gloves, and walked leisurely out of the counting-house—walked out of it to enter it no more.

I recollect that when the mill-bell rang the dinner hour, before Mr. Crimsworth entered, and the scene above related took place, I had had rather a sharp appetite, and had been waiting somewhat impatiently to hear the signal of feeding time. I forgot it now, however; the images of potatoes and roast mutton were effaced from my mind by the stir and tumult which the transaction of the last half hour had there excited. I only thought of walking, that the action of my muscles might harmonize with the action of my nerves;

and walk I did, fast and far. How could I do otherwise? A load was lifted off my heart; I felt light and liberated. I had got away from Bigben Close without a breach of resolution; without injury to my self-respect. I had not forced circumstances, circumstances had freed me. Life was again open to me; no longer was its horizon limited by the high, black wall surrounding Crimsworth's mill. Two hours had elapsed before my sensations had so far subsided as to leave me calm enough to remark for what wider and clearer boundaries I had exchanged that sooty girdle. When I did look up, lo! straight before me lay Grovetown, a village of villas about five miles out of X——. The short winter day, as I perceived from the far-declined sun, was already approaching its close; a chill frost-mist was rising from the river on which X—— stands and along whose banks the road I had taken lay; it dimmed the earth, but did not obscure the clear, icy blue of the January sky. There was a great stillness near and far; the time of the day favoured tranquillity, as the people were all employed within doors, the hour of evening release from the factories not being yet arrived; a sound of full-flowing water alone pervaded the air, for the river was deep and abundant, swelled by the melting of a late snow. I stood awhile, leaning over a wall; and looking down at the current, I watched the rapid rush of its waves. I desired memory to take a clear and permanent impression of the scene, and treasure it for future years. Grovetown church clock struck four; looking up, I beheld the last of that day's sun, glinting red through the leafless boughs of some very old oak trees surrounding the church—its light coloured and characterized the picture as I wished. I paused yet a moment, till the sweet, slow sound of the bell had quite died out of the air; then ear, eye and feeling satisfied, I quitted the wall and once more turned my face towards X——.

CHAPTER VI.

I RE-ENTERED the town a hungry man; the dinner I had forgotten recurred seductively to my recollection; and it was with a quick step and sharp appetite I ascended the narrow street leading to my lodgings. It was dark when I opened the front door and walked into the house. I wondered how my fire would be; the night was cold, and I shuddered at the prospect of a grate full of sparkless cinders. To my joyful surprise, I found, on entering my sitting-room, a good fire and a clean hearth. I had hardly noticed this phenomenon, when I became aware of another subject for wonderment; the chair I usually occupied near the hearth was already filled; a person sat there with his arms folded on his chest, and his legs stretched out on the rug. Short-sighted as I am, doubtful as was the gleam of the firelight, a moment's examination enabled me to recognise in this person my acquaintance, Mr. Hunsden. I could not of course be much pleased to see him, considering the manner in which I had parted from him the night before, and as I walked to the hearth, stirred the fire, and said coolly, "Good evening," my demeanour evinced as little cordiality as I felt; yet I wondered in my own mind what had brought him there; and I wondered, also, what motives had induced him to interfere so actively between me and Edward; it was to him, it appeared, that I owed my welcome dismissal; still I could not bring myself to ask him questions, to show any eagerness of curiosity; if he chose to explain, he might, but the explanation should be a perfectly voluntary one on his part; I thought he was entering upon it.

"You owe me a debt of gratitude," were his first words.

"Do I?" said I; "I hope it is not a large one, for I am much too poor to charge myself with heavy liabilities of any kind."

"Then declare yourself bankrupt at once, for this liability is a ton weight at least. When I came in I found your fire out, and I had it lit again, and made that sulky drab of a servant stay and blow at it with the bellows till it had burnt up properly; now, say 'Thank you!'"

"Not till I have had something to eat; I can thank nobody while I am so famished."

I rang the bell and ordered tea and some cold meat.

"Cold meat!" exclaimed Hunsden, as the servant closed the door, "what a glutton you are, man! Meat with tea! you'll die of eating too much."

"No, Mr. Hunsden, I shall not." I felt a necessity for contradicting him; I was irritated with hunger, and irritated at seeing him there, and irritated at the continued roughness of his manner.

"It is over-eating that makes you so ill tempered," said he.

"How do you know?" I demanded. "It is like you to give a pragmatical opinion without being acquainted with any of the circumstances of the case; I have had no dinner."

What I said was petulant and snappish enough, and Hunsden only replied by looking in my face and laughing.

"Poor thing!" he whined, after a pause. "It has had no dinner, has it? What! I suppose its master would not let it come home. Did Crimsworth order you to fast by way of punishment, William?"

"No, Mr. Hunsden." Fortunately, at this sulky juncture, tea was brought in, and I fell to upon some bread and butter and cold beef directly. Having cleared a plateful, I became so far humanized as to intimate to Mr. Hunsden "that he need not sit there staring, but might come to the table and do as I did, if he liked."

"But I don't like in the least," said he, and therewith he summoned the servant by a fresh pull of the bell-rope, and intimated a desire to have a glass of toast-and-water. "And some more coal," he added; "Mr. Crimsworth shall keep a good fire while I stay."

His orders being executed, he wheeled his chair round to the table, so as to be opposite me.

"Well," he proceeded. "You are out of work, I suppose."

"Yes," said I; and not disposed to show the satisfaction I felt on this point, I, yielding to the whim of the moment, took up the subject as though I considered myself aggrieved rather than benefited by what had been done. "Yes—thanks to you, I am. Crimsworth turned me off at a minute's notice, owing to some interference of yours at a public meeting, I understand."

"Ah! What! he mentioned that? He observed me signalling the lads, did he? What had he to say about his friend Hunsden—anything sweet?"

"He called you a treacherous villain."

"Oh, he hardly knows me yet! I'm one of those shy people who don't come out all at once, and he is only just beginning to make my acquaintance, but he'll find I've some good qualities—excellent ones! The Hunsdens were always unrivalled at tracking a rascal; a downright, dishonourable villain is their natural prey—they could not keep off him wherever they met him; you used the word pragmatical just now—that word is the property of our family; it has been applied to us from generation to generation; we have fine noses for abuses; we scent a scoundrel a mile off; we are reformers born, radical reformers; and it was impossible for me to live in the same town with Crimsworth, to come into weekly contact with him, to witness some of his conduct to you (for whom personally I care nothing; I only consider the brutal injustice with which he violated your natural claim to equality)—I say it was impossible for me to be thus situated and not feel the angel or the demon of my race at work within me. I followed my instinct, opposed a tyrant, and broke a chain."

Now this speech interested me much, both because it brought out Hunsden's character, and because it explained his motives; it interested me so much that I forgot to reply to it, and sat silent, pondering over a throng of ideas it had suggested.

"Are you grateful to me?" he asked, presently.

In fact I was grateful, or almost so, and I believe I half liked him at the moment, notwithstanding his proviso that what he had done was not out of regard for me. But human nature is perverse. Impossible to answer his blunt question in the affirmative, so I disclaimed all tendency to gratitude, and advised him if he expected any reward for his championship to look for it in a better world, as he was not likely to meet with it here. In reply he termed me "a dry-hearted aristocratic scamp," whereupon I again charged him with having taken the bread out of my mouth.

"Your bread was dirty, man!" cried Hunsden—"dirty and unwholesome! It came through the hands of a tyrant, for I tell you Crimsworth is a tyrant,—a tyrant to his work-people, a tyrant to his clerks, and will some day be a tyrant to his wife."

"Nonsense! bread is bread, and a salary is a salary. I've lost mine, and through your means."

"There's sense in what you say, after all," rejoined Hunsden. "I must say I am rather agreeably surprised to hear you make so practical an observation as that last. I had imagined now, from my previous observation of your character, that the sentimental delight you would have taken in your newly regained liberty would, for a while at least, have effaced all ideas of forethought and prudence. I think better of you for looking steadily to the needful."

"Looking steadily to the needful! How can I do otherwise? I must live, and to live I must have what you call 'the needful,' which I can only get by working. I repeat it, you have taken my work from me."

"What do you mean to do?" pursued Hunsden coolly. "You have influential relations; I suppose they'll soon provide you with another place."

"Influential relations? Who? I should like to know their names."

"The Seacombes."

"Stuff! I have cut them."

Hunsden looked at me incredulously.

"I have," said I, "and that definitively."

"You must mean they have cut you, William."

"As you please. They offered me their patronage on condition of my entering the Church; I declined both the terms and the recompense; I withdrew from my cold uncles, and preferred throwing myself into my elder brother's arms, from whose affectionate embrace I am now torn by the cruel intermeddling of a stranger—of yourself, in short."

I could not repress a half-smile as I said this; a similar demi-manifestation of feeling appeared at the same moment on Hunsden's lips.

"Oh, I see!" said he, looking into my eyes, and it was evident he *did* see right down into my heart. Having sat a minute or two with his chin resting on his hand, diligently occupied in the continued perusal of my countenance, he went on:—

"Seriously, have you then nothing to expect from the Seacombes?"

"Yes, rejection and repulsion. Why do you ask me twice? How can hands, stained with the ink of a counting-house, soiled with the grease of a wool-warehouse, ever again be permitted to come into contact with aristocratic palms?"

"There would be a difficulty, no doubt; still

you are such a complete Seacombe in appearance, feature, language, almost manner, I wonder they should disown you."

"They have disowned me; so talk no more about it."

"Do you regret it, William?"

"No."

"Why not, lad?"

"Because they are not people with whom I could ever have had any sympathy."

"I say you are one of them."

"That merely proves that you know nothing at all about it; I am my mother's son, but not my uncle's nephew."

"Still—one of your uncles is a lord, though rather an obscure and not a very wealthy one, and the other a right honourable: you should consider worldly interest."

"Nonsense, Mr. Hunsden. You know or may know that even had I desired to be submissive to my uncles, I could not have stooped with a good enough grace ever to have won their favour. I should have sacrificed my own comfort and not have gained their patronage in return."

"Very likely—so you calculated your wisest plan was to follow your own devices at once?"

"Exactly. I must follow my own devices—I must till the day of my death; because I can neither comprehend, adopt, nor work out those of other people."

Hunsden yawned. "Well," said he, "in all this, I see but one thing clearly—that is, that the whole affair is no business of mine." He stretched himself and again yawned. "I wonder what time it is," he went on; "I have an appointment for seven o'clock."

"Three quarters past six by my watch."

"Well, then I'll go." He got up. "You'll not meddle with trade again?" said he, leaning his elbow on the mantel-piece.

"No; I think not."

"You would be a fool if you did. Probably,

after all, you 'll think better of your uncles' proposal and go into the Church?"

"A singular regeneration must take place in my whole inner and outer man before I do that. A good clergyman is one of the best of men."

"Indeed! Do you think so?" interrupted Hunsden, scoffingly.

"I do, and no mistake. But I have not the peculiar points which go to make a good clergyman; and rather than adopt a profession for which I have no vocation, I would endure extremities of hardship from poverty."

"You 're a mighty difficult customer to suit. You won't be a tradesman or a parson; you can't be a lawyer, or a doctor, or a gentleman, because you 've no money. I'd recommend you to travel."

"What! without money?"

"You must travel in search of money, man. You can speak French — with a vile English accent, no doubt—still, you can speak it. Go on to the Continent, and see what will turn up for you there."

"God knows I should like to go!" exclaimed I with involuntary ardour.

"Go: what the deuce hinders you?" You may get to Brussels, for instance, for five or six pounds, if you know how to manage with economy."

"Necessity would teach me if I didn't."

"Go, then, and let your wits make a way for you when you get there. I know Brussels almost as well as I know X——, and I am sure it would suit such a one as you better than London."

"But occupation, Mr. Hunsden! I must go where occupation is to be had; and how could I get recommendation, or introduction, or employment at Brussels?"

"There speaks the organ of caution. You hate to advance a step before you know every inch of the way. You haven't a sheet of paper and a pen and ink?"

"I hope so," and I produced writing materials with alacrity; for I guessed what he was going to do. He sat down, wrote a few lines, folded, sealed, and addressed a letter, and held it out to me.

"There, Prudence, there's a pioneer to hew down the first rough difficulties of your path. I know well enough, lad, you are not one of those who will run their neck into a noose without seeing how they are to get it out again, and you're right there. A reckless man is my aversion, and nothing should ever persuade me to meddle with the concerns of such a one. Those who are reckless for themselves are generally ten times more so for their friends."

"This is a letter of introduction, I suppose?" said I, taking the epistle.

"Yes. With that in your pocket you will run no risk of finding yourself in a state of absolute destitution, which, I know, you will regard as a degradation—so should I, for that matter. The person, to whom you will present it, generally has two or three respectable places depending upon his recommendation."

"That will just suit me," said I.

"Well, and where's your gratitude?" demanded Mr. Hunsden; "don't you know how to say 'Thank you'?"

"I've fifteen pounds and a watch, which my godmother, whom I never saw, gave me eighteen years ago," was my rather irrelevant answer; and I further avowed myself a happy man, and professed that I did not envy any being in Christendom.

"And your gratitude?"

"I shall be off presently, Mr. Hunsden—to-morrow if all be well: I'll not stay a day longer in X—— than I am obliged."

"Very good—but it will be decent to make due acknowledgment for the assistance you have received; be quick! It is just going to strike seven: I'm waiting to be thanked."

"Just stand out of the way, will you, Mr. Hunsden: I want a key there is on the corner of the mantel-piece. I'll pack my portmanteau before I go to bed."

The house-clock struck seven.

"The lad is a heathen," said Hunsden, and taking his hat from a sideboard, he left the room laughing to himself. I had half an inclination to follow him: I really intended to leave X—— the next morning, and should certainly not have another opportunity of bidding him good-bye. The front door banged to.

"Let him go," said I, "we shall meet again some day."

CHAPTER VII.

READER, perhaps you were never in Belgium? Haply you don't know the physiognomy of the country? You have not its lineaments defined upon your memory as I have them on mine?

Three—nay four—pictures line the four-walled cell where are stored for me the records of the past. First, Eton. All in that picture is in far perspective, receding, diminutive; but freshly coloured, green, dewy, with a spring sky, piled with glittering yet showery clouds; for my childhood was not all sunshine—it had its overcast, its cold, its stormy hours. Second, X——, huge, dingy; the canvas cracked and smoked; a yellow sky, sooty clouds; no sun, no azure; the verdure of the suburbs blighted and sullied—a very dreary scene.

Third, Belgium; and I will pause before this landscape. As to the fourth, a curtain covers it, which I may hereafter withdraw, or may not, as suits my convenience and capacity. At any rate, for the present it must hang undisturbed. Belgium! name unromantic and unpoetic, yet name that whenever uttered has in my ear a sound, in my heart an echo, such as no other assemblage of syllables, however sweet or classic, can produce. Belgium! I repeat the word, now as I sit alone near midnight. It stirs my world of the past like a summons to resurrection; the graves unclose, the dead are raised; thoughts, feelings, memories that slept, are seen by me ascending from the clods—haloed most of them—but while I gaze on their vapoury forms, and strive to ascertain definitely their outline, the sound which wakened them dies, and they sink, each and all, like a light wreath of mist, absorbed in the mould, recalled to urns, re-sealed in monuments. Farewell luminous phantoms!

This is Belgium, reader. Look! don't call the picture a flat or a dull one—it was neither flat nor dull to me when I first beheld it. When I left Ostend on a mild February morning, and found myself on the road to Brussels, nothing could look vapid to me. My sense of enjoyment possessed an edge whetted to the finest, untouched, keen, exquisite. I was young; I had good health; pleasure and I had never met; no indulgence of hers had enervated or sated one faculty of my nature. Liberty I clasped in my arms for the first time, and the influence of her smile and embrace revived my life like the sun and the west wind. Yes, at that epoch I felt like a morning traveller who doubts not that from the hill he is ascending he shall behold a glorious sunrise; what if the track be strait, steep, and stony? he sees it not; his eyes are fixed on that summit, flushed already, flushed and gilded, and having gained it he is certain of the scene beyond. He knows that the sun will face him, that his chariot is even now coming over the eastern horizon, and that the herald breeze he feels on his cheek is opening for the god's career a clear, vast path of azure, amidst clouds soft as pearl and warm as flame. Difficulty and toil were to be my lot, but sustained by energy, drawn on by hopes as bright as vague, I deemed such a lot no hardship. I mounted now the hill in shade; there were pebbles, inequalities, briars in my path, but my eyes were fixed on the crimson peak above; my imagination was with the refulgent firmament beyond, and I thought nothing of the stones turning under my feet, or of the thorns scratching my face and hands.

I gazed often, and always with delight, from the window of the diligence (these, be it remembered, were not the days of trains and railroads). Well! and what did I see? I will tell you faithfully. Green, reedy swamps; fields fertile but flat, cultivated in patches that made them look like magnified kitchen-gardens; belts of cut trees, formal as pollard willows, skirting the horizon; narrow canals, gliding slow by the road-side; painted Flemish farm-houses; some very dirty hovels; a grey, dead sky; wet road, wet fields, wet house-tops: not a beautiful, scarcely a picturesque object met my eye along the whole route; yet to me, all was beautiful, all was more than picturesque. It continued fair so long as daylight lasted, though the moisture of many preceding damp days had sodden the whole country; as it grew dark, however, the rain re-commenced, and it was through streaming and starless darkness my eye caught the first gleam of the lights of Brussels. I saw little of the city but its lights that night. Having alighted from the diligence, a fiacre conveyed me to the Hotel de—— where I had been advised by a fellow traveller to put up; having eaten a traveller's supper, I retired to bed, and slept a traveller's sleep.

Next morning I awoke from prolonged and sound repose with the impression that I was yet in X——, and perceiving it to be broad daylight I started up, imagining that I had overslept myself and should be behind time at the counting-house. The momentary and painful sense of restraint vanished before the revived and reviving consciousness of freedom, as, throwing back the white curtains of my bed, I looked forth into a wide, lofty foreign chamber; how different from the small and dingy, though not uncomfortable apartment, I had occupied for a night or two at a respectable inn in London, while waiting for the sailing of the packet! Yet far be it from me to profane the memory of that little dingy room! It, too, is dear to my soul; for there, as I lay in quiet and darkness, I first heard the great bell of St. Paul's telling London it was midnight, and well do I recall the deep, deliberate tones, so full charged with colossal phlegm and force. From the small, narrow window of that room,

I first saw *the* dome, looming through a London mist. I suppose the sensations, stirred by those first sounds, first sights, are felt but once; treasure them, Memory; seal them in urns, and keep them in safe niches! Well—I rose. Travellers talk of the apartments in foreign dwellings being bare and uncomfortable; I thought my chamber looked stately and cheerful. It had such large windows—*croisées* that opened like doors, with such broad, clear panes of glass; such a great looking-glass stood on my dressing-table—such a fine mirror glittered over the mantel-piece—the painted floor looked so clean and glossy; when I had dressed and was descending the stairs, the broad marble steps almost awed me, and so did the lofty hall into which they conducted. On the first landing I met a Flemish housemaid: she had wooden shoes, a short red petticoat, a printed cotton bed-gown, her face was broad, her physiognomy eminently stupid; when I spoke to her in

French, she answered me in Flemish, with an air the reverse of civil, yet I thought her charming; if she was not pretty or polite, she was, I conceived, very picturesque; she reminded me of the female figures in certain Dutch paintings I had seen in other years at Seacombe Hall.

I repaired to the public room; that, too, was very large and very lofty, and warmed by a stove; the floor was black, and the stove was black, and most of the furniture was black; yet I never experienced a freer sense of exhilaration than when I sat down at a very long, black table (covered, however, in part by a white cloth), and, having ordered breakfast, began to pour out my coffee from a little black coffee-pot. The stove might be dismal-looking to some eyes, not to mine, but it was indisputably very warm, and there were two gentlemen seated by it talking in French; impossible to follow their rapid utterance, or comprehend much of the purport of what they said—yet French, in the mouths of Frenchmen, or Belgians (I was not then sensible of the horrors of the Belgian accent), was as music to my ears. One of these gentlemen presently discerned me to be an Englishman—no doubt from the fashion in which I addressed the waiter; for I would persist in speaking French in my execrable South-of-England style, though the man understood English. The gentleman, after looking towards me once or twice, politely accosted me in very good English; I remember I wished to God that I could speak French as well; his fluency and correct pronunciation impressed me for the first time with a due notion of the cosmopolitan character of the capital I was in; it was my first experience of that skill in living languages I afterwards found to be so general in Brussels.

I lingered over my breakfast as long as I could; while it was there on the table, and while that stranger continued talking to me, I was a free, independent traveller; but at last the things were removed, the two gentlemen left the room; suddenly the illusion ceased, reality and business came back. I, a bondsman just released from the yoke, freed for one week from twenty-one years of constraint, must, of necessity, resume the fetters of dependency. Hardly had I tasted the delight of being without a master when duty issued her stern mandate: "Go forth and seek another service." I never linger over a painful and necessary task; I never take pleasure before business, it is not in my nature to do so; impossible to enjoy a leisurely walk over the city, though I perceived the morning was very fine, until I had first presented Mr. Hunsden's letter of introduction, and got fairly on to the track of a new situation. Wrenching my mind from liberty and delight, I seized my hat, and forced my reluctant body out of the Hotel de —— into the foreign street.

It was a fine day, but I would not look at the blue sky or at the stately houses round me; my mind was bent on one thing, finding out "Mr. Brown, Numero —, Rue Royale," for so my letter was addressed. By dint of inquiry I succeeded; I stood at last at the desired door, knocked, asked for Mr. Brown, and was admitted.

Being shown into a small breakfast-room, I found myself in the presence of an elderly gentleman—very grave, business-like, and respectable-looking. I presented Mr. Hunsden's letter; he received me very civilly. After a little desultory conversation he asked me if there was anything in which his advice or experience could be of use. I said, "Yes," and then proceeded to tell him that I was not a gentleman of fortune, travelling for pleasure, but an ex-counting-house clerk, who wanted employment of some kind, and that immediately too. He replied that as a friend of Mr. Hunsden's he would be willing to assist me as well as he could. After some meditation he named a place in a mercantile house at Liège, and another in a bookseller's shop at Louvain.

"Clerk and shopman!" murmured I to myself. "No." I shook my head. I had tried the high stool; I hated it; I believed there were other occupations that would suit me better; besides I did not wish to leave Brussels.

"I know of no place in Brussels," answered Mr. Brown, "unless indeed you were disposed to turn your attention to teaching. I am acquainted with the director of a large establishment who is in want of a professor of English and Latin."

I thought two minutes, then I seized the idea eagerly.

"The very thing, sir!" said I.

"But," asked he, "do you understand French well enough to teach Belgian boys English?"

Fortunately I could answer this question in the affirmative; having studied French under a Frenchman, I could speak the language intelligibly though not fluently. I could also read it well, and write it decently.

"Then," pursued Mr. Brown, "I think I can

promise you the place, for Monsieur Pelet will not refuse a professor recommended by me, but come here again at five o'clock this afternoon, and I will introduce you to him."

The word "professor" struck me. "I am not a professor," said I.

"Oh," returned Mr. Brown, "professor, here in Belgium, means a teacher, that is all."

My conscience thus quieted, I thanked Mr. Brown, and, for the present, withdrew. This time I stepped out into the street with a relieved heart; the task I had imposed on myself for that day was executed. I might now take some hours of holiday. I felt free to look up. For the first time I remarked the sparkling clearness of the air, the deep blue of the sky, the gay clean aspect of the white-washed or painted houses; I saw what a fine street was the Rue Royale, and, walking leisurely along its broad pavement, I continued to survey its stately hotels, till the palisades, the gates, and trees of the park appearing in sight, offered to my eye a new attraction. I remember, before entering the park, I stood awhile to contemplate the statue of General Belliard, and then I advanced to the top of the great staircase just beyond, and I looked down into a narrow back street, which I afterwards learnt was called the Rue d'Isabelle. I well recollect that my eye rested on the green door of a rather large house opposite, where, on a brass plate, was inscribed, "Pensionnat de Demoiselles." Pensionnat! The word excited an uneasy sensation in my mind; it seemed to speak of restraint. Some of the demoiselles, externats no doubt, were at that moment issuing from the door—I looked for a pretty face amongst them, but their close, little French bonnets hid their features; in a moment they were gone.

I had traversed a good deal of Brussels before five o'clock arrived, but punctually as that hour struck I was again in the Rue Royale. Re-admitted to Mr. Brown's breakfast-room, I found him, as before, seated at the table, and he was not alone—a gentleman stood by the hearth. Two words of introduction designated him as my future master. "M. Pelet, Mr. Crimsworth; Mr. Crimsworth, M. Pelet." A bow on each side finished the ceremony. I don't know what sort of a bow I made; an ordinary one, I suppose, for I was in a tranquil, common-place frame of mind; I felt none of the agitation which had troubled my first interview with Edward Crimsworth. M. Pelet's bow was extremely polite, yet not theatrical, scarcely French; he and I were presently seated opposite to each other. In a pleasing voice, low, and, out of consideration to my foreign ears, very distinct and deliberate, M. Pelet intimated that he had just been receiving from "le respectable M. Brown," an account of my attainments and character, which relieved him from all scruple as to the propriety of engaging me as professor of English and Latin in his establishment; nevertheless, for form's sake, he would put a few questions to test my powers. He did, and expressed in flattering terms his satisfaction at my answers. The subject of salary next came on; it was fixed at one thousand francs per annum, besides board and lodging. "And in addition," suggested M. Pelet, "as there will be some hours in each day during which your services will not be required in my establishment, you may, in time, obtain employment in other seminaries, and thus turn your vacant moments to profitable account."

I thought this very kind, and indeed I found afterwards that the terms on which M. Pelet had engaged me were really liberal for Brussels; instruction being extremely cheap there on account of the number of teachers. It was further arranged that I should be installed in my new post the very next day, after which M. Pelet and I parted.

Well, and what was he like? and what were my impressions concerning him? He was a man of about forty years of age, of middle size, and rather emaciated figure; his face was pale, his cheeks were sunk, and his eyes hollow; his features were pleasing and regular, they had a French turn (for M. Pelet was no Fleming, but a Frenchman both by birth and parentage), yet the degree of harshness inseparable from Gallic lineaments was, in his case, softened by a mild blue eye, and a melancholy, almost suffering, expression of countenance; his physiognomy was "fine et spirituelle." I use two French words because they define better than any English terms the species of intelligence with which his features were imbued. He was altogether an interesting and prepossessing personage. I wondered only at the utter absence of all the ordinary characteristics of his profession, and almost feared he could not be stern and resolute enough for a schoolmaster. Externally at least M. Pelet presented an absolute contrast to my late master, Edward Crimsworth.

Influenced by the impression I had received of

his gentleness, I was a good deal surprised when, on arriving the next day at my new employer's house, and being admitted to a first view of what was to be the sphere of my future labours, namely the large, lofty, and well lighted school-rooms, I beheld a numerous assemblage of pupils, boys of course, whose collective appearance showed all the signs of a full, flourishing, and well disciplined seminary. As I traversed the classes in company with M. Pelet, a profound silence reigned on all sides, and if by chance a murmur or a whisper arose, one glance from the pensive eye of this most gentle pedagogue stilled it instantly. It was astonishing, I thought, how so mild a check could prove so effectual. When I had perambulated the length and breadth of the classes, M. Pelet turned and said to me—

"Would you object to taking the boys as they are, and testing their proficiency in English?"

The proposal was unexpected. I had thought I should have been allowed at least a day to prepare, but it is a bad omen to commence any career by hesitation, so I just stepped to the professor's desk near which we stood, and faced the circle of my pupils. I took a moment to collect my thoughts, and likewise to frame in French the sentence by which I proposed to open business. I made it as short as possible:—

"Messieurs, prenez vos livres de lecture."

"Anglais ou Français, monsieur?" demanded a thick set, moon-faced young Flamand in a blouse. The answer was fortunately easy:—

"Anglais."

I determined to give myself as little trouble as possible in this lesson; it would not do yet to trust my unpractised tongue with the delivery of explanations; my accent and idiom would be too open to the criticisms of the young gentlemen before me, relative to whom I felt already it would be necessary at once to take up an advantageous position, and I proceeded to employ means accordingly.

"Commencez!" cried I, when they had all produced their books. The moon-faced youth (by name Jules Vanderkelkov, as I afterwards learnt) took the first sentence. The "livre de lecture" was the "Vicar of Wakefield," much used in foreign schools because it is supposed to contain prime samples of conversational English; it might, however, have been a Runic scroll for any resemblance the words, as enunciated by Jules, bore to the language in ordinary use amongst the natives of Great Britain. My God! how he did snuffle, snort, and wheeze! All he said was said in his throat and nose, for it is thus the Flamands speak, but I heard him to the end of his paragraph without proffering a word of correction, whereat he looked vastly self-complacent, convinced, no doubt, that he had acquitted himself like a real born and bred "Anglais." In the same unmoved silence I listened to a dozen in rotation, and when the twelfth had concluded with splutter, hiss, and mumble, I solemnly laid down the book.

"Arrêtez!" said I. There was a pause, during which I regarded them all with a steady and somewhat stern gaze; a dog, if stared at hard enough and long enough, will show symptoms of embarrassment, and so at length did my bench of Belgians. Perceiving that some of the faces before me were beginning to look sullen, and others ashamed, I slowly joined my hands, and ejaculated in a deep "voix de poitrine"—

"Comme c'est affreux!"

They looked at each other, pouted, coloured, swung their heels; they were not pleased, I saw, but they were impressed, and in the way I wished them to be. Having thus taken them down a peg in their self-conceit, the next step was to raise myself in their estimation; not a very easy thing, considering that I hardly dared to speak for fear of betraying my own deficiencies.

"Ecoutez, messieurs!" said I, and I endeavoured to throw into my accents the compassionate tone of a superior being, who, touched by the extremity of the helplessness, which at first only excited his scorn, deigns at length to bestow aid. I then began at the very beginning of the "Vicar of Wakefield," and read, in a slow, distinct voice, some twenty pages, they all the while sitting mute and listening with fixed attention; by the time I had done nearly an hour had elapsed. I then rose and said:—

"C'est assez pour aujourd'hui, messieurs; demain nous recommençerons, et j'espère que tout ira bien."

With this oracular sentence I bowed, and in company with M. Pelet quitted the school-room.

"C'est bien! c'est très bien!" said my principal as we entered his parlour. "Je vois que Monsieur a de l'adresse; cela me plait, car, dans l'instruction, l'adresse fait tout autant que le savoir."

From the parlour M. Pelet conducted me to my apartment, my "chambre," as Monsieur said with a certain air of complacency. It was a very small room, with an excessively small bed, but M. Pelet gave me to understand that I was to occupy it quite alone, which was of course a great comfort. Yet, though so limited in dimensions, it had two windows. Light not being taxed in Belgium, the people never grudge its admission into their houses; just here, however, this observation is not very *apropos*, for one of these windows was boarded up; the open window looked into the boys' playground. I glanced at the other, as wondering what aspect it would present if disencumbered of the boards. M. Pelet read, I suppose, the expression of my eye; he explained:—

"La fenêtre fermée donne sur un jardin appartenant à un pensionnat de demoiselles," said he, "et les convenances exigent—enfin, vous comprenez—n'est-ce pas, monsieur?"

"Oui, oui," was my reply, and I looked of course quite satisfied; but when M. Pelet had retired and closed the door after him, the first thing I did was to scrutinize closely the nailed boards, hoping to find some chink or crevice which I might enlarge, and so get a peep at the consecrated ground. My researches were vain, for the boards were well joined and strongly nailed. It is astonishing how disappointed I felt. I thought it would have been so pleasant to have looked out upon a garden planted with flowers and trees, so amusing to have watched the demoiselles at their play; to have studied female character in a variety of phases, myself the while sheltered from view by a modest muslin curtain, whereas, owing doubtless to the absurd scruples of some old duenna of a directress, I had now only the option of looking at a bare, gravelled court, with an enormous "pas de géant" in the middle and the monotonous walls and windows of a boy's school-house round. Not only then, but many a time after, especially in moments of weariness and low spirits, did I look with dissatisfied eyes on that most tantalizing board, longing to tear it away and get a glimpse of the green region which I imagined to lie beyond. I knew a tree grew close up to the window, for though there were as yet no leaves to rustle I often heard at night the tapping of branches against the panes. In the day-time, when I listened attentively, I could hear, even through the boards, the voices of the demoiselles in their hours of recreation, and, to speak the honest truth, my sentimental reflections were occasionally a trifle disarranged by the not quite silvery, in fact the too often brazen sounds, which, rising from the unseen paradise below, penetrated clamorously into my solitude. Not to mince matters, it really seemed to me a doubtful case whether the lungs of Mdlle. Reuter's girls or those of M. Pelet's boys were the strongest, and when it came to shrieking the girls indisputably beat the boys hollow. I forgot to say, by-the-by, that Reuter was the name of the old lady who had had my window boarded up. I say old, for such I, of course, concluded her to be, judging from her cautious, chaperon-like proceedings; besides, nobody ever spoke of her as young. I remember I was very much amused when I first heard her Christian name; it was Zoraïde — Mademoiselle Zoraïde Reuter. But the continental nations do allow themselves vagaries in the choice of names, such as we sober English never run into. I think, indeed, we have too limited a list to choose from.

Meantime my path was gradually growing smooth before me. I, in a few weeks, conquered the teasing difficulties inseparable from the commencement of almost every career. Ere long I had acquired as much facility in speaking French as set me at my ease with my pupils, and as I had encountered them on a right footing at the very beginning, and continued tenaciously to retain the advantage I had early gained, they never attempted mutiny, which circumstance, all who are in any degree acquainted with the ongoings of Belgian schools, and who know the relation in which professors and pupils too frequently stand towards each other in those establishments, will consider an important and uncommon one. Before concluding this chapter I will say a word on the system I pursued with regard to my classes: my experience may possibly be of use to others.

It did not require very keen observation to detect the character of the youth of Brabant, but it needed a certain degree of tact to adopt one's measures to their capacity. Their intellectual faculties were generally weak, their animal propensities strong; thus there was at once an impotence and a kind of inert force in their natures; they were dull, but they were also singularly stubborn, heavy as lead and, like lead, most difficult to move. Such being the case, it would have been truly absurd to exact from them much in the way of mental exertion; having short memories, dense intelligence, feeble reflective powers, they recoiled with repugnance from any occupation that demanded close study or deep thought. Had the abhorred effort been extorted from them by injudicious and arbitrary measures on the part of the Professor, they would have resisted as obstinately, as clamorously, as desperate swine; and though not brave singly, they were relentless acting *en masse.*

I understood that before my arrival in M. Pelet's establishment, the combined insubordination of the pupils had effected the dismissal of more than one English master. It was necessary then to exact only the most moderate application from natures so little qualified to apply—to assist, in every practicable way, understandings so opaque and contracted—to be ever gentle, considerate, yielding even, to a certain point, with dispositions so irrationally perverse; but, having reached that culminating point of indulgence, you must fix your foot, plant it, root it in rock—become immutable as the towers of Ste. Gudule; for a step—but half a step further, and you would plunge headlong into the gulf of imbecility; there lodged, you would speedily receive proofs of Flemish gratitude and magnanimity in showers of Brabant saliva and handfuls of Low-Country mud. You might smooth to the utmost the path of learning, remove every pebble from the track; but then you must finally insist with decision on the pupil taking your arm and allowing himself to be led quietly along the prepared road. When I had brought down my lesson to the lowest level of my dullest pupil's capacity—when I had shown myself the mildest, the most tolerant of masters—a word of impertinence, a movement of disobedience, changed me at once into a despot. I offered then but one alternative—submission and acknowledgment of error, or ignominious expulsion. This system answered, and my influence, by degrees, became established on a firm basis. "The boy is father to the man," it is said; and so I often thought when I looked at my boys and remembered the political history of their ancestors. Pelet's school was merely an epitome of the Belgian nation.

CHAPTER VIII.

And Pelet himself? How did I continue to like him? Oh, extremely well! Nothing could be more smooth, gentlemanlike, and even friendly, than his demeanour to me. I had to endure from him neither cold neglect, irritating interference, nor pretentious assumption of superiority. I fear, however, two poor, hard-worked Belgian ushers in the establishment could not have said as much; to them the director's manner was invariably dry, stern, and cool. I believe he perceived once or twice that I was a little shocked at the difference he made between them and me, and accounted for it by saying, with a quiet, sarcastic smile—

"Ce ne sont que des Flamands—allez!"

And then he took his cigar gently from his lips and spat on the painted floor of the room in which we were sitting. Flamands certainly they were, and both had the true Flamand physiognomy, where intellectual inferiority is marked in lines none can mistake; still they were men, and, in the main, honest men; and I could not see why their being aboriginals of the flat, dull soil should serve as a pretext for treating them with perpetual severity and contempt. This idea of injustice somewhat poisoned the pleasure I might otherwise have derived from Pelet's soft, affable manner to myself. Certainly it was agreeable, when the day's work was over, to find in one's employer an intelligent and cheerful companion; and if he was sometimes a little sarcastic and sometimes a little too insinuating, and if I did discover that his mildness was more a matter of appearance than of reality—if I did occasionally suspect the existence of flint or steel under an external covering of velvet—still we are none of us perfect; and weary as I was of the atmosphere of brutality and insolence in which I had constantly lived at X——, I had no inclination now, on casting anchor in calmer regions, to institute at once a prying search after defects that were scrupulously withdrawn and carefully veiled from my view. I was willing to take Pelet for what he seemed—to believe him benevolent and friendly until some untoward event should prove him otherwise. He was not married, and I soon perceived he had all a Frenchman's, all a Parisian's notions about matrimony and women. I suspected a degree of laxity in his code of morals, there was something so cold and *blasé* in his tone whenever he alluded to what he called, "le beau sexe;" but he was too gentlemanlike to intrude topics I did not invite, and as he was really intelligent and really fond of intellectual subjects of discourse, he and I always found enough to talk about, without seeking themes in the mire. I hated his fashion of mentioning love; I abhorred, from my soul, mere licentiousness. He felt the difference of our notions, and, by mutual consent, we kept off ground debateable.

Pelet's house was kept and his kitchen managed by his mother, a real old Frenchwoman; she had been handsome—at least she told me so, and I strove to believe her; she was now ugly, as only continental old women can be; perhaps, though, her style of dress made her look uglier than she really was. In-doors she would go about without cap, her gray hair strangely dishevelled; then, when at home, she seldom wore a gown—only a shabby cotton camisole; shoes, too, were strangers to her feet, and in lieu of them she sported roomy slippers, trodden down at the heels. On the other hand, whenever it was her pleasure to appear abroad, as on Sundays and fête-days, she would put on some very brilliant-coloured dress, usually of thin texture, a silk bonnet with a wreath of flowers, and a very fine shawl. She was not, in the main, an ill-natured old woman, but an incessant and most indiscreet talker; she kept chiefly in and about the kitchen, and seemed rather to avoid her son's august presence; of him, indeed, she evidently stood in awe. When he reproved her, his reproofs were bitter and unsparing; but he seldom gave himself that trouble.

Madame Pelet had her own society, her own circle of chosen visitors, whom, however, I seldom saw, as she generally entertained them in what she called her "cabinet", a small den of a place adjoining the kitchen, and descending into it by one or two steps. On these steps, by the by, I have not unfrequently seen Madame Pelet seated with a trencher on her knee, engaged in the threefold employment of eating her dinner, gossiping with her favourite servant, the housemaid, and scolding her antagonist, the cook; she never dined, and seldom indeed took any meal with her son, and as to showing her face at the boys' table, that was quite out of the question. These details will sound very odd in English ears, but Belgium is not England, and its ways are not our ways.

Madame Pelet's habits of life, then, being taken into consideration, I was a good deal surprised when, one Thursday evening (Thursday was always a half-holiday), as I was sitting all alone in my apartment, correcting a huge pile of English and Latin exercises, a servant tapped at the door, and, on its being opened, presented Madame Pelet's compliments and she would be happy to see me to take my "gouter" (a meal which answers to our English "tea") with her in the dining-room.

"Plait-il? said I—for I thought I must have misunderstood, the message and invitation were so unusual; the same words were repeated. I accepted, of course, and as I descended the stairs, I wondered what whim had entered the old lady's brain; her son was out—gone to pass the evening at the salle of the Grande Harmonie or some other club of which he was a member. Just as I laid my hand on the handle of the dining-room door, a queer idea glanced across my mind.

"Surely she's not going to make love to me," said I. "I've heard of old Frenchwomen doing odd things in that line; and the goûter? They generally begin such affairs with eating and drinking, I believe."

There was a fearful dismay in this suggestion of my excited imagination, and if I had allowed myself time to dwell upon it, I should no doubt have cut there and then, rushed back to my chamber, and bolted myself in; but whenever a danger or a horror is veiled with uncertainty, the primary wish of the mind is to ascertain first the naked truth, reserving the expedient of flight for the moment when its dread anticipation shall be realized. I turned the door-handle, and in an instant had crossed the fatal threshold, closed the door behind me, and stood in the presence of Madame Pelet.

Gracious heavens! The first view of her seemed to confirm my worst apprehensions. There she sat, dressed out in a light green muslin gown, on her head a lace cap with flourishing red roses in the frill; her table was carefully spread—there were fruit, cakes, and coffee, with a bottle of something, I did not know what. Already the cold sweat started on my brow, already I glanced back over my shoulder at the closed door, when, to my unspeakable relief, my eye, wandering wildly in the direction of the stove, rested upon a second figure, seated in a large fauteuil beside it. This was a woman too, and moreover an old woman, and as fat and as rubicund as Madame Pelet was meagre and yellow; her attire was likewise very fine, and spring flowers of different hues circled in a bright wreath the crown of her violet-coloured velvet bonnet.

I had only time to make these general observations when Madame Pelet, coming forward with what she intended should be a graceful and elastic step, thus accosted me.

"Monsieur is indeed most obliging to quit his books, his studies, at the request of an insignificant person like me — will Monsieur complete his kindness by allowing me to present him to my dear friend Madame Reuter, who resides in the neighbouring house — the young ladies' school."

"Ah!" thought I, "I knew she was old," and I bowed and took my seat; Madame Reuter placed herself at the table opposite to me.

"How do you like Belgium, monsieur?" asked she in an accent of the broadest Bruxellois. I could now well distinguish the difference between the fine and pure Parisian utterance of M. Pelet, for instance, and the guttural enunciation of the Flamands. I answered politely, and then wondered how so coarse and clumsy an old woman as the one before me, should be at the head of a ladies' seminary which I had always heard spoken of in terms of high commendation. In truth there was something to wonder at. Madame Reuter looked more like a joyous, free-living old Flemish fermière, or even a maîtresse d'auberge, than a staid, grave, rigid directrice de pensionnat. In general the Continental, or at least the Belgian old women permit themselves a license of manners, speech, and aspect, such as our venerable grand-dames would recoil from as absolutely disreputable, and Madame Reuter's jolly face bore evidence that she was no exception to the rule of her country; there was a twinkle and leer in her left eye; her right she kept habitually half shut, which I thought very odd indeed. After several vain attempts to comprehend the motives of these two droll old creatures for inviting me to join them at their goûter, I, at last, fairly gave it up, and resigning myself to inevitable mystification, I sat and looked first at one, then at the other, taking care meantime to do justice to the confitures, cakes, and coffee, with which they amply supplied me. They, too, ate, and that with no delicate appetite, and having demolished a large portion of the solids, they proposed a "petit verre." I declined—not so Mesdames Pelet and Reuter; each mixed herself what I thought rather a stiff tumbler of punch, and placing it on a stand near the stove, they drew up their chairs to that convenience, and invited me to do the same; I obeyed, and being seated fairly between them, I was thus addressed first by Madame Pelet, then by Madame Reuter.

"We will now speak of business," said Madame Pelet, and she went on to make an elaborate speech, which, being interpreted, was to the effect that she had asked for the pleasure of my company that evening in order to give her friend Madame Reuter an opportunity of broaching an important proposal which might turn out greatly to my advantage.

"Pourvu que vous soyez sage," said Madame Reuter, "et à vrai dire, vous en avez bien l'air.

Take one drop of the punch (or ponche, as she pronounced it); it is an agreeable and wholesome beverage after a full meal."

I bowed, but again declined it. She went on:—

"I feel," said she, after a solemn sip—"I feel profoundly the importance of the commission with which my dear daughter has entrusted me, for you are aware, monsieur, that it is my daughter who directs the establishment in the next house?"

"Ah! I thought it was yourself, madame." Though, indeed, at that moment, I recollected that it was called Mademoiselle, not Madame Reuter's pensionnat.

"I! oh no! I manage the house and look after the servants, as my friend Madame Pelet does for Monsieur her son—nothing more. Ah! you thought I gave lessons in class—did you?"

And she laughed, loud and long, as though the idea tickled her fancy amazingly.

"Madame is in the wrong to laugh," I observed,

"if she does not give lessons, I am sure it is not because she cannot," and I whipped out a white pocket-handkerchief and wafted it, with a French grace, past my nose, bowing at the same time.

"Quel charmant jeune homme!" murmured Madame Pelet in a low voice. Madame Reuter, being less sentimental, as she was Flamand and not French, only laughed again.

"You are a dangerous person I fear," said she; "if you can forge compliments at that rate Zoraïde will positively be afraid of you, but if you are good, I will keep your secret, and not tell her how well you can flatter. Now, listen what sort of a proposal she makes to you. She has heard that you are an excellent professor, and as she wishes to get the very best masters for her school (car Zoraïde fait tout comme une reine, c'est une véritable maîtresse-femme), she has commissioned me to step over this afternoon, and sound Madame Pelet as to the possibility of engaging you. Zoraïde is a wary general; she never advances without first examining well her ground. I don't think she would be pleased if she knew I had already disclosed her intentions to you; she did not order me to go so far, but I thought there would be no harm in letting you into the secret, and Madame Pelet was of the same opinion. Take care, however, you don't betray either of us to Zoraïde—to my daughter, I mean; she is so discreet and circumspect herself, she cannot understand that one should find a pleasure in gossiping a little ——"

"C'est absolument comme mon fils!" cried Madame Pelet.

"All the world is so changed since our girlhood!" rejoined the other: "young people have such old heads now. But to return, monsieur. Madame Pelet will mention the subject of your giving lessons in my daughter's establishment to her son, and he will speak to you; and then, to-morrow, you will step over to our house, and ask to see my daughter, and you will introduce the subject as if the first intimation of it had reached you from M. Pelet himself, and be sure you never mention my name, for I would not displease Zoraïde on any account.

"Bien! bien!" interrupted I—for all this chatter and circumlocution began to bore me very much; "I will consult M. Pelet, and the thing shall be settled as you desire. Good evening, mesdames—I am infinitely obliged to you."

"Comment! vous vous en allez dêjá?" exclaimed Madame Pelet.

"Prenez encore quelquechose, monsieur; une pomme cuite, des biscuits, encore une tasse de café?"

"Merci, merci, madame—au revoir." And I backed at last out of the apartment.

Having regained my own room, I set myself to turn over in my mind the incident of the evening. It seemed a queer affair altogether, and queerly managed; the two old women had made quite a little intricate mess of it; still I found that the uppermost feeling in my mind on the subject was one of satisfaction. In the first place it would be a change to give lessons in another seminary, and then to teach young ladies would be an occupation so interesting—to be admitted at all into a ladies' boarding-school would be an incident so new in my life. Besides, thought I, as I glanced at the boarded window, "I shall now at last see the mysterious garden: I shall gaze both on the angels and their Eden."

CHAPTER IX.

M. Pelet could not of course object to the proposal made by Mdlle. Reuter; permission to accept such additional employment, should it offer, having formed an article of the terms on which he had engaged me. It was, therefore, arranged in the course of next day that I should be at liberty to give lessons in Mdlle. Reuter's establishment four afternoons in every week.

When evening came I prepared to step over in order to seek a conference with Mademoiselle herself on the subject; I had not had time to pay the visit before, having been all day closely occupied in class. I remember very well that before quitting my chamber, I held a brief debate with myself as to whether I should change my ordinary attire for something smarter. At last I concluded it would be a waste of labour. "Doubtless," thought I, "she is some stiff old maid, for though the daughter of Madame Reuter, she may well number upwards of forty winters; besides, if it were otherwise, if she be both young and pretty, I am not handsome, and no dressing can make me so, therefore I'll go as I am." And off I started, cursorily glancing sideways as I passed the toilet-table, surmounted by a looking-glass; a thin irregular face I saw, with sunk, dark eyes under a large, square forehead, complexion destitute of bloom or attraction; something young but not youthful, no object to win a lady's love, no butt for the shafts of Cupid.

I was soon at the entrance of the Pensionnat, in a moment I had pulled the bell; in another moment the door was opened, and within appeared a passage paved alternately with black and white marble; the walls were painted in imitation of marble also; and at the far end opened a glass door, through which I saw shrubs and a grass-plat, looking pleasant in the sunshine of the mild spring evening—for it was now the middle of April.

This then was my first glimpse of *the* garden; but I had not time to look long, the portress, after having answered in the affirmative my question as to whether her mistress was at home, opened the folding-doors of a room to the left, and having ushered me in, closed them behind me. I found myself in a salon with a very well painted, highly varnished floor; chairs and sofas covered with white draperies, a green porcelain stove, walls hung with pictures in gilt frames, a gilt pendule, and other ornaments on the mantel-piece, a large lustre pendent from the centre of the ceiling, mirrors, consoles, muslin curtains, and a handsome centre table completed the inventory of furniture. All looked extremely clean and glittering, but the general effect would have been somewhat chilling had not a second large pair of folding-doors, standing wide open, and disclosing another and smaller salon, more snugly furnished, offered some relief to the eye. This room was carpeted, and therein was a piano, a couch, a chiffonnière—above all, it contained a lofty window with a crimson curtain, which, being undrawn, afforded another glimpse of the garden, through the large, clear panes, round which some leaves of ivy, some tendrils of vine were trained.

"Monsieur Creemsvort, n'est ce pas?" said a voice behind me; and, starting involuntarily, I turned. I had been so taken up with the contemplation of the pretty little salon that I had not noticed the entrance of a person into the larger room. It was, however, Mdlle. Reuter who now addressed me, and stood close beside me; and when I had bowed with instantaneously recovered *sang froid*—for I am not easily embarrassed—I commenced the conversation by remarking on the pleasant aspect of her little cabinet, and the advantage she had over M. Pelet in possessing a garden.

"Yes," she said, "she often thought so;" and added, "it is my garden, monsieur, which makes me retain this house, otherwise I should probably have removed to larger and more commodious premises long since; but you see I could not take my garden with me, and I should scarcely find one so large and pleasant anywhere else in town."

I approved her judgment.

"But you have not seen it yet," said she, rising; "come to the window and take a better view." I followed her; she opened the sash, and leaning out, I saw in full the enclosed demesne which had hitherto been to me an unknown region. It was a long, not very broad strip of cultured ground, with an alley bordered by enormous old fruit trees down the middle; there was a sort of lawn, a parterre of rose-trees, some flower-borders, and, on the far side, a thickly planted copse of lilacs, laburnums, and acacias. It looked pleasant, to me

—very pleasant, so long a time had elapsed since I had seen a garden of any sort. But it was not only on Mddle. Reuter's garden that my eyes dwelt; when I had taken a view of her well-trimmed beds and budding shrubberies, I allowed my glance to come back to herself, nor did I hastily withdraw it.

I had thought to see a tall, meagre, yellow, conventual image in black, with a close white cap, bandaged under the chin like a nun's head-gear; whereas, there stood by me a little and roundly formed woman, who might indeed be older than I, but was still young; she could not, I thought, be more than six or seven and twenty; she was as fair as a fair Englishwoman; she had no cap; her hair was nut-brown, and she wore it in curls; pretty her features were not, nor very soft, nor very regular, but neither were they in any degree plain, and I already saw cause to deem them expressive. What was their predominant cast? Was it sagacity?—sense? Yes, I thought so; but

I could scarcely as yet be sure. I discovered, however, that there was a certain serenity of eye, and freshness of complexion, most pleasing to behold. The colour on her cheek was like the bloom on a good apple, which is as sound at the core as it is red on the rind.

Mdlle. Reuter and I entered upon business. She said she was not absolutely certain of the wisdom of the step she was about to take, because I was so young, and parents might possibly object to a professor like me for their daughters: "But it is often well to act on one's own judgment," said she, "and to lead parents, rather than be led by them. The fitness of a professor is not a matter of age; and, from what I have heard, and from what I observe myself, I would much rather trust you than M. Ledru, the music-master, who is a married man of near fifty."

I remarked that I hoped she would find me worthy of her good opinion; that, if I knew myself, I was incapable of betraying any confidence reposed in me. "Du reste," said she, "the surveillance will be strictly attended to." And then she proceeded to discuss the subject of terms. She was very cautious, quite on her guard; she did not absolutely bargain, but she warily sounded me to find out what my expectations might be; and when she could not get me to name a sum, she reasoned and reasoned with a fluent yet quiet circumlocution of speech, and at last nailed me down to five hundred francs per annum—not too much, but I agreed. Before the negotiation was completed, it began to grow a little dusk. I did not hasten it, for I liked well enough to sit and hear her talk; I was amused with the sort of business talent she displayed. Edward could not have shown himself more practical, though he might have evinced more coarseness and urgency; and then she had so many reasons, so many explanations; and, after all, she succeeded in proving herself quite disinterested and even liberal. At last she concluded, she could say no more, because, as I acquiesced in all things, there was no further ground for the exercise of her parts of speech. I was obliged to rise. I would rather have sat a little longer; what had I to return to but my small, empty room? And my eyes had a pleasure in looking at Mdlle. Reuter, especially now, when the twilight softened her features a little, and, in the doubtful dusk, I could fancy her forehead as open as it was really elevated, her mouth touched with turns of sweetness as well as defined in lines of sense. When I rose to go, I held out my hand, on purpose, though I knew it was contrary to the etiquette of foreign habits; she smiled and said—

"Ah! c'est comme tous les Anglais;" but gave me her hand very kindly.

"It is the privilege of my country, Mademoiselle," said I; "and, remember, I shall always claim it."

She laughed a little, quite good naturedly, and with the sort of tranquillity obvious in all she did—a tranquillity which soothed and suited me singularly, at least I thought so that evening. Brussels seemed a very pleasant place to me when I got out again into the street, and it appeared as if some cheerful, eventful, upward-tending career were even then opening to me, on that self-same mild, still April night. So impressionable a being is man, or at least such a man as I was in those days.

CHAPTER X.

Next day the morning hours seemed to pass very slowly at M. Pelet's; I wanted the afternoon to come that I might go again to the neighbouring pensionnat and give my first lesson within its pleasant precincts; for pleasant they appeared to me. At noon the hour of recreation arrived; at one o'clock we had lunch; this got on the time, and at last St. Gudule's deep bell, tolling slowly two, marked the moment for which I had been waiting.

At the foot of the narrow back-stairs that descended from my room, I met M. Pelet.

"Comme vous avez l'air rayonnant!" said he. "Je ne vous ai jamais vu aussi gai que s'est-il donc passé?"

"Apparemment que j'aime les changements," replied I.

"Ah! je comprends—c'est cela—soyez sage seulement. Vous êtes bien jeune—trop jeune pour le rôle que vous allez jouer; il faut prendre garde—savez-vous?"

"Mais quel danger y a-t-il?"

"Je n'en sais rien—ne vous laissez pas aller à de vives impressions—voilà tout."

I laughed; a sentiment of exquisite pleasure played over my nerves at the thought that "vives impressions" were likely to be created; it was the deadness, the sameness of life's daily ongoings that had hitherto been my bane; my blouse-clad élèves in the boy's seminary never stirred in me any "vives impressions," except it might be occasionally some of anger. I broke from M. Pelet, and as I strode down the passage he followed me with one of his laughs—a very French, rakish, mocking sound.

Again I stood at the neighbouring door, and

soon was re-admitted into the cheerful passage with its clear, dove-colour, imitation marble walls. I followed the portress, and descending a step, and making a turn, I found myself in a sort of corridor; a side-door opened, Mdlle. Reuter's little figure, as graceful as it was plump, appeared. I could now see her dress in full daylight; a neat, simple mousseline-laine gown fitted her compact, round shape to perfection—delicate little collar and manchettes of lace, trim Parisian brodequins showed her neck, wrists, and feet, to complete advantage; but how grave was her face as she came suddenly upon me! Solicitude and business were in her eye—on her forehead; she looked almost stern. Her "bon jour, monsieur," was quite polite, but so orderly, so common-place; it spread directly a cool, damp towel over my "vives impressions." The servant turned back when her mistress appeared, and I walked slowly along the corridor, side by side with Mdlle. Reuter.

"Monsieur will give a lesson in the first class to-day," said she; "dictation or reading will perhaps be the best thing to begin with, for those are the easiest forms of communicating instruction in a foreign language; and, at the first, a master naturally feels a little unsettled."

She was quite right, as I had found from experience; it only remained for me to acquiesce. We proceeded now in silence. The corridor terminated in a hall, large, lofty, and square; a glass door on one side showed within a long, narrow refectory, with tables, an armoire, and two lamps; it was empty; large glass doors, in front, opened on the play-ground and garden; a broad staircase ascended spirally on the opposite side; the remaining wall showed a pair of great folding-doors, now closed, and admitting, doubtless, to the classes.

Mdlle. Reuter turned her eye laterally on me, to ascertain, probably, whether I was collected enough to be ushered into her sanctum sanctorum.

I suppose she judged me to be in a tolerable state of self-government, for she opened the door, and I followed her through. A rustling sound of uprising greeted our entrance; without looking to the right or left, I walked straight up the lane between two sets of benches and desks, and took possession of the empty chair and isolated desk raised on an estrade of one step high, so as to command one division; the other division being under the surveillance of a maîtresse, similarly elevated. At the back of the estrade, and attached to a moveable partition dividing this school-room from another beyond, was a large tableau of wood painted black and varnished; a thick crayon of white chalk lay on my desk for the convenience of elucidating any grammatical or verbal obscurity which might occur in my lessons by writing it upon the tableau, a wet sponge appeared beside the chalk to enable me to efface the marks when they had served the purpose intended.

I carefully and deliberately made these observations before allowing myself to take one glance at the benches before me; having handled the crayon, looked back at the tableau, fingered the sponge in order to ascertain that it was in a right state of moisture, I found myself cool enough to admit of looking calmly up and gazing deliberately round me.

And first I observed that Mdlle. Reuter had already glided away, she was nowhere visible; a maîtresse or teacher, the one who occupied the corresponding estrade to my own, alone remained to keep guard over me; she was a little in the shade, and, with my short sight, I could only see that she was of a thin, bony figure, and rather tallowy complexion, and that her attitude, as she sat, partook equally of listlessness and affectation. More obvious, more prominent, shone on by the full light of the large window, were the occupants of the benches just before me, of whom some were girls of fourteen, fifteen, sixteen, some young women from eighteen (as it appeared to me) up to twenty; the most modest attire, the simplest fashion of wearing the hair, were apparent in all, and good features, ruddy, blooming complexions, large and brilliant eyes, forms full, even to solidity, seemed to abound. I did not bear the first view like a stoic; I was dazzled, my eyes fell, and in a voice somewhat too low I murmured—

"Prenez vos cahiers de dictée, mesdemoiselles."

Not so had I bid the boys at Pelet's take their reading-books. A rustle followed, and an opening of desks; behind the lifted lids which momentarily screened the heads bent down to search for exercise-books, I heard tittering and whispers.

"Eulalie, je suis prête à pâmer de rire," observed one.

"Comme il a rougi en parlant!"

"Oui, c'est un véritable blanc-bec."

"Tais-toi, Hortense—il nous écoute."

And now the lids sank and the heads reappeared; I had marked three, the whisperers, and I did not scruple to take a very steady look at them as they emerged from their temporary eclipse. It is astonishing what ease and courage their little phrases of flippancy had given me; the idea by which I had been awed was that the youthful beings before me, with their dark nun-like robes and softly braided hair, were a kind of half-angels. The light titter, the giddy whisper, had already in some measure relieved my mind of that fond and oppressive fancy.

The three I allude to were just in front, within half a yard of my estrade, and were among the most womanly-looking present. Their names I knew afterwards, and may as well mention now; they were Eulalie, Hortense, Caroline. Eulalie was tall, and very finely shaped: she was fair, and her features were those of a Low-country Madonna; many a "figure de vierge" have I seen in Dutch pictures, exactly resembling hers; there were no angles in her shape or in her face, all was curve and roundness—neither thought, sentiment, nor passion, disturbed by line or flush the equality of her pale, clear skin; her noble bust heaved with her regular breathing, her eyes moved a little—by these evidences of life alone, could I have distinguished her from some large handsome figure, moulded in wax. Hortense was of middle size and stout, her form was ungraceful, her face striking, more alive and brilliant than Eulalie's, her hair was dark brown, her complexion richly coloured; there were frolic and mischief in her eye: consistency and good sense she might possess, but none of her features betokened those qualities.

Caroline was little, though evidently full grown; raven-black hair, very dark eyes, absolutely regular features, with a colourless olive complexion, clear as to the face and sallow about the neck, formed in her that assemblage of points whose union many persons regard as the perfection of beauty. How, with the tintless pallor of her skin and the classic straightness of her lineaments, she managed to look sensual, I don't know. I think her lips and eyes contrived the affair between them, and the result left no uncertainty on the beholder's mind. She was sensual now, and in ten years' time she would be coarse—promise plain was written in her face of much future folly.

If I looked at these girls with little scruplé, they looked at me with still less. Eulalie raised her unmoved eye to mine, and seemed to expect, passively but securely, an impromptu tribute to her majestic charms. Hortense regarded me boldly and giggled at the same time, while she said with an air of impudent freedom—

"Dictez-nous quelquechose de facile pour commençer, monsieur."

Caroline shook her loose ringlets of abundant but somewhat coarse hair over her rolling black eyes; parting her lips, as full as those of a hot-blooded Maroon, she showed her well-set teeth sparkling between them, and treated me at the same time to a smile "de sa façon." Beautiful as

Pauline Borghese, she looked at the moment scarcely purer than Lucrèce de Borgia. Caroline was of noble family. I heard her lady-mother's character afterwards, and then I ceased to wonder at the precocious accomplishments of the daughter. These three, I at once saw, deemed themselves the queens of the school, and conceived that by their splendour they threw all the rest into the shade. In less than five minutes they had thus revealed to me their characters, and in less than five minutes I had buckled on a breast-plate of steely indifference, and let down a visor of impassible austerity.

"Take your pens and commence writing," said I, in as dry and trite a voice as if I had been addressing only Jules Vanderkelkov and Co.

The dictée now commenced. My three belles interrupted me perpetually with little, silly questions and uncalled-for remarks, to some of which I made no answer, and to others, replied very quietly and briefly.

"Comment dît-on point et virgule en Anglais, monsieur?"

"Semi-colon, mademoiselle."

"Semi-collong? Ah comme c'est drôle!" (giggle.)

"J'ai une si mauvaise plume — impossible d'écrire!"

"Mais, monsieur—je ne sais pas suivre—vous allez si vîte."

"Je n'ai rien compris, moi!"

Here a general murmur arose, and the teacher, opening her lips for the first time, ejaculated—

"Silence, mesdemoiselles!"

No silence followed—on the contrary, the three ladies in front began to talk more loudly.

"C'est si difficile, l'Anglais!"

"Je déteste la dictée."

"Quel ennui d'écrire quelquechose que l'on ne comprend pas!"

Some of those behind laughed: a degree of

confusion began to pervade the class; it was necessary to take prompt measures.

"Donnez-moi votre cahier," said I to Eulalie in an abrupt tone; and bending over, I took it before she had time to give it.

"Et vous, mademoiselle—donnez-moi le vôtre," continued I, more mildly, addressing a little pale, plain-looking girl who sat in the first row of the other division, and whom I had remarked as being at once the ugliest and the most attentive in the room; she rose up, walked over to me, and delivered her book with a grave, modest curtsey. I glanced over the two dictations; Eulalie's was slurred, blotted, and full of silly mistakes—Sylvie's (such was the name of the ugly little girl) was clearly written, it contained no error against sense, and but few faults of orthography. I coolly read aloud both exercises, marking the faults—then I looked at Eulalie:

"C'est honteux!" said I, and I deliberately tore her dictation in four parts, and presented her with the fragments. I returned Sylvie her book with a smile, saying—

"C'est bien—je suis content de vous."

Sylvie looked calmly pleased, Eulalie swelled like an incensed turkey, but the mutiny was quelled: the conceited coquetry and futile flirtation of the first bench were exchanged for a taciturn sullenness, much more convenient to me, and the rest of my lesson passed without interruption.

A bell clanging out in the yard announced the moment for the cessation of school labours. I heard our own bell at the same time, and that of a certain public college immediately after. Order dissolved instantly; up started every pupil, I hastened to seize my hat, bow to the maîtresse, and quit the room before the tide of externats should pour from the inner class, where I knew near a hundred were prisoned, and whose rising tumult I already heard.

I had scarcely crossed the hall and gained the corridor, when Mdlle. Reuter came again upon me.

"Step in here a moment," said she, and she held open .the door of the side-room from whence she had issued on my arrival; it was a *salle-a-manger*, as appeared from the beaufet and the armoire vitrée, filled with glass and china, which formed part of its furniture. Ere she had closed the door on me and herself, the corridor was already filled with day-pupils, tearing down their cloaks, bonnets, and cabas from the wooden pegs on which they were suspended; the shrill voice of a maîtresse was heard at intervals vainly endeavouring to enforce some sort of order; vainly, I say: discipline there was none in these rough ranks, and yet this was considered one of the best conducted schools in Brussels.

"Well, you have given your first lesson," began Mdlle. Reuter in the most calm, equable voice, as though quite unconscious of the chaos from which we were separated only by a single wall.

"Were you satisfied with your pupils, or did

any circumstance in their conduct give you cause for complaint? Conceal nothing from me, repose in me entire confidence."

Happily, I felt in myself complete power to manage my pupils without aid; the enchantment, the golden haze which had dazzled my perspicuïty at first, had been a good deal dissipated. I cannot say I was chagrined or downcast by the contrast which the reality of a pensionnat de demoiselles presented to my vague ideal of the same community; I was only enlightened and amused; consequently, I felt in no disposition to complain to Mdlle. Reuter, and I received her considerate invitation to confidence with a smile.

"A thousand thanks, mademoiselle, all has gone very smoothly."

She looked more than doubtful.

"Et les trois demoiselles du premier banc?" said she.

"Ah! tout va au mieux!" was my answer, and Mdlle. Reuter ceased to question me; but her eye—not large, not brilliant, not melting, or kindling, but astute, penetrating, practical, showed she was even with me; it let out a momentary gleam, which said plainly, "Be as close as you like, I am not dependent on your candour; what you would conceal I already know."

By a transition so quiet as to be scarcely perceptible, the directress's manner changed; the anxious, business-air passed from her face, and she began chatting about the weather and the town, and asking in neighbourly wise after M. and Madame Pelet. I answered all her little questions; she prolonged her talk, I went on following its many little windings; she sat so long, said so much, varied so often the topics of discourse, that it was not difficult to perceive she had a particular aim in thus detaining me. Her mere words could have afforded no clue to this aim, but her countenance aided; while her lips uttered only affable commonplaces, her eyes reverted continually to my face. Her glances were not given in full, but out of the corners, so quietly, so stealthily, yet I think I lost not one. I watched her as keenly as she watched me; I perceived soon that she was feeling after my real character; she was searching for salient points, and weak points, and eccentric points; she was applying now this test, now that, hoping in the end to find some chink, some niche, where she could put in her little firm foot and stand upon my neck—mistress of my nature. Do not mistake me, reader, it was no amorous influence she wished to gain—at that time it was only the power of the politician to which she aspired; I was now installed as a professor in her establishment, and she wanted to know where her mind was superior to mine—by what feeling or opinion she could lead me.

I enjoyed the game much, and did not hasten its conclusion; sometimes I gave her hopes, beginning a sentence rather weakly, when her shrewd eye would light up—she thought she had me; having led her a little way, I delighted to turn round and finish with sound, hard sense, whereat her countenance would fall. At last a servant entered to announce dinner; the conflict being thus necessarily terminated, we parted without having gained any advantage on either side: Mdlle Reuter had not even given me an opportunity of attacking her with feeling, and I had managed to baffle her little schemes of craft. It was a regular drawn battle. I again held out my hand when I left the room, she gave me hers; it was a small and white hand but how cool! I met her eye too in full—obliging her to give me a straightforward look; this last test went against me: it left her as it found her—moderate, temperate, tranquil; me it disappointed.

"I am growing wiser," thought I, as I walked back to M. Pelet's. "Look at this little woman; is she like the women of novelists and romancers? To read of female character as depicted in Poetry, and Fiction, one would think it was made up of sentiment, either for good or bad—here is a specimen, and a most sensible and respectable specimen, too, whose staple ingredient is abstract reason. No Talleyrand was ever more passionless than Zoraïde Reuter!" So I thought then; I found afterwards that blunt susceptibilities are very consistent with strong propensities.

CHAPTER XI.

I HAD indeed had a very long talk with the crafty little politician, and on regaining my quarters, I found that dinner was half over. To be late at meals was against a standing rule of the establishment, and, had it been one of the Flemish ushers who thus entered after the removal of the soup and the commencement of the first course, M. Pelet would probably have greeted him with a public rebuke, and would certainly have mulcted him both of soup and fish; as it was, that polite though partial gentleman only shook his head, and as I took my place, unrolled my napkin, and said my heretical grace to myself, he civilly despatched a servant to the kitchen, to bring me a plate of "purée aux carrottes" (for this was a maigre-day) and before sending away the first course, reserved for me a portion of the stock-fish of which it consisted. Dinner being over, the boys rushed out for their evening play; Kint and Vandam (the two ushers) of course followed them. Poor fellows! if they had not looked so very heavy, so very soulless, so very indifferent to all things in heaven above or in the earth beneath, I could have pitied them greatly for the obligation they were under to trail after those rough lads everywhere and at all times; even as it was, I felt disposed to scout myself as a privileged prig when I turned to ascend to my chamber, sure to find there, if not enjoyment, at least liberty; but this evening (as had often happened before) I was to be still further distinguished.

"Eh bien mauvais sujet!" said the voice of M. Pelet behind me, as I set my foot on the first step of the stair. "Où allez-vous? Venez à la salle-à manger, que je vous gronde un peu."

"I beg pardon, monsieur," said I, as I followed him to his private sitting-room, "for having returned so late—it was not my fault."

"That is just what I want to know," rejoined M. Pelet, as he ushered me into the comfortable parlour with a good wood-fire—for the stove had now been removed for the season. Having rung the bell he ordered "Coffee for two," and presently he and I were seated, almost in English comfort, one on each side of the hearth, a little round table between us with a coffee-pot, a sugar-basin, and two large white china cups. While M. Pelet employed himself in choosing a cigar from a box, my thoughts reverted to the two outcast ushers, whose voices I could hear even now crying hoarsely for order in the play-ground.

"C'est une grande responsabilité, que la surveillance," observed I.

"Plait-il?" dit M. Pelet.

I remarked that I thought Messieurs Vandam

and Kint must sometimes be a little fatigued with their labours.

"Des bêtes de somme,—des bêtes de somme," murmured scornfully the director. Meantime I offered him his cup of coffee.

"Servez-vous, mon garçon," said he blandly, when I had put a couple of huge lumps of continental sugar into his cup. "And now tell me why you stayed so long at Mdlle. Reuter's. I know that lessons conclude, in her establishment as in mine, at four o'clock, and when you returned it was past five."

"Mdlle. wished to speak with me, monsieur."

"Indeed! on what subject? if one may ask."

"Mademoiselle talked about nothing, monsieur."

"A fertile topic! And did she discourse thereon in the school-room, before the pupils?"

"No; like you, monsieur, she asked me to walk into her parlour."

"And Madame Reuter—the old duenna—my mother's gossip, was there, of course?"

"No, monsieur; I had the honour of being quite alone with Mademoiselle."

"C'est joli—cela," observed M. Pelet, and he smiled and looked into the fire.

"Honi soit qui mal y pense," murmured I significantly.

"Je connais un peu ma petite voisine—voyez-vous."

"In that case Monsieur will be able to aid me in finding out what was Mademoiselle's reason for making me sit before her sofa, one mortal hour, listening to the most copious and fluent dissertation on the merest frivolities."

"She was sounding your character."

"I thought so, monsieur."

"Did she find out your weak point?"

"What is my weak point?"

"Why the sentimental. Any woman, sinking her shaft deep enough, will at last reach a fathomless spring of sensibility in thy breast, Crimsworth."

I felt the blood stir about my heart and rise warm to my cheek.

" Some women might, monsieur."

" Is Mdlle. Reuter of the number? Come, speak frankly, mon fils; elle est encore jeune, plus agée que toi peutêtre, mais juste assez pour unir la tendresse d'une petite maman à l'amour d'une épouse dévouée; n'est-ce pas que cela t'irait supérieurement?"

" No, monsieur; I should like my wife to be my wife, and not half my mother."

" She is then a little too old for you?"

" No, monsieur, not a day too old if she suited me in other things."

" In what does she not suit you, William? She is personally agreeable, is she not?"

" Very; her hair and complexion are just what I admire, and her turn of form, though quite Belgian, is full of grace."

" Bravo! and her face? her features? How do you like them?"

"A little harsh, especially her mouth."

"Ah, yes! her mouth," said M. Pelet, and he chuckled inwardly. "There is character about her mouth—firmness—but she has a very pleasant smile; don't you think so?"

"Rather crafty."

"True, but that expression of craft is owing to her eyebrows; have you remarked her eyebrows?"

I answered that I had not.

"You have not seen her looking down then?" said he.

"No."

"It is a treat, notwithstanding. Observe her when she has some knitting, or some other woman's work in hand, and sits the image of peace, calmly intent on her needles and her silk, some discussion meantime going on around her, in the course of which peculiarities of character are being developed, or important interests canvassed; she takes no part in it; her humble, feminine mind is wholly with her knitting; none of her features move; she neither presumes to smile approval, nor frown disapprobation; her little hands assiduously ply their unpretending task; if she can only get this purse finished, or this bonnet-grec completed, it is enough for her. If gentlemen approach her chair, a deeper quiescence, a meeker modesty settles on her features, and clothes her general mien; observe then her eyebrows, et dîtes-moi s'il n'y a pas du chat dans l'un et du renard dans l'autre."

"I will take careful notice the first opportunity," said I.

"And then," continued M. Pelet, "the eyelid will flicker, the light-coloured lashes be lifted a second, and a blue eye, glancing out from under the screen, will take its brief, sly, searching survey, and retreat again."

I smiled, and so did Pelet, and after a few minutes' silence I asked:—

"Will she ever marry, do you think?"

"Marry! Will birds pair? Of course it is both her intention and resolution to marry when she finds a suitable match, and no one is better aware than herself of the sort of impression she is capable of producing; no one likes better to captivate in a quiet way. I am mistaken if she will not yet leave the print of her stealing steps on thy heart, Crimsworth."

"Of her steps? Confound it, no! My heart is not a plank to be walked on."

"But the soft touch of a patte de velours will do it no harm?"

"She offers me no patte de velours; she is all form and reserve with me."

"That to begin with; let respect be the foundation, affection the first floor, love the superstructure; Mdlle. Reuter is a skilful architect."

"And interest, M. Pelet—interest. Will not Mademoiselle consider that point?"

"Yes, yes, no doubt; it will be the cement

between every stone. And now we have discussed the directress, what of the pupils? N'y-a-t-il pas de belles études parmi ces jeunes têtes?"

"Studies of character? Yes; curious ones, at least, I imagine; but one cannot divine much from a first interview."

"Ah, you affect discretion; but tell me now, were you not a little abashed before those blooming young creatures?"

"At first, yes; but I rallied and got through with all due sang froid."

"I don't believe you."

"It is true notwithstanding. At first I thought them angels, but they did not leave me long under that delusion; three of the eldest and handsomest undertook the task of setting me right, and they managed so cleverly that in five minutes I knew *them*, at least, for what they were—three arrant coquettes."

"Je les connais!" exclaimed M. Pelet. "Elles sont toujours au premier rang à l'eglise et à la promenade; une blonde superbe, une jolie espiègle, une belle brune."

"Exactly."

"Lovely creatures all of them—heads for artists; what a group they would make, taken together! Eulalie (I know their names), with her smooth, braided hair, and calm, ivory brow. Hortense, with her rich chestnut locks so luxuriantly knotted, plaited, twisted, as if she did not know how to dispose of all their abundance, with her vermillion lips, damask cheek, and roguish laughing eye. And Caroline de Blémont! Ah there is beauty! beauty in perfection. What a cloud of sable curls about the face of a houri! What fascinating lips! What glorious black eyes! Your Byron would have worshipped her, and you—you cold frigid islander!—you played the austere, the insensible in the presence of an Aphrodite so exquisite?"

I might have laughed at the director's enthusiasm had I believed it real, but there was something in his tone which indicated got-up raptures· I felt he was only affecting fervour in order to put me off my guard, to induce me to come out in return, so I scarcely even smiled. He went on :—

" Confess, William, do not the mere good looks of Zoraïde Reuter appear dowdyish and commonplace compared with the splendid charms of some of her pupils ?"

The question discomposed me, but I now felt plainly that my principal was endeavouring (for reasons best known to himself—at that time I could not fathom them) to excite ideas and wishes in my mind alien to what was right and honourable. The iniquity of the instigation proved its antidote, and when he further added :—

" Each of those three beautiful girls will have a handsome fortune; and with a little address, a gentlemanlike, intelligent young fellow like you might make himself master of the hand, heart, and purse of any one of the trio."

I replied by a look and an interrogative, "Monsieur?" which startled him.

He laughed a forced laugh, affirmed that he had only been joking, and demanded whether I could possibly have thought him in earnest. Just then the bell rang; the play-hour was over; it was an evening on which M. Pelet was accustomed to read passages from the drama and the belles lettres to his pupils. He did not wait for my answer, but rising left the room, humming as he went some gay strain of Béranger's.

CHAPTER XII.

DAILY, as I continued my attendance at the seminary of Mdlle. Reuter, did I find fresh occasions to compare the ideal with the real. What had I known of female character previously to my arrival at Brussels? Precious little. And what was my notion of it? Something vague, slight, gauzy, glittering; now when I came in contact with it I found it to be a palpable substance enough; very hard too sometimes, and often heavy; there was metal in it, both lead and iron.

Let the idealists, the dreamers about earthly angels and human flowers, just look here while I open my portfolio and show them a sketch or two, pencilled after nature. I took these sketches in the second-class school-room of Mdlle. Reuter's establishment, where about a hundred specimens of the genus "jeune fille" collected together, offered a fertile variety of subject. A miscellaneous assortment they were, differing both in caste and country; as I sat on my estrade and glanced over the long range of desks, I had under my eye French, English, Belgians, Austrians, and Prussians. The majority belonged to the class bourgeois; but there were many comtesses, there were the daughters of two generals and of several colonels, captains, and Government employés; these ladies sat side by side with young females destined to be demoiselles de magasins, and with some Flamandes, genuine aborigines of the country. In dress all were nearly similar, and in manners there was small difference; exceptions there were to the general rule, but the majority gave the tone to the establishment, and that tone was rough, boisterous, marked by a point-blank disregard of all forbearance towards each other or their teachers; an eager pursuit by each individual of her own interest and convenience; and a coarse indifference to the interest and convenience of every one else. Most of them could lie with audacity when it appeared advantageous to do so. All understood the art of speaking fair when a point was to be gained, and could with consummate skill and at a moment's notice turn the cold shoulder the instant civility ceased to be profitable. Very little open quarrelling ever took place amongst them; but backbiting and tale-bearing were universal. Close friendships were forbidden by the rules of the school, and no one girl seemed to cultivate more regard for another than was just necessary to secure a companion when solitude would have been irksome. They were each and all supposed to have been reared in utter unconsciousness of vice. The precautions used to keep them ignorant, if not innocent, were innumerable. How was it, then, that scarcely one of those girls having attained the age of fourteen could look a man in the face with modesty and propriety? An air of bold, impudent flirtation, or a loose, silly leer, was sure to answer the most ordinary glance from a masculine eye. I know nothing of the arcana of the Roman Catholic religion, and I am not a bigot in matters of theology, but I suspect the root of this precocious impurity, so obvious, so general in Popish countries, is to be found in the discipline, if not the doctrines of the Church of Rome. I record what I have seen: these girls belonged to what are called the respectable ranks of society; they had all been carefully brought up, yet was the mass of them mentally depraved. So much for the general view: now for one or two selected specimens.

The first picture is a full length of Aurelia Koslow, a German fräulein, or rather a half-breed between German and Russian. She is eighteen years of age, and has been sent to

Brussels to finish her education; she is of middle size, stiffly made, body long, legs short, bust much developed but not compactly moulded, waist disproportionately compressed by an inhumanly braced corset, dress carefully arranged, large feet tortured into small bottines, head small, hair smoothed, braided, oiled, and gummed to perfection; very low forehead, very diminutive and vindictive gray eyes, somewhat Tartar features, rather flat nose, rather high-cheek bones, yet the ensemble not positively ugly; tolerably good complexion. So much for person. As to mind deplorably ignorant and ill-informed; incapable of writing or speaking correctly even German, her native tongue, a dunce in French, and her attempts at learning English a mere farce, yet she has been at school twelve years; but as she invariably gets her exercises, of every description, done by a fellow pupil, and reads her lessons off a book concealed in her lap, it is not wonderful that her progress has been so snail-like. I do not know what Aurelia's daily habits of life are, because I have not the opportunity of observing her at all times; but from what I see of the state of her desk, books and papers, I should say she is slovenly and even dirty; her outward dress, as I have said, is well attended to, but in passing behind her bench, I have remarked that her neck is gray for want of washing, and her hair, so glossy with gum and grease, is not such as one feels tempted to pass the hand over, much less to run the fingers through. Aurelia's conduct in class, at least when I am present, is something extraordinary, considered as an index of girlish innocence. The moment I enter the room, she nudges her next neighbour and indulges in a half-suppressed laugh. As I take my seat on the estrade, she fixes her eye on me; she seems resolved to attract, and, if possible, monopolize my notice: to this end she launches at me all sorts of looks, languishing, provoking, leering, laughing. As I am found quite proof against this sort of artillery—for we scorn what, unasked, is lavishly offered—she has recourse to the expedient of making noises; sometimes she sighs, sometimes groans, sometimes utters inarticulate sounds, for which language has no name. If, in walking up the school-room, I pass near her, she puts out her foot that it may touch mine; if I do not happen to observe the manœuvre, and my boot comes in contact with her brodequin, she affects to fall into convulsions of suppressed laughter; if I notice the snare and avoid it, she expresses her mortification in sullen muttering, where I hear myself abused in bad French, pronounced with an intolerable low German accent.

Not far from Mdlle. Koslow sits another young lady by name Adèle Dronsart: this is a Belgian, rather low of stature, in form heavy, with broad waist, short neck and limbs, good red and white complexion, features well chiselled and regular, well-cut eyes of a clear brown colour, light brown hair, good teeth, age not much above fifteen, but as full-grown as a stout young Englishwoman of twenty. This portrait gives the idea of a somewhat dumpy but good-looking damsel, does it not? Well, when I looked along the row of young heads, my eye generally stopped at this of Adèle's; her gaze was ever waiting for mine, and it frequently succeeded in arresting it. She was an unnatural-looking being—so young, fresh, blooming, yet so Gorgon-like. Suspicion, sullen ill-temper were on her forehead, vicious propensities in her eye, envy and panther-like deceit about her mouth. In general she sat very still; her massive shape looked as if it could not bend much, nor did her large head—so broad at the base, so narrow towards the top—seem made to turn readily on her short neck. She had but two varieties of expression; the prevalent one a forbidding, dissatisfied scowl, varied sometimes by a most pernicious and perfidious smile. She was shunned by her fellow-pupils, for, bad as many of them were, few were as bad as she.

Aurelia and Adèle were in the first division of the second class; the second division was headed by a pensionnaire named Juanna Trista. This girl was of mixed Belgian and Spanish origin; her Flemish mother was dead, her Catalonian father was a merchant, residing in the —— Isles, where Juanna had been born and whence she was sent to Europe to be educated. I wonder that any one, looking at that girl's head and countenance, would have received her under their roof. She had precisely the same shape of skull as Pope Alexander the Sixth; her organs of benevolence, veneration, conscientiousness, adhesiveness, were singularly small, those of self-esteem, firmness, destructiveness, combativeness, preposterously large; her head sloped up in the penthouse shape, was contracted about the forehead, and prominent behind; she had rather good, though large and marked features; her temperament was fibrous and bilious, her complexion pale and dark, hair and eyes black, form angular and rigid but proportionate, age fifteen.

Juanna was not very thin but she had a gaunt visage, and her "regard" was fierce and hungry; narrow as was her brow, it presented space enough for the legible graving of two words, Mutiny and Hate; in some one of her other lineaments—I think the eye—cowardice had also its distinct cipher. Mdlle. Trista thought fit to trouble my first lessons with a coarse, work-day sort of turbulence; she made noises with her mouth like a horse, she ejected her saliva, she uttered brutal expressions; behind and below her were seated a band of very vulgar, inferior-looking Flamandes, including two or three examples of that deformity of person, and imbecility of intellect, whose frequency in the Low Countries would seem to furnish proof that the climate is such as to induce degeneracy of the human mind and body; these, I soon found, were completely under her influence, and with their aid she got up and sustained a swinish tumult, which I was constrained at last to quell by ordering her and two of her tools to rise from their seats, and, having kept them standing five minutes, turning them bodily out of the school-room: the accomplices into a large place adjoining called the grande salle; the principal into a cabinet, of which I closed the door and pocketed the key. This judgment I executed in the presence of Mdlle. Reuter, who looked much aghast at beholding so decided a proceeding—the most severe that had ever been ventured on in her establishment. Her look of affright I answered with one of composure, and finally with a smile which perhaps flattered and certainly soothed her. Juanna Trista remained in Europe long enough to repay, by malevolence and ingratitude, all who had ever done her a good turn, and she then went to join her father in the —— Isles, exulting in the thought that she should there have slaves, whom, as she said, she could kick and strike at will.

These three pictures are from the life. I possess others, as marked and as little agreeable, but I will spare my reader the exhibition of them.

Doubtless it will be thought that I ought now, by way of contrast, to show something charming; some gentle virgin head, circled with a halo, some sweet personification of innocence, clasping the dove of peace to her bosom. No; I saw nothing of the sort, and therefore cannot portray it. The pupil in the school possessing the happiest disposition was a young girl from the country, Louise Path; she was sufficiently benevolent and obliging, but not well taught, nor well mannered; moreover, the plague-spot of dissimulation was in her also; honour and principle were unknown to her, she had scarcely heard their names. The least exceptionable pupil was the poor little Sylvie I have mentioned once before. Sylvie was gentle in manners, intelligent in mind; she was even sincere, as far as her religion would permit her to be so, but her physical organization was defective; weak health stunted her growth and chilled her spirits, and then, destined as she was for the cloister, her whole soul was warped to a conventual bias, and in the tame, trained subjection of her manner, one read that she had already prepared herself for her future course of life, by giving up her independence of thought and action into the hands of some despotic confessor. She permitted herself no original opinion, no preference of companion or employment; in everything she was guided by another. With a pale, passive, automaton air, she went about all day long doing what she was bid; never what she liked, or what, from innate conviction, she thought it right to do. The poor little future religieuse had been early taught to make the dictates of her own reason and conscience quite subordinate to the will of her spiritual director. She was the model pupil of Mdlle. Reuter's establishment; pale, blighted image, where life lingered feebly, but whence the soul had been conjured by Romish wizard-craft!

A few English pupils there were in this school, and these might be divided into two classes. 1st, The continental English — the daughters chiefly of broken adventurers whom debt or dishonour had driven from their own country. These poor girls had never known the advantages of settled homes, decorous example, or honest Protestant education; resident a few months now in one Catholic school, now in another, as their parents wandered from land to land—from France to Germany, from Germany to Belgium — they had picked up some scanty instruction, many bad habits, losing every notion even of the first elements of religion and morals, and acquiring an imbecile indifference to every sentiment that can elevate humanity; they were distinguishable by an habitual look of sullen dejection, the result of crushed self-respect and constant brow-beating from their Popish fellow-pupils, who hated them as English, and scorned them as heretics.

The second class were British English. Of these I did not encounter half a dozen during the whole time of my attendance at the seminary; their characteristics were clean but careless dress, ill-arranged hair (compared with the tight and trim foreigners), erect carriage, flexible figures, white and taper hands, features more irregular, but also more intellectual than those of the Belgians, grave and modest countenances, a general air of native propriety and decency; by this last circumstance alone I could at a glance distinguish the daughter of Albion and nursling of Protestantism from the foster-child of Rome, the *protégée* of Jesuitry: proud, too, was the aspect of these British girls; at once envied and ridiculed by their continental associates, they warded off insult with austere civility, and met hate with mute disdain; they eschewed company-keeping, and in the midst of numbers seemed to dwell isolated.

The teachers presiding over this mixed multitude were three in number, all French—their names Mdlles. Zéphyrine, Pélagie, and Suzette, the two last were common-place personages enough; their look was ordinary, their manner was ordinary, their temper was ordinary, their thoughts, feelings, and views were all ordinary—were I to write a chapter on the subject I could not elucidate it further. Zéphyrine was somewhat more distinguished in appearance and deportment than Pélagie and Suzette, but in character a genuine Parisian coquette, perfidious, mercenary, and dry-hearted. A fourth maîtresse I sometimes saw who seemed to come daily to teach needlework, or netting, or lace-mending, or some such flimsy art, but of her I never had more than a passing glimpse, as she sat in the carré, with her frames and some dozen of the elder pupils about her, consequently I had no opportunity of studying her character, or even of observing her person much; the latter, I remarked, had a very girlish air for a maîtresse, otherwise it was not striking; of character I should think she possessed but little, as her pupils seemed constantly "en revolte" against her authority. She did not reside in the house; her name, I think, was Mdlle. Henri.

Amidst this assemblage of all that was insignificant and defective, much that was vicious and repulsive (by that last epithet many would have described the two or three stiff, silent, decently behaved, ill-dressed British girls), the sensible, sagacious, affable directress shone like a steady star over a marsh full of Jack-o'-lanthorns; profoundly aware of her superiority, she derived an inward bliss from that consciousness which sustained her under all the care and responsibility inseparable from her position; it kept her temper calm, her brow smooth, her manner tranquil. She liked—as who would not?—on entering the school-room, to feel that her sole presence sufficed to diffuse that order and quiet which all the remonstrances, and even commands, of her underlings frequently failed to enforce; she liked to stand in comparison, or rather contrast, with those who surrounded her, and to know that in personal as well as mental advantages, she bore away the undisputed palm of preference—(the three teachers were all plain.) Her pupils she managed with such indulgence and address, taking always on herself the office of recompenser and eulogist, and abandoning to her subalterns every invidious task of blame and punishment, that they all regarded her with deference, if not with affection; her teachers did not love her, but they submitted because they were her inferiors in everything; the various masters who attended her school were each and all in some way or other under her influence: over one she had acquired power by her skilful management of his bad temper; over another by little attentions to his petty caprices; a third she had subdued by flattery; a fourth—a timid man—she kept in awe by a sort of austere decision of mien; me, she still watched, still tried by the most ingenious tests—she roved round me, baffled, yet persevering; I believe she thought I was like a smooth and bare precipice, which offered neither jutting stone nor tree-root, nor tuft of grass to aid the climber. Now she flattered with exquisite tact, now she moralized, now she tried how far I was accessible to mercenary motives, then she disported on the brink of affectation—knowing that some men are won by weakness—anon, she talked excellent sense, aware that others have the folly to admire judgment. I found it at once pleasant and easy to evade all these efforts; it was sweet, when she thought me nearly won, to turn round and to smile in her very eyes, half scornfully, and then to witness her scarcely veiled, though mute mortification. Still she persevered, and at last, I am bound to confess it, her finger, essaying, proving every atom of the casket, touched its secret spring, and for a moment the lid sprung open; she laid her hand on the jewel within; whether she stole and broke it, or whether the lid shut again with a snap on her fingers, read on, and you shall know.

It happened that I came one day to give a lesson when I was indisposed; I had a bad cold and a cough; two hours' incessant talking left me very hoarse and tired; as I quitted the school-room, and was passing along the corridor, I met Mdlle. Reuter; she remarked, with an anxious air, that I looked very pale and tired. "Yes," I said, "I was fatigued;" and then, with increased interest, she rejoined, "You shall not go away till you have had some refreshment." She persuaded me to step into the parlour, and was very kind and gentle while I stayed. The next day she was kinder still; she came herself into the class to see that the windows were closed, and that there was no draught; she exhorted me with friendly earnestness not to over-exert myself; when I went away, she gave me her hand unasked, and I could not but mark, by a respectful and gentle pressure, that I was sensible of the favour, and grateful for it. My modest demonstration kindled a little merry smile on her countenance; I thought her almost charming. During the remainder of the evening, my mind was full of impatience for the afternoon of the next day to arrive, that I might see her again.

I was not disappointed, for she sat in the class during the whole of my subsequent lesson, and often looked at me almost with affection. At four o'clock she accompanied me out of the school-room, asking with solicitude after my health, then scolding me sweetly because I spoke too loud and gave myself too much trouble; I stopped at the glass-door which led into the garden, to hear her lecture to the end; the door was open, it was a very fine day, and while I listened to the soothing reprimand, I looked at the sunshine and flowers, and felt very happy. The day-scholars began to pour from the school-rooms into the passage.

"Will you go into the garden a minute or two," asked she, "till they are gone?"

I descended the steps without answering, but I looked back as much as to say—

"You will come with me?"

In another minute I and the directress were walking side by side down the alley bordered with fruit-trees, whose white blossoms were then in full blow as well as their tender green leaves. The sky was blue, the air still, the May afternoon was full of brightness and fragrance. Released from the stifling class, surrounded with flowers and foliage, with a pleasing, smiling, affable woman at my side—how did I feel? Why, very enviably. It seemed as if the romantic visions my imagination had suggested of this garden, while it was yet hidden from me by the jealous boards, were more than realized; and, when a turn in the alley shut out the view of the house, and some tall shrubs excluded M. Pelet's mansion, and screened us momentarily from the other houses, rising amphitheatre-like round this green spot, I gave my arm to Mdlle. Reuter, and led her to a garden-chair, nestled under some lilacs near. She sat down; I took my place at her side. She went on talking to me with that ease which communicates ease, and, as I listened, a revelation dawned in my mind that I was on the brink of falling in love. The dinner-bell rang, both at her house and M. Pelet's; we were obliged to part; I detained her a moment as she was moving away.

"I want something," said I.

"What?" asked Zoraïde naïvely.

"Only a flower."

"Gather it then—or two, or twenty, if you like."

"No—one will do—but you must gather it, and give it to me."

"What a caprice!" she exclaimed, but she raised herself on her tip-toes, and, plucking a beautiful branch of lilac, offered it to me with grace. I took it, and went away, satisfied for the present, and hopeful for the future.

Certainly that May day was a lovely one, and it closed in a moonlight night of summer warmth and serenity. I remember this well; for, having sat up late that evening, correcting devoirs, and feeling weary and a little oppressed with the closeness of my small room, I opened the often-mentioned boarded window, whose boards, however, I had persuaded old Madame Pelet to have removed since I had filled the post of professor in the pensionnat de demoiselles, as, from that time, it was no longer "inconvenient" for me to overlook my own pupils at their sports. I sat down in the window-seat, rested my arm on the sill, and leaned out: above me was the clear-obscure of a cloudless night sky—splendid moonlight subdued the tremulous sparkle of the stars—below lay the garden, varied with silvery lustre and deep shade, and all fresh with dew—a grateful perfume exhaled from the closed blossoms of the fruit-trees—not a leaf stirred, the night was breezeless. My window looked directly down upon a certain walk of Mdlle. Reuter's garden, called "l'allée défendue," so named because the pupils were forbidden to enter it on account of its proximity to the boys' school. It was here that the lilacs and laburnums grew especially thick; this was the most sheltered nook in the enclosure, its shrubs screened the garden-chair where that afternoon I had sat with the young directress. I need not say that my thoughts were chiefly with her as I leaned from the lattice, and let my eye roam, now over the walks and borders of the garden, now along the many windowed front of the house, which rose white beyond the masses of foliage. I wondered in what part of the building was situated her apartment; and a single light, shining through the persiennes of one croisée, seemed to direct me to it.

"She watches late," thought I, "for it must be now near midnight. She is a fascinating little woman," I continued in voiceless soliloquy; "her image forms a pleasant picture in memory; I know she is not what the world calls pretty—no matter, there is harmony in her aspect, and I like it; her brown hair, her blue eye, the freshness of her cheek, the whiteness of her neck, all suit my taste. Then I respect her talent; the idea of marrying a doll or a fool was always abhorrent to me: I know that a pretty doll, a fair fool, might do well enough for the honeymoon; but when passion cooled, how dreadful to find a lump of wax and wood laid in my bosom, a half idiot clasped in my arms, and to remember that I had made of this my equal—nay, my idol—to know that I must pass the rest of my dreary life with a creature incapable of understanding what I said, of appreciating what I thought, or of sympathising with what I felt! "Now, Zoraïde Reuter," thought I, "has tact, 'caractère,' judgment, discretion; has she heart? What a good, simple little smile played about her lips when she gave me the branch of lilacs! I have thought her crafty, dissembling, interested sometimes, it is true; but may not much that looks like cunning and dissimulation in her conduct be only the efforts made by a bland temper to traverse quietly perplexing difficulties. And as to interest, she wishes to make her way in the world, no doubt, and who can blame her? Even if she be truly deficient in sound principle, is it not rather her misfortune than her fault? She has been brought up a Catholic: had she been born an Englishwoman, and reared a Protestant, might she not have added straight integrity to all her other excellences? Supposing she were to marry an English and Protestant husband, would she not, rational, sensible as she is, quickly acknowledge the superiority of right over expediency, honesty over policy? It would be worth a man's while to try the experiment; to-morrow I will renew my observations. She knows that I watch her: how calm she is under scrutiny! it seems rather to gratify than annoy her." Here a strain of music stole in upon my monologue, and suspended it; it was a bugle, very skilfully played, in the neighbourhood of the park, I thought, or on the Place Royale. So sweet were the tones, so subduing their effect at that hour, in the midst of silence and under the quiet reign of moonlight, I ceased to think, that I might listen more intently. The strain retreated, its sound waxed fainter and was soon gone; my ear prepared to repose on the absolute hush of midnight once more. No. What murmur was that which, low, and yet near and approaching nearer, frustrated the expectation of total silence? It was some one conversing—yes, evidently, an audible though subdued voice spoke in the garden immediately below me. Another answered: the first voice was that of a man, the second that of a woman; and a man and a woman I saw coming slowly down the alley. Their forms were at first in shade, I could but discern a dusk outline of each, but a ray of moonlight met them at the termination of the walk, when they were under my very nose, and revealed very plainly, very unequivocally, Mdlle. Zoraïde Reuter, arm-in-arm, or hand-in-hand (I forget which) with my principal, confidant, and counsellor, M. François Pelet. And M. Pelet was saying—

"A quand donc le jour des noces, ma bien-aimée?"

And Mdlle. Reuter answered—

"Mais, François, tu sais bien qu'il me serait impossible de me marier avant les vacances."

"June, July, August, a whole quarter!" exclaimed the director. "How can I wait so long?—I who am ready, even now, to expire at your feet with impatience!"

"Ah! if you die, the whole affair will be settled without any trouble about notaries and contracts; I shall only have to order a slight mourning dress, which will be much sooner prepared than the nuptial trousseau."

"Cruel Zoraïde; you laugh at the distress of one who loves you so devotedly as I do: my torment is your sport; you scruple not to stretch my soul on the rack of jealousy; for, deny it as you will, I am certain you have cast encouraging glances on that school-boy, Crimsworth; he has presumed to fall in love, which he dared not have done unless you had given him room to hope."

"What do you say, François? Do you say Crimsworth is in love with me?"

"Over head and ears."

"Has he told you so?"

"No—but I see it in his face: he blushes whenever your name is mentioned."

A little laugh of exulting coquetry announced Mdlle. Reuter's gratification at this piece of intelligence (which was a lie, by-the-bye—I had never been so far gone as that, after all). M. Pelet proceeded to ask what she intended to do with me, intimating pretty plainly, and not very gallantly, that it was nonsense for her to think of taking such a "blanc-bec" as a husband, since she must be at least ten years older than I (was she then thirty-two? I should not have thought it). I heard her disclain any intentions on the subject—the director, however, still pressed her to give a definite answer.

"François," said she, "you are jealous," and still she laughed; then, as if suddenly recollecting that this coquetry was not consistent with the character for modest dignity she wished to establish, she proceeded, in a demure voice: "Truly, my dear François, I will not deny that this young Englishman may have made some attempts to ingratiate himself with me; but, so far from giving him any encouragement, I have always treated him with as much reserve as it was possible to combine with civility; affianced as I am to you, I would give no man false hopes; believe me, dear friend."

Still Pelet uttered murmurs of distrust—so I judged, at least, from her reply.

"What folly! How could I prefer an unknown foreigner to you? And then—not to flatter your vanity—Crimsworth could not bear comparison with you either physically or mentally; he is not a handsome man at all; some may call him gentleman-like and intelligent-looking, but for my part.——"

The rest of the sentence was lost in the distance, as the pair, rising from the chair in which they had been seated, moved away. I waited their return, but soon the opening and shutting of a door informed me that they had re-entered the house; I listened a little longer, all was perfectly still; I listened more than an hour—at last I heard M. Pelet come in and ascend to his chamber. Glancing once more towards the long front of the garden-house, I perceived that its solitary light was at length extinguished; so, for a time, was my faith in love and friendship. I went to bed, but something feverish and fiery had got into my veins which prevented me from sleeping much that night.

CHAPTER XIII.

Next morning I rose with the dawn, and having dressed myself and stood half-an-hour, my elbow leaning on the chest of drawers, considering what means I should adopt to restore my spirits, fagged with sleeplessness, to their ordinary tone—for I had no intention of getting up a scene with M. Pelet, reproaching him with perfidy, sending him a challenge, or performing other gambadoes of the sort—I hit at last on the expedient of walking out in the cool of the morning to a neighbouring establishment of baths, and treating myself to a bracing plunge. The remedy produced the desired effect. I came back at seven o'clock steadied and invigorated, and was able to greet M. Pelet, when he entered to breakfast, with an unchanged and tranquil countenance; even a cordial offering of the hand and the flattering appellation of "mon fils," pronounced in that caressing tone with which Monsieur had, of late days especially, been accustomed to address me, did not elicit any external sign of the feeling which, though subdued, still glowed at my heart. Not that I nursed vengeance—no; but the sense of insult and treachery lived in me like a kindling, though as yet smothered coal. God knows I am not by nature vindictive; I would not hurt a man because I can no longer trust or like him; but neither my reason nor feelings are of the vacillating order—they are not of that sand-like sort where impressions, if soon made, are as soon effaced. Once convinced that my friend's disposition is incompatible with my own, once assured that he is indelibly stained with certain defects obnoxious to my principles, and I dissolve the conection. I did so with Edward. As to Pelet, the discovery was yet new; should I act thus with him? It was the question I placed before my mind as I stirred my cup of coffee with a half-pistolet (we never had spoons), Pelet meantime being seated opposite, his pallid face looking as knowing and more haggard than usual, his blue eye turned, now sternly on his boys and ushers, and now graciously on me.

"Circumstances must guide me," said I; and meeting Pelet's false glance and insinuating smile, I thanked heaven that I had last night opened my window and read by the light of a full moon the true meaning of that guileful countenance. I felt half his master, because the reality of his nature was now known to me; smile and flatter as he would, I saw his soul lurk behind his smile, and heard in every one of his smooth phrases a voice interpreting their treacherous import.

But Zoraïde Reuter? Of course her defection had cut me to the quick? That sting must have gone too deep for any consolations of philosophy to be available in curing its smart? Not at all.

The night fever over, I looked about for balm to that wound also, and found some nearer home than at Gilead. Reason was my physician; she began by proving that the prize I had missed was of little value: she admitted that, physically, Zoraïde might have suited me, but affirmed that our souls were not in harmony, and that discord must have resulted from the union of her mind with mine. She then insisted on the suppression of all repining, and commanded me rather to rejoice that I had escaped a snare. Her medicament did me good. I felt its strengthening effect when I met the directress the next day; its stringent operation on the nerves suffered no trembling, no faltering; it enabled me to face her with firmness, to pass her with ease. She had held out her hand to me—that I did not choose to see. She had greeted me with a charming smile—it fell on my heart like light on stone. I passed on to the estrade, she followed me; her eye, fastened on my face, demanded of every feature the meaning of my changed and careless manner. "I will give her an answer," thought I; and, meeting her gaze full, arresting, fixing her glance, I shot into her eyes, from my own, a look, where there was no respect, no love, no tenderness, no gallantry; where the strictest analysis could detect nothing but scorn, hardihood, irony. I made her bear it, and feel it; her steady countenance did not change, but her colour rose, and she approached me as if fascinated. She stepped on to the estrade, and stood close by my side; she had nothing to say. I would not relieve her embarrassment, and negligently turned over the leaves of a book.

"I hope you feel quite recovered to-day," at last she said, in a low tone.

"And I, mademoiselle, hope that you took no cold last night in consequence of your late walk in the garden."

Quick enough of comprehension, she understood me directly: her face became a little blanched—a very little—but no muscle in her rather marked features moved; and, calm and self-possessed, she retired from the estrade, taking her seat quietly at a little distance, and occupying herself with netting a purse. I proceeded to give my lesson; it was a "Composition," *i. e.*, I dictated certain general questions, of which the pupils were to compose the answers from memory, access to books being forbidden. While Mdlle. Eulalie, Hortense, Caroline, &c., were pondering over the string of rather abstruse grammatical interrogatories I had propounded, I was at liberty to employ the vacant half hour in further observing the directress herself. The green silk purse was progressing fast in her hands; her eyes were bent upon it; her attitude, as she sat netting within two yards of me, was still yet guarded; in her whole person were expressed, at once, and with equal clearness, vigilance, and repose—a rare union! Looking at her, I was forced, as I had often been before, to offer her good sense, her wondrous self-control, the tribute of involuntary admiration.

She had felt that I had withdrawn from her my esteem; she had seen contempt and coldness in my eye, and to her, who coveted the approbation of all around her, who thirsted after universal good opinion, such discovery must have been an acute wound. I had witnessed its effect in the momentary pallor of her cheek—cheek unused to vary; yet how quickly, by dint of self-control, had she recovered her composure! With what quiet dignity she now sat, almost at my side, sustained by her sound and vigorous sense; no trembling in her somewhat lengthened, though shrewd upper lip, no coward shame on her austere forehead.

"There is metal there," I said, as I gazed. "Would that there were fire also, living ardour to make the steel glow—then I could love her."

Presently I discovered that she knew I was watching her, for she stirred not, she lifted not her crafty eyelid; she had glanced down from her netting to her small foot, peeping from the soft folds of her purple merino gown; thence her eye reverted to her hand, ivory white, with a bright garnet ring on the forefinger, and a light frill of lace round the wrist; with a scarcely perceptible movement she turned her head, causing her nut-brown curls to wave gracefully. In these slight signs I read that the wish of her heart, the design of her brain, was to lure back the game she had scared. A little incident gave her the opportunity of addressing me again.

While all was silence in the class—silence, but for the rustling of copy-books and the travelling of pens over their pages—a leaf of the large folding-door, opening from the hall, unclosed, admitting a pupil who, after making a hasty obeisance, ensconced herself with some appearance of trepidation, probably occasioned by her entering so late, in a vacant seat at the desk nearest the door. Being seated, she proceeded, still with an air of hurry and embarrassment, to open her cabas, to take out her books; and, while I was waiting for her to look up, in order to make out her identity—for, short-sighted as I was, I had not recognised her at her entrance—Mdlle. Reuter, leaving her chair, approached the estrade.

"Monsieur Creemsvort," said she, in a whisper; for when the school-rooms were silent, the directress always moved with velvet tread, and spoke in the most subdued key, enforcing order and stillness fully as much by example as precept; "Monsieur Creemsvort, that young person, who has just entered, wishes to have the advantage of taking lessons with you in English; she is not a pupil of the house; she is, indeed, in one sense, a teacher, for she gives instruction in lace-mending, and in little varieties of ornamental needle-work. She very properly proposes to qualify herself for a higher department of education, and has asked permission to attend your lessons, in order to perfect her knowledge of English, in which language she has, I believe, already made some progress; of course it is my wish to aid her in an effort so praiseworthy; you will permit her then to benefit by your instruction—n'est ce pas, monsieur?" And Mdlle. Reuter's eyes were raised to mine with a look at once naïve, benign, and beseeching.

I replied, "Of course," very laconically, almost abruptly.

"Another word," she said, with softness; "Mdlle. Henri has not received a regular education; perhaps her natural talents are not of the highest order: but I can assure you of the excellence of her intentions, and even of the amiability of her disposition. Monsieur will then, I am sure, have the goodness to be considerate with her at first, and not expose her backwardness, her inevitable deficiencies, before the young ladies, who, in a sense, are her pupils. Will Monsieur Creemsvort favour me by attending to this hint?" I nodded. She continued with subdued earnestness—

"Pardon me, monsieur, if I venture to add that what I have just said is of importance to the poor girl; she already experiences great difficulty in impressing these giddy young things with a due degree of deference for her authority, and should that difficulty be increased by new discoveries of her incapacity, she might find her position in my establishment too painful to be retained; a circumstance I should much regret for her sake, as she can ill afford to lose the profits of her occupation here."

Mdlle. Reuter possessed marvellous tact; but tact the most exquisite, unsupported by sincerity, will sometimes fail of its effect; thus, on this occasion, the longer she preached about the necessity of being indulgent to the governess-pupil, the more impatient I felt as I listened. I discerned so clearly that while her professed motive was a wish to aid the dull, though well-meaning Mdlle. Henri, her real one was no other than a design to impress me with an idea of her own exalted goodness and tender considerateness; so having again hastily nodded assent to her remarks, I obviated their renewal by suddenly demanding the compositions, in a sharp accent, and stepping from the estrade, I proceeded to collect them. As I passed the governess-pupil, I said to her—

"You have come in too late to receive a lesson to-day; try to be more punctual next time."

I was behind her, and could not read in her face the effect of my not very civil speech. Probably I should not have troubled myself to do so, had I been full in front; but I observed that she immediately began to slip her books into her cabas again; and, presently, after I had returned to the estrade, while I was arranging the mass of compositions, I heard the folding-door again open and close; and, on looking up, I perceived her place vacant. I thought to myself, "She will consider her first attempt at taking a lesson in English something of a failure;" and I wondered whether she had departed in the sulks, or whether stupidity had induced her to take my words too literally, or, finally, whether my irritable tone had wounded her feelings. The last notion I dismissed almost as soon as I had conceived it, for not having seen any appearance of sensitiveness in any human face since my arrival in Belgium, I had begun to regard it almost as a fabulous quality. Whether her physiognomy announced it I could not tell, for her speedy exit had allowed me no time to ascertain the circumstance. I had, indeed, on two or three previous occasions, caught a passing view of her (as I believe has been mentioned before); but I had never stopped to scrutinize either her face or person, and had but the most vague idea of her general appearance. Just as I had finished rolling up the compositions, the four o'clock bell rang; with my accustomed alertness in obeying that signal, I grasped my hat and evacuated the premises.

CHAPTER XIV.

If I was punctual in quitting Mdlle. Reuter's domicile, I was at least equally punctual in arriving there; I came the next day at five minutes before two, and on reaching the schoolroom door, before I opened it, I heard a rapid, gabbling sound, which warned me that the "prière du midi" was not yet concluded. I waited the termination thereof; it would have been impious to intrude my heretical presence during its progress. How the repeater of the prayer did cackle and splutter! I never before or since heard language enounced with such steam-engine haste. "Notre père qui êtes au ciel" went off like a shot; then followed an address to Marie, "vièrge céleste, reine des anges, maison d'or, tour d'ivoire!" and then an invocation to the saint of the day; and then down they all sat, and the solemn (?) rite was over; and I entered, flinging the door wide and striding in fast, as it was my wont to do now; for I had found that in entering with aplomb, and mounting the estrade with emphasis, consisted the grand secret of ensuring immediate silence. The folding-doors between the two classes, opened for the prayer, were instantly closed; a maîtresse, work-box in hand, took her seat at her appropriate desk; the pupils sat still with their pens and books before them; my three beauties in the van, now well-humbled by a demeanour of consistent coolness, sat erect with their hands folded quietly on their knees; they had given up giggling and whispering to each other, and no longer ventured to utter pert speeches in my presence; they now only talked to me occasionally with their eyes, by means of which organs they could still, however, say very audacious and coquettish things. Had affection, goodness, modesty, real talent, ever employed those bright orbs as interpreters, I do not think I could have refrained from giving a kind and encouraging, perhaps an ardent reply now and then; but as it was, I found pleasure in answering the glance of vanity with the gaze of stoicism. Youthful, fair, brilliant, as were many of my pupils, I can truly say that in me they never saw any other bearing than such as an austere, though just guardian, might have observed towards them. If any doubt the accuracy of this assertion, as inferring more conscientious self-denial or Scipio-like self-control than they feel disposed to give me credit for, let them take into consideration the following circumstances, which, while detracting from my merit, justify my veracity.

Know, O incredulous reader! that a master stands in a somewhat different relation towards a pretty, light-headed, probably ignorant girl, to that occupied by a partner at a ball, or a gallant on the promenade. A professor does not meet his pupil to see her dressed in satin and muslin, with hair perfumed and curled, neck scarcely shaded by aerial lace, round white arms circled with bracelets, feet dressed for the gliding dance. It is not his business to whirl her through the waltz, to feed her with compliments, to heighten her beauty by the flush of gratified vanity. Neither does he encounter her on the smooth-rolled, tree-shaded Boulevard, in the green and sunny park, whither she repairs clad in her becoming walking dress, her scarf thrown with grace over her shoulders, her little bonnet scarcely screening her curls, the red rose under its brim adding a new tint to the softer rose on her cheek; her face and eyes, too, illumined with smiles, perhaps as transient as the sunshine of the gala-day, but also quite as brilliant; it is not his office to walk by her side, to listen to her lively chat, to carry her parasol, scarcely larger than a broad green leaf, to lead in a ribbon her Blenheim spaniel or Italian greyhound. No; he finds her in the school-room, plainly dressed, with books before her. Owing to her education or her nature books are to her a nuisance, and she opens them with aversion, yet her teacher must instil into her mind the contents of these books; that mind resists the admission of grave information, it recoils, it grows restive, sullen tempers are shown, disfiguring frowns spoil the symmetry of the face, sometimes coarse gestures banish grace from the deportment, while muttered expressions, redolent of native and ineradicable vulgarity, desecrate the sweetness of the voice. Where the temperament is serene though the intellect be sluggish, an unconquerable dullness opposes every effort to instruct. Where there is cunning but not energy, dissimulation, falsehood, a thousand schemes and tricks are put in play to evade the necessity of application; in short, to the tutor, female youth, female charms are like tapestry hangings, of which the wrong side is continually turned towards him: and even when he sees the smooth, neat, external surface he so well knows what knots, long stitches, and jagged ends are behind that he has scarce a temptation to admire too fondly the seemly forms and bright colours exposed to general view.

Our likings are regulated by our circumstances. The artist prefers a hilly country because it is picturesque; the engineer a flat one because it is convenient; the man of pleasure likes what he calls "a fine woman"—she suits him; the fashionable young gentleman admires the fashionable young lady—she is of his kind; the toil-worn, fagged, probably irritable tutor, blind almost to beauty, insensible to airs and graces, glories chiefly in certain mental qualities; application, love of knowledge, natural capacity, docility, truthfulness, gratefulness, are the charms that attract his notice and win his regard. These he seeks, but seldom meets; these, if by chance he finds, he would fain retain for ever, and when separation deprives him of them he feels as if some ruthless hand had snatched from him his only ewe-lamb. Such being the case, and the case it is, my readers will agree with me that there was nothing either very meritorious or very marvellous in the integrity and moderation of my conduct at Mdlle. Reuter's pensionnat de demoiselles.

My first business this afternoon consisted in reading the list of places for the month, determined by the relative correctness of the compositions given the preceding day. The list was headed, as usual, by the name of Sylvie, that plain, quiet little girl I have described before as being at once the best and ugliest pupil in the establishment: the second place had fallen to the lot of a certain Léonie Ledru, a diminutive, sharp-featured, and parchment-skinned creature of quick wits, frail conscience, and indurated feelings; a lawyer-like thing, of whom I used to say that, had she been a boy, she would have made a model of an unprincipled, clever attorney. Then came Eulalie, the proud beauty, the Juno of the school, whom six long years of drilling in the simple grammar of the English language had compelled, despite the stiff phlegm of her intellect, to acquire a mechanical acquaintance with most of its rules. No smile, no trace of pleasure or satisfaction appeared in Sylvie's nun-like and passive face as she heard her name read first. I always felt saddened by the sight of that poor girl's absolute quiescence on all occasions, and it was my custom to look at her, to address her, as seldom as possible; her extreme docility, her assiduous perseverance, would have recommended her warmly to my good opinion; her modesty, her intelligence, would have induced me to feel most kindly—most affectionately towards her, notwithstanding the almost ghastly plainness of her features, the disproportion of her form, the corpse-like lack of animation in her countenance, had I not been aware that every friendly word, every kindly action, would be reported by her to her confessor, and by him misinterpreted and poisoned. Once I laid my hand on her head, in token of approbation; I thought Sylvie was going to smile, her dim eye almost kindled; but, presently, she shrunk from me; I was a man and a heretic; she, poor child! a destined nun and devoted Catholic: thus a fourfold wall of separation divided her mind from mine. A pert smirk, and a hard glance of triumph, was Léonie's method of testifying her gratification; Eulalie looked sullen and envious—she had hoped to be first. Hortense and Caroline exchanged a reckless grimace on hearing their names read out somewhere near the bottom of the list; the brand of mental inferiority was considered by them as no disgrace, their hopes for the future being based solely on their personal attractions.

This affair arranged, the regular lesson followed. During a brief interval, employed by the pupils in ruling their books, my eye, ranging carelessly over the benches, observed, for the first time, that the farthest seat in the farthest row—a seat usually vacant—was again filled by the new scholar, the Mdlle. Henri so ostentatiously recommended to me by the directress. To-day I had on my spectacles; her appearance, therefore, was clear to me at the first glance; I had not to puzzle over it. She looked young; yet, had I been required to name her exact age, I should have been somewhat nonplussed; the slightness of her figure might have suited seventeen; a certain anxious and pre-occupied expression of face seemed the indication of riper years. She was dressed, like all the rest, in a dark stuff gown and a white collar; her features were dissimilar to any there, not so rounded, more defined, yet scarcely regular. The shape of her head too was different, the superior part more developed, the base considerably less. I felt assured, at first sight, that she was not a Belgian; her complexion, her countenance, her lineaments, her figure, were all distinct from theirs, and, evidently, the type of another race—of a race less gifted with fullness of flesh and plenitude of blood; less jocund, material, unthinking. When I first cast my eyes on her, she sat looking fixedly down, her chin resting on her hand, and she did not change her attitude till I commenced the lesson. None of the Belgian girls would have retained one position, and that a reflective one, for the same length of time. Yet, having intimated that her appearance was peculiar, as being unlike that of her Flemish companions, I have little more to say respecting it; I can pronounce no encomiums on her beauty, for she was not beautiful; nor offer condolence on her plainness, for neither was she plain; a care-worn character of forehead, and a corresponding moulding of the mouth, struck me with a sentiment resembling surprise, but these traits would probably have passed unnoticed by any less crotchetty observer.

Now, reader, though I have spent a page and a half in describing Mdlle. Henri, I know well enough that I have left on your mind's eye no distinct picture of her; I have not painted her complexion, nor her eyes, nor her hair, nor even drawn the outline of her shape. You cannot tell whether her nose was aquiline or retroussé, whether her chin was long or short, her face square or oval; nor could I the first day, and it is not my intention to communicate to you at once a knowledge I myself gained by little and little.

I gave a short exercise which they all wrote down. I saw the new pupil was puzzled at first with the novelty of the form and language; once or twice she looked at me with a sort of painful solicitude, as not comprehending at all what I meant; then she was not ready when the others were, she could not write her phrases so fast as they did; I would not help her, I went on relentless. She looked at me; her eye said most plainly, "I cannot follow you." I disregarded the appeal, and, carelessly leaning back in my chair, glancing from time to time with a *nonchalant* air out of the window, I dictated a little faster. On looking towards her again, I perceived her face clouded with embarrassment, but she was still writing on most diligently; I paused a few seconds; she employed the interval in hurriedly re-perusing what she had written, and shame and discomfiture were apparent in her countenance; she evidently found she had made great nonsense of it. In ten minutes more the dictation was complete, and, having allowed a brief space in which to correct it, I took their books; it was with a reluctant hand Mdlle. Henri gave up hers, but, having once yielded it to my possession, she composed her anxious face, as if, for the present, she had resolved to dismiss regret, and had made up her mind to be thought unprecedentedly stupid. Glancing over her exercise, I found that several lines had been omitted, but what was written contained very few faults; I instantly inscribed "Bon" at the bottom of the page, and returned it to her; she smiled, at first incredulously, then as if re-assured, but did not lift her eyes; she could look at me, it seemed, when perplexed and bewildered, but not when gratified; I thought that scarcely fair.

CHAPTER XV.

Some time elapsed before I again gave a lesson in the first class; the holiday of Whitsuntide occupied three days, and on the fourth it was the turn of the second division to receive my instructions. As I made the transit of the carré, I observed, as usual, the band of sewers surrounding Mdlle. Henri; there were only about a dozen of them, but they made as much noise as might have sufficed for fifty; they seemed very little under her control; three or four at once assailed her with importunate requirements; she looked harassed, she demanded silence, but in vain. She saw me, and I read in her eye pain that a stranger should witness the insubordination of her pupils; she seemed to entreat order—her prayers were useless; then I remarked that she compressed her lips and contracted her brow; and her countenance, if I read it correctly, said—"I have done my best; I seem to merit blame notwithstanding; blame me then who will." I passed on; as I closed the school-room door, I heard her say, suddenly and sharply, addressing one of the eldest and most turbulent of the lot—

"Amélie Müllenberg, ask me no question, and request of me no assistance, for a week to come; during that space of time I will neither speak to you nor help you."

The words were uttered with emphasis—nay, with vehemence—and a comparative silence followed; whether the calm was permanent, I know not; two doors now closed between me and the carré.

Next day was appropriated to the first class; on my arrival, I found the directress seated, as usual, in a chair between the two estrades, and before her was standing Mdlle. Henri, in an attitude (as it seemed to me) of somewhat reluctant attention. The directress was knitting and talking at the same time. Amidst the hum of a large school-room, it was easy so to speak in the ear of one person, as to be heard by that person alone, and it was thus Mdlle. Reuter parleyed with her teacher. The face of the latter was a little flushed, not a little troubled; there was vexation in it, whence resulting I know not, for the directress looked very placid indeed; she could not be scolding in such gentle whispers, and with so equable a mien; no, it was presently proved that her discourse had been of the most friendly tendency, for I heard the closing words—

"C'est assez, ma bonne amie; à present je ne veux pas vous retenir davantage."

Without reply, Mdlle. Henri turned away; dissatisfaction was plainly evinced in her face, and a smile, slight and brief, but bitter, distrustful, and, I thought, scornful, curled her lip as she took her place in the class; it was a secret, involuntary smile, which lasted but a second; an air of depression succeeded, chased away presently by one of attention and interest, when I gave the word for all the pupils to take their reading-books. In general I hated the reading-lesson, it was such a torture to the ear to listen to their uncouth mouthing of my native tongue, and no effort of example or precept on my part ever seemed to effect the slightest improvement in their accent. To-day, each in her appropriate key, lisped, stuttered, mumbled, and jabbered as usual; about fifteen had racked me in turn, and my auricular nerve was expecting with resignation the discords of the sixteenth, when a full, though low voice, read out, in clear correct English—

"On his way to Perth, the king was met by a Highland woman, calling herself a prophetess; she stood at the side of the ferry by which he was about to travel to the north, and cried with a loud voice, 'My lord the king, if you pass this water you will never return again alive!' "—(*Vide* the history of Scotland.)

I looked up in amazement; the voice was a voice of Albion; the accent was pure and silvery; it only wanted firmness, and assurance, to be the counterpart of what any well educated lady in Essex or Middlesex might have enounced, yet the speaker or reader was no other than Mdlle. Henri, in whose grave, joyless face I saw no mark of consciousness that she had performed any extraordinary feat. No one else evinced surprise either. Mdlle Reuter knitted away assiduously; I was aware, however, that at the conclusion of the paragraph, she had lifted her eyelid and honoured me with a glance sideways; she did not know the full excellency of the teacher's style of reading, but she perceived that her accent was not that of the others, and wanted to discover what I thought; I masked my visage with indifference, and ordered the next girl to proceed.

When the lesson was over, I took advantage of the confusion caused by breaking up, to approach Mdlle. Henri; she was standing near the window and retired as I advanced; she thought I wanted to look out, and did not imagine that I could have anything to say to her. I took her exercise-book out of her hand; as I turned over the leaves I addressed her:—

"You have had lessons in English before?" I asked.

"No, sir."

"No! you read it well; you have been in England?"

"Oh no!" with some animation.

"You have been in English families?"

Still in the answer was "No." Here my eye, resting on the fly-leaf of the book, saw written, "Frances Evans Henri."

"Your name?" I asked.

"Yes, sir."

My interrogations were cut short; I heard a

little rustling behind me, and close at my back was the directress, professing to be examining the interior of a desk.

"Mademoiselle," said she, looking up and addressing the teacher, "will you have the goodness to go and stand in the corridor, while the young ladies are putting on their things, and try to keep some order."

Mdlle. Henri obeyed.

"What splendid weather!" observed the directress cheerfully, glancing at the same time from the window. I assented and was withdrawing. "What of your new pupil, monsieur?" continued she, following my retreating steps. "Is she likely to make progress in English?"

"Indeed I can hardly judge. She possesses a pretty good accent; of her real knowledge of the language I have as yet had no opportunity of forming an opinion."

"And her natural capacity, monsieur? I have

had my fears about that: can you relieve me by an assurance at least of its average power?"

"I see no reason to doubt its average power, mademoiselle, but really I scarcely know her, and have not had time to study the calibre of her capacity. I wish you a very good afternoon."

She still pursued me. "You will observe, monsieur, and tell me what you think; I could so much better rely on your opinion than on my own; women cannot judge of these things as men can, and, excuse my pertinacity, monsieur, but it is natural I should feel interested about this poor little girl (pauvre petite); she has scarcely any relations, her own efforts are all she has to look to, her acquirements must be her sole fortune; her present position has once been mine, or nearly so; it is then but natural I should sympathize with her; and sometimes, when I see the difficulty she has in managing pupils, I feel quite chagrined. I doubt not she does her best, her intentions are excellent; but, monsieur, she wants tact and firmness. I have talked to her on the subject, but I am not fluent, and probably did not express myself with clearness; she never appears to comprehend me. Now, would you occasionally, when you see an opportunity, slip in a word of advice to her on the subject; men have so much more influence than women have—they argue so much more logically than we do; and you, monsieur, in particular, have so paramount a power of making yourself obeyed; a word of advice from you could not but do her good; even if she were sullen and headstrong (which I hope she is not) she would scarcely refuse to listen to you; for my own part, I can truly say that I never attend one of your lessons without deriving benefit from witnessing your management of the pupils. The other masters are a constant source of anxiety to me: they cannot impress the young ladies with sentiments of respect, nor restrain the levity natural to youth: in you, monsieur, I feel the most absolute confidence; try then to put this poor child into the way of controlling our giddy, high-spirited Brabantoises. But, monsieur, I would add one word more; don't alarm her *amour propre*; beware of inflicting a wound there. I reluctantly admit that in that particular she is blameably—some would say ridiculously—susceptible. I fear I have touched this sore point inadvertently, and she cannot get over it."

During the greater part of this harangue my hand was on the lock of the outer door; I now turned it.

"Au revoir, mademoiselle," said I, and I escaped. I saw the directress's stock of words was yet far from exhausted. She looked after me, she would fain have detained me longer. Her manner towards me had been altered ever since I had begun to treat her with hardness and indifference: she almost cringed to me on every occasion; she consulted my countenance incessantly, and beset me with innumerable little officious attentions.

Servility creates despotism. This slavish homage, instead of softening my heart, only pampered whatever was stern and exacting in its mood. The very circumstance of her hovering round me like a fascinated bird, seemed to transform me into a rigid pillar of stone; her flatteries irritated my scorn, her blandishments confirmed my reserve. At times I wondered what she meant by giving herself such trouble to win me, when the more profitable Pelet was already in her nets, and when too she was aware that I possessed her secret, for I had not scrupled to tell her as much: but the fact is that as it was her nature to doubt the reality and undervalue the worth of modesty, affection, disinterestedness—to regard these qualities as foibles of character—so it was equally her tendency to consider pride, hardness, selfishness, as proofs of strength. She would trample on the neck of humility, she would kneel at the feet of disdain; she would meet tenderness with secret contempt, indifference she would woo with ceaseless assiduities. Benevolence, devotedness, enthusiasm, were her antipathies; for dissimulation and self-interest she had a preference—they were real wisdom in her eyes; moral and physical degradation, mental and bodily inferiority, she regarded with indulgence; they were foils capable of being turned to good account as set-offs for her own endowments. To violence, injustice, tyranny, she succumbed—they were her natural masters; she had no propensity to hate, no impulse to resist them; the indignation their behests awake in some hearts was unknown in hers. From all this it resulted that the false and selfish called her wise, the vulgar and debased termed her charitable, the insolent and unjust dubbed her amiable, the conscientious and benevolent generally at first accepted as valid her claim to be considered one of themselves; but ere long the plating of pretension wore off, the real mate:ial appeared below, and they laid her aside as a deception.

CHAPTER XVI.

In the course of another fortnight I had seen sufficient of Frances Evans Henri, to enable me to form a more definite opinion of her character. I found her possessed in a somewhat remarkable degree of at least two good points, viz., perseverance and a sense of duty; I found she was really capable of applying to study, of contending with difficulties. At first I offered her the same help which I had always found it necessary to confer on the others; I began with unloosing for her each knotty point, but I soon discovered that such help was regarded by my new pupil as degrading; she recoiled from it with a certain proud impatience. Hereupon I appointed her long lessons, and left her to solve alone any perplexities they might present. She set to the task with serious ardour, and having quickly accomplished one labour, eagerly demanded more. So much for her perseverance; as to her sense of duty, it evinced itself thus: she liked to learn, but hated to teach; her progress as a pupil depended upon herself, and I saw that on herself she could calculate with certainty; her success as a teacher rested partly, perhaps chiefly, upon the will of others; it cost her a most painful effort to enter into conflict with this foreign will, to endeavour to bend it into subjection to her own; for in what regarded people in general the action of her will was impeded by many scruples; it was as unembarrassed as strong where her own affairs were concerned, and to it she could at any time subject her inclination, if that inclination went counter to her convictions of right; yet when called upon to wrestle with the propensities, the habits, the faults of others, of children especially, who are deaf to reason, and, for the most part, insensate to persuasion, her will sometimes almost refused to act; then came in the sense of duty and forced the reluctant will into operation. A wasteful expense of energy and labour was frequently the consequence; Frances toiled for and with her pupils like a drudge, but it was long ere her conscientious exertions were rewarded by anything like docility on their part, because they saw that they had power over her, inasmuch as by resisting her painful attempts to convince, persuade, control—by forcing her to the employment of coercive measures—they could inflict upon her exquisite suffering. Human beings—human children especially—seldom deny themselves the pleasure of exercising a power which they are conscious of possessing, even though that power consist only in a capacity to make others wretched; a pupil whose sensations are duller than those of his instructor, while his nerves are tougher and his bodily strength perhaps greater, has an immense advantage over that instructor, and he will generally use it relentlessly, because the very young, very healthy, very thoughtless, know neither how to sympathize nor how to spare. Frances, I fear, suffered much; a continual weight seemed to oppress her spirits; I have said she did not live in the house, and whether in her own abode, wherever that might be, she wore the same pre-occupied, unsmiling, sorrowfully resolved air that always shaded her features under the roof of Mdlle. Reuter, I could not tell.

One day I gave, as a devoir, the trite little anecdote of Alfred tending cakes in the herdsman's hut, to be related with amplifications. A singular affair most of the pupils made of it; brevity was what they had chiefly studied; the majority of the narratives were perfectly unintelligible; those of Sylvie and Lèonie Ledru alone pretended to anything like sense and connection. Eulalie, indeed, had hit upon a clever expedient for at once ensuring accuracy and saving trouble; she had obtained access somehow to an abridged history of England, and had copied the anecdote out fair. I wrote on the margin of her production "Stupid and deceitful," and then tore it down the middle.

Last in the pile of single-leaved devoirs, I found one of several sheets, neatly written out and stitched together; I knew the hand, and scarcely needed the evidence of the signature, "Frances Evans Henri," to confirm my conjecture as to the writer's identity.

Night was my usual time for correcting devoirs, and my own room the usual scene of such task—task most onerous hitherto; and it seemed strange to me to feel rising within me an incipient sense of interest, as I snuffed the candle and addressed myself to the perusal of the poor teacher's manuscript.

"Now," thought I, "I shall see a glimpse of what she really is; I shall get an idea of the nature and extent of her powers; not that she can be expected to express herself well in a foreign tongue, but still, if she has any mind, here will be a reflection of it."

The narrative commenced by a description of a Saxon peasant's hut, situated within the confines of a great, leafless, winter forest; it represented an evening in December; flakes of snow were falling, and the herdsman foretold a heavy storm; he summoned his wife to aid him in collecting their flock, roaming far away on the pastoral banks of the Thone; he warns her that it will be late ere they return. The good woman is reluctant to quit her occupation of baking cakes for the evening meal; but acknowledging the primary importance of securing the herds and flocks, she puts on her sheep-skin mantle; and, addressing a stranger who rests half-reclined on a bed of rushes near the hearth, bids him mind the bread till her return.

"Take care, young man," she continues, "that you fasten the door well after us; and, above all, open to none in our absence; whatever sound you hear, stir not, and look not out. The night will soon fall; this forest is most wild and lonely; strange noises are often heard therein after sunset; wolves haunt these glades, and Danish warriors infest the country; worse things are talked of; you might chance to hear, as it were, a child cry, and on opening the door to afford it succour, a great black bull, or a shadowy goblin dog, might rush over the threshold; or, more awful still, if something flapped, as with wings, against the lattice, and then a raven or a white dove flew in and settled on the hearth, such a visitor would be a sure sign of misfortune to the house; therefore, heed my advice, and lift the latchet for nothing."

Her husband calls her away, both depart. The stranger, left alone, listens awhile to the muffled snow-wind, the remote, swollen sound of the river, and then he speaks.

"It is Christmas Eve," says he, "I mark the date; here I sit alone on a rude couch of rushes, sheltered by the thatch of a herdsman's hut; I, whose inheritance was a kingdom, owe my night's harbourage to a poor serf; my throne is usurped, my crown presses the brow of an invader; I have no friends; my troops wander broken in the hills of Wales; reckless robbers spoil my country; my subjects lie prostrate, their breasts crushed by the heel of the brutal Dane. Fate—thou hast done thy worst, and now thou standest before me resting thy hand on thy blunted blade. Ay; I see thine eye confront mine and demand why I still live, why I still hope. Pagan demon, I credit not thine omnipotence, and so cannot succumb to thy power. My God, whose Son, as on this night, took on Him the form of man, and for man vouchsafed to suffer and bleed, controls thy hand, and without His behest thou canst not strike a stroke. My God is sinless, eternal, all-wise—in Him is my trust; and though stripped and crushed by thee — though naked, desolate, void of resource—I do not despair, I cannot despair: were the lance of Guthrum now wet with my blood, I should not despair. I watch, I toil, I hope, I pray; Jehovah, in his own time, will aid."

I need not continue the quotation; the whole devoir was in the same strain. There were errors of orthography, there were foreign idioms, there were some faults of construction, there were verbs irregular transformed into verbs regular; it was mostly made up, as the above example shows, of short and somewhat rude sentences, and the style stood in great need of polish and sustained dignity; yet such as it was, I had hitherto seen nothing like it in the course of my professoral experience. The girl's mind had conceived a picture of the hut, of the two peasants, of the crownless king; she had imagined the wintry forest, she had recalled the old Saxon ghost legends, she had appreciated Alfred's courage under calamity, she had remembered his Christian education, and had shown him, with the rooted confidence of those primitive days, relying on the scriptural Jehovah for aid against the mythological Destiny. This she had done without a hint from me: I had given the subject, but not said a word about the manner of treating it.

"I will find, or make, an opportunity of speaking to her," I said to myself as I rolled the devoir up; "I will learn what she has of English in her besides the name of Frances Evans; she is no novice in the language, that is evident, yet she told me she had neither been in England, nor taken lessons in English, nor lived in English families."

In the course of my next lesson, I made a report of the other devoirs, dealing out praise and blame in very small retail parcels, according to my custom, for there was no use in blaming severely, and high encomiums were rarely merited. I said nothing of Mdlle. Henri's exercise, and, spectacles on nose, I endeavoured to decipher in her countenance her sentiments at the omission. I wanted to find out whether in her existed a consciousness of her own talents. "If she thinks she did a clever thing in composing that devoir, she will now look mortified," thought I. Grave as usual, almost sombre, was her face; as usual her eyes were fastened on the cahier open before her; there was something, I thought, of expectation in her attitude as I concluded a brief review of the last devoir, and when, casting it from me and rubbing my hands, I bade them take their grammars, some slight change did pass over her air and mien, as though she now relinquished a faint prospect of pleasant excitement; she had been waiting for something to be discussed in which she had a degree of interest; the discussion was not to come on, so expectation sank back, shrunk and sad, but attention, promptly filling up the void, repaired in a moment the transient collapse of feature; still, I felt, rather than saw, during the whole course of the lesson, that a hope had been wrenched from her, and that if she did not show distress, it was because she would not.

At four o'clock, when the bell rang and the room was in immediate tumult, instead of taking my hat and starting from the estrade, I sat still a moment. I looked at Frances, she was putting her books into her cabas; having fastened the button, she raised her head; encountering my eye, she made a quiet, respectful obeisance, as bidding good afternoon, and was turning to depart:—

"Come here," said I, lifting my finger at the same time. She hesitated; she could not hear the words amidst the uproar now pervading both school-rooms; I repeated the sign; she approached, again she paused, within half a yard of the estrade, and looked shy, and still doubtful whether she had mistaken my meaning.

"Step up," I said, speaking with decision. It is the only way of dealing with diffident, easily embarrassed characters, and with some slight manual aid I presently got her placed just where I wanted her to be, that is, between my desk and the window, where she was screened from the rush of the second division, and where no one could sneak behind her to listen.

"Take a seat," I said, placing a tabouret; and I made her sit down. I knew what I was doing, would be considered a very strange thing, and, what was more, I did not care. Frances knew it also, and, I fear, by an appearance of agitation and trembling, that she cared much. I drew from my pocket the rolled-up devoir.

"This is yours, I suppose?" said I, addressing her in English, for I now felt sure she could speak English.

"Yes," she answered distinctly; and as I unrolled it and laid it out flat on the desk before her with my hand upon it, and a pencil in that hand, I saw her moved, and, as it were, kindled; her depression beamed as a cloud might behind which the sun is burning.

"This devoir has numerous faults," said I. "It will take you some years of careful study before you are in a condition to write English with absolute correctness. Attend; I will point out some principal defects." And I went through it carefully, noting every error, and demonstrating why they were errors, and how the words or phrases ought to have been written. In the course of this sobering process she became calm. I now went on:—

"As to the substance of your devoir, Mdlle. Henri, it has surprised me; I perused it with pleasure, because I saw in it some proofs of taste and fancy. Taste and fancy are not the highest gifts of the human mind, but such as they are you possess them—not probably in a paramount degree, but in a degree beyond what the majority can boast. You may then take courage; cultivate the faculties that God and nature have bestowed on you, and do not fear in any crisis of suffering, under any pressure of injustice, to derive free and full consolation from the consciousness of their strength and rarity."

"Strength and rarity!" I repeated to myself;

"ay, the words are probably true," for on looking up, I saw the sun had dissevered its screening cloud, her countenance was transfigured, a smile shone in her eyes—a smile almost triumphant; it seemed to say—

"I am glad you have been forced to discover so much of my nature; you need not so carefully moderate your language. Do you think I am myself a stranger to myself? What you tell me in terms so qualified, I have known fully from a child."

She did say this as plainly as a frank and flashing glance could, but in a moment the glow of her complexion, the radiance of her aspect had subsided; if strongly conscious of her talents, she was equally conscious of her harassing defects, and the remembrance of these, obliterated for a single second, now reviving with sudden force, at once subdued the too vivid characters in which her sense of her powers had been expressed. So quick was the revulsion of feeling, I had not time to check her triumph by reproof; ere I could contract my brows to a frown she had become serious, and almost mournful-looking.

"Thank you, sir," said she, rising; there was gratitude both in her voice and in the look with which she accompanied it. It was time indeed for our conference to terminate, for, when I glanced around, behold all the boarders (the day-scholars had departed) were congregated within a yard or two of my desk, and stood staring with eyes and mouths wide open; the three maîtresses formed a whispering knot in one corner, and, close at my elbow, was the directress, sitting on a low chair, calmly clipping the tassels of her finished purse.

CHAPTER XVII.

After all I had profited but imperfectly by the opportunity I had so boldly achieved of speaking to Mdlle. Henri; it was my intention to ask her how she came to be possessed of two English baptismal names, Frances and Evans, in addition to her French surname, also whence she derived her good accent. I had forgotten both points, or, rather, our colloquy had been so brief that I had not had time to bring them forward; moreover, I had not half tested her powers of speaking English; all I had drawn from her in that language were the words "Yes," and "Thank you, sir." "No matter," I reflected. "What has been left incomplete now, shall be finished another day." Nor did I fail to keep the promise thus made to myself. It was difficult to get even a few words of particular conversation with one pupil among so many; but, according to the old proverb, "Where there is a will, there is a way;" and again and again I managed to find an opportunity for exchanging a few words with Mdlle. Henri, regardless that envy stared and detraction whispered whenever I approached her.

"Your book an instant." Such was the mode in which I often began these brief dialogues; the time was always just at the conclusion of the lesson; and motioning to her to rise, I installed myself in her place, allowing her to stand deferentially at my side; for I esteemed it wise and right in her case to enforce strictly all forms ordinarily in use between master and pupil; the rather because I perceived that in proportion as my manner grew austere and magisterial, hers became easy and self-possessed—an odd contradiction, doubtless, to the ordinary effect in such cases; but so it was.

"A pencil," said I, holding out my hand without looking at her. (I am now about to sketch a brief report of the first of these conferences.) She gave me one, and while I underlined some errors in a grammatical exercise she had written, I observed—

"You are not a native of Belgium?"

"No."

"Nor of France?"

"No."

"Where then is your birth-place?"

"I was born at Geneva."

"You don't call Frances and Evans Swiss names, I presume?"

"No, sir; they are English names."

"Just so; and is it the custom of the Genevese to give their children English appellatives?"

"Non, monsieur; mais—"

"Speak English, if you please."

"Mais—"

"English—"

"But—" (slowly and with embarrassment)—"my parents were not all the two Genevese."

"Say *both*, instead of 'all the two,' mademoiselle."

"Not *both* Swiss: my mother was English."

"Ah! and of English extraction?"

"Yes—her ancestors were all English."

"And your father?"

"He was Swiss."

"What besides? What was his profession?"

"Ecclesiastic—pastor—he had a church."

"Since your mother is an Englishwoman, why do you not speak English with more facility?"

"Maman est morte, il y a dix ans."

"And you do homage to her memory by forgetting her language. Have the goodness to put French out of your mind so long as I converse with you—keep to English."

"C'est si difficile, monsieur, quand on n'en a plus l' habitude."

"You had the habitude formerly, I suppose? Now answer me in your mother-tongue."

"Yes, sir, I spoke the English more than the French when I was a child."

"Why do you not speak it now?"

"Because I have no English friends."

"You live with your father, I suppose?"

"My father is dead."

"You have brothers and sisters?"

"Not one."

"Do you live alone?"

"No—I have an aunt—ma tante Julienne."

"Your father's sister?"

"Justement, monsieur."

"Is that English?"

"No—but I forget—"

"For which, mademoiselle, if you were a child I should certainly devise some slight punishment; at your age—you must be two or three and twenty, I should think?"

"Pas encore, monsieur—en un mois j'aurai dix-neuf ans."

"Well, nineteen is a mature age, and, having attained it, you ought to be so solicitous for your own improvement, that it should not be needful for a master to remind you twice of the expediency of your speaking English whenever practicable."

To this wise speech I received no answer; and, when I looked up, my pupil was smiling to herself a much-meaning, though not very gay smile; it seemed to say "He talks of he knows not what:" it said this so plainly, that I determined to request information on the point concerning which my ignorance seemed to be thus tacitly affirmed.

"Are you solicitous for your own improvement?"

"Rather."

"How do you prove it, mademoiselle?"

An odd question, and bluntly put; it excited a second smile.

"Why, monsieur, I am not inattentive—am I? I learn my lessons well—"

"Oh, a child can do that! and what more do you do?"

"What more can I do?"

"Oh, certainly, not much; but you are a teacher, are you not, as well as a pupil?"

"Yes."

"You teach lace-mending?"

"Yes."

"A dull, stupid occupation; do you like it?"

"No—it is tedious."

"Why do you pursue it? Why do you not rather teach history, geography, grammar, even arithmetic?"

"Is Monsieur certain that I am myself thoroughly acquainted with these studies?"

"I don't know; you ought to be at your age."

"But I never was at school, monsieur—"

"Indeed! What then were your friends—

what was your aunt about? She is very much to blame."

"No, monsieur, no—my aunt is good—she is not to blame—she does what she can; she lodges and nourishes me" (I report Mdlle. Henri's phrases literally, and it was thus she translated from the French). "She is not rich; she has only an annuity of twelve hundred francs, and it would be impossible for her to send me to school."

"Rather," thought I to myself on hearing this, but I continued, in the dogmatical tone I had adopted:—

"It is sad, however, that you should be brought up in ignorance of the most ordinary branches of education; had you known something of history and grammar you might, by degrees, have relinquished your lace-mending drudgery, and risen in the world."

"It is what I mean to do."

"How? By a knowledge of English alone? That will not suffice; no respectable family will receive a governess whose whole stock of knowledge consists in a familiarity with one foreign language."

"Monsieur, I know other things."

"Yes, yes, you can work with Berlin wools, and embroider handkerchiefs and collars — that will do little for you."

Mdlle. Henri's lips were unclosed to answer, but she checked herself, as thinking the discussion had been sufficiently pursued, and remained silent.

"Speak," I continued impatiently; "I never like the appearance of acquiescence when the reality is not there, and you had a contradiction at your tongue's end."

"Monsieur, I have had many lessons both in grammar, history, geography, and arithmetic. I have gone through a course of each study."

"Bravo! but how did you manage it, since your aunt could not afford to send you to school?"

"By lace-mending; by the thing Monsieur despises so much."

"Truly! And now, mademoiselle, it will be a good exercise for you to explain to me in English how such a result was produced by such means."

"Monsieur, I begged my aunt to have me taught lace-mending soon after we came to Brussels, because I knew it was a métier, a trade which was easily learnt, and by which I could earn some money very soon. I learnt it in a few days, and I quickly got work, for all the Brussels ladies have old lace—very precious—which must be mended all the times it is washed. I earned money a little, and this money I gave for lessons in the studies I have mentioned; some of it I spent in buying books, English books especially; soon I shall try to find a place of governess, or school-teacher, when I can write and speak English well; but it will be difficult, because those who know I have been a lace-mender will despise me, as the pupils here despise me. Pourtant j'ai mon projet," she added in a lower tone.

"What is it?"

"I will go and live in England; I will teach French there."

The words were pronounced emphatically. She said "England" as you might suppose an Israelite of Moses' days would have said Canaan.

"Have you a wish to see England?"

"Yes, and an intention."

And here a voice, the voice of the directress, interposed:—

"Mademoiselle Henri, je crois qu'il va pleuvoir; vous feriez bien, ma bonne amie, de retourner chez vous tout de suite."

In silence, without a word of thanks for this officious warning, Mdlle. Henri collected her books; she moved to me respectfully, endeavoured to move to her superior, though the endeavour was almost a failure, for her head seemed as if it would not bend, and thus departed.

Where there is one grain of perseverance or wilfulness in the composition, trifling obstacles are ever known rather to stimulate than discourage. Mdlle. Reuter might as well have spared herself the trouble of giving that intimation about the weather (by-the-by her prediction was falsified by the event—it did not rain that evening). At the close of the next lesson I was again at Mdlle. Henri's desk. Thus did I accost her:—

"What is your idea of England, mademoiselle? Why do you wish to go there?"

Accustomed by this time to the calculated abruptness of my manner, it no longer discomposed or surprised her, and she answered with only so much of hesitation as was rendered inevitable by the difficulty she experienced in improvising the translation of her thoughts from French to English.

"England is something unique, as I have heard and read; my idea of it is vague, and I want to go there to render my idea clear, definite."

"Hum! How much of England do you suppose you could see if you went there in the capacity of a teacher? A strange notion you must have of getting a clear and definite idea of a country! All you could see of Great Britain would be the interior of a school, or at most of one or two private dwellings."

"It would be an English school; they would be English dwellings."

"Indisputably; but what then? What would be the value of observations made on a scale so narrow?"

"Monsieur, might not one learn something by analogy? An—échantillon—a—a sample often serves to give an idea of the whole; besides, narrow and wide are words comparative, are they not? All my life would perhaps seem narrow in your eyes—all the life of a—that little animal subterranean—une taupe—comment dit-on?"

"Mole."

"Yes—a mole, which lives underground, would seem narrow even to me.

"Well, mademoiselle—what then? Proceed."

"Mais, monsieur, vous me comprenez."

"Not in the least; have the goodness to explain."

"Why, monsieur, it is just so. In Switzerland I have done but little, learnt but little, and seen but little; my life there was in a circle; I walked the same round every day; I could not get out of it; had I rested—remained there even till my death, I should never have enlarged it, because I am poor and not skilful, I have not great acquirements; when I was quite tired of this round, I begged my aunt to go to Brussels; my existence is no larger here, because I am no richer or higher; I walk in as narrow a limit, but the scene is changed; it would change again if I went to England. I knew something of the bourgeois of Geneva, now I know something of the bourgeois of Brussels; if I went to

London, I should know something of the bourgeois of London. Can you make any sense out of what I say, monsieur, or is it all obscure?"

"I see, I see—now let us advert to another subject; you propose to devote your life to teaching, and you are a most unsuccessful teacher; you cannot keep your pupils in order."

A flush of painful confusion was the result of this harsh remark; she bent her head to the desk, but soon raising it, replied—

"Monsieur, I am not a skilful teacher, it is true, but practice improves; besides, I work under difficulties; here I only teach sewing, I can show no power in sewing, no superiority—it is a subordinate art; then I have no associates in this house, I am isolated; I am too a heretic, which deprives me of influence."

"And in England you would be a foreigner; that too would deprive you of influence, would effectually separate you from all round you; in England you would have as few connections, as little importance as you have here."

"But I should be learning something; for the rest, there are probably difficulties for such as I everywhere, and if I must contend, and perhaps be conquered, I would rather submit to English pride than to Flemish coarseness; besides, monsieur ——."

She stopped—not evidently from any difficulty in finding words to express herself, but because discretion seemed to say, "You have said enough."

"Finish your phrase," I urged.

"Besides, monsieur, I long to live once more among Protestants; they are more honest than Catholics; a Romish school is a building with porous walls, a hollow floor, a false ceiling; every room in this house, monsieur, has eye-holes and ear-holes, and what the house is, the inhabitants are, very treacherous; they all think it lawful to tell lies; they all call it politeness to profess friendship where they feel hatred."

"All?" said I; "you mean the pupils—the mere children—inexperienced, giddy things, who have not learnt to distinguish the difference between right and wrong?"

"On the contrary, monsieur—the children are the most sincere; they have not yet had time to become accomplished in duplicity; they will tell lies, but they do it inartificially, and you know they are lying; but the grown-up people are very false; they deceive strangers, they deceive each other ——."

A servant here entered:—

"Mdlle. Henri—Mdlle. Reuter vous prie de vouloir bien conduire la petite de Dorlodot chez elle, elle vous attend dans le cabinet de Rosalie la portière—c'est que sa bonne n'est pas venue la chercher—voyez-vous."

"Eh bien! est-ce que je suis sa bonne—moi?" demanded Mdlle. Henri, then smiling, with that same bitter, derisive smile I had seen on her lips once before, she hastily rose and made her exit.

END OF VOL. I.

THE PROFESSOR,

A Tale

THE PROFESSOR,

A Tale.

BY

CURRER BELL
(Charlotte Brontë)

IN TWO VOLUMES.

VOL. II.

GYAN

Published by

Gyan Publishing House
5, Ansari Road
Daryaganj, New Delhi-110002
Phone: 011-47034999, 9811692060
E-mail: books@gyanbooks.com

Distribution Network
gyanbooks.com
India, USA, Canada, UK, Australia

ISBN: 978-81-212-0651-8 (Set)
978-81-212-0664-8 (HB)
First Published, 1857

2nd Impression 2024

Printed at: Gyan Press, Delhi.

THE PROFESSOR, A TALE (VOL. II.)
Author: CURRER BELL (CHARLOTTE BRONTË)

THE PROFESSOR;

A Tale.

THE PROFESSOR,

A Tale.

BY

CURRER BELL,

AUTHOR OF "JANE EYRE," "SHIRLEY," "VILLETTE," &c.

IN TWO VOLUMES.

VOL. II.

LONDON:

SMITH, ELDER & CO., 65, CORNHILL.

1857.

THE PROFESSOR.

CHAPTER XVIII.

The young Anglo-Swiss evidently derived both pleasure and profit from the study of her mother-tongue. In teaching her I did not, of course, confine myself to the ordinary school routine; I made instruction in English a channel for instruction in literature. I prescribed to her a course of reading; she had a little selection of English classics, a few of which had been left her by her mother, and the others she had purchased with her own penny-fee. I lent her some more modern works; all these she read with avidity, giving me, in writing, a clear summary of each work when she had perused it. Composition, too, she delighted in. Such occupation seemed the very breath of her nostrils, and soon her improved productions wrung from me the avowal that those qualities in her I had termed taste and fancy ought rather to have been denominated judgment and imagination. When I intimated so much, which I did as usual in dry and stinted phrase, I looked for the radiant and exulting smile my one word of eulogy had elicited before; but Frances coloured. If she did smile, it was very softly and shyly; and instead of looking up to me with a conquering glance, her eyes rested on my hand, which, stretched over her shoulder, was writing some directions with a pencil on the margin of her book.

"Well, are you pleased that I am satisfied with your progress?" I asked.

"Yes," said she slowly, gently, the blush that had half subsided returning.

"But I do not say enough, I suppose?" I continued. "My praises are too cool?"

She made no answer, and, I thought, looked a little sad. I divined her thoughts, and should much have liked to have responded to them, had it been expedient so to do. She was not now very ambitious of my admiration—not eagerly desirous of dazzling me; a little affection—ever so little—pleased her better than all the panegyrics in the world. Feeling this, I stood a good while behind her, writing on the margin of her book. I could hardly quit my station or relinquish my occupation; something retained me bending there, my head very near hers, and my hand near hers too; but the margin of a copy-book is not an illimitable space—so, doubtless, the directress thought; and she took occasion to walk past in order to ascertain by what art I prolonged so disproportionately the period necessary for filling it. I was obliged to go. Distasteful effort—to leave what we most prefer!

Frances did not become pale or feeble in consequence of her sedentary employment; perhaps the stimulus it communicated to her mind counterbalanced the inaction it imposed on her body. She changed, indeed, changed obviously and rapidly; but it was for the better. When I first saw her, her countenance was sunless, her complexion colourless; she looked like one who had no source of enjoyment, no store of bliss anywhere in the world; now the cloud had passed from her mien, leaving space for the dawn of hope and interest, and those feelings rose like a clear morning, animating what had been depressed, tinting what had been pale. Her eyes, whose colour I had not at first known, so dim were they with repressed tears, so shadowed with ceaseless dejection, now, lit by a ray of the sunshine that cheered her heart, revealed irids of bright hazel—irids large and full, screened with long lashes; and pupils instinct with fire. That look of wan emaciation which anxiety or low spirits often communicates to a thoughtful, thin face, rather long than round, having vanished from hers; a clearness of skin almost bloom, and a plumpness almost embonpoint, softened the decided lines of her features. Her figure shared in this beneficial change; it became rounder, and as the harmony of her form was complete and her stature of the graceful middle height, one did not regret (or at least *I* did not regret) the absence of confirmed fulness, in contours, still slight, though compact, elegant, flexible—the exquisite turning of waist, wrist, hand, foot and ankle satisfied completely my notions of symmetry, and allowed a lightness and freedom of movement which corresponded with my ideas of grace.

Thus improved, thus wakened to life, Mdlle. Henri began to take a new footing in the school; her mental power, manifested gradually but steadily, ere long extorted recognition even from the envious; and when the young and healthy saw that she could smile brightly, converse gaily, move with vivacity and alertness, they acknowledged in her a sisterhood of youth and health, and tolerated her as of their kind accordingly.

To speak truth, I watched this change much as a gardener watches the growth of a precious plant, and I contributed to it too, even as the said gardener contributes to the development of his favourite. To me it was not difficult to discover how I could best foster my pupil, cherish her starved feelings, and induce the outward manifestation of that inward vigour which sunless drought and blighting-blast had hitherto forbidden to expand. Constancy of attention—a kindness as mute as watchful, always standing by her, cloaked in the rough garb of austerity, and making its real nature known only by a rare glance of interest, or a cordial and gentle word; real respect masked with seeming imperiousness, directing, urging her actions, yet helping her too, and that with devoted care: these were the means I used, for these means best suited Frances' feelings, as susceptible as deep-vibrating—her nature, at once proud and shy.

The benefits of my system became apparent also in her altered demeanour as a teacher; she now took her place amongst her pupils with an air of spirit and firmness which assured them at once that she meant to be obeyed—and obeyed she was. They felt they had lost their power over her. If any girl had rebelled, she would no longer have taken her rebellion to heart; she possessed a source of comfort they could not drain, a pillar of support they could not overthrow; formerly, when insulted, she wept; now, she smiled.

The public reading of one of her devoirs achieved the revelation of her talents to all and sundry; I remember the subject—it was an emigrant's letter to his friends at home. It opened with simplicity; some natural and graphic touches disclosed to the reader the scene of virgin forest and great, New-World river—barren of sail and flag—amidst which the epistle was supposed to be indited. The difficulties and dangers that attend a settler's life were hinted at; and in the few words said on that subject, Mdlle. Henri failed not to render audible the voice of resolve, patience, endeavour. The disasters which had driven him from his native country were alluded to; stainless honour, inflexible independence, indestructible self-respect there took the word. Past days were spoken of; the grief of parting, the regrets of absence, were touched upon; feeling, forcible and fine, breathed eloquent in every period. At the close, consolation was suggested; religious faith became there the speaker, and she spoke well.

The devoir was powerfully written in language at once chaste and choice, in a style nerved with vigour and graced with harmony.

Mdlle. Reuter was quite sufficiently acquainted with English to understand it when read or spoken in her presence, though she could neither speak nor write it herself. During the perusal of this devoir, she sat placidly busy, her eyes and fingers occupied with the formation of a "rivière," or open-work hem round a cambric handkerchief; she said nothing, and her face and forehead, clothed with a mask of purely negative expression, were as blank of comment as her lips. As neither surprise, pleasure, approbation, nor interest were evinced in her countenance, so no more were disdain, envy, annoyance, weariness; if that inscrutable mien said anything, it was simply this—

"The matter is too trite to excite an emotion, or call forth an opinion."

As soon as I had done, a hum rose; several of the pupils, pressing round Mdlle. Henri, began to beset her with compliments; the composed voice of the directress was now heard:—

"Young ladies, such of you as have cloaks and umbrellas will hasten to return home before the shower becomes heavier" (it was raining a little), "the remainder will wait till their respective servants arrive to fetch them." And the school dispersed, for it was four o'clock.

"Monsieur, a word," said Mdlle. Reuter, stepping on to the estrade, and signifying, by a movement of the hand, that she wished me to relinquish, for an instant, the castor I had clutched.

"Mademoiselle, I am at your service."

"Monsieur, it is of course an excellent plan to encourage effort in young people by making conspicuous the progress of any particularly industrious pupil, but do you not think that in the present instance, Mdlle. Henri can hardly be considered as a concurrent with the other pupils? She is older than most of them and has had advantages of an exclusive nature for acquiring a knowledge of English; on the other hand, her sphere of life is somewhat beneath theirs; under these circumstances, a public distinction, conferred upon Mdlle. Henri, may be the means of suggesting comparisons, and exciting feelings such as would be far from advantageous to the individual forming their object. The interest I take in Mdlle. Henri's real welfare makes me desirous of screening her from annoyances of this sort; besides, monsieur, as I have before hinted to you, the sentiment of *amour-propre* has a somewhat marked preponderance in her character; celebrity has a tendency to foster this sentiment, and in her it should be rather repressed—she rather needs keeping down than bringing forward; and then I think, monsieur—it appears to me that ambition, *literary* ambition especially, is not a feeling to be cherished in the mind of a woman; would not Mdlle. Henri be much safer and happier if taught to believe that in the quiet discharge of social duties consists her real vocation, than if stimulated to aspire after applause and publicity? She may never marry; scanty as are her resources, obscure as are her connections, uncertain as is her health (for I think her consumptive, her mother died of that complaint), it is more than probable she never will; I do not see how she can rise to a position, whence such a step would be possible; but even in celibacy it would be better for her to retain the character and habits of a respectable, decorous female."

"Indisputably, mademoiselle," was my answer. "Your opinion admits of no doubt," and, fearful of the harangue being renewed, I retreated under cover of that cordial sentence of assent.

At the date of a fortnight after the little incident noted above, I find it recorded in my diary that a hiatus occurred in Mdlle. Henri's usually regular attendance in class. The first day or two I wondered at her absence, but did not like to ask an explanation of it; I thought indeed some chance word might be dropped which would afford me the information I wished to obtain, without my running the risk of exciting silly smiles and gossiping whispers by demanding it. But when a week passed and the seat at the desk near the door still remained vacant, and when no allusion was made to the circumstance by any individual of the class—when, on the contrary, I found that all observed a marked silence on the point—I determined, *coûte qui coûte*, to break the ice of this silly reserve. I selected Sylvie as my informant, because from her I knew that I should at least get a sensible answer, unaccompanied by wriggle, titter, or other flourish of folly.

"Où donc est Mdlle. Henri?" I said one day as I returned an exercise-book I had been examining.

"Elle est partie, monsieur."

"Partie! et pour combien de temps? Quand reviendra-t-elle?"

"Elle est partie pour toujours, monsieur; elle ne reviendra plus."

"Ah!" was my involuntary exclamation; then after a pause:—

"En êtes-vous bien sûre, Sylvie?"

"Oui, oui, monsieur, mademoiselle la directrice nous l'a dit elle-même il y a deux ou trois jours."

And I could pursue my inquiries no further; time, place, and circumstances, forbade my adding another word. I could neither comment on what had been said, nor demand further particulars. A question as to the reason of the teacher's departure, as to whether it had been voluntary or otherwise, was indeed on my lips, but I suppressed it—there were listeners all round. An hour after, in passing Sylvie in the corridor as she was putting on her bonnet, I stopped short and asked:—

"Sylvie, do you know Mdlle. Henri's address? I have some books of hers," I added carelessly, "and I should wish to send them to her."

"No, monsieur," replied Sylvie, "but perhaps Rosalie, the portress, will be able to give it you."

Rosalie's cabinet was just at hand; I stepped in and repeated the inquiry. Rosalie—a smart French grisette—looked up from her work with a knowing smile, precisely the sort of smile I had been so desirous to avoid exciting. Her answer was prepared; she knew nothing whatever of Mdlle. Henri's address—had never known it. Turning from her with impatience—for I believed she lied and was hired to lie — I almost knocked down some one who had been standing at my back; it was the directress. My abrupt movement made her recoil two or three steps. I was obliged to apologize, which I did more concisely than politely. No man likes to be dogged, and in the very irritable mood in which I then was the sight of Mdlle. Reuter thoroughly incensed me. At the moment I turned her countenance looked hard, dark, and inquisitive; her eyes were bent upon me with an expression of almost hungry curiosity. I had scarcely caught this phase of physiognomy ere it had vanished; a bland smile played on her features; my harsh apology was received with good-humoured facility.

"Oh, don't mention it, monsieur; you only touched my hair with your elbow; it is no worse, only a little dishevelled." She shook it back, and passing her fingers through her curls, loosened them into more numerous and flowing ringlets. Then she went on with vivacity:—

"Rosalie, I was coming to tell you to go instantly and close the windows of the salon; the wind is rising, and the muslin curtains will be covered with dust."

Rosalie departed. "Now," thought I, "this will not do; Mdlle. Reuter thinks her meanness in eaves-dropping is screened by her art in devising a pretext, whereas the muslin curtains she speaks of are not more transparent than this same pretext." An impulse came over me to thrust the flimsy screen aside, and confront her craft boldly with a word or two of plain truth. "The rough-shod foot treads most firmly on slippery ground," thought I, so I began:—

"Mademoiselle Henri has left your establishment—been dismissed, I presume?"

"Ah, I wished to have a little conversation

with you, monsieur," replied the directress with the most natural and affable air in the world; "but we cannot talk quietly here; will Monsieur step into the garden a minute?" And she preceded me, stepping out through the glass-door I have before mentioned.

"There," said she, when we had reached the centre of the middle alley, and when the foliage of shrubs and trees, now in their summer pride, closing behind and around us, shut out the view of the house, and thus imparted a sense of seclusion even to this little plot of ground in the very core of a capital.

"There, one feels quiet and free when there are only pear-trees and rose-bushes about one; I daresay you, like me, monsieur, are sometimes tired of being eternally in the midst of life; of having human faces always round you, human eyes always upon you, human voices always in your ear. I am sure I often wish intensely for liberty to spend a whole month in the country at some little farm-house, bien gentille, bien propre, tout entourée de champs et de bois; quelle vie charmante que la vie champêtre! N'est-ce pas, monsieur?"

"Cela dépend, mademoiselle."

"Que le vent est bon et frais!" continued the directress; and she was right there, for it was a south wind, soft and sweet. I carried my hat in my hand, and this gentle breeze, passing through my hair, soothed my temples like balm. Its refreshing effect, however, penetrated no deeper than the mere surface of the frame; for as I walked by the side of Mdlle. Reuter, my heart was still hot within me, and while I was musing the fire burned, then spake I with my tongue:—

"I understand Mdlle. Henri is gone from hence, and will not return?"

"Ah, true! I meant to have named the subject to you some days ago, but my time is so completely taken up, I cannot do half the things I wish; have you never experienced what it is, monsieur, to find the day too short by twelve hours for your numerous duties?"

"Not often. Mdlle. Henri's departure was not voluntary, I presume? If it had been, she would certainly have given me some intimation of it, being my pupil."

"Oh, did she not tell you? that was strange; for my part, I never thought of adverting to the subject; when one has so many things to attend to, one is apt to forget little incidents that are not of primary importance."

"You consider Mdlle. Henri's dismission, then, as a very insignificant event?"

"Dismission? Ah! she was not dismissed; I can say with truth, monsieur, that since I became the head of this establishment no master or teacher has ever been *dismissed* from it."

"Yet some have left it, mademoiselle?"

"Many; I have found it necessary to change frequently—a change of instructors is often beneficial to the interests of a school; it gives life and variety to the proceedings; it amuses the pupils, and suggests to the parents the idea of exertion and progress."

"Yet when you are tired of a professor or maîtresse, you scruple to dismiss them?"

"No need to have recourse to such extreme measures, I assure you. Allons, monsieur le professeur—asseyons-nous; je vais vous donner une petite leçon dans votre état d'instituteur." (I wish I might write all she said to me in French—it loses sadly by being translated into English.) We had now reached *the* garden-chair; the directress sat down, and signed to me to sit by her, but I only rested my knee on the seat, and stood leaning my head and arm against the embowering branch of a huge laburnum, whose golden flowers, blent with the dusky green leaves of a lilac-bush, formed a mixed arch of shade and sunshine over the retreat. Mdlle. Reuter sat silent a moment; some novel movements were evidently working in her mind, and they showed their nature on her astute brow; she was meditating some *chef d'œuvre* of policy. Convinced by several months' experience that the affectation of virtues she did not possess was unavailing to ensnare me—aware that I had read her real nature, and would believe nothing of the character she gave out as being hers—she had determined, at last, to try a new key, and see if the lock of my heart would yield to that; a little audacity, a word of truth, a glimpse of the real. "Yes, I will try," was her inward resolve; and then her blue eye glittered upon me—it did not flash—nothing of flame ever kindled in its temperate gleam.

"Monsieur fears to sit by me?" she inquired playfully.

"I have no wish to usurp Pelet's place," I answered, for I had got the habit of speaking to her bluntly—a habit begun in anger, but continued because I saw that, instead of offending, it fascinated her. She cast down her eyes, and drooped her eyelids; she sighed uneasily; she turned with an anxious gesture, as if she would give me the idea of a bird that flutters in its cage, and would fain fly from its jail and jailor, and seek its natural mate and pleasant nest.

"Well—and your lesson?" I demanded briefly.

"Ah!" she exclaimed, recovering herself, "you are so young, so frank and fearless, so talented, so impatient of imbecility, so disdainful of vulgarity, you need a lesson; here it is then: far more is to be done in this world by dexterity than by strength; but, perhaps, you knew that before, for there is delicacy as well as power in your character—policy, as well as pride?"

"Go on," said I; and I could hardly help smiling, the flattery was so piquant, so finely seasoned. She caught the prohibited smile, though I passed my hand over my mouth to conceal it; and again she made room for me to sit beside her. I shook my head, though temptation penetrated to my senses at the moment, and once more I told her to go on.

"Well, then, if ever you are at the head of a large establishment, dismiss nobody. To speak truth, monsieur (and to you I will speak truth), I despise people who are always making rows, blustering, sending off one to the right, and another to the left, urging, and hurrying circumstances. I'll tell you what I like best to do, monsieur, shall I?" She looked up again; she had compounded her glance well this time—much archness, more deference, a spicy dash of coquetry, an unveiled consciousness of capacity. I nodded; she treated me like the great Mogul; so I became the great Mogul as far as she was concerned.

"I like, monsieur, to take my knitting in my hands, and to sit quietly down in my chair; circumstances defile past me; I watch their march; so long as they follow the course I wish, I say nothing, and do nothing; I don't clap my hands, and cry out 'Bravo! How lucky I am!' to attract the attention and envy of my neighbours—I am merely passive; but when events fall out ill—when circumstances become adverse—I watch very vigilantly; I knit on still, and still I hold my tongue; but every now and then, monsieur, I just put my toe out—so—and give the rebellious circumstance a little secret push, without noise, which sends it the way I wish, and I am successful after all, and nobody has seen my expedient. So, when teachers or masters become troublesome and inefficient—when, in short, the interests of the school would suffer from their retaining their places—I mind my knitting, events progress, circumstances glide past; I see one which, if pushed ever so little awry, will render untenable the post I wish to have vacated—the deed is done—the stumbling-block removed—and no one saw me: I have not made an enemy, I am rid of an incumbrance."

A moment since, and I thought her alluring; this speech concluded, I looked on her with distaste. "Just like you," was my cold answer. "And in this way you have ousted Mdlle. Henri? You wanted her office, therefore you rendered it intolerable to her?"

"Not at all, monsieur, I was merely anxious about Mdlle. Henri's health; no, your moral sight is clear and piercing, but there you have failed to discover the truth. I took—I have always taken a real interest in Mdlle. Henri's welfare; I did not like her going out in all weathers; I thought it would be more advantageous for her to obtain a permanent situation; besides, I considered her now qualified to do something more than teach sewing. I reasoned with her; left the decision to herself; she saw the correctness of my views, and adopted them."

"Excellent! and now, mademoiselle, you will have the goodness to give me her address."

"Her address!" and a sombre and stony change came over the mien of the directress. "Her address? Ah!—well—I wish I could oblige you, monsieur, but I cannot, and I will tell you why; whenever I myself asked her for her address, she always evaded the inquiry. I thought—I may be wrong—but I *thought* her motive for doing so, was a natural, though mistaken reluctance to introduce me to some, probably, very poor abode; her means were narrow, her origin obscure; she lives somewhere, doubtless, in the 'basse ville.'"

"I'll not lose sight of my best pupil yet," said I, "though she were born of beggars and lodged in a cellar; for the rest, it is absurd to make a bugbear of her origin to me—I happen to know that she was a Swiss pastor's daughter, neither more nor less; and, as to her narrow means, I care nothing for the poverty of her purse so long as her heart overflows with affluence."

"Your sentiments are perfectly noble, monsieur," said the directress, affecting to suppress a yawn; her sprightliness was now extinct, her temporary candour shut up; the little, red-coloured, piratical-looking pennon of audacity she had allowed to float a minute in the air, was furled, and the broad, sober-hued flag of dissimulation again hung low over the citadel. I did not like her thus, so I cut short the *tête-à-tête* and departed.

CHAPTER XIX.

Novelists should never allow themselves to weary of the study of real life, If they observed this duty conscientiously, they would give us fewer pictures chequered with vivid contrasts of light and shade; they would seldom elevate their heroes and heroines to the heights of rapture—still seldomer sink them to the depths of despair; for if we rarely taste the fulness of joy in this life, we yet more rarely savour the acrid bitterness of hopeless anguish; unless, indeed, we have plunged like beasts into sensual indulgence, abused, strained, stimulated, again overstrained, and, at last, destroyed our faculties for enjoyment; then, truly, we may find ourselves without support, robbed of hope. Our agony is great, and how can it end? We have broken the spring of our powers; life must be all suffering—too feeble to conceive faith—death must be darkness—God, spirits, religion can have no place in our collapsed minds, where linger only hideous and polluting recollections of vice; and time brings us on to the brink of the grave, and dissolution flings us in—a rag eaten through and through with disease, wrung together with pain, stamped into the churchyard sod by the inexorable heel of despair.

But the man of regular life and rational mind never despairs. He loses his property—it is a blow—he staggers a moment; then, his energies, roused by the smart, are at work to seek a remedy; activity soon mitigates regret. Sickness affects him; he takes patience—endures what he cannot cure. Acute pain racks him; his writhing limbs know not where to find rest; he leans on Hope's anchor. Death takes from him what he loves; roots up, and tears violently away the stem round which his affections were twined—a dark, dismal time, a frightful wrench—but some morning Religion looks into his desolate house with sunrise, and says, that in another world, another life, he shall meet his kindred again. She speaks of that world as a place unsullied by sin—of that life, as an era unembittered by suffering; she mightily strengthens her consolation by connecting with it two ideas—which mortals cannot comprehend, but on which they love to repose—Eternity, Immortality; and the mind of the mourner, being filled with an image, faint yet glorious, of heavenly hills all light and peace—of a spirit resting there in bliss—of a day when his spirit shall also alight there, free and disembodied—of a reunion perfected by love, purified from fear—he takes courage—goes out to encounter the necessities and discharge the duties of life; and, though sadness may never lift her burden from his mind, Hope will enable him to support it.

Well—and what suggested all this? and what

is the inference to be drawn therefrom? What suggested it, is the circumstance of my best pupil —my treasure—being snatched from my hands, and put away out of my reach; the inference to be drawn from it is—that, being a steady, reasonable man, I did not allow the resentment, disappointment, and grief, engendered in my mind by this evil chance, to grow there to any monstrous size; nor did I allow them to monopolize the whole space of my heart; I pent them, on the contrary, in one strait and secret nook. In the day-time, too, when I was about my duties, I put them on the silent system; and it was only after I had closed the door of my chamber at night that I somewhat relaxed my severity towards these morose nurslings, and allowed vent to their language of murmurs; then, in revenge, they sat on my pillow, haunted my bed, and kept me awake with their long, midnight cry.

A week passed. I had said nothing more to Mdlle. Reuter. I had been calm in my demeanour to her though, stony cold and hard. When I looked at her, it was with the glance fitting to be bestowed on one who I knew had consulted jealousy as an adviser, and employed treachery as an instrument—the glance of quiet disdain and rooted distrust. On Saturday evening, ere I left the house, I stept into the *salle-à-manger*, where she was sitting alone, and, placing myself before her, I asked, with the same tranquil tone and manner that I should have used had I put the question for the first time—

"Mademoiselle, will you have the goodness to give me the address of Frances Evans Henri?"

A little surprised, but not disconcerted, she smilingly disclaimed any knowledge of that address, adding, "Monsieur has perhaps forgotten that I explained all about that circumstance before—a week ago?"

"Mademoiselle," I continued, "you would greatly oblige me by directing me to that young person's abode."

She seemed somewhat puzzled; and, at last, looking up with an admirably counterfeited air of naïveté, she demanded, "Does Monsieur think I am telling an untruth?"

Still avoiding to give her a direct answer, I said, "It is not then your intention, mademoiselle, to oblige me in this particular?"

"But, monsieur, how can I tell you what I do not know?"

"Very well; I understand you perfectly, mademoiselle, and now I have only two or three words to say. This is the last week in July; in another month the vacation will commence; have the goodness to avail yourself of the leisure it will afford you to look out for another English master—at the close of August, I shall be under the necessity of resigning my post in your establishment."

I did not wait for her comments on this announcement, but bowed and immediately withdrew.

That same evening, soon after dinner, a servant brought me a small packet; it was directed in a hand I knew, but had not hoped so soon to see again; being in my own apartment and alone, there was nothing to prevent my immediately opening it; it contained four five-franc pieces, and a note in English.

"MONSIEUR,

"I came to Mdlle. Reuter's house yesterday, at the time when I knew you would be just about finishing your lesson, and I asked if I might go into the school-room and speak to you. Mdlle. Reuter came out and said you were already gone; it had not yet struck four, so I thought she must be mistaken, but concluded it would be vain to call another day on the same errand. In one sense a note will do as well—it will wrap up the 20 francs, the price of the lessons I have received from you; and if it will not fully express the thanks I owe you in addition—

if it will not bid you good-bye as I could wish to have done—if it will not tell you, as I long to do, how sorry I am that I shall probably never see you more—why, spoken words would hardly be more adequate to the task. Had I seen you, I should probably have stammered out something feeble and unsatisfactory—something belying my feelings rather than explaining them; so it is perhaps as well that I was denied admission to your presence. You often remarked, monsieur, that my devoirs dwelt a great deal on fortitude in bearing grief—you said I introduced that theme too often: I find indeed that it is much easier to write about a severe duty than to perform it, for I am oppressed when I see and feel to what a reverse fate has condemned me; you were kind to me, monsieur—very kind; I am afflicted—I am heart-broken to be quite separated from you; soon I shall have no friend on earth. But it is useless troubling you with my distresses. What claim have I on your sympathy? None; I will then say no more.

Farewell, Monsieur.

F. E. Henri.

I put up the note in my pocket-book. I slipped the five-franc pieces into my purse—then I took a turn through my narrow chamber.

"Mdlle. Reuter talked about her poverty," said I, "and she is poor; yet she pays her debts and more. I have not yet given her a quarter's lessons, and she has sent me a quarter's due. I wonder of what she deprived herself to scrape together the twenty francs—I wonder what sort of a place she has to live in, and what sort of a woman her aunt is, and whether she is likely to get employment to supply the place she has lost. No doubt she will have to trudge about long enough from school to school, to inquire here, and apply there—be rejected in this place, disappointed in that. Many an evening she'll go to her bed tired and unsuccessful. And the directress would not let her in to bid me good-bye? I might not have the chance of standing with her for a few minutes at a window in the school-room and exchanging some half-dozen of sentences—getting to know where she lived—putting matters in train for having all things arranged to my mind? No address on the note"—I continued, drawing it again from the pocket-book and examining it on each side of the two leaves: "women are women, that is certain, and always do business like women; men mechanically put a date and address to their communications. And these five-franc pieces?"—(I hauled them forth from my purse)—"if she had offered me them herself instead of tying them up with a thread of green silk in a kind of Lilliputian packet, I could have thrust them back into her little hand, and shut up the small, taper fingers over them—so—and compelled her shame, her pride, her shyness all to yield to a little bit of determined

Will—now where is she? How can I get at her?"

Opening my chamber-door I walked down into the kitchen.

"Who brought the packet?" I asked of the servant who had delivered it to me.

"Un petit commissionaire, monsieur."

"Did he say anything?"

"Rien."

And I wended my way up the back-stairs, wondrously the wiser for my inquiries.

"No matter," said I to myself, as I again closed the door. "No matter—I'll seek her through Brussels."

And I did. I sought her day by day whenever I had a moment's leisure, for four weeks; I sought her on Sundays all day long; I sought her on the Boulevards, in the Allée Verte, in the Park; I sought her in Ste. Gudule and St. Jacques; I sought her in the two Protestant chapels; I attended these latter at the German, French, and

English services, not doubting that I should meet her at one of them. All my researches were absolutely fruitless; my security on the last point was proved by the event to be equally groundless with my other calculations. I stood at the door of each chapel after the service, and waited till every individual had come out, scrutinizing every gown draping a slender form, peering under every bonnet covering a young head. In vain; I saw girlish figures pass me, drawing their black scarfs over their sloping shoulders, but none of them had the exact turn and air of Mdlle. Henri's; I saw pale and thoughtful faces "encadrées" in bands of brown hair, but I never found her forehead, her eyes, her eyebrows. All the features of all the faces I met seemed frittered away, because my eye failed to recognise the peculiarities it was bent upon; an ample space of brow and a large, dark, and serious eye, with a fine but decided line of eye-brow traced above.

"She has probably left Brussels—perhaps is

gone to England, as she said she would," muttered I inwardly, as on the afternoon of the fourth Sunday I turned from the door of the chapel royal which the door-keeper had just closed and locked, and followed in the wake of the last of the congregation, now dispersed and dispersing over the square. I had soon outwalked the couples of English gentlemen and ladies. (Gracious goodness! why don't they dress better? My eye is yet filled with visions of the high-flounced, slovenly, and tumbled dresses in costly silk and satin, of the large unbecoming collars in expensive lace; of the ill-cut coats and strangely fashioned pantaloons which every Sunday, at the English service, filled the choirs of the chapel-royal, and after it, issuing forth into the square, came into disadvantageous contrast with freshly and trimly attired foreign figures, hastening to attend salut at the church of Coburg). I had passed these pairs of Britons, and the groups of pretty British children, and the British footmen and waiting-maids; I had crossed the Place Royale, and got into the Rue Royale, thence I had diverged into the Rue de Louvain—an old and quiet street. I remember that, feeling a little hungry, and not desiring to go back and take my share of the "goûter," now on the refectory-table at Pelet's—to wit, pistolets and water—I stepped into a baker's and refreshed myself on a *couc* (?) (it is a Flemish word, I don't know how to spell it) *à Corinthe—anglice,* a currant bun—and a cup of coffee; and then I strolled on towards the Porte de Louvain. Very soon I was out of the city, and slowly mounting the hill, which ascends from the gate, I took my time; for the afternoon, though cloudy, was very sultry, and not a breeze stirred to refresh the atmosphere. No inhabitant of Brussels need wander far to search for solitude; let him but move half a league from his own city and he will find her brooding still and blank over the wide fields, so drear though so fertile, spread out treeless and trackless round the capital of Brabant.

Having gained the summit of the hill, and having stood and looked long over the cultured but lifeless campaign, I felt a wish to quit the high road, which I had hitherto followed, and get in among those tilled grounds—fertile as the beds of a Brobdignagian kitchen-garden—spreading far and wide even to the boundaries of the horizon, where, from a dusk green, distance changed them to a sullen blue, and confused their tints with those of the livid and thunderous-looking sky. Accordingly I turned up a by-path to the right; I had not followed it far ere it brought me, as I expected, into the fields, amidst which, just before me, stretched a long and lofty white wall enclosing, as it seemed from the foliage showing above, some thickly planted nursery of yew and cypress, for of that species were the branches resting on the pale parapets, and crowding gloomily about a massive cross, planted doubtless on a central eminence and extending its arms, which seemed of black marble, over the summits of those sinister trees. I approached, wondering to what house this well-protected garden appertained; I turned the angle of the wall, thinking to see some stately residence; I was close upon great iron gates; there was a hut serving for a lodge near, but I had no occasion to apply for the key—the gates were open; I pushed one leaf back, rain had rusted its hinges, for it groaned dolefully as they revolved. Thick planting embowered the entrance. Passing up the avenue I saw objects on each hand which, in their own mute language of inscription and sign, explained clearly to what abode I had made my way. This was the house appointed for all living; crosses, monuments, and garlands of everlastings announced, "The Protestant Cemetery, outside the gate of Louvain."

The place was large enough to afford half an hour's strolling without the monotony of treading continually the same path, and, for those who love to peruse the annals of grave-yards, here was variety of inscription enough to occupy the attention for double or treble that space of time. Hither people of many kindreds, tongues, and nations, had brought their dead for interment; and here, on pages of stone, of marble, and of brass, were written names, dates, last tributes of pomp or love, in English, in French, in German, and Latin. Here the Englishman had erected a marble monument over the remains of his Mary Smith or Jane Brown, and inscribed it only with her name. There the French widower had shaded the grave of his Elmire or Celestine with a brilliant thicket of roses, amidst which a little tablet rising, bore an equally bright testimony to her countless virtues. Every nation, tribe, and kindred, mourned after its own fashion, and how soundless was the mourning of all! My own tread, though slow and upon smooth-rolled paths, seemed to startle, because it formed the sole break to a silence otherwise total. Not only the winds, but the very fitful, wandering airs, were that afternoon, as by common consent, all fallen asleep in their various quarters; the north was hushed, the south silent, the east sobbed not, nor did the west whisper. The clouds in heaven were condensed and dull, but apparently quite motionless. Under the trees of this cemetery nestled a warm, breathless gloom, out of which the cypresses stood up straight and mute, above which the willows hung low and still; where the flowers, as languid as fair, waited listless for night dew or thunder-shower; where the tombs, and those they hid, lay impassible to sun or shadow, to rain or drought.

Importuned by the sound of my own footsteps, I turned off upon the turf, and slowly advanced to a grove of yews; I saw something stir among the stems; I thought it might be a broken branch swinging, my short-sighted vision had caught no form, only a sense of motion, but the dusky shade passed on, appearing and disappearing at the openings in the avenue. I soon discerned it was a living thing, and a human thing; and, drawing nearer, I perceived it was a woman, pacing slowly to and fro, and evidently deeming herself alone as I had deemed myself alone, and meditating as I had been meditating. Ere long, she returned to a seat which I fancy she had but just quitted, or I should have caught sight of her before. It was in a nook, screened by a clump of trees; there was the white wall before her, and a little stone set up against the wall, and, at the foot of the stone, was an allotment of turf freshly turned up, a new-made grave. I put on my spectacles, and passed softly close behind her; glancing at the inscription on the stone, I read, "Julienne Henri, died at Brussels, aged sixty. August 10th, 18—." Having perused the inscription, I looked down at the form sitting bent and thoughtful just under my eyes, unconscious of the vicinity of any living thing; it was a slim, youthful figure in mourning apparel of the plainest black stuff, with a little simple black crape bonnet; I felt, as well as saw, who it was; and, moving neither hand nor foot, I stood some moments enjoying the security of conviction. I had sought her for a month, and had never discovered one of her traces—never met a hope, or seized a chance of encountering her anywhere. I had been forced to loosen my grasp on expectation; and, but an hour ago, had sunk slackly under the discouraging thought that the current of life, and the impulse of destiny, had swept her for ever from my reach; and, behold, while bending sullenly earthward beneath the pressure of despondency—while following with my eyes the track of sorrow on the turf of a grave-yard—here was my lost jewel dropped on the tear-fed herbage, nestling in the mossy and mouldy roots of yew-trees

Frances sat very quiet, her elbow on her knee, and her head on her hand. I knew she could retain a thinking attitude a long time without change; at last, a tear fell; she had been looking at the name on the stone before her, and her heart had no doubt endured one of those constrictions with which the desolate living, regretting the dead, are, at times, so sorely oppressed. Many tears rolled down, which she wiped away, again and again, with her handkerchief; some distressed sobs escaped her, and then, the paroxysm over, she sat quiet as before. I put my hand gently on her shoulder; no need further to prepare her, for she was neither hysterical nor liable to fainting-fits; a sudden push, indeed, might have startled her, but the contact of my quiet touch merely woke attention as I wished; and, though she turned quickly, yet so lightning-swift is thought—in some minds especially—I believe the wonder of what—the consciousness of who it was that thus stole unawares on her solitude, had passed through her brain, and flashed into her heart, even before she had effected that hasty movement; at least, Amazement had hardly opened her eyes and raised them to mine, ere Recognition informed their irids with most speaking brightness. Nervous surprise had hardly discomposed her features ere a sentiment of most vivid joy shone clear and warm on her whole countenance. I had hardly time to observe that she was wasted and pale, ere called to feel a responsive inward pleasure by the sense of most full and exquisite pleasure glowing in the animated flush, and shining in the expansive light, now diffused over my pupil's face. It was the summer sun flashing out after the heavy summer shower; and what fertilizes more rapidly than that beam, burning almost like fire in its ardour?

I hate boldness—that boldness which is of the brassy brow and insensate nerves; but I love the courage of the strong heart, the fervour of the generous blood; I loved with passion the light of Frances Evans' clear hazel eye when it did not fear to look straight into mine; I loved the tones with which she uttered the words—

"Mon maître! mon maître!"

I loved the movement with which she confided her hand to my hand; I loved her as she stood there, pennyless and parentless; for a sensualist charmless, for me a treasure—my best object of sympathy on earth, thinking such thoughts as I thought, feeling such feelings as I felt; my ideal of the shrine in which to seal my stores of love; personification of discretion and forethought, of diligence and perseverance, of self-denial and self-control—those guardians, those trusty keepers of the gift I longed to confer on her—the gift of all my affections; model of truth and honour, of independence and conscientiousness—those refiners and sustainers of an honest life; silent possessor of a well of tenderness, of a flame, as genial as still, as pure as quenchless, of natural feeling, natural passion—those sources of refreshment and comfort to the sanctuary of home. I knew how quietly and how deeply the well bubbled in her heart; I knew how the more dangerous flame burned safely under the eye of reason; I had seen when the fire shot up a moment high and vivid, when the accelerated heat troubled life's current in its channels; I had seen reason reduce the rebel, and humble its blaze to embers. I had confidence in Frances Evans; I had respect for her, and as I drew her arm through mine, and led her out of the cemetery, I felt I had another sentiment, as strong as confidence, as firm as respect, more fervid than either—that of love.

"Well, my pupil," said I, as the ominous-sounding gate swung to behind us—"Well, I have found you again: a month's search has seemed long, and I little thought to have discovered my lost sheep straying amongst graves."

Never had I addressed her but as "Mademoiselle" before, and to speak thus was to take up a tone new to both her and me. Her answer apprised me that this language ruffled none of her feelings, woke no discord in her heart:—

"Mon maître," she said, "have you troubled

yourself to seek me? I little imagined you would think much of my absence, but I grieved bitterly to be taken away from you. I was sorry for that circumstance when heavier troubles ought to have made me forget it."

"Your aunt is dead?"

"Yes, a fortnight since, and she died full of regret, which I could not chase from her mind; she kept repeating, even during the last night of her existence, 'Frances, you will be so lonely when I am gone, so friendless: she wished too that she could have been buried in Switzerland, and it was I who persuaded her in her old age to leave the banks of Lake Leman, and to come, only as it seems to die, in this flat region of Flanders. Willingly would I have observed her last wish, and taken her remains back to our own country, but that was impossible; I was forced to lay her here."

"She was ill but a short time, I presume?"

"But three weeks. When she began to sink

I asked Mdlle. Reuter's leave to stay with her and wait on her; I readily got leave."

"Do you return to the pensionnat?" I demanded hastily.

"Monsieur, when I had been at home a week Mdlle. Reuter called one evening, just after I had got my aunt to bed; she went into her room to speak to her, and was extremely civil and affable, as she always is; afterwards she came and sat with me a long time, and, just as she rose to go away, she said: 'Mademoiselle, I shall not soon cease to regret your departure from my establishment, though indeed it is true that you have taught your class of pupils so well that they are all quite accomplished in the little works you manage so skilfully, and have not the slightest need of further instruction; my second teacher must in future supply your place, with regard to the younger pupils, as well as she can, though she is indeed an inferior artiste to you, and doubtless it will be your part now to assume a higher position in your calling; I am sure you will everywhere find schools and families willing to profit by your talents.' And then she paid me my last quarter's salary. I asked, as Mademoiselle would no doubt think, very bluntly, if she designed to discharge me from the establishment. She smiled at my inelegance of speech, and answered that 'our connection as employer and employed was certainly dissolved, but that she hoped still to retain the pleasure of my acquaintance; she should always be happy to see me as a friend;' and then she said something about the excellent condition of the streets, and the long continuance of fine weather, and went away quite cheerful."

I laughed inwardly; all this was so like the directress—so like what I had expected and guessed of her conduct; and then the exposure and proof of her lie, unconsciously afforded by Frances:—"She had frequently applied for Mdlle. Henri's address," forsooth; "Mdlle. Henri had always evaded giving it," &c., &c., and here I found her a visitor at the very house of whose locality she had professed absolute ignorance!

Any comments I might have intended to make on my pupil's communication, were checked by the plashing of large rain-drops on our faces and on the path, and by the muttering of a distant but coming storm. The warning obvious in stagnant air and leaden sky had already induced me to take the road leading back to Brussels, and now I hastened my own steps and those of my companion, and, as our way lay downhill, we got on rapidly. There was an interval after the fall of the first broad drops before heavy rain came on; in the meantime we had passed through the Porte de Louvain, and were again in the city.

"Where do you live?" I asked; "I will see you safe home."

"Rue Notre Dame aux Neiges," answered Frances.

It was not far from the Rue de Louvain, and we stood on the door-steps of the house we sought ere the clouds, severing with loud peal and shattered cataract of lightning, emptied their livid folds in a torrent, heavy, prone, and broad.

"Come in! come in!" said Frances, as, after putting her into the house, I paused ere I followed: the word decided me; I stepped across the threshold, shut the door on the rushing, flashing, whitening storm, and followed her upstairs to her apartments. Neither she nor I were wet; a projection over the door had warded off the straight-descending flood; none but the first, large drops had touched our garments; one minute more and we should not have had a dry thread on us.

Stepping over a little mat of green wool, I found myself in a small room with a painted floor and a square of green carpet in the middle; the articles of furniture were few, but all bright and exquisitely clean; order reigned through its narrow limits — such order as it soothed my punctilious soul to behold. And I had hesitated to enter the abode, because I apprehended after all that Mdlle. Reuter's hint about its extreme poverty might be too well-founded, and I feared to embarrass the lace-mender by entering her lodgings unawares! Poor the place might be; poor truly it was; but its neatness was better than elegance, and, had but a bright little fire shone on that clean hearth, I should have deemed it more attractive than a palace. No fire was there, however, and no fuel laid ready to light; the lace-mender was unable to allow herself that indulgence, especially now when, deprived by death of her sole relative, she had only her own unaided exertions to rely on. Frances went into an inner room to take off her bonnet, and she came out a model of frugal neatness, with her well-fitting black stuff dress, so accurately defining her elegant bust and taper waist, with her spotless white collar turned back from a fair and shapely neck, with her plenteous brown hair arranged in smooth bands on her temples, and in a large Grecian plat behind: ornaments she had none—neither brooch, ring, nor ribbon; she did well enough without them—perfection of fit, proportion of form, grace of carriage, agreeably supplied their place. Her eye, as she re-entered the small sitting-room, instantly sought mine, which was just then lingering on the hearth; I knew she read at once the sort of inward ruth and pitying pain which the chill vacancy of that hearth stirred in my soul: quick to penetrate, quick to determine, and quicker to put in practice, she had in a moment tied a holland apron round her waist; then she disappeared, and re-appeared with a basket; it had a cover; she opened it, and produced wood and coal; deftly and compactly she arranged them in the grate.

"It is her whole stock, and she will exhaust it out of hospitality," thought I.

"What are you going to do?" I asked: "not

surely to light a fire this hot evening? I shall be smothered."

"Indeed, monsieur, I feel it very chilly since the rain began; besides, I must boil the water for my tea, for I take tea on Sundays; you will be obliged to try and bear the heat."

She had struck a light; the wood was already in a blaze; and truly, when contrasted with the darkness, the wild tumult of the tempest without, that peaceful glow which began to beam on the now animated hearth, seemed very cheering. A low, purring sound, from some quarter, announced that another being, besides myself, was pleased with the change; a black cat, roused by the light from its sleep on a little cushioned foot-stool, came and rubbed its head against Frances' gown as she knelt; she caressed it, saying it had been a favourite with her "pauvre tante Julienne."

The fire being lit, the hearth swept, and a small kettle of a very antique pattern, such as

I thought I remembered to have seen in old farm-houses in England, placed over the now ruddy flame, Frances' hands were washed, and her apron removed in an instant; then she opened a cupboard, and took out a tea-tray, on which she had soon arranged a china tea-equipage, whose pattern, shape, and size, denoted a remote antiquity; a little, old-fashioned silver spoon was deposited in each saucer; and a pair of silver tongs, equally old-fashioned, were laid on the sugar-basin; from the cupboard, too, was produced a tidy silver cream-ewer, not larger than an egg-shell. While making these preparations, she chanced to look up, and, reading curiosity in my eyes, she smiled and asked—

"Is this like England, monsieur?"

"Like the England of a hundred years ago," I replied.

"Is it truly? Well, everything on this tray is at least a hundred years old: these cups, these spoons, this ewer, are all heir-looms; my great-grandmother left them to my grandmother, she to my mother, and my mother brought them with her from England to Switzerland, and left them to me; and, ever since I was a little girl, I have thought I should like to carry them back to England, whence they came."

She put some pistolets on the table; she made the tea, as foreigners do make tea—*i. e.*, at the rate of a teaspoonful to half a dozen cups; she placed me a chair, and, as I took it, she asked, with a sort of exultation—

"Will it make you think yourself at home for a moment?"

"If I had a home in England, I believe it would recall it," I answered; and, in truth, there was a sort of illusion in seeing the fair-complexioned, English-looking girl presiding at the English meal, and speaking in the English language.

"You have then no home?" was her remark.

"None, nor ever have had. If ever I possess a home, it must be of my own making, and the task is yet to begin." And, as I spoke, a pang, new to me, shot across my heart: it was a pang of mortification at the humility of my position, and the inadequacy of my means; while with that pang was born a strong desire to do more, earn more, be more, possess more; and in the increased possessions, my roused and eager spirit panted to include the home I had never had, the wife I inwardly vowed to win.

Frances' tea was little better than hot water, sugar, and milk; but I liked it, and it cheered me; and her pistolets, with which she could not offer me butter, were sweet to my palate as manna.

The repast over, and the treasured plate and porcelain being washed and put by, the bright table rubbed still brighter, "le chat de ma tante Julienne" also being fed with provisions brought forth on a plate for its special use, a few stray cinders, and a scattering of ashes too, being swept from the hearth, Frances at last sat down; and then, as she took a chair opposite to me, she betrayed, for the first time, a little embarrassment; and no wonder, for indeed I had unconsciously watched her rather too closely, followed all her steps and all her movements a little too perseveringly with my eyes, for she mesmerized me by the grace and alertness of her action—by the deft, cleanly, and even decorative effect resulting from each touch of her slight and fine fingers; and when, at last, she subsided to stillness, the intelligence of her face seemed beauty to me, and I dwelt on it accordingly. Her colour, however, rising, rather than settling with repose, and her eyes remaining downcast, though I kept waiting for the lids to be raised that I might drink a ray of the light I loved—a light where fire dissolved in softness, where affection tempered penetration, where, just now at least, pleasure played with thought—this expectation not being gratified, I began at last to suspect that I had probably myself to blame for the disappointment; I must cease gazing, and begin talking, if I wished to break the spell under which she now sat motionless; so recollecting the composing effect which an authoritative tone and manner had ever been wont to produce on her, I said—

"Get one of your English books, mademoiselle, for the rain yet falls heavily, and will probably detain me half an hour longer."

Released, and set at ease, up she rose, got her book, and accepted at once the chair I placed for her at my side. She had selected "Paradise Lost" from her shelf of classics, thinking, I suppose, the religious character of the book best adapted it to Sunday; I told her to begin at the beginning, and while she read Milton's invocation to that heavenly muse, who on the "secret top of Oreb or Sinai" had taught the Hebrew shepherd how in the womb of chaos, the conception of a world had originated and ripened, I enjoyed, undisturbed, the treble pleasure of having her near me, hearing the sound of her voice—a sound sweet and satisfying in my ear—and looking, by intervals, at her face: of this last privilege, I chiefly availed myself when I found fault with an intonation, a pause, or an emphasis; as long as I dogmatized, I might also gaze, without exciting too warm a flush.

"Enough," said I, when she had gone through some half dozen pages (a work of time with her, for she read slowly and paused often to ask and receive information)—"enough; and now the rain is ceasing, and I must soon go." For, indeed, at that moment, looking towards the window, I saw it all blue; the thunder-clouds were broken and scattered, and the setting August sun sent a gleam like the reflection of rubies through the lattice. I got up; I drew on my gloves.

"You have not yet found another situation to supply the place of that from which you were dismissed by Mdlle. Reuter?"

"No, monsieur; I have made inquiries everywhere, but they all ask me for references; and to speak truth, I do not like to apply to the directress, because I consider she acted neither justly nor honourably towards me; she used underhand means to set my pupils against me, and thereby render me unhappy while I held my place in her establishment, and she eventually deprived me of it by a masked and hypocritical manœuvre, pretending that she was acting for my good, but really snatching from me my chief means of subsistence, at a crisis when not only my own life, but that of another, depended on my exertions: of her I will never more ask a favour.

"How, then, do you propose to get on? How do you live now?"

"I have still my lace-mending trade; with care it will keep me from starvation, and I doubt not by dint of exertion to get better employment yet; it is only a fortnight since I began to try; my courage or hopes are by no means worn out yet."

"And if you get what you wish, what then? what are your ultimate views?"

"To save enough to cross the channel; I always look to England as my Canaan."

"Well, well—ere long I shall pay you another visit; good evening now," and I left her rather abruptly; I had much ado to resist a strong inward impulse, urging me to take a warmer, a more expressive leave: what so natural as to fold her for a moment in a close embrace, to imprint one kiss on her cheek or forehead? I was not unreasonable—that was all I wanted; satisfied in that point, I could go away content, and Reason denied me even this; she ordered me to turn my eyes from her face, and my steps from her apartment—to quit her as dryly and coldly as I would have quitted old Madame Pelet. I obeyed, but I swore rancorously to be avenged one day. "I'll earn a right to do as I please in this matter, or I'll die in the contest. I have one object before me now—to get that Genevese girl for my wife; and my wife she shall be—that is, provided she has as much, or half as much regard for her master as he has for her. And would she be so docile, so smiling, so happy under my instructions if she had not? Would she sit at my side when I dictate or correct, with such a still, contented, halcyon mien?" For I had ever remarked, that however sad or harassed her countenance might be when I entered a room, yet after I had been near her, spoken to her a few words, given her some directions, uttered perhaps some reproofs, she would, all at once, nestle into a nook of happiness, and look up serene and revived. The reproofs suited her best of all: while I scolded she would chip away with her pen-knife at a pencil or a pen; fidgetting a little, pouting a little, defending herself by monosyllables, and when I deprived her of the pen or pencil, fearing it would be all cut away, and when I interdicted even the monosyllabic defence, for the purpose of working up the subdued excitement a little higher, she would at last raise her eyes and give me a certain glance, sweetened with gaiety, and pointed with defiance, which, to speak truth, thrilled me as nothing had ever done, and made me, in a fashion (though happily she did not know it), her subject, if not her slave. After such little scenes, her spirits would maintain their flow, often for some hours, and, as I remarked before, her health therefrom took a sustenance and vigour which, previously to the event of her aunt's death and her dismissal, had almost recreated her whole frame.

It has taken me several minutes to write these last sentences; but I had thought all their purport during the brief interval of descending the stairs from Frances' room. Just as I was opening the outer door, I remembered the twenty francs which I had not restored; I paused: impossible to carry them away with me; difficult to force them back on their original owner; I had now seen her in her own humble abode, witnessed the dignity of her poverty, the pride of order, the fastidious care of conservatism, obvious in the arrangement and economy of her little home; I was sure she would not suffer herself to be excused paying her debts; I was certain the favour of indemnity would be accepted from no hand, perhaps least of all from mine: yet these four five-franc pieces were a burden to my self-respect, and I must get rid of them. An expedient—a clumsy one no doubt, but the best I could devise—suggested itself to me. I darted up the stairs, knocked, re-entered the room as if in haste:—

"Mademoiselle, I have forgotten one of my gloves; I must have left it here."

She instantly rose to seek it; as she turned her back, I—being now at the hearth—noiselessly lifted a little vase, one of a set of china ornaments, as old-fashioned as the tea-cups—slipped the money under it, then saying—"Oh here is my glove! I had dropped it within the fender; good evening, mademoiselle," I made my second exit.

Brief as my impromptu return had been, it had afforded me time to pick up a heart-ache; I remarked that Frances had already removed the red embers of her cheerful little fire from the grate: forced to calculate every item, to save in every detail, she had instantly on my departure retrenched a luxury too expensive to be enjoyed alone.

"I am glad it is not yet winter," thought I; "but in two months more come the winds and rains of November; would to God that before then I could earn the right, and the power, to shovel coals into that grate *ad libitum*!"

Already the pavement was drying; a balmy and fresh breeze stirred the air, purified by lightning: I felt the West behind me, where spread a sky like opal; azure immingled with crimson: the enlarged sun, glorious in Tyrian tints, dipped his brim already; stepping, as I was, eastward, I faced a vast bank of clouds, but also I had before me the arch of an evening rainbow;

a perfect rainbow—high, wide, vivid. I looked long; my eye drank in the scene, and I suppose my brain must have absorbed it; for that night, after lying awake in pleasant fever a long time, watching the silent sheet-lightning, which still played among the retreating clouds, and flashed silvery over the stars, I at last fell asleep; and then in a dream were reproduced the setting sun, the bank of clouds, the mighty rainbow. I stood, methought, on a terrace; I leaned over a parapeted wall; there was space below me, depth I could not fathom, but hearing an endless dash of waves, I believed it to be the sea; sea spread to the horizon; sea of changeful green and intense blue: all was soft in the distance; all vapour-veiled. A spark of gold glistened on the line between water and air, floated up, approached, enlarged, changed; the object hung midway between heaven and earth, under the arch of the rainbow; the soft but dusk clouds diffused behind. It hovered as on wings; pearly, fleecy, gleaming air streamed like raiment round it; light, tinted with carnation, coloured what seemed face and limbs; a large star shone with still lustre on an angel's forehead; an upraised arm and hand, glancing like a ray, pointed to the bow overhead, and a voice in my heart whispered—

"Hope smiles on Effort!"

CHAPTER XX.

A COMPETENCY was what I wanted; a competency it was now my aim and resolve to secure; but never had I been farther from the mark. With August the school-year (l'année scolaire) closed, the examinations concluded, the prizes were adjudged, the schools dispersed, the gates of all colleges, the doors of all pensionnats shut, not to be re-opened till the beginning or middle of October. The last day of August was at hand, and what was my position? Had I advanced a step since the commencement of the past quarter? On the contrary, I had receded one. By renouncing my engagement as English master in Mdlle. Reuter's establishment, I had voluntarily cut off 20*l.* from my yearly income; I had diminished my 60*l.* per annum to 40*l.*, and even that sum I now held by a very precarious tenure.

It is some time since I made any reference to M. Pelet. The moonlight walk is, I think, the last incident recorded in this narrative where that gentleman cuts any conspicuous figure: the fact is, since that event, a change had come over the spirit of our intercourse. He, indeed, ignorant that the still hour, a cloudless moon, and an open lattice, had revealed to me the secret of his selfish love and false friendship, would have continued smooth and complaisant as ever; but I grew spiny as a porcupine, and inflexible as a blackthorn cudgel; I never had a smile for his raillery, never a moment for his society; his invitations to take coffee with him in his parlour were invariably rejected, and very stiffly and sternly rejected too; his jesting allusions to the directress (which he still continued) were heard with a grim calm very different from the petulant pleasure they were formerly wont to excite. For a long time Pelet bore with my frigid demeanour very patiently; he even increased his attentions, but finding that even a cringing politeness failed to thaw or move me, he at last altered too; in his turn he cooled; his invitations ceased; his countenance became suspicious and overcast, and I read in the perplexed yet brooding aspect of his brow, a constant examination and comparison of premises, and an anxious endeavour to draw thence some explanatory inference. Ere long, I fancy, he succeeded, for he was not without penetration; perhaps, too, Mdlle. Zoraïde might have aided him in the solution of the enigma; at any rate I soon found that the uncertainty of doubt had vanished from his manner; renouncing all pretence of friendship and cordiality, he adopted a reserved, formal, but still scrupulously polite deportment. This was the point to which I had wished to bring him, and I was now again comparatively at my ease. I did not, it is true, like my position in his house, but being freed from the annoyance of false professions and double-dealing I could endure it, especially as no heroic sentiments of hatred or jealousy of the director distracted my philosophical soul; he had not, I found, wounded me in a very tender point, the wound was so soon and so radically healed, leaving only a sense of contempt for the treacherous fashion in which it had been inflicted, and a lasting mistrust of the hand which I had detected attempting to stab in the dark.

This state of things continued till about the middle of July, and then there was a little change; Pelet came home one night, an hour after his usual time, in a state of unequivocal intoxication, a thing anomalous with him; for if he had some of the worst faults of his countrymen he had also one at least of their virtues, *i.e.* sobriety. So drunk, however, was he upon this occasion that after having roused the whole establishment (except the pupils, whose dormitory being over the classes in a building apart from the dwelling-house, was consequently out of the reach of disturbance) by violently ringing the hall-bell and ordering lunch to be brought in immediately, for he imagined it was noon, whereas the city bells had just tolled midnight; after having furiously rated the servants for their want of punctuality, and gone near to chastise his poor old mother, who advised him to go to bed, he began raving dreadfully about "le maudit Anglais, Creemsvort." I had not yet retired; some German books I had got hold of had kept me up late; I heard the uproar below, and could distinguish the director's voice exalted in a manner as appalling as it was unusual. Opening my door a little, I became aware of a demand on his part for "Creemsvort" to be brought down to him that he might cut his throat on the hall-table and wash his honour, which he affirmed to be in a dirty condition, in infernal British blood. "He is either mad or drunk," thought I, "and in either case the old woman and the servants will be the better of a man's assistance," so I descended straight to the hall. I found him staggering about, his eyes in a fine frenzy rolling —a pretty sight he was, a just medium between the fool and the lunatic.

"Come, M. Pelet," said I, "you had better go to bed," and I took hold of his arm. His excitement, of course, increased greatly at sight and touch of the individual for whose blood he had been making application: he struggled and struck with fury—but a drunken man is no match for a sober one; and, even in his normal state, Pelet's worn-out frame could not have stood against my sound one. I got him up-stairs, and, in process of time, to bed. During the operation he did not fail to utter comminations which, though broken, had a sense in them; while stigmatizing me as the treacherous spawn of a perfidious country, he, in the same breath, anathematized Zoraïde Reuter; he termed her "femme sotte et vicieuse," who, in a fit of lewd caprice, had thrown herself away on an unprincipled adventurer; directing the point of the last appellation by a furious blow, obliquely aimed at me. I left him in the act of bounding elastically out of the bed into which I had tucked him; but, as I took the precaution of turning the key in the door behind me, I retired to my own room, assured of his safe custody till the morning, and free to draw undisturbed conclusions from the scene I had just witnessed.

Now, it was precisely about this time that the directress, stung by my coldness, bewitched by my scorn, and excited by the preference she suspected me of cherishing for another, had fallen into a snare of her own laying—was herself caught in the meshes of the very passion with which she wished to entangle me. Conscious of the state of things in that quarter, I gathered, from the condition in which I saw my employer, that his ladye-love had betrayed the alienation of her affections—inclinations, rather, I would say; affection is a word at once too warm and too pure for the subject—had let him see that the cavity of her hollow heart, emptied of his image, was now occupied by that of his usher. It was not without some surprise that I found myself obliged to entertain this view of the case; Pelet, with his old-established school, was so convenient, so profitable a match—Zoraïde was so calculating, so interested a woman—I wondered mere personal preference could, in her mind, have prevailed for a moment over worldly advantage: yet, it was evident, from what Pelet said, that, not only had she repulsed him, but had even let slip expressions of partiality for me. One of his drunken exclamations was, "And the jade doats on your youth, you raw blockhead! and talks of your noble deportment, as she calls your accursed English formality—and your pure morals, forsooth! des mœurs de Caton à-t-elle dit—sotte!" Hers, I thought, must be a curious soul, where, in spite of a strong, natural tendency to estimate unduly advantages of wealth and station, the sardonic disdain of a fortuneless subordinate had wrought a deeper impression than could be imprinted by the most flattering assiduities of a prosperous *chef d'institution.* I smiled inwardly; and strange to say, though my *amour propre* was excited not disagreeably by the conquest, my better feelings remained untouched. Next day, when I saw the directress, and when she made an excuse to meet me in the corridor, and besought my notice by a demeanour and look subdued to Helot humility, I could not love, I could scarcely pity her. To answer briefly and dryly some interesting inquiry about my health—to pass her by with a stern bow—was all I could; her presence and manner had then, and for some time previously and consequently, a singular effect upon me: they sealed up all that was good, elicited all that was noxious in my nature; sometimes they enervated my senses, but they always hardened my heart. I was aware of the detriment done, and quarrelled with myself for the change. I had ever hated a tyrant; and, behold, the possession of a slave, self-given, went near to transform me into what I abhorred! There was at once a sort of low gratification in receiving this luscious incense from an attractive and still young worshipper; and an irritating sense of degradation in the very experience of the pleasure. When she stole about me with the soft step of a slave, I felt at once barbarous and sensual as a pasha. I endured her homage sometimes; sometimes I rebuked it. My indifference or harshness served equally to increase the evil I desired to check.

"Que le dédain lui sied bien!" I once overheard her say to her mother: "il est beau comme Apollon quand il sourit de son air hautain."

And the jolly old dame laughed, and said she thought her daughter was bewitched, for I had no point of a handsome man about me, except being straight and without deformity. "Pour moi," she continued, "il me fait tout l'effet d'un chat-huant, avec ses bésicles."

Worthy old girl! I could have gone and kissed her had she not been a little too old, too fat, and too red-faced; her sensible, truthful words seemed so wholesome, contrasted with the morbid illusions of her daughter.

When Pelet awoke on the morning after his frenzy fit, he retained no recollection of what had happened the previous night, and his mother fortunately had the discretion to refrain from informing him that I had been a witness of his degradation. He did not again have recourse to wine for curing his griefs, but even in his sober mood he soon showed that the iron of jealousy had entered into his soul. A thorough Frenchman, the national characteristic of ferocity had not been omitted by nature in compounding the ingredients of his character; it had appeared first in his access of drunken wrath, when some of his demonstrations of hatred to my person were of a truly fiendish character, and now it was more covertly betrayed by momentary contractions of the features, and flashes of fierceness in his light blue eyes, when their glance chanced to encounter mine. He absolutely avoided speaking to me; I was now spared even the falsehood of his politeness. In this state of our mutual relations, my soul rebelled, sometimes almost ungovernably, against living in the house and discharging the service of such a man; but who is free from the constraint of circumstances? At that time, I was not: I used to rise each morning eager to shake off his yoke, and go out with my portmanteau under my arm, if a beggar, at least a freeman; and in the evening, when I came back from the pensionnat de demoiselles, a certain pleasant voice in my ear; a certain face, so intelligent, yet so docile, so reflective, yet so soft, in my eyes; a certain cast of character, at once proud and pliant, sensitive and sagacious, serious and ardent, in my head; a certain tone of feeling, fervid and modest, refined and practical, pure and powerful, delighting and troubling my memory—visions of new ties I longed to contract, of new duties I longed to undertake, had taken the rover and the rebel out of me, and had shown endurance of my hated lot in the light of a Spartan virtue.

But Pelet's fury subsided; a fortnight sufficed for its rise, progress, and extinction: in that space of time the dismissal of the obnoxious teacher had been effected in the neighbouring house, and in the same interval I had declared my resolution to follow and find out my pupil, and upon my application for her address being refused, I had summarily resigned my own post. This last act seemed at once to restore Mdlle. Reuter to her senses; her sagacity, her judgment, so long misled by a fascinating delusion, struck again into the right track the moment that delusion vanished.

By the right track, I do not mean the steep and difficult path of principle—in that path she never trod; but the plain high-way of common sense, from which she had of late widely diverged. When there she carefully sought, and having found, industriously pursued the trail of her old suitor, M. Pelet. She soon overtook him What arts she employed to soothe and blind him I know not, but she succeeded both in allaying his wrath, and hoodwinking his discernment, as was soon proved by the alteration in his mien and manner; she must have managed to convince him that I neither was, nor ever had been, a rival of his, for the fortnight of fury against me terminated in a fit of exceeding graciousness and amenity, not unmixed with a dash of exulting self-complacency, more ludicrous than irritating. Pelet's bachelor's life had been passed in proper French style with due disregard to moral restraint, and I thought his married life promised to be very French also. He often boasted to me what a terror he had been to certain husbands of his acquaintance; I perceived it would not now be difficult to pay him back in his own coin.

The crisis drew on. No sooner had the holidays commenced than note of preparation for some momentous event sounded all through the premises of Pelet: painters, polishers, and upholsterers were immediately set to work, and there was talk of "la chambre de Madame," "le salon de Madame." Not deeming it probable that the old duenna at present graced with that title in our house, had inspired her son with such enthusiasm of filial piety, as to induce him to fit up apartments expressly for her use, I concluded, in common with the cook, the two house-maids, and the kitchen-scullion, that a new and more juvenile Madame was destined to be the tenant of these gay chambers.

Presently official announcement of the coming event was put forth. In another week's time

M. François Pelet, directeur, and Mdlle. Zoraïde Reuter, directrice, were to be joined together in the bands of matrimony. Monsieur, in person, heralded the fact to me; terminating his communication by an obliging expression of his desire that I should continue, as heretofore, his ablest assistant and most trusted friend; and a proposition to raise my salary by an additional two hundred francs per annum. I thanked him, gave no conclusive answer at the time, and, when he had left me, threw off my blouse, put on my coat, and set out on a long walk outside the porte de Flandre, in order, as I thought, to cool my blood, calm my nerves, and shake my disarranged ideas into some order. In fact, I had just received what was virtually my dismissal. I could not conceal, I did not desire to conceal from myself the conviction that, being now certain that Mdlle. Reuter was destined to become Madame Pelet, it would not do for me to remain a dependent dweller in the house which was soon to be hers. Her present demeanour towards me was deficient, neither in dignity nor propriety; but I knew her former feeling was unchanged. Decorum now repressed, and Policy masked it, but Opportunity would be too strong for either of these—Temptation would shiver their restraints.

I was no pope—I could not boast infallibility: in short, if I stayed, the probability was that, in three months' time, a practical modern French novel would be in full process of concoction under the roof of the unsuspecting Pelet. Now, modern French novels are not to my taste, either practically or theoretically. Limited as had yet been my experience of life, I had once had the opportunity of contemplating, near at hand, an example of the results produced by a course of interesting and romantic domestic treachery. No golden halo of fiction was about this example, I saw it bare and real, and it was very loathsome. I saw a mind degraded by the practice of mean subterfuge, by the habit of perfidious deception, and a body depraved by the infectious influence of the vice-polluted soul. I had suffered much from the forced and prolonged view of this spectacle; those sufferings I did not now regret, for their simple recollection acted as a most wholesome antidote to temptation. They had inscribed on my reason the conviction that unlawful pleasure, trenching on another's rights, is delusive and envenomed pleasure—its hollowness disappoints at the time, its poison cruelly tortures afterwards, its effects deprave for ever.

From all this resulted the conclusion that I must leave Pelet's, and that instantly; "but," said Prudence, "you know not where to go, nor how to live;" and then the dream of true love came over me: Frances Henri seemed to stand at my side; her slender waist to invite my arm; her hand to court my hand; I felt it was made to nestle in mine; I could not relinquish my right to it, nor could I withdraw my eyes for ever from hers, where I saw so much happiness, such a correspondence of heart with heart; over whose expression I had such influence; where I could kindle bliss, infuse awe, stir deep delight, rouse sparkling spirit, and sometimes waken pleasurable dread. My hopes to win and possess, my resolutions to work and rise, rose in array against me; and here I was about to plunge into the gulf of absolute destitution; "and all this," suggested an inward voice, "because you fear an evil which may never happen!" "It will happen; you *know* it will;" answered that stubborn monitor, Conscience. "Do what you feel is right; obey me, and even in the sloughs of want I will plant for you firm footing." And then, as I walked fast along the road, there rose upon me a strange, inly-felt idea of some Great Being, unseen, but all present; who, in his beneficence, desired only my welfare, and now watched the struggle of good and evil in my heart, and waited to see whether I should obey his voice, heard in the whispers of my conscience, or lend an ear to the sophisms by which his enemy and mine, the Spirit of evil, sought to lead me astray. Rough and steep was the path indicated by divine suggestion; mossy and declining the green way along which Temptation strewed flowers; but whereas, methought, the Deity of love, the Friend of all that exists, would smile well-pleased were I to gird up my loins and address myself to the rude ascent, so, on the other hand, each inclination to the velvet declivity seemed to kindle a gleam of triumph on the brow of the man-hating, God-defying demon. Sharp and short I turned round; fast I retraced my steps; in half an hour I was again at M. Pelet's: I sought him in his study; brief parley, concise explanation sufficed; my manner proved that I was resolved; he, perhaps, at heart approved my decision. After twenty minutes' conversation I re-entered my own room, self-deprived of the means of living, self-sentenced to leave my present home, with the short notice of a week in which to provide another.

CHAPTER XXI.

Directly as I closed the door, I saw laid on the table two letters; my thought was, that they were notes of invitation from the friends of some of my pupils; I had received such marks of attention occasionally, and with me, who had no friends, correspondence of more interest was out of the question; the postman's arrival had never yet been an event of interest to me since I came to Brussels. I laid my hand carelessly on the documents, and coldly and slowly glancing at them, I prepared to break the seals; my eye was arrested and my hand too; I saw what excited me, as if I had found a vivid picture where I expected only to discover a blank page:

on one cover was an English post-mark; on the other, a lady's clear, fine autograph; the last I opened first:—

"MONSIEUR,

"I found out what you had done the very morning after your visit to me; you might be sure I should dust the china every day; and, as no one but you had been in my room for a week, and as fairy-money is not current in Brussels, I could not doubt who left the twenty francs on the chimney-piece. I thought I heard you stir the vase when I was stooping to look for your glove under the table, and I wondered you should imagine it had got into such a little cup. Now, monsieur, the money is not mine, and I shall not keep it; I will not send it in this note because it might be lost—besides, it is heavy; but I will restore it to you the first time I see you, and you must make no difficulties about taking it; because, in the first place, I am sure, monsieur, you can understand that one likes to pay one's debts; that it is satisfactory to owe no man anything; and, in the second place, I can now very well afford to be honest, as I am provided with a situation. This last circumstance is, indeed, the reason of my writing to you, for it is pleasant to communicate good news; and, in these days, I have only my master to whom I can tell anything.

"A week ago, monsieur, I was sent for by a Mrs. Wharton, an English lady; her eldest daughter was going to be married, and some rich relation having made her a present of a veil and dress in costly old lace, as precious, they said, almost as jewels, but a little damaged by time, I was commissioned to put them in repair. I had to do it at the house; they gave me, besides, some embroidery to complete, and nearly a week elapsed before I had finished everything. While I worked, Miss Wharton often came into the room and sat with me, and so did Mrs. Wharton; they made me talk English; asked how I had learned to speak it so well; then they inquired what I knew besides—what books I had read; soon they seemed to make a sort of wonder of me, considering me no doubt as a learned grisette. One afternoon, Mrs. Wharton brought in a Parisian lady to test the accuracy of my knowledge of French; the result of it was that, owing probably in a great degree to the mother's and daughter's good humour about the marriage, which inclined them to do beneficent deeds, and partly, I think, because they are naturally benevolent people, they decided that the wish I had expressed to do something more than mend lace was a very legitimate one; and the same day they took me in their carriage to Mrs. D.'s, who is the directress of the first English school at Brussels. It seems she happened to be in want of a French lady to give lessons in geography, history, grammar, and composition, in the French language. Mrs. Wharton recommended me very warmly; and, as two of her younger daughters are pupils in the house, her patronage availed to get me the lace. It was settled that I am to attend six hours daily (for, happily, it was not required that I should live in the house; I should have been sorry to leave my lodgings), and, for this, Mrs. D. will give me twelve hundred francs per annum.

"You see, therefore, monsieur, that I am now rich; richer almost than I ever hoped to be: I feel thankful for it, especially as my sight was beginning to be injured by constant working at fine lace; and I was getting, too, very weary of sitting up late at nights, and yet not being able to find time for reading or study. I began to fear that I should fall ill, and be unable to pay my way; this fear is now, in a great measure, removed; and, in truth, monsieur, I am very grateful to God for the relief; and I feel it necessary, almost, to speak of my happiness to some one who is kind-hearted enough to derive joy from seeing others joyful. I could not, therefore, resist the temptation of writing to you; I argued with myself it is very pleasant for me to write, and it will not be exactly painful, though it may be tiresome to Monsieur to read. Do not be too angry with my circumlocution and inelegancies of expression, and, believe me

"Your attached pupil,

"F. E. Henri."

Having read this letter, I mused on its contents for a few moments — whether with sentiments pleasurable or otherwise I will hereafter note — and then took up the other. It was directed in a hand to me unknown — small, and rather neat; neither masculine nor exactly feminine; the seal bore a coat of arms, concerning which I could only decipher that it was not that of the Seacombe family, consequently the epistle could be from none of my almost forgotten, and certainly quite forgetting patrician relations. From whom, then, was it? I removed the envelope; the note folded within ran as follows:—

"I have no doubt in the world that you are doing well in that greasy Flanders; living probably on the fat of the unctuous land; sitting like a black-haired, tawny-skinned, long-nosed Israelite by the flesh-pots of Egypt; or like a rascally son of Levi near the brass cauldrons of the sanctuary, and every now and then plunging in a consecrated hook, and drawing out of the sea of broth the fattest of heave-shoulders and the fleshiest of wave-breasts. I know this, because you never write to any one in England. Thankless dog that you are! I, by the sovereign efficacy of my recommendation, got you the place where you are now living in clover, and yet not a word of gratitude, or even acknowledgment, have you ever offered in return; but I am coming to see you, and small conception can you, with your addled aristocratic brains, form of the sort of moral kicking I have, ready packed in my carpet-bag, destined to be presented to you immediately on my arrival.

"Meantime I know all about your affairs, and have just got information, by Brown's last letter, that you are said to be on the point of forming an advantageous match with a pursy, little Belgian schoolmistress—a Mdlle. Zénobie, or some such name. Won't I have a look at her when I come over? And this you may rely on: if she pleases my taste, or if I think it worth while in a pecuniary point of view, I'll pounce on your prize and bear her away triumphant in spite of your teeth. Yet I don't like dumpies either, and Brown says she is little and stout—the better fitted for a wiry, starved-looking chap like you.

"Be on the look-out, for you know neither the day nor hour when your —— (I don't wish to blaspheme, so I'll leave a blank) cometh.

"Yours truly,

"Hunsden Yorke Hunsden."

"Humph!" said I; and ere I laid the letter down, I again glanced at the small, neat handwriting, not a bit like that of a mercantile man, nor, indeed, of any man except Hunsden himself. They talk of affinities between the autograph and the character: what affinity was there here? I recalled the writer's peculiar face and certain traits I suspected, rather than knew, to appertain to his nature, and I answered, "a great deal."

Hunsden, then, was coming to Brussels, and coming I knew not when; coming charged with the expectation of finding me on the summit of prosperity, about to be married, to step into a warm nest, to lie comfortably down by the side of a snug, well-fed little mate.

"I wish him joy of the fidelity of the picture he has painted," thought I. "What will he say when, instead of a pair of plump turtle-doves, billing and cooing in a bower of roses, he finds a single lean cormorant, standing mateless and shelterless on poverty's bleak cliff? Oh, confound him! Let him come, and let him laugh at the contrast between rumour and fact. Were he the devil himself, instead of being merely very like him, I'd not condescend to get out of his way, or to forge a smile or a cheerful word wherewith to avert his sarcasm."

Then I recurred to the other letter: that struck a chord whose sound I could not deaden by thrusting my fingers into my ears, for it vibrated within; and though its swell might be exquisite music, its cadence was a groan.

That Frances was relieved from the pressure of want, that the curse of excessive labour was taken off her, filled me with happiness; that her first thought in prosperity should be to augment her joy by sharing it with me, met and satisfied the wish of my heart. Two results of her letter were then pleasant, sweet as two draughts of nectar; but applying my lips for the third time to the cup, and they were excoriated as with vinegar and gall.

Two persons whose desires are moderate may live well enough in Brussels on an income which would scarcely afford a respectable maintenance for one in London: and that, not because the necessaries of life are so much dearer in the latter capital, or taxes so much higher than in the former, but because the English surpass in folly all the nations on God's earth, and are more abject slaves to custom, to opinion, to the desire to keep up a certain appearance, than the Italians are to priestcraft, the French to vain glory, the Russians to their Czar, or the Germans to black beer. I have seen a degree of sense in the modest arrangement of one homely Belgian household, that might put to shame the elegance, the superfluities, the luxuries, the strained refinements of a hundred genteel English mansions. In Belgium, provided you can make money, you may save it; this is scarcely possible in England; ostentation there lavishes in a month what industry has earned in a year. More shame to all classes in that most bountiful and beggarly country for their servile following of Fashion; I could write a chapter or two on this subject, but must forbear, at least for the present. Had I retained my 60*l.* per annum I could, now that Frances was in possession of 50*l.*, have gone straight to her this very evening, and spoken out the words which, repressed, kept fretting my heart with fever; our united income would, as we should have managed it, have sufficed well for our mutual support; since we lived in a country where economy was not confounded with meanness, where frugality in dress, food, and furniture, was not synonymous with vulgarity in these various points. But the placeless usher, bare of resource, and unsupported by connections, must not think of this; such a sentiment as love, such a word as marriage, were misplaced in his heart, and on his lips. Now for the first time did I truly feel what it was to be poor; now did the sacrifice I had made in casting from me the means of living put on a new aspect; instead of a correct, just, honourable act, it seemed a deed at once light and fanatical: I took several turns in my room, under the goading influence of most poignant remorse; I walked a quarter of an hour from the wall to the window; and at the window, self-reproach seemed to face me; at the wall, self-disdain: all at once out spoke Conscience:—

"Down stupid tormentors!" cried she; "the man has done his duty; you shall not bait him thus by thoughts of what might have been; he relinquished a temporary and contingent good to avoid a permanent and certain evil; he did well. Let him reflect now, and when your blinding dust and deafening hum subside, he will discover a path."

I sat down; I propped my forehead on both my hands; I thought and thought an hour—two hours; vainly. I seemed like one sealed in a subterranean vault, who gazes at utter blackness; at blackness ensured by yard-thick stone walls around, and by piles of building above, expecting light to penetrate through granite, and through cement firm as granite. But there are chinks, or there may be chinks, in the best adjusted masonry; there was a chink in my cavernous cell; for, eventually, I saw, or seemed to see, a ray—pallid, indeed, and cold, and doubtful, but still a ray, for it showed that narrow path which conscience had promised. After two, three hours' torturing research in brain and memory, I disinterred certain remains of circumstances, and conceived a hope that by putting them together an expedient might be framed, and a resource discovered. The circumstances were briefly these:—

Some three months ago M. Pelet had, on the occasion of his fête, given the boys a treat, which treat consisted in a party of pleasure to a certain place of public resort in the outskirts of Brussels, of which I do not at this moment remember the name, but near it were several of those lakelets called étangs; and there was one étang, larger than the rest, where on holidays people were accustomed to amuse themselves by rowing round it in little boats. The boys having eaten an unlimited quantity of "gaufres," and drank several bottles of Louvain beer, amid the shades of a garden made and provided for such crams, petitioned the director for leave to take a row on the étang. Half a dozen of the eldest succeeded in obtaining leave, and I was commissioned to accompany them as surveillant. Among the half dozen happened to be a certain Jean Baptiste Vandenhuten, a most ponderous young Flamand, not tall, but even now, at the early age of sixteen, possessing a breadth and depth of personal development truly national. It chanced that Jean was the first lad to step into the boat; he stumbled, rolled to one side, the boat revolted at his weight and capsized. Vandenhuten sank like lead, rose, sank again. My coat and waistcoat were off in an instant; I had not been brought up at Eton and boated and bathed and swam there ten long years for nothing; it was a natural and easy act for me to leap to the rescue. The lads and the boatmen yelled; they thought there would be two deaths by drowning instead of one; but as Jean rose the third time, I clutched him by one leg and the collar, and in three minutes more both he and I were safe landed. To speak heaven's truth my merit in the action was small indeed, for I had run no risk, and subsequently did not even catch cold from the wetting; but when M. and Madame Vandenhuten, of whom Jean Baptiste was the sole hope, came to hear of the exploit, they seemed to think I had evinced a bravery and devotion which no thanks could sufficiently repay. Madame, in particular, was "certain I must have dearly loved their sweet son, or I would not thus have hazarded my own life to save his." Monsieur, an honest-looking though phlegmatic man, said very little, but he would not suffer me to leave the room, till I had promised that in case I ever stood in need of help I would, by applying to him, give him a chance of discharging the obligation under which he affirmed I had laid him. These words, then, were my glimmer of light; it was here I found my sole outlet; and in truth, though the cold light roused, it did not cheer me; nor did the outlet seem such as I should like to pass through. Right I had none to M. Vandenhuten's good offices; it was not on the ground of merit I could apply to him; no, I must stand on that of necessity: I had no work; I wanted work; my best chance of obtaining it lay in securing his recommendation. This I knew could be had by asking for it; not to ask, because the request revolted my pride and contradicted my habits, would, I felt, be an indulgence of false and indolent fastidiousness. I might repent the omission all my life; I would not then be guilty of it.

That evening I went to M. Vandenhuten's;

but I had bent the bow and adjusted the shaft in vain; the string broke. I rang the bell at the great door (it was a large, handsome house in an expensive part of the town); a man-servant opened; I asked for M. Vandenhuten; M. Vandenhuten and family were all out of town—gone to Ostend—did not know when they would be back. I left my card, and retraced my steps.

CHAPTER XXII.

A WEEK is gone; *le jour des noces* arrived; the marriage was solemnized at St. Jacques; Mdlle. Zoraïde became Madame Pelet, *née* Reuter; and, in about an hour after this transformation, "the happy pair," as newspapers phrase it, were on their way to Paris; where, according to previous arrangement, the honeymoon was to be spent. The next day I quitted the pensionnat. Myself and my chattels (some books and clothes) were soon transferred to a modest lodging I had hired in a street not far off. In half an hour my clothes were arranged in a commode, my books on a shelf, and the "flitting" was effected. I should not have been unhappy that day had not one pang tortured me—a longing to go to the Rue Notre Dame aux Neiges, resisted, yet irritated by an inward resolve to avoid that street till such time as the mist of doubt should clear from my prospects.

It was a sweet September evening—very mild, very still; I had nothing to do; at that hour I knew Frances would be equally released from occupation; I thought she might possibly be wishing for her master, I knew I wished for my pupil. Imagination began with her low whispers, infusing into my soul the soft tale of pleasures that might be.

"You will find her reading or writing," said she; "you can take your seat at her side; you need not startle her peace by undue excitement; you need not embarrass her manner by unusual action or language. Be as you always are; look over what she has written; listen while she reads; chide her, or quietly approve; you know the effect of either system; you know her smile when pleased, you know the play of her looks when roused; you have the secret of awakening what expression you will, and you can choose amongst that pleasant variety. With you she will sit silent as long as it suits you to talk alone; you can hold her under a potent spell: intelligent as she is, eloquent as she can be, you can seal her lips, and veil her bright countenance with diffidence; yet, you know, she is not all monotonous mildness; you have seen, with a sort of strange pleasure, revolt, scorn, austerity, bitterness, lay energetic claim to a place in her feelings and physiognomy; you know that few could rule her as you do; you know she might break, but never bend under the hand of Tyranny and Injustice, but Reason and Affection can guide her by a sign. Try their influence now. Go—they are not passions; you may handle them safely."

"I will *not* go," was my answer to the sweet temptress. "A man is master of himself to a certain point, but not beyond it. Could I seek Frances to-night, could I sit with her alone in a quiet room, and address her only in the language of Reason and Affection?"

"No," was the brief, fervent reply of that Love which had conquered and now controlled me.

Time seemed to stagnate; the sun would not go down; my watch ticked, but I thought the hands were paralyzed.

"What a hot evening!" I cried, throwing open the lattice; for, indeed, I had seldom felt so feverish. Hearing a step ascending the common stair, I wondered whether the "locataire," now mounting to his apartments, were as unsettled in mind and condition as I was, or whether he lived in the calm of certain resources, and in the freedom of unfettered feelings. What! was he coming in person to solve the problen hardly proposed in inaudible thought? He had actually knocked at the door—at *my* door; a smart, prompt rap; and, almost before I could invite him in, he was over the threshold, and had closed the door behind him.

"And how are you?" asked an indifferent, quiet voice, in the English language; while my visitor, without any sort of bustle or introduction, put his hat on the table, and his gloves into his hat, and drawing the only arm-chair the room afforded a little forward, seated himself tranquilly therein.

"Can't you speak?" he inquired in a few moments, in a tone whose nonchalance seemed to intimate that it was much the same thing whether I answered or not. The fact is, I found it desirable to have recourse to my good friends "les bésicles;" not exactly to ascertain the identity of my visitor—for I already knew him, confound his impudence! but to see how he looked—to get a clear notion of his mien and countenance. I wiped the glasses very deliberately, and put them on quite as deliberately; adjusting them so as not to hurt the bridge of my nose, or get entangled in my short tufts of dun hair. I was sitting in the window-seat, with my back to the light, and I had him *vis-à-vis;* a position he would much rather have had reversed; for, at any time, he preferred scrutinizing to being scrutinized. Yes, it was *he*, and no mistake, with his six feet of length arranged in a sitting attitude; with his dark travelling surtout with its velvet collar, his gray pantaloons, his black stock, and *his* face, the most original one Nature ever modelled, yet the least obtrusively so; not one feature that could be termed marked or odd, yet the effect of the whole unique. There is no use in attempting to describe what is indescribable. Being in no hurry to address him, I sat and stared at my ease.

"Oh, that's your game—is it?" said he at last. "Well, we'll see which is soonest tired." And he slowly drew out a fine cigar-case, picked one to his taste, lit it, took a book from the shelf convenient to his hand, then leaning back, proceeded to smoke and read as tranquilly as if he had been in his own room, in Grove-street, X——shire, England. I knew he was capable of continuing in that attitude till midnight, if he conceived the whim, so I rose, and taking the book from his hand, I said:—

"You did not ask for it, and you shall not have it."

"It is silly and dull," he observed, "so I have not lost much;" then the spell being broken, he went on. "I thought you lived at Pelet's; I went there this afternoon, expecting to be starved to death by sitting in a boarding-school drawing-room, and they told me you were gone, had departed this morning; you had left your address behind you though, which I wondered at; it was a more practical and sensible precaution than I should have imagined you capable of. Why did you leave?"

"Because M. Pelet has just married the lady

whom you and Mr. Brown assigned to me as my wife."

"Oh indeed!" replied Hunsden with a short laugh; "so you've lost both your wife and your place?"

"Precisely so."

I saw him give a quick, covert glance all round my room; he marked its narrow limits, its scanty furniture: in an instant he had comprehended the state of matters—had absolved me from the crime of prosperity. A curious effect this discovery wrought in his strange mind; I am morally certain that if he had found me installed in a handsome parlour, lounging on a soft couch, with a pretty, wealthy wife at my side, he would have hated me; a brief, cold, haughty visit, would in such a case have been the extreme limit of his civilities, and never would he have come near me more, so long as the tide of fortune bore me smoothly on its surface; but the painted furniture, the bare walls, the cheerless solitude of my room relaxed his rigid pride, and I know not what softening change had taken place both in his voice and look ere he spoke again.

"You have got another place?"

"No."

"You are in the way of getting one?"

"No."

"That is bad; have you applied to Brown?"

"No indeed."

"You had better; he often has it in his power to give useful information in such matters."

"He served me once very well; I have no claim on him, and am not in the humour to bother him again."

"Oh, if you 're bashful, and dread being intrusive, you need only commission me. I shall see him to-night; I can put in a word."

"I beg you will not, Mr. Hunsden; I am in your debt already; you did me an important service when I was at X——; got me out of a den where I was dying: that service I have never repaid, and at present I decline positively adding another item to the account."

"If the wind sits that way, I'm satisfied. I thought my unexampled generosity in turning you out of that accursed counting-house would be duly appreciated some day; 'Cast your bread on the waters, and it shall be found after many days,' say the Scriptures. Yes, that's right, lad—make much of me—I'm a nonpareil: there's nothing like me in the common herd. In the meantime, to put all humbug aside and talk sense for a few moments, you would be greatly the better of a situation, and what is more, you are a fool if you refuse to take one from any hand that offers it."

"Very well, Mr. Hunsden; now you have settled that point, talk of something else. What news from X——?"

"I have not settled that point, or at least there is another to settle before we get to X——. Is this Miss Zénobie" (Zoraïde, interposed I)"—"well, Zoraïde—is she really married to Pelet?"

"I tell you yes—and if you don't believe me, go and ask the curé of St. Jacques."

"And your heart is broken?"

"I am not aware that it is; it feels all right—beats as usual."

"Then your feelings are less superfine than I took them to be; you must be a coarse, callous character, to bear such a thwack without staggering under it."

"Staggering under it? What the deuce is there to stagger under in the circumstance of a Belgian schoolmistress marrying a French schoolmaster? The progeny will doubtless be a strange hybrid race; but that 's their look out—not mine."

"He indulges in scurrilous jests, and the bride was his affianced one!"

"Who said so?"

"Brown."

"I 'll tell you what, Hunsden—Brown is an old gossip."

"He is; but in the meantime, if his gossip be founded on less than fact—if you took no particular interest in Miss Zoraïde—why, O youthful pedagogue! did you leave your place in consequence of her becoming Madame Pelet?"

"Because—" I felt my face a grow a little hot; "because—in short, Mr. Hunsden, I decline answering any more questions," and I plunged my hands deep in my breeches pocket.

Hunsden triumphed: his eyes — his laugh announced victory.

"What the deuce are you laughing at, Mr. Hunsden?"

"At your exemplary composure. Well, lad, I'll not bore you; I see how it is: Zoraïde has jilted you—married some one richer, as any sensible woman would have done if she had had the chance."

I made no reply—I let him think so, not feeling

inclined to enter into an explanation of the real state of things, and as little to forge a false account; but it was not easy to blind Hunsden; my very silence, instead of convincing him that he had hit the truth, seemed to render him doubtful about it; he went on:—

"I suppose the affair has been conducted as such affairs always are amongst rational people: you offered her your youth and your talents—such as they are—in exchange for her position and money: I don't suppose you took appearance, or what is called *love*, into the account—for I understand she is older than you, and Brown says, rather sensible-looking than beautiful. She, having then no chance of making a better bargain, was at first inclined to come to terms with you, but Pelet—the head of a flourishing school—stepped in with a higher bid; she accepted, and he has got her: a correct transaction—perfectly so—business-like and legitimate. And now we'll talk of something else."

"Do," said I, very glad to dismiss the topic, and especially glad to have baffled the sagacity of my cross-questioner—if, indeed, I had baffled it; for though his words now led away from the dangerous point, his eyes, keen and watchful, seemed still pre-occupied with the former idea.

"You want to hear news from X——? And what interest can you have in X——? You left no friends there, for you made none. Nobody ever asks after you—neither man nor woman; and if I mention your name in company, the men look as if I had spoken of Prester John; and the women sneer covertly. Our X—— belles must have disliked you. How did you excite their displeasure?"

"I don't know. I seldom spoke to them—they were nothing to me. I considered them only as something to be glanced at from a distance; their dresses and faces were often pleasing enough to the eye: but I could not understand their conversation, nor even read their countenances. When

I caught snatches of what they said, I could never make much of it; and the play of their lips and eyes did not help me at all."

"That was your fault, not theirs. There are sensible, as well as handsome women in X——; women it is worth any man's while to talk to, and with whom I can talk with pleasure: but you had and have no pleasant address; there is nothing in you to induce a woman to be affable. I have remarked you sitting near the door in a room full of company, bent on hearing, not on speaking; on observing, not on entertaining; looking frigidly shy at the commencement of a party, confusingly vigilant about the middle, and insultingly weary towards the end. Is that the way, do you think, ever to communicate pleasure or excite interest? No; and if you are generally unpopular, it is because you deserve to be so."

"Content!" I ejaculated.

"No, you are not content; you see beauty always turning its back on you; you are mortified and then you sneer. I verily believe all that is desirable on earth—wealth, reputation, love—will for ever to you be the ripe grapes on the high trellis: you'll look up at them; they will tantalize in you the lust of the eye; but they are out of reach: you have not the address to fetch a ladder, and you'll go away calling them sour."

Cutting as these words might have been under some circumstances, they drew no blood now. My life was changed; my experience had been varied since I left X——, but Hunsden could not know this; he had seen me only in the character of Mr. Crimsworth's clerk—a dependent amongst wealthy strangers, meeting disdain with a hard front, conscious of an unsocial and unattractive exterior, refusing to sue for notice which I was sure would be withheld, declining to evince an admiration which I knew would be scorned as worthless. He could not be aware that since then youth and loveliness had been to me every-day objects; that I had studied them at leisure and closely, and had seen the plain texture of truth under the embroidery of appearance; nor could he, keen-sighted as he was, penetrate into my heart, search my brain, and read my peculiar sympathies and antipathies; he had not known me long enough, or well enough, to perceive how low my feelings would ebb under some influences, powerful over most minds; how high, how fast they would flow under other influences, that perhaps acted with the more intense force on me, because they acted on me alone. Neither could he suspect for an instant the history of my communications with Mdlle. Reuter; secret to him and to all others was the tale of her strange infatuation: her blandishments, her wiles had been seen but by me, and to me only were they known; but they had changed me, for they had proved that I *could* impress. A sweeter secret nestled deeper in my heart; one full of tenderness and as full of strength: it took the sting out of Hunsden's sarcasm; it kept me unbent by shame, and unstirred by wrath. But of all this I could say nothing—nothing decisive at least; uncertainty sealed my lips, and during the interval of silence by which alone I replied to Mr. Hunsden, I made up my mind to be for the present wholly misjudged by him, and misjudged I was; he thought he had been rather too hard upon me, and that I was crushed by the weight of his upbraidings; so to re-assure me he said, doubtless I should mend some day; I was only at the beginning of life yet; and since happily I was not quite without sense, every false step I made would be a good lesson.

Just then I turned my face a little to the light; the approach of twilight, and my position in the window-seat, had, for the last ten minutes, prevented him from studying my countenance; as I moved, however, he caught an expression which he thus interpreted:—

"Confound it! How doggedly self-approving the lad looks! I thought he was fit to die with shame, and there he sits grinning smiles, as good as to say, 'Let the world wag as it will, I've the philosopher's stone in my waistcoat-pocket, and the elixir of life in my cupboard; I'm independent of both Fate and Fortune!"

"Hunsden—you spoke of grapes; I was thinking of a fruit I like better than your X—— hot-house grapes—an unique fruit, growing wild, which I have marked as my own, and hope one day to gather and taste. It is of no use your offering me the draught of bitterness, or threatening me with death by thirst: I have the anticipation of sweetness on my palate; the hope of freshness on my lips; I can reject the unsavoury, and endure the exhausting."

"For how long?"

"Till the next opportunity for effort; and as the prize of success will be a treasure after my own heart, I'll bring a bull's strength to the struggle."

"Bad luck crushes bulls as easily as bullaces; and, I believe, the fury dogs you: you were born with a wooden spoon in your mouth, depend on it."

"I believe you; and I mean to make my wooden spoon do the work of some people's silver ladles: grasped firmly, and handled nimbly, even a wooden spoon will shovel up broth."

Hunsden rose: "I see," said he; "I suppose you 're one of those who develope best unwatched, and act best unaided—work your own way. Now, I 'll go." And, without another word, he was going; at the door he turned:

"Crimsworth Hall is sold," said he.

"Sold!" was my echo.

"Yes; you know, of course, that your brother failed three months ago?"

"What! Edward Crimsworth?"

"Precisely; and his wife went home to her father's; when affairs went awry, his temper sympathized with them; he used her ill; I told you he would be a tyrant to her some day; as to him——"

"Ay, as to him—what is become of him?"

"Nothing extraordinary—don't be alarmed; he put himself under the protection of the court, compounded with his creditors—tenpence in the pound; in six weeks set up again, coaxed back his wife, and is flourishing like a green bay-tree."

"And Crimsworth Hall—was the furniture sold too?"

"Everything—from the grand piano down to the rolling-pin."

"And the contents of the oak dining-room—were they sold?"

"Of course, why should the sofas and chairs of that room be held more sacred than those of any other?"

"And the pictures?"

"What pictures? Crimsworth had no special collection that I know of—he did not profess to be an amateur."

"There were two portraits, one on each side the mantel-piece; you cannot have forgotten them,

Mr. Hunsden; you once noticed that of the lady——"

"Oh, I know! the thin-faced gentlewoman with a shawl put on like drapery.—Why, as a matter of course, it would be sold among the other things. If you had been rich, you might have bought it, for I remember you said it represented your mother: you see what it is to be without a sou."

I did. "But surely," I thought to myself, "I shall not always be so poverty-stricken; I may one day buy it back yet.—Who purchased it? do you know?" I asked.

"How is it likely? I never inquired who purchased anything; there spoke the unpractical man—to imagine all the world is interested in what interests himself! Now, good night—I'm off for Germany to-morrow morning; I shall be back here in six weeks, and possibly I may call and see you again; I wonder whether you'll be still out of place!" he laughed, as mockingly, as heartlessly as Mephistopheles, and so laughing, vanished.

Some people, however indifferent they may become after a considerable space of absence, always contrive to leave a pleasant impression just at parting; not so Hunsden; a conference with him affected one like a draught of Peruvian bark; it seemed a concentration of the specially harsh, stringent, bitter; whether, like bark, it invigorated, I scarcely knew.

A ruffled mind makes a restless pillow; I slept little on the night after this interview; towards morning I began to doze, but hardly had my slumber become sleep, when I was roused from it by hearing a noise in my sitting-room, to which my bed-room adjoined—a step, and a shoving of furniture; the movement lasted barely two minutes; with the closing of the door it ceased. I listened; not a mouse stirred; perhaps I had dreamt it; perhaps a *locataire* had made a mistake, and entered my apartment instead of his own. It was yet but five o'clock; neither I nor the day were wide awake; I turned, and was soon unconscious. When I did rise, about two hours later, I had forgotten the circumstance; the first thing I saw, however, on quitting my chamber, recalled it; just pushed in at the door of my sitting-room, and still standing on end, was a wooden packing-case—a rough deal affair, wide but shallow; a porter had doubtless shoved it forward, but seeing no occupant of the room, had left it at the entrance.

"That is none of mine," thought I, approaching; "it must be meant for somebody else." I stooped to examine the address:—

"Wm. Crimsworth, Esq., No. —, —— St., Brussels."

I was puzzled, but concluding that the best way to obtain information was to ask within, I cut the cords and opened the case. Green baize enveloped its contents, sewn carefully at the sides; I ripped the pack-thread with my pen-knife, and still, as the seam gave way, glimpses of gilding appeared through the widening interstices. Boards and baize being at length removed, I lifted from the case a large picture, in a magnificent frame; leaning it against a chair, in a position where the light from the window fell favourably upon it, I stepped back—already I had mounted my spectacles. A portrait-painter's sky (the most sombre and threatening of welkins), and distant trees of a conventional depth of hue, raised in full relief a pale, pensive-looking female face, shadowed with soft dark hair, almost blending with the equally dark clouds; large, solemn eyes looked reflectively into mine; a thin cheek rested on a delicate little hand; a shawl, artistically draped, half hid, half showed a slight figure. A listener (had there been one) might have heard me, after ten minutes' silent gazing, utter the word "Mother!" I might have said more—but with me, the first word uttered aloud in soliloquy rouses consciousness; it reminds me that only crazy people talk to themselves, and then I think out my monologue, instead of speaking it. I had thought a long while, and a long while had contemplated the intelligence, the sweetness, and—alas! the sadness also of those fine, grey eyes, the mental power of that forehead, and the rare sensibility of that serious mouth, when my glance, travelling downwards, fell on a narrow billet, stuck in the corner of the picture, between the frame and the canvas. Then I first asked, "Who sent this picture? Who thought of me, saved it out of the wreck of Crimsworth Hall, and now commits it to the care of its natural keeper?" I took the note from its niche; thus it spoke:—

"There is a sort of stupid pleasure in giving a child sweets, a fool his bells, a dog a bone. You are repaid by seeing the child besmear his face with sugar; by witnessing how the fool's ecstasy makes a greater fool of him than ever; by watching the dog's nature come out over his bone. In giving William Crimsworth his mother's picture, I give him sweets, bells, and bone, all in one; what grieves me is, that I cannot behold the result; I would have added five shillings more to my bid if the auctioneer could only have promised me that pleasure.

H. Y. H.

P.S.—You said last night you positively declined adding another item to your account with me; don't you think I've saved you that trouble?"

I muffled the picture in its green baize covering, restored it to the case, and having transported the whole concern to my bed-room, put it out of sight under my bed. My pleasure was now poisoned by pungent pain; I determined to look no more till I could look at my ease. If Hunsden had come in at that moment, I should have said to him, "I owe you nothing, Hunsden—not a fraction of a farthing: you have paid yourself in taunts."

Too anxious to remain any longer quiescent, I had no sooner breakfasted, than I repaired once more to M. Vandenhuten's, scarcely hoping to find him at home; for a week had barely elapsed since my first call: but fancying I might be able to glean information as to the time when his return was expected. A better result awaited me than I had anticipated, for though the family were yet at Ostend, M. Vandenhuten had come over to Brussels on business for the day. He received me with the quiet kindness of a sincere though not excitable man. I had not sat five minutes alone with him in his bureau, before I became aware of a sense of ease in his presence, such as I rarely experienced with strangers. I was surprised at my own composure, for, after all, I had come on business to me exceedingly painful—that of soliciting a favour. I asked on what basis the calm rested—I feared it might be deceptive.

Ere long I caught a glimpse of the ground, and at once I felt assured of its solidity; I knew where I was.

M. Vandenhuten was rich, respected, and influential; I, poor, despised and powerless; so we stood to the world at large as members of the world's society; but to each other, as a pair of human beings, our positions were reversed. The Dutchman (he was not Flamand, but pure Hollandais) was slow, cool, of rather dense intelligence, though sound and accurate judgment; the Englishman far more nervous, active, quicker both to plan and to practise, to conceive and to realize. The Dutchman was benevolent, the Englishman susceptible; in short our characters dovetailed, but my mind having more fire and action than his, instinctively assumed and kept the predominance.

This point settled, and my position well ascertained, I addressed him on the subject of my affairs with that genuine frankness which full confidence can alone inspire. It was a pleasure to him to be so appealed to; he thanked me for giving him this opportunity of using a little exertion in my behalf. I went on to explain to him that my wish was not so much to be helped, as to be put into the way of helping myself; of him I did not want exertion—that was to be my part—but only information and recommendation. Soon after I rose to go. He held out his hand at parting—an action of greater significance with foreigners than with Englishmen. As I exchanged a smile with him, I thought the benevolence of his truthful face was better than the intelligence of my own. Characters of my order experience a balm-like solace in the contact of such souls as animated the honest breast of Victor Vandenhuten.

The next fortnight was a period of many alternations; my existence during its lapse resembled a sky of one of those autumnal nights which are specially haunted by meteors and falling stars. Hopes and fears, expectations and disappointments, descended in glancing showers from zenith to horizon; but all were transient, and darkness followed swift each vanishing apparition. M. Vandenhuten aided me faithfully; he set me on the track of several places, and himself made efforts to secure them for me; but for a long time solicitation and recommendation were vain—the door either shut in my face when I was about to walk in, or another candidate, entering before me, rendered my further advance useless. Feverish and roused, no disappointment arrested me; defeat following fast on defeat served as stimulants to will. I forgot fastidiousness, conquered reserve, thrust pride from me: I asked, I persevered, I remonstrated, I dunned. It is so that openings are forced into the guarded circle where Fortune sits dealing favours round. My perseverance made me known; my importunity made me remarked. I was inquired about; my former pupils' parents, gathering the reports of their children, heard me spoken of as talented, and they echoed the word: the sound, bandied about at random, came at last to ears which, but for its universality, it might never have reached; and at the very crisis when I had tried my last effort and knew not what to do, Fortune looked in at me one morning, as I sat in drear and almost desperate deliberation on my bedstead, nodded with the familiarity of an old acquaintance—though God knows I had never met her before—and threw a prize into my lap.

In the second week of October, 18—, I got the appointment of English professor to all the classes of —— College, Brussels, with a salary of three thousand francs per annum; and the certainty of being able, by dint of the reputation and publicity accompanying the position, to make as much more by private lessons. The official notice, which communicated this information, mentioned also that it was the strong recommendation of M. Vandenhuten, négociant, which had turned the scale of choice in my favour.

No sooner had I read the announcement than I hurried to M. Vandenhuten's bureau, pushed the document under his nose, and when he had perused it, took both his hands, and thanked him with unrestrained vivacity. My vivid words and emphatic gesture moved his Dutch calm to unwonted sensation. He said he was happy—glad to have served me; but he had done nothing meriting such thanks. He had not laid out a centime—only scratched a few words on a sheet of paper.

Again I repeated to him—

"You have made me quite happy, and in a way that suits me; I do not feel an obligation irksome, conferred by your kind hand; I do not feel disposed to shun you because you have done me a favour; from this day you must consent to admit me to your intimate acquaintance, for I shall hereafter recur again and again to the pleasure of your society."

"Ainsi soit-il," was the reply, accompanied by a smile of benignant content. I went away with its sunshine in my heart.

CHAPTER XXIII.

It was two o'clock when I returned to my lodgings; my dinner, just brought in from a neighbouring hotel, smoked on the table; I sat down, thinking to eat—had the plate been heaped with potsherds and broken glass, instead of boiled beef and haricots, I could not have made a more signal failure: appetite had forsaken me. Impatient of seeing food which I could not taste, I put it all aside into a cupboard, and then demanded, "What shall I do till evening?" for before six P. M. it would be vain to seek the Rue Notre Dame aux Neiges; its inhabitant (for me it had but one) was detained by her vocation elsewhere. I walked in the streets of Brussels, and I walked in my own room from two o'clock till six; never once in that space of time did I sit down. I was in my chamber when the last named hour struck; I had just bathed my face and feverish hands, and was standing near the glass; my cheek was crimson, my eye was flame, still all my features looked quite settled and calm. Descending swiftly the stair and stepping out, I was glad to see Twilight drawing on in clouds; such shade was to me like a grateful screen, and the chill of latter Autumn, breathing in a fitful wind from the north-west, met me as a refreshing coolness. Still I saw it was cold to others, for the women I passed were wrapped in shawls, and the men had their coats buttoned close.

When are we quite happy? Was I so then? No; an urgent and growing dread worried my nerves, and had worried them since the first moment good tidings had reached me. How was Frances? It was ten weeks since I had seen her, six since I had heard from her, or of her. I had answered her letter by a brief note, friendly but calm, in which no mention of continued correspondence or further visits was made. At that hour my bark hung on the topmost curl of a wave of fate, and I knew not on what shoal the onward rush of the billow might hurl it; I would not then attach her destiny to mine by the slightest thread; if doomed to split on the rock, or run aground on the sand-bank, I was resolved no other vessel should share my disaster: but six weeks was a long time; and could it be that she was still well and doing well? Were not all sages agreed in declaring that happiness finds no climax on earth? Dared I think that but half a street now divided me from the full cup of contentment—the draught drawn from waters said to flow only in heaven?

I was at the door; I entered the quiet house; I mounted the stairs; the lobby was void and still, all the doors closed; I looked for the neat green mat; it lay duly in its place.

"Signal of hope!" I said, and advanced. "But I will be a little calmer; I am not going to rush in, and get up a scene directly." Forcibly staying my eager step, I paused on the mat.

"What an absolute hush! Is she in? Is anybody in?" I demanded to myself. A little tinkle, as of cinders falling from a grate, replied; a movement—a fire was gently stirred; and the slight rustle of life continuing, a step paced equably backwards and forwards, backwards and forwards, in the apartment. Fascinated, I stood, more fixedly fascinated when a voice rewarded the attention of my strained ear—so low, so self-addressed, I never fancied the speaker otherwise than alone; solitude might speak thus in a desert, or in the hall of a forsaken house.

"'And ne'er but once, my son,' he said,
Was yon dark cavern trod;
In persecution's iron days,
When the land was left by God.

From Bewley's bog, with slaughter red,
  A wanderer hither drew;
And oft he stopped and turned his head.
  As by fits the night-winds blew.
For trampling round by Cheviot-edge,
  Were heard the troopers keen;
And frequent from the Whitelaw ridge
  The death-shot flashed between." &c., &c.

The old Scotch ballad was partly recited, then dropt; a pause ensued; then another strain followed, in French, of which the purport, translated, ran as follows:—

I gave, at first, attention close;
  Then interest warm ensued;
From interest as improvement rose,
  Succeeded gratitude.

Obedience was no effort soon,
  And labour was no pain;
If tired, a word, a glance alone
  Would give me strength again.

From others of the studious band,
  Ere long he singled me;
But only by more close demand,
  And sterner urgency.

The task he from another took,
  From me he did reject;
He would no slight omission brook,
  And suffer no defect.

If my companions went astray,
  He scarce their wanderings blamed;
If I but faltered in the way,
  His anger fiercely flamed.

Something stirred in an adjoining chamber; it would not do to be surprised eaves-dropping; I tapped hastily, and as hastily entered. Frances was just before me; she had been walking slowly in her room, and her step was checked by my advent: Twilight only was with her, and tranquil, ruddy Firelight; to these sisters, the Bright and the Dark, she had been speaking, ere I entered, in poetry. Sir Walter Scott's voice, to her a foreign far-off sound, a mountain-echo, had uttered itself in the first stanzas; the second, I thought, from the style and the substance, was the language of her own heart. Her face was grave, its expression concentrated; she bent on me an unsmiling eye—an eye just returning from abstraction, just awaking from dreams: well-arranged was her simple attire, smooth her dark hair, orderly her tranquil room; but what—with her thoughtful look, her serious self-reliance, her bent to meditation and haply inspiration—what had she to do with love? "Nothing," was the answer of her own sad, though gentle countenance; it seemed to say, "I must cultivate fortitude and cling to poetry; one is to be my support and the other my solace through life. Human affections do not bloom, nor do human passions glow for me." Other women have such thoughts. Frances, had she been as desolate as she deemed, would not have been worse off than thousands of her sex.

Look at the rigid and formal race of old maids—the race whom all despise; they have fed themselves, from youth upwards, on maxims of resignation and endurance. Many of them get ossified with the dry diet; self-control is so continually their thought, so perpetually their object, that at last it absorbs the softer and more agreeable qualities of their nature; and they die mere models of austerity, fashioned out of a little parchment and much bone. Anatomists will tell you that there is a heart in the withered old maid's carcase—the same as in that of any cherished wife or proud mother in the land. Can this be so? I really don't know; but feel inclined to doubt it.

I came forward, bade Frances "good evening," and took my seat. The chair I had chosen was one she had probably just left; it stood by a little table where were her open desk and papers. I know not whether she had fully recognised me at first, but she did so now; and in a voice, soft but quiet, she returned my greeting. I had shown no eagerness; she took her cue from me, and evinced no surprise. We met as we had always met, as master and pupil—nothing more. I proceeded to handle the papers; Frances, observant and serviceable, stepped into an inner room, brought a candle, lit it, placed it by me; then drew the curtain over the lattice, and having added a little fresh fuel to the already bright fire, she drew a second chair to the table and sat down at my right hand, a little removed. The paper on the top was a translation of some grave French author into English, but underneath lay a sheet with stanzas; on this I laid hands. Frances half rose, made a movement to recover the captured spoil, saying, that was nothing—a mere copy of verses. I put by resistance with the decision I knew she never long opposed; but on this occasion her fingers had fastened on the paper. I had quietly to unloose them; their hold dissolved to my touch; her hand shrunk away; my own would fain have followed it, but for the present I forbade such impulse. The first page of the sheet was occupied with the lines I had overheard; the sequel was not exactly the writer's own experience, but a composition by portions of that experience suggested. Thus while egotism was avoided, the fancy was exercised, and the heart satisfied. I translate as before, and my translation is nearly literal; it continued thus:—

When sickness stayed awhile my course,
  He seemed impatient still,
Because his pupil's flagging force
  Could not obey his will.

One day when summoned to the bed,
  Where Pain and I did strive,
I heard him, as he bent his head,
  Say, "God, she *must* revive!"

I felt his hand, with gentle stress,
  A moment laid on mine,
And wished to mark my consciousness
  By some responsive sign.

But pow'rless then to speak or move,
  I only felt, within,
The sense of Hope, the strength of Love,
  Their healing work begin.

And as he from the room withdrew,
  My heart his steps pursued;
I longed to prove, by efforts new,
  My speechless gratitude.

When once again I took my place,
  Long vacant, in the class,
Th' unfrequent smile across his face
  Did for one moment pass.

The lessons done; the signal made
  Of glad release and play,
He, as he passed, an instant stayed
  One kindly word to say.

"Jane, till to-morrow you are free
  From tedious task and rule;
This afternoon I must not see
  That yet pale face in school.

"Seek in the garden-shades a seat,
Far from the play-ground din;
The sun is warm, the air is sweet:
Stay till I call you in."

A long and pleasant afternoon
I passed in those green bowers;
All silent, tranquil, and alone
With birds, and bees, and flowers.

Yet, when my master's voice I heard
Call, from the window, "Jane!"
I entered, joyful, at the word,
The busy house again.

He, in the hall, paced up and down;
He paused as I passed by;
His forehead stern relaxed its frown:
He raised his deep-set eye.

"Not quite so pale," he murmured low.
"Now, Jane, go rest awhile."
And as I smiled, his smoothened brow
Returned as glad a smile.

My perfect health restored, he took
His mien austere again;
And, as before, he would not brook
The slightest fault from Jane.

The longest task, the hardest theme
Fell to my share as erst,
And still I toiled to place my name
In every study first.

He yet begrudged and stinted praise,
But I had learnt to read
The secret meaning of his face,
And that was my best meed.

Even when his hasty temper spoke
In tones that sorrow stirred,
My grief was lulled as soon as woke
By some relenting word.

And when he lent some precious book,
Or gave some fragrant flower,
I did not quail to Envy's look,
Upheld by Pleasure's power.

At last our school ranks took their ground;
  The hard-fought field I won ;
The prize, a laurel-wreath, was bound
  My throbbing forehead on.

Low at my master's knee I bent,
  The offered crown to meet ;
Its green leaves through my temples sent
  A thrill as wild as sweet.

The strong pulse of Ambition struck
  In every vein I owned ;
At the same instant, bleeding broke
  A secret, inward wound.

The hour of triumph was to me
  The hour of sorrow sore ;
A day hence I must cross the sea,
  Ne'er to recross it more.

An hour hence, in my master's room,
  I with him sat alone,
And told him what a dreary gloom
  O'er joy had parting thrown.

He little said; the time was brief,
  The ship was soon to sail,
And while I sobbed in bitter grief,
  My master but looked pale.

They called in haste; he bade me go,
  Then snatched me back again;
He held me fast and murmured low
  "Why will they part us, Jane?"

"Were you not happy in my care?
  Did I not faithful prove?
Will others to my darling bear
  As true, as deep a love?

"O God, watch o'er my foster child!
  O guard her gentle head!
When winds are high and tempests wild
  Protection round her spread!

"They call again; leave then my breast;
  Quit thy true shelter, Jane;
But when deceived, repulsed, opprest,
  Come home to me again!"

I read—then dreamily made marks on the margin with my pencil; thinking all the while of other things; thinking that "Jane" was now at my side; no child, but a girl of nineteen; and she might be mine, so my heart affirmed; Poverty's curse was taken off me; Envy and Jealousy were far away, and unapprised of this our quiet meeting; the frost of the Master's manner might melt; I felt the thaw coming fast, whether I would or not; no further need for the eye to practise a hard look, for the brow to compress its expanse into a stern fold: it was now permitted to suffer the outward revelation of the inward glow—to seek, demand, elicit an answering ardour. While musing thus, I thought that the grass on Hermon never drank the fresh dews of sunset more gratefully than my feelings drank the bliss of this hour.

Frances rose, as if restless; she passed before me to stir the fire, which did not want stirring: she lifted and put down the little ornaments on the mantel-piece; her dress waved within a yard of me; slight, straight, and elegant, she stood erect on the hearth.

There are impulses we can control; but there are others which control us, because they attain us with a tiger-leap, and are our masters ere we have seen them. Perhaps though, such impulses are seldom altogether bad; perhaps Reason, by a process as brief as quiet, a process that is finished ere felt, has ascertained the sanity of the deed Instinct meditates, and feels justified in remaining passive while it is performed. I know I did not reason, I did not plan or intend, yet, whereas one moment I was sitting solus on the chair near the table, the next, I held Frances on my knee, placed there with sharpness and decision, and retained with exceeding tenacity.

"Monsieur!" cried Frances, and was still: not another word escaped her lips; sorely confounded she seemed during the lapse of the first few moments; but the amazement soon subsided; terror did not succeed, nor fury: after all, she was only a little nearer than she had ever been before, to one she habitually respected and trusted; embarrassment might have impelled her to contend, but self-respect checked resistance where resistance was useless.

"Frances, how much regard have you for me?" was my demand. No answer; the situation was yet too new and surprising to permit speech. On this consideration, I compelled myself for some seconds to tolerate her silence, though impatient of it: presently, I repeated the same question—probably, not in the calmest of tones; she looked at me; my face, doubtless, was no model of composure, my eyes no still wells of tranquillity.

"Do speak," I urged; and a very low, hurried, yet still arch voice said—

"Monsieur, vous me faîtes mal; de grâce lâchez un peu ma main droite."

In truth I became aware that I was holding the said "main droite" in a somewhat ruthless grasp: I did as desired; and, for the third time, asked more gently—

"Frances, how much regard have you for me?"

"Mon maître, j'en ai beaucoup," was the truthful rejoinder.

"Frances, have you enough to give yourself to me as my wife?—to accept me as your husband?"

I felt the agitation of the heart, I saw "the purple light of love" cast its glowing reflection on cheek, temples, neck; I desired to consult the eye, but sheltering lash and lid forbade.

"Monsieur," said the soft voice at last,—"Monsieur désire savoir si je consens—si—enfin, si je veux me marier avec lui?"

"Justement."

"Monsieur sera-t-il aussi bon mari qu'il a été bon maître?"

"I will try, Frances."

A pause; then with a new, yet still subdued inflexion of the voice—an inflexion which provoked while it pleased me—accompanied, too, by a "sourire à la fois fin et timide" in perfect harmony with the tone:—

"C'est à dire, monsieur sera toujours un peu entêté, exigeant, volontaire ——?"

"Have I been so, Frances?"

"Mais oui; vous le savez bien."

"Have I been nothing else?"

"Mais oui; vous avez été mon meilleur ami."

"And what, Frances, are you to me?"

"Votre dévouée élève, qui vous aime de tout son cœur."

"Will my pupil consent to pass her life with me? Speak English now, Frances."

Some moments were taken for reflection; the answer, pronounced slowly, ran thus:—

"You have always made me happy; I like to hear you speak; I like to see you; I like to be near you; I believe you are very good, and very superior; I know you are stern to those who are careless and idle, but you are kind, very kind to the attentive and industrious, even if they are not clever. Master, I should be *glad* to live with you always;" and she made a sort of movement, as if she would have clung to me, but restraining herself she only added with earnest emphasis—"Master, I consent to pass my life with you."

"Very well, Frances."

I drew her a little nearer to my heart; I took a first kiss from her lips, thereby sealing the compact, now framed between us; afterwards she and I were silent, nor was our silence brief. Frances' thoughts, during this interval, I know not, nor did I attempt to guess them; I was not occupied in searching her countenance, nor in otherwise troubling her composure. The peace I felt, I wished her to feel; my arm, it is true, still detained her; but with a restraint that was gentle enough, so long as no opposition tightened it. My gaze was on the red fire; my heart was measuring its own content; it sounded and sounded, and found the depth fathomless.

"Monsieur," at last said my quiet companion, as stirless in her happiness as a mouse in its terror. Even now in speaking she scarcely lifted her head.

"Well, Frances?" I like unexaggerated intercourse; it is not my way to overpower with amorous epithets, any more than to worry with selfishly importunate caresses.

"Monsieur est raisonnable, n'est-ce pas?"

"Yes; especially when I am requested to be so in English: but why do you ask me? You see nothing vehement or obtrusive in my manner; am I not tranquil enough?"

"Ce n'est pas cela—" began Frances.

"English!" I reminded her.

"Well, monsieur, I wished merely to say, that I should like, of course, to retain my employment of teaching. You will teach still, I suppose, monsieur?"

"Oh, yes! It is all I have to depend on."

"Bon!—I mean good. Thus we shall have both the same profession. I like that; and my efforts to get on will be as unrestrained as yours—will they not, monsieur?"

"You are laying plans to be independent of me," said I.

"Yes, monsieur; I must be no incumbrance to you—no burden in any way."

"But, Frances, I have not yet told you what my prospects are. I have left M. Pelet's; and after nearly a month's seeking, I have got another place, with a salary of three thousand francs a year, which I can easily double by a little additional exertion. Thus you see it would be useless for you to fag yourself by going out to give lessons; on six thousand francs you and I can live, and live well."

Frances seemed to consider. There is something flattering to man's strength, something consonant to his honourable pride, in the idea of becoming the providence of what he loves—feeding and clothing it, as God does the lilies of the field. So, to decide her resolution, I went on:—

"Life has been painful and laborious enough to you so far, Frances; you require complete rest; your twelve hundred francs would not form a very important addition to our income, and what sacrifice of comfort to earn it! Relinquish your labours: you must be weary, and let me have the happiness of giving you rest."

I am not sure whether Frances had accorded due attention to my harangue; instead of answering me with her usual respectful promptitude, she only sighed and said—

"How rich you are, monsieur!" and then she stirred uneasy in my arms. "Three thousand francs!" she murmured, "while I get only twelve hundred!" She went on faster. "However it must be so for the present; and, monsieur, were you not saying something about my giving up my place? Oh no! I shall hold it fast;" and her little fingers emphatically tightened on mine.

"Think of my marrying you to be kept by you, monsieur! I could not do it; and how dull my days would be! You would be away teaching in close, noisy school-rooms, from morning till evening, and I should be lingering at home, unemployed and solitary; I should get depressed and sullen, and you would soon tire of me."

"Frances, you could read and study—two things you like so well."

"Monsieur, I could not; I like a contemplative life, but I like an active life better; I must act in some way, and act with you. I have taken notice, monsieur, that people who are only in each other's company for amusement, never really like each other so well, or esteem each other so highly, as those who work together, and perhaps suffer together."

"You speak God's truth," said I at last,

"and you shall have your own way, for it is the best way. Now, as a reward for such ready consent, give me a voluntary kiss."

After some hesitation, natural to a novice in the art of kissing, she brought her lips into very shy and gentle contact with my forehead; I took the small gift as a loan, and repaid it promptly, and with generous interest.

I know not whether Frances was really much altered since the time I first saw her; but, as I looked at her now, I felt that she was singularly changed for me; the sad eye, the pale cheek, the dejected and joyless countenance I remembered as her early attributes, were quite gone, and now I saw a face dressed in graces; smile, dimple, and rosy tint, rounded its contours and brightened its hues. I had been accustomed to nurse a flattering idea that my strong attachment to her proved some particular perspicacity in my nature; she was not handsome, she was not rich, she was not even accomplished, yet was she my life's treasure; I must then be a man of peculiar discernment. To-night my eyes opened on the mistake I had made; I began to suspect that it was only my tastes which were unique, not my power of discovering and appreciating the superiority of moral worth over physical charms. For me Frances had physical charms: in her there was no deformity to get over; none of those prominent defects of eyes, teeth, complexion, shape, which hold at bay the admiration of the boldest male champions of intellect (for women can love a downright ugly man if he be but talented); had she been either "édentée, myope, rugueuse, ou bossue," my feelings towards her might still have been kindly, but they could never have been impassioned; I had affection for the poor little misshapen Sylvie, but for her I could never have had love. It is true Frances' mental points had been the first to interest me, and they still retained the strongest hold on my preference; but I liked the graces of her person too. I derived a pleasure, purely material, from contemplating the clearness of her brown eyes, the fairness of her fine skin, the purity of her well-set teeth, the proportion of her delicate form; and that pleasure I could ill have dispensed with. It appeared, then, that I too was a sensualist, in my temperate and fastidious way.

Now, reader, during the last two pages I have been giving you honey fresh from flowers, but you must not live entirely on food so luscious; taste then a little gall—just a drop, by way of change.

At a somewhat late hour, I returned to my lodgings: having temporarily forgotten that man had any such coarse cares as those of eating and drinking, I went to bed fasting. I had been excited and in action all day, and had tasted no food since eight that morning; besides, for a fortnight past, I had known no rest either of body or mind; the last few hours had been a sweet delirium, it would not subside now, and.

till long after midnight, broke with troubled ecstacy the rest I so much needed. At last I dozed, but not for long; it was yet quite dark when I awoke, and my waking was like that of Job when a spirit passed before his face, and like him, "the hair of my flesh stood up." I might continue the parallel, for in truth, though I saw nothing, yet "a thing was secretly brought unto me, and mine ear received a little thereof; there was silence, and I heard a voice," saying—

"In the midst of life, we are in death."

That sound, and the sensation of chill anguish accompanying it, many would have regarded as supernatural; but I recognised it at once as the effect of reaction. Man is ever clogged with his mortality, and it was my mortal nature which now faltered and plained; my nerves, which jarred and gave a false sound, because the soul, of late rushing headlong to an aim, had overstrained the body's comparative weakness. A horror of great darkness fell upon me; I felt my chamber invaded by one I had known formerly, but had thought for ever departed. I was temporarily a prey to Hypochondria.

She had been my acquaintance, nay, my guest, once before in boyhood; I had entertained her at bed and board for a year; for that space of time I had her to myself in secret; she lay with me, she ate with me, she walked out with me, showing me nooks in woods, hollows in hills, where we could sit together, and where she could drop her drear veil over me, and so hide sky and sun, grass and green tree; taking me entirely to her death-cold bosom, and holding me with arms of bone. What tales she would tell me at such hours! What songs she would recite in my ears! How she would discourse to me of her own country—the Grave—and again and again promise to conduct me there ere long; and, drawing me to the very brink of a black, sullen river, show me, on the other side, shores unequal with mound, monument and tablet, standing up in a glimmer more hoary than moonlight. "Necropolis!" she would whisper, pointing to the pale piles, and add, "It contains a mansion prepared for you."

But my boyhood was lonely, parentless; uncheered by brother or sister; and there was no marvel that, just as I rose to youth, a sorceress, finding me lost in vague mental wanderings, with many affections and few objects, glowing aspirations and gloomy prospects, strong desires and slender hopes, should lift up her illusive lamp to me in the distance, and lure me to her vaulted home of horrors. No wonder her spells *then* had power; but *now*, when my course was widening, my prospect brightening; when my affections had found a rest; when my desires, folding wings, weary with long flight, had just alighted on the very lap of Fruition, and nestled there warm, content, under the caress of a soft hand—why did Hypochondria accost me now?

I repulsed her, as one would a dreaded and

ghastly concubine coming to embitter a husband's heart towards his young bride; in vain; she kept her sway over me for that night and the next day, and eight succeeding days. Afterwards, my spirits began slowly to recover their tone; my appetite returned, and in a fortnight I was well. I had gone about as usual all the time, and had said nothing to anybody of what I felt, but I was glad when the evil spirit departed from me, and I could again seek Frances, and sit at her side, freed from the dreadful tyranny of my demon.

CHAPTER XXIV.

One fine, frosty Sunday in November, Frances and I took a long walk; we made the tour of the city by the Boulevards; and, afterwards, Frances being a little tired, we sat down on one of those wayside seats placed under the trees, at intervals, for the accommodation of the weary. Frances was telling me about Switzerland; the subject animated her; and I was just thinking that her eyes spoke full as eloquently as her tongue, when she stopped and remarked—

"Monsieur, there is a gentleman who knows you."

I looked up; three fashionably dressed men were just then passing—Englishmen, I knew by their air and gait as well as by their features; in the tallest of the trio I at once recognised Mr. Hunsden; he was in the act of lifting his hat to Frances; afterwards, he made a grimace at me, and passed on.

"Who is he?"

"A person I knew in England."

"Why did he bow to me? He does not know me."

"Yes he does know you, in his way."

"How, monsieur?" (she still called me "monsieur;" I could not persuade her to adopt any more familiar term.)

"Did you not read the expression of his eyes?"

"Of his eyes? No. What did they say?"

"To you they said, 'How do you do, Wilhelmina Crimsworth?' To me, 'So you have found your counterpart at last; there she sits, the female of your kind!'"

"Monsieur, you could not read all that in his eyes; he was so soon gone."

"I read that and more, Frances; I read that he will probably call on me this evening, or on some future occasion shortly; and I have no doubt he will insist on being introduced to you; shall I bring him to your rooms?"

"If you please, monsieur—I have no objection; I think, indeed, I should rather like to see him nearer; he looks so original."

As I had anticipated, Mr. Hunsden came that evening. The first thing he said was:—

"You need not begin boasting, Monsieur le Professeur; I know about your appointment to ——— College, and all that; Brown has told me." Then he intimated that he had returned from Germany but a day or two since; afterwards, he abruptly demanded whether that was Madame Pelet-Reuter with whom he had seen me on the Boulevards. I was going to utter a rather emphatic negative, but on second thoughts I checked myself, and, seeming to assent, asked what he thought of her?

"As to her, I'll come to that directly; but first I've a word for you. I see you are a scoundrel; you've no business to be promenading about with another man's wife. I thought you had sounder sense than to get mixed up in foreign hodge-podge of this sort."

"But the lady?"

"She's too good for you evidently; she is like you, but something better than you—no beauty, though; yet when she rose (for I looked back to see you both walk away) I thought her figure and carriage good. These foreigners understand grace. What the devil has she done with Pelet? She has not been married to him three months—he must be a spoon!"

I would not let the mistake go too far; I did not like it much.

"Pelet? How your head runs on M. and Madame Pelet! You are always talking about them. I wish to the gods you had wed Mdlle. Zoraïde yourself!"

"Was that young gentlewoman not Mdlle. Zoraïde?"

"No; nor Madame Zoraïde either."

"Why did you tell a lie, then?"

"I told no lie; but you are in such a hurry. She is a pupil of mine—a Swiss girl."

"And of course you are going to be married to her? Don't deny that."

"Married! I think I shall—if Fate spares us both ten weeks longer. That is my little wild strawberry, Hunsden, whose sweetness made me careless of your hot-house grapes."

"Stop! No boasting—no heroics; I won't bear them. What is she? To what *caste* does she belong?"

I smiled. Hunsden unconsciously laid stress on the word *caste*, and, in fact, republican, lord-hater as he was, Hunsden was as proud of his old —— shire blood, of his descent and family standing, respectable and respected through long generations back, as any peer in the realm of his

Norman race and Conquest-dated title. Hunsden would as little have thought of taking a wife from a *caste* inferior to his own, as a Stanley would think of mating with a Cobden. I enjoyed the surprise I should give; I enjoyed the triumph of my practice over his theory; and leaning over the table, and uttering the words slowly but with repressed glee, I said concisely—

"She is a lace-mender."

Hunsden examined me. He did not *say* he was surprised, but surprised he was; he had his own notions of good breeding. I saw he suspected I was going to take some very rash step; but repressing declamation or remonstrance, he only answered—

"Well, you are the best judge of your own affairs. A lace-mender may make a good wife as well as a lady; but of course you have taken care to ascertain thoroughly that since she has not education, fortune or station, she is well furnished with such natural qualities as you think most likely to conduce to your happiness. Has she many relations?"

"None in Brussels."

"That is better. Relations are often the real evil in such cases. I cannot but think that a train of inferior connections would have been a bore to you to your life's end."

After sitting in silence a little while longer, Hunsden rose, and was quietly bidding me good evening; the polite, considerate manner in which he offered me his hand (a thing he had never done before), convinced me that he thought I had made a terrible fool of myself; and that, ruined and thrown away as I was, it was no time for sarcasm or cynicism, or indeed for anything but indulgence and forbearance.

"Good night, William," he said, in a really soft voice, while his face looked benevolently compassionate. "Good night, lad. I wish you and your future wife much prosperity; and I hope she will satisfy your fastidious soul."

I had much ado to refrain from laughing as I beheld the magnanimous pity of his mien; maintaining, however, a grave air, I said—

"I thought you would have liked to have seen Mdlle. Henri?"

"Oh that is the name! Yes—if it would be convenient I should like to see her—but——." He hesitated.

"Well?"

"I should on no account wish to intrude."

"Come then," said I. We set out. Hunsden no doubt regarded me as a rash, imprudent man, thus to show my poor little grisette sweetheart, in her poor little unfurnished grenier; but he prepared to act the real gentleman, having, in fact, the kernel of that character, under the harsh husk it pleased him to wear by way of mental mackintosh. He talked affably, and even gently, as we went along the street; he had never been so civil to me in his life. We reached the house, entered, ascended the stair; on gaining the lobby, Hunsden turned to mount a narrower stair which led to a higher story; I saw his mind was bent on the attics.

"Here, Mr. Hunsden," said I quietly, tapping at Frances' door. He turned; in his genuine politeness he was a little disconcerted at having made the mistake; his eye reverted to the green mat, but he said nothing.

We walked in, and Frances rose from her seat near the table to receive us; her mourning attire gave her a recluse, rather conventual, but withal very distinguished look; its grave simplicity added nothing to beauty but much to dignity; the finish of the white collar and manchettes sufficed for a relief to the merino gown of solemn black; ornament was forsworn. Frances curtsied with sedate grace, looking, as she always did look, when one first accosted her, more a woman to respect than to love; I introduced Mr. Hunsden, and she expressed her happiness at making his acquaintance in French.

The pure and polished accent, the low yet sweet and rather full voice, produced their effect immediately; Hunsden spoke French in reply; I had not heard him speak that language before; he managed it very well. I retired to the window-seat; Mr. Hunsden, at his hostess's invitation, occupied a chair near the hearth; from my position I could see them both, and the room too, at a glance. The room was so clean and bright, it looked like a little polished cabinet; a glass filled with flowers in the centre of the table, a fresh rose in each china cup on the mantel-piece, gave it an air of *fête*. Frances was serious, and Mr. Hunsden subdued, but both mutually polite; they got on at the French swimmingly: ordinary topics were discussed with great state and decorum; I thought I had never seen two such models of propriety, for Hunsden (thanks to the constraint of the foreign tongue) was obliged to shape his phrases, and measure his sentences, with a care that forbade any eccentricity. At last England was mentioned, and Frances proceeded to ask questions. Animated by degrees, she began to change, just as a grave night-sky changes at the approach of sunrise: first it seemed as if her forehead cleared, then her eyes glittered, her features relaxed, and became quite mobile; her subdued complexion grew warm and transparent; to me, she now looked pretty; before, she had only looked ladylike.

She had many things to say to the Englishman just fresh from his island-country, and she urged him with an enthusiasm of curiosity, which ere long thawed Hunsden's reserve as fire thaws a congealed viper. I use this not very flattering comparison because he vividly reminded me of a snake waking from torpor, as he erected his tall form, reared his head, before a little declined, and putting back his hair from his broad Saxon forehead, showed unshaded the gleam of almost savage satire which his interlocutor's tone of eagerness and look of ardour had sufficed at once to kindle in his soul and elicit from his eyes: he was himself, as Frances was herself, and in none but his own language would he now address her.

"You understand English?" was the prefatory question.

"A little."

"Well, then, you shall have plenty of it; and first, I see you've not much more sense than some others of my acquaintance" (indicating me with his thumb), "or else you'd never turn rabid about that dirty little country called England; for rabid, I see you are; I read Anglophobia in your looks and hear it in your words. Why, mademoiselle, is it possible that anybody with a grain of rationality should feel enthusiasm about a mere name, and that name England? I thought you were a lady-abbess five minutes ago, and respected you accordingly; and now I see you are a sort of Swiss sybil, with high Tory and high Church principles!"

"England is your country?" asked Frances.

"Yes."

"And you don't like it?"

"I'd be sorry to like it! A little corrupt, venal, lord-and-king-cursed nation, full of mucky pride (as they say in ——shire), and helpless pauperism; rotten with abuses, worm-eaten with prejudices!"

"You might say so of almost every state; there are abuses and prejudices everywhere, and I thought fewer in England than in other countries."

"Come to England and see. Come to Birmingham and Manchester; come to St. Giles in London, and get a practical notion of how our system works. Examine the foot-prints of our august aristocracy; see how they walk in blood, crushing hearts as they go. Just put your head in at English cottage doors; get a glimpse of Famine crouched torpid on black hearth-stones; of Disease lying bare on beds without coverlets; of Infamy wantoning viciously with Ignorance, though indeed Luxury is her favourite paramour, and princely halls are dearer to her than thatched hovels ——"

"I was not thinking of the wretchedness and vice in England; I was thinking of the good side—of what is elevated in your character as a nation."

"There is no good side—none at least of which you can have any knowledge; for you cannot appreciate the efforts of industry, the achievements of enterprise, or the discoveries of science; narrowness of education and obscurity of position quite incapacitate you from understanding those points; and as to historical and poetical associations, I will not insult you, mademoiselle, by supposing that you alluded to such humbug."

"But I did, partly."

Hunsden laughed—his laugh of unmitigated scorn.

"I did, Mr. Hunsden. Are you of the number of those to whom such associations give no pleasure?"

"Mademoiselle, what is an association? I never saw one. What is its length, breadth, weight, value—ay *value?* What price will it bring in the market?"

"Your portrait, to any one who loved you, would, for the sake of association, be without price."

That inscrutable Hunsden heard this remark and felt it rather acutely, too, somewhere; for he coloured—a thing not unusual with him, when hit unawares on a tender point. A sort of trouble momentarily darkened his eye, and I believe he filled up the transient pause succeeding his antagonist's home-thrust, by a wish that some one did love him as he would like to be loved—some one whose love he could unreservedly return.

The lady pursued her temporary advantage.

"If your world is a world without associations, Mr. Hunsden, I no longer wonder that you hate England so. I don't clearly know what Paradise is, and what angels are; yet taking it to be the most glorious region I can conceive, and angels the most elevated existences—if one of them—if Abdiel the Faithful himself" (she was thinking of Milton) "were suddenly stripped of the faculty of association, I think he would soon rush forth from 'the ever-during gates,' leave heaven, and seek what he had lost in hell. Yes, in the very hell from which he turned 'with retorted scorn.'"

Frances' tone in saying this was as marked as her language, and it was when the word "hell" twanged off from her lips, with a somewhat startling emphasis, that Hunsden deigned to bestow one slight glance of admiration. He liked something strong, whether in man or woman; he liked whatever dared to clear conventional limits. He had never before heard a lady say "hell" with that uncompromising sort of accent, and the sound pleased him from a lady's lips; he would fain have had Frances to strike the string again, but it was not in her way. The display of eccentric vigour never gave her pleasure, and it only sounded in her voice or flashed in her countenance when extraordinary circumstances—and those generally painful—forced it out of the depths where it burned latent. To me, once or twice, she had in intimate conversation, uttered venturous thoughts in nervous language; but when the hour of such manifestation was past, I could not recall it; it came of itself and of itself departed. Hunsden's excitations she put by soon with a smile, and recurring to the theme of disputation, said—

"Since England is nothing, why do the continental nations respect her so?"

"I should have thought no child would have asked that question," replied Hunsden, who never at any time gave information without reproving for stupidity those who asked it of him; "if you had been my pupil, as I suppose you once had the misfortune to be that of a deplorable character not a hundred miles off, I would have put you in the corner for such a confession of ignorance. Why, mademoiselle, can't you see that it is our *gold* which buys us French politeness, German good-will, and Swiss servility?" And he sneered diabolically.

"Swiss!" said Frances, catching the word "servility." "Do you call my countrymen servile?" And she started up. I could not suppress a low laugh; there was ire in her glance and defiance in her attitude. "Do you abuse Switzerland to me, Mr. Hunsden? Do you think I have no associations? Do you calculate that I am prepared to dwell only on what vice and degradation may be found in Alpine villages, and to leave quite out of my heart the social greatness of my countrymen, and our blood-earned freedom, and the natural glories of our mountains? You 're mistaken—you 're mistaken."

"Social greatness? Call it what you will, your countrymen are sensible fellows; they make a marketable article of what to you is an abstract idea; they have, ere this, sold their social greatness and also their blood-earned freedom to be the servants of foreign kings."

"You never were in Switzerland?"

"Yes—I have been there twice."

"You know nothing of it."

"I do."

"And you say the Swiss are mercenary, as a parrot says 'Poor Poll,' or as the Belgians here say the English are not brave, or as the French accuse them of being perfidious: there is no justice in your dictums."

"There is truth."

"I tell you, Mr. Hunsden, you are a more unpractical man than I am an unpractical woman, for you don't acknowedge what really exists; you want to annihilate individual patriotism and national greatness as an Atheist would annihilate God and his own soul, by denying their existence."

"Where are you flying to? You are off at a

tangent—I thought we were talking about the mercenary nature of the Swiss."

"We were—and if you proved to me that the Swiss are mercenary to-morrow (which you cannot do) I should love Switzerland still."

"You would be mad, then—mad as a March hare—to indulge in a passion for millions of ship-loads of soil, timber, snow and ice."

"Not so mad as you who love nothing."

"There's a method in my madness; there 's none in yours."

"Your method is to squeeze the sap out of creation and make manure of the refuse, by way of turning it to what you call use."

"You cannot reason at all," said Hunsden; "there is no logic in you."

"Better to be without logic than without feeling," retorted Frances, who was now passing backwards and forwards from her cupboard to the table, intent, if not on hospitable thoughts at least on hospitable deeds, for she was laying the cloth, and putting plates, knives and forks thereon.

"Is that a hit at me, mademoiselle? Do you suppose I am without feeling?"

"I suppose you are always interfering with your own feelings, and those of other people, and dogmatizing about the irrationality of this, that, and the other sentiment, and then ordering it to be suppressed because you imagine it to be inconsistent with logic."

"I do right."

Frances had stept out of sight into a sort of little pantry; she soon re-appeared.

"You do right? Indeed, no! You are much mistaken if you think so. Just be so good as to let me get to the fire, Mr. Hunsden; I have something to cook." (An interval occupied in settling a casserole on the fire; then, while she stirred its contents:) "Right! as if it were right to crush any pleasurable sentiment that God has given to man, especially any sentiment that, like patriotism, spreads man's selfishness in wider circles" (fire stirred, dish put down before it).

"Were you born in Switzerland?"

"I should think so, or else why should I call it my country?"

"And where did you get your English features and figure?"

"I am English too; half the blood in my veins is English; thus I have a right to a double power of patriotism, possessing an interest in two noble, free, and fortunate countries."

"You had an English mother?"

"Yes, yes; and you, I suppose, had a mother from the moon or from Utopia, since not a nation in Europe has a claim on your interest."

"On the contrary, I'm a universal patriot, if you could understand me rightly; my country is the world."

"Sympathies so widely diffused must be very shallow: will you have the goodness to come to table. Monsieur" (to me who appeared to be now absorbed in reading by moonlight)—" Monsieur, supper is served."

This was said in quite a different voice to that in which she had been bandying phrases with Mr. Hunsden—not so short, graver and softer.

" Frances, what do you mean by preparing supper; we had no intention of staying."

" Ah, monsieur, but you have stayed, and supper is prepared; you have only the alternative of eating it."

The meal was a foreign one of course; it consisted in two small but tasty dishes of meat prepared with skill and served with nicety; a salad and " fromage françois," completed it. The business of eating interposed a brief truce between the belligerents, but no sooner was supper disposed of than they were at it again. The fresh subject of dispute ran on the spirit of religious intolerance which Mr. Hunsden affirmed to exist strongly in Switzerland, notwithstanding the professed attachment of the Swiss to freedom. Here Frances had greatly the worst of it, not only because she was unskilled to argue, but because her own real opinions on the point in question happened to coincide pretty nearly with Mr. Hunsden's, and she only contradicted him out of opposition. At last she gave in, confessing that she thought as he thought, but bidding him take notice that she did not consider herself beaten.

"No more did the French at Waterloo," said Hunsden.

"There is no comparison between the cases," rejoined Frances; "mine was a sham fight."

"Sham or real, it 's up with you."

"No; though I have neither logic nor wealth of words, yet in a case where my opinion really differed from yours, I would adhere to it when I had not another word to say in its defence; you should be baffled by dumb determination. You speak of Waterloo; your Wellington ought to have been conquered there, according to Napoleon; but he persevered in spite of the laws of war, and was victorious in defiance of military tactics. I would do as he did."

"I'll be bound for it you would; probably you have some of the same sort of stubborn stuff in you."

"I should be sorry if I had not; he and Tell were brothers, and I'd scorn the Swiss, man or woman, who had none of the much-enduring nature of our heroic William in his soul."

"If Tell was like Wellington, he was an ass."

"Does not *ass* mean *baudet?*" asked Frances, turning to me.

"No, no," replied I, "it means an *esprit-fort;* and now," I continued, as I saw that fresh occasion of strife was brewing between these two, "it is high time to go."

Hunsden rose. "Good bye," said he to Frances, "I shall be off for this glorious England to-morrow, and it may be twelve months or more before I come to Brussels again; whenever I do come I'll seek you out, and you shall see if I don't find means to make you fiercer than a dragon. You 've done pretty well this evening, but next interview you shall challenge me outright. Meantime you 're doomed to become Mrs. William Crimsworth, I suppose; poor young lady! but you have a spark of spirit; cherish it, and give the Professor the full benefit thereof."

"Are you married, Mr. Hunsden?" asked Frances, suddenly.

"No. I should have thought you might have guessed I was a Benedick by my look."

"Well, whenever you marry don't take a wife out of Switzerland; for if you begin blaspheming Helvetia, and cursing the cantons—above all, if you mention the word *ass* in the same breath with the name Tell (for ass *is* baudet, I know; though Monsieur is pleased to translate it *esprit-fort*) your mountain maid will some night smother her Breton-bretonnant, even as your own Shakspeare's Othello smothered Desdemona."

"I am warned," said Hunsden; "and so are you,

lad" (nodding to me). "I hope yet to hear of a travesty of the Moor and his gentle lady, in which the parts shall be reversed according to the plan just sketched—you, however, being in my night-cap. Farewell, mademoiselle!" He bowed on her hand, absolutely like Sir Charles Grandison on that of Harriet Byron; adding—"Death from such fingers would not be without charms."

"Mon Dieu!" murmured Frances, opening her large eyes and lifting her distinctly arched brows; "c'est qu'il fait des compliments! je ne m'y suis pas attendu." She smiled half in ire, half in mirth, curtsied with foreign grace, and so they parted.

No sooner had we got into the street than Hunsden collared me.

"And that is your lace-mender?" said he; "and you reckon you have done a fine, magnanimous thing in offering to marry her? You, a scion of Seacombe, have proved your disdain of social distinctions by taking up with an *ouvrière!*

And I pitied the fellow, thinking his feelings had misled him, and that he had hurt himself by contracting a low match!"

"Just let go my collar, Hunsden."

On the contrary he swayed me to and fro; so I grappled him round the waist. It was dark; the street lonely and lampless. We had then a tug for it; and after we had both rolled on the pavement and with difficulty picked ourselves up, we agreed to walk on more soberly.

"Yes, that's my lace-mender," said I; "and she is to be mine for life—God willing."

"God is not willing—you can't suppose it; what business have you to be suited so well with a partner? And she treats you with a sort of respect too, and says, 'Monsieur,' and modulates her tone in addressing you, actually as if you were something superior! She could not evince more deference to such a one as me, were she favoured by Fortune to the supreme extent of being my choice instead of yours."

"Hunsden, you 're a puppy. But you 've only seen the title-page of my happiness; you don't know the tale that follows; you cannot conceive the interest and sweet variety and thrilling excitement of the narrative."

Hunsden—speaking low and deep, for we had now entered a busier street—desired me to hold my peace, threatening to do something dreadful if I stimulated his wrath further by boasting. I laughed till my sides ached. We soon reached his hotel; before he entered it, he said—

"Don't be vain-glorious. Your lace-mender is too good for you, but not good enough for me; neither physically nor morally does she come up to my ideal of a woman. No; I dream of something far beyond that pale-faced, excitable little Helvetian (by-the-by she has infinitely more of the nervous, mobile Parisienne in her than of the robust 'jungfrau'). Your Mdlle. Henri is in person *chétive,* in mind *sans caractère,* compared with the queen of my visions. You, indeed, may put up with that *minois chiffonné*; but when I marry I must have straighter and more harmonious features, to say nothing of a nobler and better developed shape than that perverse, ill-thriven child can boast."

"Bribe a seraph to fetch you a coal of fire from heaven if you will," said I, "and with it kindle life in the tallest, fattest, most boneless, fullest-blooded of Rubens' painted women—leave me only my Alpine peri, and I'll not envy you."

With a simultaneous movement, each turned his back on the other. Neither said "God bless you;" yet on the morrow the sea was to roll between us.

CHAPTER XXV.

In two months more Frances had fulfilled the time of mourning for her aunt. One January morning—the first of the new year holidays—I went in a fiacre, accompanied only by M. Vandenhuten, to the Rue Notre Dame aux Neiges, and having alighted alone and walked upstairs, I found Frances apparently waiting for me, dressed in a style scarcely appropriate to that cold, bright, frosty day. Never till now had I seen her attired in any other than black or sad-coloured stuff; and there she stood by the window, clad all in white, and white of a most diaphanous texture; her array was very simple to be sure, but it looked imposing and festal because it was so clear, full, and floating; a veil shadowed her head, and hung below her knee; a little wreath of pink flowers fastened it to her thickly tressed Grecian plat, and thence it fell softly on each side of her face. Singular to state, she was, or had been crying; when I asked her if she were ready she said "Yes, monsieur," with something very like a checked sob; and when I took a shawl, which lay on the table, and folded it round her, not only did tear after tear course unbidden down her cheek, but she shook to my ministration like a reed. I said I was sorry to see her in such low spirits, and requested to be allowed an insight into the origin thereof. She only said, "It was impossible to help it," and then voluntarily though hurriedly putting her hand into mine, accompanied me out of the room, and ran down-stairs with a quick, uncertain step, like one who was eager to get some formidable piece of business over. I put her into the fiacre. M. Vandenhuten received her and seated her beside himself; we drove all together to the Protestant chapel, went through a certain service in the Common Prayer Book, and she and I came out married. M. Vandenhuten had given the bride away.

We took no bridal trip; our modesty, screened by the peaceful obscurity of our station, and the pleasant isolation of our circumstances, did not exact that additional precaution. We repaired at once to a small house I had taken in the faubourg nearest to that part of the city where the scene of our avocations lay.

Three or four hours after the wedding ceremony, Frances, divested of her bridal snow, and attired in a pretty lilac gown of warmer materials, a piquant black silk apron, and a lace collar with some finishing decoration of lilac ribbon, was kneeling on the carpet of a neatly furnished though not spacious parlour, arranging on the shelves of a chiffonière some books, which I handed to her from the table. It was snowing fast out of doors; the afternoon had turned out wild and cold; the leaden sky seemed full of drifts, and the street was already ankle-deep in the white down-fall. Our fire burned bright, our new habitation looked brilliantly clean and fresh, the furniture was all arranged, and there were but some articles of glass, china, books, &c., to put in order. Frances found in this business occupation till tea-time, and then, after I had distinctly instructed her how to make a cup of tea in rational English style, and after she had got over the dismay occasioned by seeing such an extravagant amount of material put into the pot, she administered to me a proper British repast, at which there wanted neither candles nor urn, fire-light nor comfort.

Our week's holiday glided by, and we re-addressed ourselves to labour. Both my wife and I began in good earnest with the notion that we were working people, destined to earn our bread by exertion, and that of the most assiduous kind. Our days were thoroughly occupied; we used to part every morning at eight o'clock, and not meet again till five P.M.; but into what sweet rest did the turmoil of each busy day decline! Looking down the vista of memory, I see the evenings passed in that little parlour like a long string of rubies circling the dusk brow of the past. Unvaried were they as each cut gem, and like each gem brilliant and burning.

A year and a half passed. One morning (it was a *fête*, and we had the day to ourselves) Frances said to me, with a suddenness peculiar to her when she had been thinking long on a subject, and at last, having come to a conclusion, wished to test its soundness by the touchstone of my judgment."

"I don't work enough."

"What now?" demanded I, looking up from my coffee, which I had been deliberately stirring while enjoying, in anticipation, a walk I proposed to take with Frances, that fine summer day (it was June), to a certain farm-house in the country, where we were to dine. "What now?" and I saw at once, in the serious ardour of her face, a project of vital importance.

"I am not satisfied," returned she: "you are now earning eight thousand francs a year" (it was true; my efforts, punctuality, the fame of my pupils' progress, the publicity of my station, had so far helped me on), "while I am still at my miserable twelve hundred francs. I *can* do better, and I *will*."

"You work as long and as diligently as I do, Frances."

"Yes, monsieur, but I am not working in the right way, and I am convinced of it."

"You wish to change—you have a plan for progress in your mind; go and put on your bonnet; and, while we take our walk, you shall tell me of it."

"Yes, monsieur."

She went—as docile as a well trained child; she was a curious mixture of tractability and firmness: I sat thinking about her, and wondering what her plan could be, when she re-entered.

"Monsieur, I have given Minnie" (our bonne) "leave to go out too, as it is so very fine; so will you be kind enough to lock the door, and take the key with you?"

"Kiss me, Mrs. Crimsworth," was my not very apposite reply; but she looked so engaging in her light summer dress and little cottage bonnet, and her manner in speaking to me was then, as always, so unaffectedly and suavely respectful, that my heart expanded at the sight of her, and a kiss seemed necessary to content its importunity.

"There, monsieur."

"Why do you always call me 'Monsieur?' Say, 'William.'"

"I cannot pronounce your W; besides, 'Monsieur' belongs to you; I like it best."

Minnie having departed in clean cap and smart shawl, we, too, set out, leaving the house solitary and silent—silent, at least, but for the ticking of the clock. We were soon clear of Brussels; the fields received us, and then the lanes, remote from carriage-resounding *chaussées*. Ere long we came upon a nook, so rural, green, and secluded, it might have been a spot in some pastoral English province; a bank of short and mossy grass, under a hawthorn, offered a seat too tempting to be declined; we took it, and when we had admired and examined some English-looking wild-flowers growing at our feet, I recalled Frances' attention and my own to the topic touched on at breakfast.

"What was her plan?" A natural one—the next step to be mounted by us, or, at least, by her, if she wanted to rise in her profession. She proposed to begin a school. We already had the means for commencing on a careful scale, having lived greatly within our income. We possessed, too, by this time, an extensive and eligible connection, in the sense advantageous to our business; for, though our circle of visiting acquaintance continued as limited as ever, we were now widely known in schools and families as teachers. When Frances had developed her plan, she intimated, in some closing sentences, her hopes for the future. If we only had good health and tolerable success, we might, she was sure, in time realize an independency; and that, perhaps, before we were too old to enjoy it; then both she and I would rest; and what was to hinder us from going to live in England? England was still her Promised Land.

I put no obstacle in her way; raised no objection; I knew she was not one who could live quiescent and inactive, or even comparatively inactive. Duties she must have to fulfil, and important duties; work to do—and exciting, absorbing, profitable work; strong faculties stirred in her frame, and they demanded full nourishment, free exercise: mine was not the hand ever to starve or cramp them; no, I delighted in offering them sustenance, and in clearing them wider space for action.

"You have conceived a plan, Frances," said I, "and a good plan; execute it; you have my free consent, and wherever and whenever my assistance is wanted, ask and you shall have."

Frances' eyes thanked me almost with tears; just a sparkle or two, soon brushed away; she possessed herself of my hand too, and held it for some time very close clasped in both her own, but she said no more than "Thank you, monsieur."

We passed a divine day, and came home late, lighted by a full summer moon.

Ten years rush now upon me with dusty, vibrating, unresting wings; years of bustle, action, unslacked endeavour; years in which I and my wife, having launched ourselves in the full career of progress, as progress whirls on in European capitals, scarcely knew repose, were strangers to amusement, never thought of indulgence, and yet, as our course ran side by side, as we marched hand in hand, we neither murmured, repented, nor faltered. Hope indeed cheered us; health kept us up; harmony of thought and deed smoothed many difficulties, and finally, success bestowed every now and then encouraging reward on diligence. Our school became one of the most popular in Brussels, and as by degrees we raised our terms and elevated our system of education, our choice of pupils grew more select, and at length included the children of the best families in Belgium. We had too an excellent connection in England, first opened by the unsolicited recommendation of Mr. Hunsden, who having been over, and having abused me for my prosperity in set terms, went back, and soon after sent a leash of young ——shire heiresses—his cousins; as he said "to be polished off by Mrs. Crimsworth."

As to this same Mrs. Crimsworth, in one sense she was become another woman, though in another she remained unchanged. So different was she under different circumstances, I seemed to possess two wives. The faculties of her nature, already disclosed when I married her, remained fresh and fair; but other faculties shot up strong, branched out broad, and quite altered the external character of the plant. Firmness, activity, and enterprise, covered with grave foliage poetic feeling and fervour; but these flowers were still there, preserved pure and dewy under the umbrage of later growth and hardier nature: perhaps I only in the world knew the secret of their existence, but to me they were ever ready to yield an exquisite fragrance and present a beauty as chaste as radiant.

In the day-time my house and establishment were conducted by Madame the directress, a stately and elegant woman, bearing much anxious thought on her large brow; much calculated dignity in her serious mien: immediately after breakfast I used to part with this lady; I went to my college, she to her school-room; returning for an hour in the course of the day, I found her always in class, intently occupied; silence, industry, observance, attending on her presence. When not actually teaching, she was overlooking and guiding by eye and gesture; she then appeared vigilant and solicitous. When communicating instruction, her aspect was more animated; she seemed to feel a certain enjoyment in the occupation. The language in which she addressed her pupils, though simple and unpretending, was never trite or dry; she did not speak from routine-formulas—she made her own phrases as she went on, and very nervous and impressive phrases they frequently were; often, when elucidating favourite points of history, or geography, she would wax genuinely eloquent in her earnestness. Her pupils, or at least the elder and more intelligent amongst them, recognised well the language of a superior mind; they felt too, and some of them received the impression of elevated sentiments; there was little fondling between mistress and girls, but some of Frances' pupils in time learnt to love her sincerely, all of them beheld her with respect: her general demeanour towards them was serious; sometimes benignant when they pleased her with their progress and attention, always scrupulously refined and considerate. In cases where reproof or punishment was called for she was usually forbearing enough; but if any took advantage of that forbearance, which sometimes happened, a sharp, sudden, and lightning-like severity taught the culprit the extent of the mistake committed. Sometimes a gleam of tenderness softened her eyes and manner, but this was rare; only when a pupil was sick, or when it pined after home, or in the case of some little motherless child, or of one much poorer than its companions, whose scanty wardrobe and mean appointments brought on it the contempt of the jewelled young countesses and silk-clad misses. Over such feeble fledglings the directress spread a wing of kindliest protection: it was to their bedsides she came at night to tuck them warmly in; it was after them she looked in winter to see that they always had a comfortable seat by the stove; it was they who by turns were summoned to the salon to receive some little dole of cake or fruit—to sit on a foot-stool at the fire-side—to enjoy home-comforts, and almost home-liberty, for an evening together—to be spoken to gently and softly, comforted, encouraged, cherished—and when bed-time came, dismissed with a kiss of true tenderness. As to Julia and Georgiana G——, daughters of an English baronet, as to Mdlle. Mathilde de——, heiress of a Belgian count, and sundry other children of patrician race, the directress was careful of them as of the others, anxious for their progress, as for that of the rest—but it never seemed to enter her head to distinguish them by a mark of preference; one girl of noble blood she loved dearly—a young Irish baroness—Lady

Catherine ——; but it was for her enthusiastic heart and clever head, for her generosity and her genius, the title and rank went for nothing.

My afternoons were spent also in college, with the exception of an hour that my wife daily exacted of me for her establishment, and with which she would not dispense. She said that I must spend that time amongst her pupils to learn their characters, to be "*au courant*" with every thing that was passing in the house, to become interested in what interested her, to be able to give her my opinion on knotty points when she required it, and this she did constantly, never allowing my interest in the pupils to fall asleep, and never making any change of importance without my cognizance and consent. She delighted to sit by me when I gave my lessons (lessons in literature), her hands folded on her knee, the most fixedly attentive of any present. She rarely addressed me in class; when she did it was with an air of marked deference; it was her pleasure, her joy to make me still the master in all things.

At six o'clock P.M. my daily labours ceased. I then came home, for my home was my heaven; ever at that hour, as I entered our private sitting-room, the lady-directress vanished from before my eyes, and Frances Henri, my own little lace-mender, was magically restored to my arms; much disappointed she would have been if her master had not been as constant to the tryste as herself, and if his truthful kiss had not been prompt to answer her soft, " Bon soir, monsieur."

Talk French to me she would, and many a punishment she has had for her wilfulness. I fear the choice of chastisement must have been injudicious, for instead of correcting the fault, it seemed to encourage its renewal. Our evenings were our own; that recreation was necessary to refresh our strength for the due discharge of our duties; sometimes we spent them all in conversation, and my young Genevese, now that she was thoroughly accustomed to her English professor, now that she loved him too absolutely to fear him much, reposed in him a confidence so unlimited that topics of conversation could no more be wanting with him than subjects for communion with her own heart. In those moments, happy as a bird with its mate, she would show me what she had of vivacity, of mirth, of originality in her well-dowered nature. She would show, too, some stores of raillery, of "malice," and would vex, tease, pique me sometimes about what she called my "bizarreries anglaises," my "caprices insulaires," with a wild and witty wickedness that made a perfect white demon of her while it lasted. This was rare, however, and the elfish freak was always short: sometimes when driven a little hard in the war of words, for her tongue did ample justice to the pith, the point, the delicacy of her native French, in which language she always attacked me, I used to turn upon her with my old decision, and arrest bodily the sprite that teased me. Vain idea! no sooner had I grasped hand or arm than the elf was gone; the provocative smile quenched in the expressive brown eyes, and a ray of gentle homage shone under the lids in its place. I had seized a mere vexing fairy, and found a submissive and supplicating little mortal woman in my arms. Then I made her get a book, and read English to me for an hour by way of penance. I frequently dosed her with Wordsworth in this way, and Wordsworth steadied her soon; she had a difficulty in comprehending his deep, serene, and sober mind; his language, too, was not facile to her; she had to ask questions, to sue for explanations, to be like a child and a novice, and to acknowledge me as her senior and director. Her instinct instantly penetrated and possessed the meaning of more ardent and imaginative writers. Byron excited her; Scott she loved; Wordsworth only she puzzled at, wondered over, and hesitated to pronounce an opinion upon.

But whether she read to me, or talked with me; whether she teased me in French, or entreated me in English; whether she jested with wit, or inquired with deference; narrated with interest, or listened with attention; whether she smiled *at* me or *on* me, always at nine o'clock I was left—abandoned. She would extricate herself from my arms, quit my side, take her lamp, and be gone. Her mission was up-stairs; I have followed her sometimes and watched her. First she opened the door of the dortoir (the pupils' chamber), noiselessly she glided up the long room between the two rows of white beds, surveyed all the sleepers; if any were wakeful, especially if any were sad, spoke to them and soothed them; stood some minutes to ascertain that all was safe and tranquil; trimmed the watch-light which burned in the apartment all night, then withdrew, closing the door behind her without sound. Thence she glided to our own chamber; it had a little cabinet within; this she sought; there, too, appeared a bed, but one, and that a very small one; her face (the night I followed and observed her) changed as she approached this tiny couch; from grave it warmed to earnest; she shaded with one hand the lamp she held in the other; she bent above the pillow and hung over a child asleep; its slumber (that evening at least, and usually, I believe) was sound and calm; no tear wet its dark eyelashes; no fever heated its round cheek; no ill dream discomposed its budding features. Frances gazed, she did not smile, and yet the deepest delight filled, flushed her face; feeling, pleasurable, powerful, worked in her whole frame, which still was motionless. I saw, indeed, her heart heave, her lips were a little apart, her breathing grew somewhat hurried; the child smiled; then at last the mother smiled too, and said in low soliloquy, "God bless my little son!" She stooped closer over him, breathed the softest of kisses on his brow, covered his minute hand with hers, and at last started up and came away. I regained the parlour before her. Entering it two minutes later she said quietly as she put down her extinguished lamp—

"Victor rests well: he smiled in his sleep; he has your smile, monsieur."

The said Victor was of course her own boy, born in the third year of our marriage: his Christian name had been given him in honour of M. Vandenhuten, who continued always our trusty and well-beloved friend.

Frances was then a good and dear wife to me, because I was to her a good, just, and faithful husband. What she would have been had she married a harsh, envious, careless man—a profligate, a prodigal, a drunkard, or a tyrant, is another question, and one which I once propounded to her; her answer, given after some reflection, was—

"I should have tried to endure the evil or cure it for awhile; and when I found it intolerable and incurable, I should have left my torturer suddenly and silently."

"And if law or might had forced you back again?"

"What, to a drunkard, a profligate, a selfish spendthrift, an unjust fool?"

"Yes."

"I would have gone back; again assured myself whether or not his vice and my misery were capable of remedy; and if not, have left him again."

"And if again forced to return, and compelled to abide?"

"I don't know," she said hastily. "Why do you ask me, monsieur?"

I would have an answer, because I saw a strange kind of spirit in her eye, whose voice I determined to waken.

"Monsieur, if a wife's nature loathes that of the man she is wedded to, marriage must be slavery. Against slavery all right thinkers revolt, and though torture be the price of resistance, torture must be dared: though the only road to freedom lie through the gates of death, those gates must be passed; for freedom is indispensable. Then, monsieur, I would resist as far as my strength permitted; when that strength failed I should be sure of a refuge. Death would certainly screen me both from bad laws and their consequences."

"Voluntary death, Frances?"

"No, monsieur. I'd have courage to live out every throe of anguish Fate assigned me, and principle to contend for justice and liberty to the last."

"I see you would have made no patient Grizzle. And, now, supposing Fate had merely assigned you the lot of an old maid, what then? How would you have liked celibacy?"

"Not much, certainly. An old maid's life must doubtless be void and vapid—her heart strained and empty. Had I been an old maid I should have spent existence in efforts to fill the void and ease the aching. I should have probably failed, and died weary and disappointed, despised and of no account, like other single women. But I 'm not an old maid," she added quickly. "I should have been, though, but for my master. I should never have suited any man but Professor Crimsworth—no other gentleman, French, English, or Belgian, would have thought me amiable or handsome; and I doubt whether I should have cared for the approbation of many others, if I could have obtained it. Now, I have been Professor Crimsworth's wife eight years, and what is he in my eyes? Is he honourable, beloved——?" She stopped, her voice was cut off, her eyes suddenly suffused. She and I were standing side by side; she threw her arms round me and strained me to her heart with passionate earnestness: the energy of her whole being glowed in her dark and then dilated eye, and crimsoned her animated cheek; her look and movement were like inspiration; in one there was such a flash, in the other such a power. Half an hour afterwards, when she had become calm, I asked where all that wild vigour was gone which had transformed her erewhile and made her glance so thrilling and ardent—her action so rapid and strong. She looked down, smiling softly and passively:—

"I cannot tell where it is gone, monsieur," said she, "but I know that, whenever it is wanted, it will come back again."

Behold us now at the close of the ten years, and we have realized an independency. The rapidity with which we attained this end had its origin in three reasons:—Firstly, we worked so hard for it; secondly, we had no incumbrances to delay success; thirdly, as soon as we had capital to invest, two well-skilled counsellors, one in Belgium, one in England, viz., Vandenhuten and Hunsden, gave us each a word of advice as to the sort of investment to be chosen. The suggestion made was judicious; and, being promptly acted on, the result proved gainful—I need not say how gainful; I communicated details to Messrs. Vandenhuten and

Hunsden; nobody else can be interested in hearing them.

Accounts being wound up, and our professional connection disposed of, we both agreed that, as Mammon was not our master, nor his service that in which we desired to spend our lives; as our desires were temperate, and our habits unostentatious, we had now abundance to live on—abundance to leave our boy; and should besides always have a balance on hand, which, properly managed by right sympathy and unselfish activity, might help Philanthropy in her enterprises, and put solace into the hand of Charity.

To England we now resolved to take wing; we arrived there safely; Frances realized the dream of her life-time. We spent a whole summer and autumn in travelling from end to end of the British islands; and, afterwards, passed a winter in London. Then we thought it high time to fix our residence; my heart yearned towards my native county of ——shire; and it is in ——shire I now live; it is in the library of my own home I am now writing. That home lies amid a sequestered and rather hilly region, thirty miles removed from X——; a region whose verdure the smoke of mills has not yet sullied, whose waters still run pure, whose swells of moorland preserve in some ferny glens, that lie between them, the very primal wildness of nature, her moss, her bracken, her blue-bells; her scents of reed and heather; her free and fresh breezes. My house is a picturesque and not too spacious dwelling, with low and long windows, a trellised and leaf-veiled porch over the front-door; just now, on this summer evening, looking like an arch of roses and ivy. The garden is chiefly laid out in lawn, formed of the sod of the hills, with herbage short and soft as moss, full of its own peculiar flowers, tiny and starlike, embedded in the minute embroidery of their fine foliage. At the bottom of the sloping garden there is a wicket, which opens upon a lane as green as the lawn, very long, shady, and little frequented; on the turf of this lane generally appear the first daisies of spring—whence its name—Daisy Lane; serving also as a distinction to the house.

It terminates (the lane I mean) in a valley full of wood; which wood—chiefly oak and beech—spreads shadowy about the vicinage of a very old mansion, one of the Elizabethan structures, much larger, as well as more antique than Daisy Lane, the property and residence of an individual familiar both to me and to the reader. Yes, in Hunsden Wood—for so are those glades and that grey building, with many gables and more chimneys, named—abides Yorke Hunsden, still unmarried; never, I suppose, having yet found his ideal, though I know at least a score of young ladies within a circuit of forty miles, who would be willing to assist him in the search.

The estate fell to him by the death of his

father, five years since; he has given up trade, after having made by it sufficient to pay off some incumbrances by which the family heritage was burdened. I say he abides here, but I do not think he is resident above five months out of the twelve; he wanders from land to land, and spends some part of each winter in town: he frequently brings visitors with him when he comes to ——shire, and these visitors are often foreigners; sometimes he has a German metaphysician, sometimes a French savant; he had once a dissatisfied and savage-looking Italian, who neither sang nor played, and of whom Frances affirmed that he had "tout l'air d'un conspirateur."

What English guests Hunsden invites, are all either men of Birmingham or Manchester—hard men, seemingly knit up in one thought, whose talk is of free trade. The foreign visitors, too, are politicians; they take a wider theme—European progress—the spread of liberal sentiments over the Continent; on their mental tablets, the names of Russia, Austria, and the Pope, are inscribed in red ink. I have heard some of them talk vigorous sense—yea, I have been present at polyglot discussions in the old, oak-lined dining-room at Hunsden Wood, where a singular insight was given of the sentiments entertained by resolute minds respecting old northern despotisms, and older southern superstitions: also, I have heard much twaddle, enounced chiefly in French and Deutsch, but let that pass. Hunsden himself tolerated the drivelling theorists; with the practical men he seemed leagued hand and heart.

When Hunsden is staying alone at the Wood, (which seldom happens) he generally finds his way two or three times a week to Daisy Lane. He has a philanthropic motive for coming to smoke his cigar in our porch on summer evenings; he says he does it to kill the earwigs amongst the roses, with which insects, but for his benevolent fumigations, he intimates we should certainly be over-run. On wet days, too, we are almost sure to see him; according to him, it gets on time to work me into lunacy by treading on my mental corns, or to force from Mrs. Crimsworth revelations of the dragon within her, by insulting the memory of Hofer and Tell.

We also go frequently to Hunsden Wood, and both I and Frances relish a visit there highly. If there are other guests, their characters are an interesting study; their conversation is exciting and strange; the absence of all local narrowness both in the host and his chosen society gives a metropolitan, almost a cosmopolitan freedom and largeness to the talk. Hunsden himself is a polite man in his own house; he has, when he chooses to employ it, an inexhaustible power of entertaining guests; his very mansion too is interesting, the rooms look storied, the passages legendary, the low ceiled chambers, with their long rows of diamond-paned lattices, have an old-world, haunted air: in his travels he has collected store of articles of *vertu*, which are well and tastefully disposed in his panelled or tapestried rooms: I have seen there one or two pictures, and one or two pieces of statuary which many an aristocratic connoisseur might have envied.

When I and Frances have dined and spent an evening with Hunsden, he often walks home with us. His wood is large, and some of the timber is old and of huge growth. There are winding ways in it which, pursued through glade and brake, make the walk back to Daisy Lane a somewhat long one. Many a time, when we have had the benefit of a full moon, and when the night has been mild and balmy, when, moreover, a certain nightingale has been singing, and a certain stream, hid in alders, has lent the song a soft accompaniment, the remote church-bell of the one hamlet in a district of ten miles, has tolled midnight ere the lord of the wood left us at our porch. Free-flowing was his talk at such hours, and far more quiet and gentle than in the day-time and before numbers. He would then forget politics and discussion, and would dwell on the past times of his house, on his family history, on himself and his own feelings—subjects each and all invested with a peculiar zest, for they were each and all unique. One glorious night in June, after I had been taunting him about his ideal bride and asking him when she would come and graft her foreign beauty on the old Hunsden oak, he answered suddenly—

"You call her ideal; but see, here is her shadow; and there cannot be a shadow without a substance."

He had led us from the depth of the "winding way" into a glade from whence the beeches withdrew, leaving it open to the sky; an unclouded moon poured her light into this glade, and Hunsden held out under her beam an ivory miniature.

Frances, with eagerness, examined it first; then she gave it to me—still, however, pushing her little face close to mine, and seeking in my eyes what I thought of the portrait. I thought it represented a very handsome and very individual-looking female face, with, as he had once said, "straight and harmonious features." It was dark; the hair, raven-black, swept not only from the brow, but from the temples—seemed thrust away carelessly, as if such beauty dispensed with, nay, despised arrangement. The Italian eye looked straight into you, and an independent, determined eye it was; the mouth was as firm as fine; the chin ditto. On the back of the miniature was gilded "Lucia."

"That is a real head," was my conclusion.

Hunsden smiled.

"I think so," he replied. "All was real in Lucia."

"And she was somebody you would have liked to marry—but could not?"

"I should certainly have liked to marry her, and that I *have* not done so is a proof that I *could* not."

He repossessed himself of the miniature, now again in Frances' hand, and put it away.

"What do *you* think of it?" he asked of my wife, as he buttoned his coat over it.

"I am sure Lucia once wore chains and broke them," was the strange answer. "I do not mean matrimonial chains," she added, correcting herself, as if she feared misinterpretation, "but social chains of some sort. The face is that of one who has made an effort, and a successful and triumphant effort, to wrest some vigorous and valued faculty from insupportable constraint; and when Lucia's faculty got free, I am certain it spread wide pinions and carried her higher than—" she hesitated.

"Than what?" demanded Hunsden.

"Than 'les convenances' permitted you to follow."

"I think you grow spiteful—impertinent."

"Lucia has trodden the stage," continued Frances. "You never seriously thought of marrying her; you admired her originality, her fearlessness, her energy of body and mind; you delighted in her talent whatever that was, whether song, dance, or dramatic representation; you worshipped her beauty, which was of the sort after your own heart: but I am sure she filled a sphere from whence you would never have thought of taking a wife."

"Ingenious," remarked Hunsden; "whether true or not is another question. Meantime, don't you feel your little lamp of a spirit wax very pale beside such a girandole as Lucia's?"

"Yes."

"Candid, at least; and the Professor will soon be dissatisfied with the dim light you give?"

"Will you, monsieur?"

"My sight was always too weak to endure a blaze, Frances," and we had now reached the wicket.

I said, a few pages back, that this is a sweet summer evening; it is—there has been a series of lovely days, and this is the loveliest; the hay is just carried from my fields, its perfume still lingers in the air. Frances proposed to me, an hour or two since, to take tea out on the lawn; I see the round table, loaded with china, placed under a certain beech; Hunsden is expected—nay, I hear he is come—there is his voice, laying down the law on some point with authority; that of Frances replies; she opposes him of course. They are disputing about Victor, of whom Hunsden affirms that his mother is making a milksop. Mrs. Crimsworth retaliates:—

"Better a thousand times he should be a milksop than what he, Hunsden, calls 'a fine lad'; and moreover she says that if Hunsden were to become a fixture in the neighbourhood, and were not a mere comet, coming and going, no one knows how, when, where, or why, she should be quite uneasy till she had got Victor away to a school at least a hundred miles off; for that with his mutinous maxims and unpractical dogmas, he would ruin a score of children."

I have a word to say of Victor ere I shut this manuscript in my desk—but it must be a brief one, for I hear the tinkle of silver on porcelain.

Victor is as little of a pretty child as I am of a handsome man, or his mother of a fine woman; he is pale and spare, with large eyes, as dark as those of Frances, and as deeply set as mine. His shape is symmetrical enough, but slight; his health is good. I never saw a child smile less than he does, nor one who knits such a formidable brow when sitting over a book that interests him, or while listening to tales of adventure, peril, or wonder, narrated by his mother, Hunsden, or myself. But though still, he is not unhappy—though serious, not morose; he has a susceptibility to pleasurable sensations almost too keen, for it amounts to enthusiasm. He learned to read in the old-fashioned way out of a spelling-book at his mother's knee, and as he got on without driving by that method, she thought it unnecessary to buy him ivory letters, or to try any of the other inducements to learning now deemed indispensable. When he could read, he became a glutton of books, and is so still. His toys have been few, and he has never wanted more; for those he possesses, he seems to have contracted a partiality amounting to affection; this feeling, directed towards one or two living animals of the house, strengthens almost to a passion.

Mr. Hunsden gave him a mastiff cub, which he called Yorke, after the donor; it grew to a superb dog, whose fierceness, however, was much modified by the companionship and caresses of its young master. He would go nowhere, do nothing without Yorke; Yorke lay at his feet while he learned his lessons, played with him in the garden, walked with him in the lane and wood, sat near his chair at meals, was fed always by his own hand, was the first thing he sought in the morning, the last he left at night. Yorke accompanied Mr. Hunsden one day to X——, and was bitten in the street by a dog in a rabid state. As soon as Hunsden had brought him home, and had informed me of the circumstance, I went into the yard and shot him where he lay licking his wound: he was dead in an instant; he had not seen me level the gun; I stood behind him. I had scarcely been ten minutes in the house, when my ear was struck with sounds of anguish: I repaired to the yard once more, for they proceeded thence. Victor was kneeling beside his dead mastiff, bent over it, embracing its bull-like neck, and lost in a passion of the wildest woe: he saw me.

"Oh, papa; I'll never forgive you! I'll never forgive you!" was his exclamation. "You shot Yorke—I saw it from the window. I never believed you could be so cruel—I can love you no more!"

I had much ado to explain to him, with a steady voice, the stern necessity of the deed;

he still, with that inconsolable and bitter accent which I cannot render, but which pierced my heart, repeated—

"He might have been cured—you should have tried—you should have burnt the wound with a hot iron, or covered it with caustic. You gave no time; and now it is too late—he is dead!"

He sank fairly down on the senseless carcase; I waited patiently a long while, till his grief had somewhat exhausted him; and then I lifted him in my arms and carried him to his mother, sure that she would comfort him best. She had witnessed the whole scene from a window; she would not come out for fear of increasing my difficulties by her emotion, but she was ready now to receive him. She took him to her kind heart, and on to her gentle lap; consoled him but with her lips, her eyes, her soft embrace, for some time; and then, when his sobs diminished, told him that Yorke had felt no pain in dying; and that if he had been left to expire naturally, his end would have been most horrible; above all, she told him that I was not cruel (for that idea seemed to give exquisite pain to poor Victor), that it was my affection for Yorke and him which had made me act so, and that I was now almost heart-broken to see him weep thus bitterly.

Victor would have been no true son of his father, had these considerations, these reasons, breathed in so low, so sweet a tone—married to caresses so benign, so tender—to looks so inspired with pitying sympathy—produced no effect on him. They did produce an effect: he grew calmer, rested his face on her shoulder, and lay still in her arms. Looking up, shortly, he asked his mother to tell him over again what she had said about Yorke having suffered no pain, and my not being cruel; the balmy words being repeated, he again pillowed his cheek on her breast, and was again tranquil.

Some hours after, he came to me in my library, asked if I forgave him, and desired to be reconciled. I drew the lad to my side, and there I kept him a good while, and had much talk with him; in the course of which he disclosed many points of feeling and thought I approved of in my son. I found, it is true, few elements of the "good fellow" or the "fine fellow" in him; scant sparkles of the spirit which loves to flash over the wine cup, or which kindles the passions to a destroying fire; but I saw in the soil of his heart healthy and swelling germs of compassion, affection, fidelity. I discovered in the garden of his intellect a rich growth of wholesome principles—reason, justice, moral courage, promised, if not blighted, a fertile bearing. So I bestowed on his large forehead, and on his cheek—still pale with tears—a proud and contented kiss, and sent him away comforted. Yet I saw him the next day laid on the mound under which Yorke had been buried, his face covered with his hands; he was melancholy for some weeks; and more than a year elapsed before he would listen to any proposal of having another dog.

Victor learns fast. He must soon go to Eton, where, I suspect, his first year or two will be utter wretchedness: to leave me, his mother, and his home, will give his heart an agonized wrench; then, the fagging will not suit him—but emulation, thirst after knowledge, the glory of success, will stir and reward him in time. Meantime, I feel in myself a strong repugnance to fix the hour which will uproot my sole olive branch, and transplant it far from me; and, when I speak to Frances on the subject, I am heard with a kind of patient pain, as though I alluded to some fearful operation, at which her nature shudders, but from which her fortitude will not permit her to recoil. The step must, however, be taken, and it *shall* be; for, though Frances will not make a milksop of her son, she will accustom him to a style of treatment, a forbearance, a congenial tenderness, he will meet with from none else.

She sees, as I also see, a something in Victor's temper—a kind of electrical ardour and power—which emits, now and then, ominous sparks; Hunsden calls it his spirit, and says it should not be curbed. I call it the leaven of the offending Adam, and consider that it should be, if not *whipped* out of him, at least soundly disciplined; and that he will be cheap of any amount of either bodily or mental suffering which will ground him radically in the art of self-control. Frances gives this *something* in her son's marked character no name; but when it appears in the grinding of his teeth, in the glittering of his eye, in the fierce revolt of feeling against disappointment, mischance, sudden sorrow, or supposed injustice, she folds him to her breast, or takes him to walk with her alone in the wood; then she reasons with him like any philosopher, and to reason Victor is ever accessible; then she looks at him with eyes of love, and by love Victor can be infallibly subjugated; but will reason or love be the weapons with which in future the world will meet his violence? Oh, no! for that flash in his black eye—for that cloud on his bony brow—for that compression of his statuesque lips, the lad will some day get blows instead of blandishments—kicks instead of kisses; then for the fit of mute fury which will sicken his body and madden his soul; then for the ordeal of merited and salutary suffering, out of which he will come (I trust) a wiser and a better man.

I see him now; he stands by Hunsden, who is seated on the lawn under the beech; Hunsden's hand rests on the boy's collar, and he is instilling God knows what principles into his ear. Victor looks well just now, for he listens with a sort of smiling interest; he never looks so like his mother as when he smiles—pity the sunshine breaks out so rarely! Victor has a preference for Hunsden, full as strong as I deem desirable, being considerably more potent, decided, and indiscriminating, than any I ever entertained for that personage myself. Frances, too, regards it with a sort of unexpressed anxiety; while her son leans on Hunsden's knee, or rests against his shoulder, she roves with restless movement round, like a dove guarding its young from a hovering hawk; she says she wishes Hunsden had children of his own, for then he would better know the danger of inciting their pride and indulging their foibles.

Frances approaches my library window; puts aside the honeysuckle which half covers it, and tells me tea is ready; seeing that I continue busy she enters the room, comes near me quietly, and puts her hand on my shoulder.

"Monsieur est trop appliqué."

"I shall soon have done."

She draws a chair near, and sits down to wait till I have finished; her presence is as pleasant to my mind as the perfume of the fresh hay and spicy flowers, as the glow of the westering sun, as the repose of the midsummer eve are to my senses.

But Hunsden comes; I hear his step, and there he is, bending through the lattice, from which he has thrust away the woodbine with unsparing hand, disturbing two bees and a butterfly.

"Crimsworth! I say, Crimsworth! take that pen out of his hand, mistress, and make him lift up his head."

"Well, Hunsden? I hear you—"

"I was at X—— yesterday; your brother Ned is getting richer than Crœsus by railway speculations; they call him in the Piece-Hall a stag of ten; and I have heard from Brown. M. and Madame Vandenhuten and Jean Baptiste talk of coming to see you next month. He mentions the Pelets too; he says their domestic harmony is not the finest in the world, but in business they are doing "on ne peut mieux," which circumstance he concludes will be a sufficient consolation to both for any little crosses in the affections. Why don't you invite the Pelets to ——shire, Crimsworth? I should so like to see your first flame,

Zoraïde. Mistress, don't be jealous, but he loved that lady to distraction; I know it for a fact. Brown says she weighs twelve stones now; you see what you've lost, Mr. Professor. Now, Monsieur and Madame, if you don't come to tea, Victor and I will begin without you."

"Papa, come!"

THE END.

UNIFORM EDITION

OF THE

WORKS OF CURRER BELL,

AUTHOR OF "JANE EYRE," ETC.

I.

JANE EYRE. By Currer Bell.

In One Volume. *Tenth Thousand.*

"'Jane Eyre' is a remarkable production. Freshness and originality, truth and passion, singular felicity in the description of natural scenery and in the analysation of human thought, enable this tale to stand boldly out from the mass, and to assume its own place in the bright field of romantic literature."—*Times.*

"'Jane Eyre' is a book of decided power. The thoughts are true, sound, and original; and the style is resolute, straightforward, and to the purpose. The object and moral of the work are excellent. As an analysis of a single mind, as an elucidation of its progress from childhood to full age, it may claim comparison with any work of the same species."—*Examiner.*

"A very pathetic tale; very singular, and so like truth that it is difficult to avoid believing that much of the characters and incidents are taken from life. It is an episode in this work-a-day world, most interesting, and touched at once with a daring and delicate hand. The execution of the painting is as perfect as the conception. It is a book for the enjoyment of a feeling heart and vigorous understanding."—*Blackwood's Magazine.*

"For many years there has been no work of such power, piquancy, and originality. Its very faults are on the side of vigour, and its beauties are all original. From out the depths of a sorrowing experience here is a voice speaking to the experience of thousands. It is a book of singular fascination."—*Edinburgh Review.*

"Almost all that we require in a novelist the writer has; perception of character and power of delineating it; picturesqueness, passion, and knowledge of life. Reality—deep, significant reality—is the characteristic of this book."—*Fraser's Magazine.*

2.

SHIRLEY. By Currer Bell.

A New Edition, in one Volume.

"The peculiar power which was so greatly admired in 'Jane Eyre' is not absent from this book. It possesses deep interest, and an irresistible grasp of reality. There is a vividness and distinctness of conception in it quite marvellous. The power of graphic delineation and expression is intense. There are scenes which, for strength and delicacy of emotion, are not transcended in the range of English fiction."—*Examiner.*

"'Shirley' is an admirable book; totally free from cant, affectation, or conventional tinsel of any kind; genuine English in the independence and uprightness of the tone of thought, in the purity of heart and feeling which pervade it; genuine English in the masculine vigour or rough originality of its conception of character; and genuine English in style and diction. It is a tale of passion and character rather than of incident; and, thus considered, it is a veritable triumph of psychology."—*Morning Chronicle.*

"The same piercing and loving eye, and the same bold and poetic imagery, are exhibited here as in 'Jane Eyre.' Similar power is manifested in the delineation of character. With a few brief, vigorous touches, the picture starts into distinctness."—*Edinburgh Review.*

"'Shirley is very clever. It could not be otherwise. The faculty of graphic description, strong imagination, fervid and masculine diction, analytic skill, all are visible. . . . . Gems of rare thought and glorious passion shine here and there."—*Times.*

"We like the book as a whole: we like its spirit. The character of 'Shirley' is excellently conceived and well sustained; and touching is the story of Caroline. We sympathise with the author's general charity, with her special love for the old country, the old church, and the old duke; we kindle with her fervid bursts of eloquence, and recognise the truth of her pictures from life."—*Fraser's Magazine.*

"'Shirley' is a book demanding close perusal and careful consideration. The writer's main purpose has been to trace the fortunes and feelings of two girls: the one is tender, the other is sparkling; both suffer from the malady of unrest and dissatisfaction, and in both the desolateness and the fever are assuaged by one and the same master-enchanter—Love."—*Athenæum.*

"'Shirley' is a novel of remarkable power and brilliancy; it is calculated to rouse attention, excite the imagination, and keep the faculties in eager and impatient suspense. It will unquestionably add to the reputation of the author. Currer Bell's powers of description are displayed to greater advantage in this novel than in its predecessor."—*Morning Post.*

"'Shirley' is the anatomy of the female heart. It is a book which indicates exquisite feeling, and very great power of mind in the writer. The women are all divine."—*Daily News.*

"The novel before us is Yorkshire throughout—racy of the soil. There is something in it of kin to Jane Austen's books, or Maria Edgeworth's, or Walter Scott's. There is human life as it is in England, in the thoughtful and toiling, the employing and labouring classes, with the women and clergy thereto appurtenant."—*Globe.*

3.

VILLETTE. By Currer Bell.

A New Edition, in one Volume.

"'Villette' is a most remarkable work—a production altogether *sui generis.* Fullness and vigour of thought mark almost every sentence, and there is a sort of easy power pervading the whole narrative such as we have rarely met. The characters are sketched with a bold and free pencil, and their indiyiduality is sustained with a consistency which marks a master's hand. The descriptions, too, are wonderfully graphic."—*Edinburgh Review.*

"This novel amply sustains the fame of the author of 'Jane Eyre' and 'Shirley' as an original and powerful writer. 'Villette' is a most admirably written novel, everywhere original, everywhere shrewd, and at heart everywhere kindly. The men, women, and children who figure throughout it have flesh and blood in them, and all are worked out in such a way as to evince a very keen spirit of observation, and a fine sense of the picturesque in character."—*Examiner.*

"There is throughout a charm of freshness which is infinitely delightful: freshness in observation, freshness in feeling, freshness in expression. Brain and heart are both held in suspense by the fascinating power of the writer."—*Literary Gazette.*

"The tale is one of the affections, and remarkable as a picture of manners. A burning heart glows throughout it, and one brilliantly distinct character keeps it alive."—*Athenæum.*

"Of interesting scenes and well-drawn characters there is abundance. The characters are various, happily conceived, and some of them painted with a truth of detail rarely surpassed."—*Spectator.*

"A work of astonishing power and passion. In it we read the actual thoughts and feelings of a strong, struggling soul." *Westminster Review.*

"'Villette' is not only a very able but a very pleasant book. It is a tale which, though here and there it is dashed with wonder and melancholy, is as a whole cheerful and piquant; abundant in clear, clean-cut, strongly drawn etchings, presenting so pleasant and effective a transcript of manners, English and Continental, that its success cannot fail to be remarkable." —*Morning Chronicle.*

"Everything written by Currer Bell is remarkable. She can touch nothing without leaving on it the stamp of originality. Of her three novels this is perhaps the strangest, the most astonishing, though not the best. The sustained ability is perhaps greater in 'Villette' than in its two predecessors. It is crowded with beauties, with good things, for which we look to the clear sight, deep feeling, and singular though not extensive experience of life, which we associate with the name of Currer Bell."—*Daily News.*

"'Villette' is entitled to take a very high place in the literature of fiction. The reader will find character nicely conceived and powerfully depicted; he will discover much quiet humour, a lively wit, brilliant dialogue, vivid descriptions, reflections both new and true, sentiment free from cant and conventionality, and bursts of eloquence and poetry, flashing here and there."—*Critic.*

"The fascination of genius dwells in this book, which is, in our judgment, superior to any of Currer Bell's previous efforts. For originality of conception, grasp of character, elaboration and consistency of detail, and picturesque force of expression, few works in the English language can stand the test of comparison with it."—*Morning Post.*

"A fiction of extraordinary literary power, and of singular fascination; it is one of the most absorbing of books, one of the most interesting of stories."—*Globe.*

"'Villette' may claim the unhesitating commendations of readers and critics. The autobiography of the heroine is at once natural, interesting, cheerful, piquant, and thoughtful."—*Britannia.*

4.

WUTHERING HEIGHTS and AGNES GREY. By Ellis and Acton Bell.

A New Edition, with a Selection of their Literary Remains, and a Biographical Notice of both Authors, by CURRER BELL. In One Volume.

"'Wuthering Heights' is strangely original. It bears a resemblance to some of those irregular German tales in which the writers, giving the reins to their fancy, represent personages as swayed and impelled to evil by supernatural influences. But they give spiritual identity to evil impulses, while Ellis Bell more naturally shows them as the offspring of the unregenerated heart. He displays considerable power in his creations. They have all the angularity of misshapen growth, and form in this respect a striking contrast to those regular forms we are accustomed to meet with in English fiction. They exhibit nothing of the composite character. There is in them no trace of ideal models. They are so new, so wildly grotesque, so entirely without art, that they strike us as proceeding from a mind of limited experience, but of original energy, and of a singular and distinctive cast. We do not know whether the author writes with any purpose; but we can speak of one effect of his production. It strongly shows the brutalising influence of unchecked passion. His characters are a commentary on the truth that there is no tyranny in the world like that which thoughts of evil exercise in the daring and reckless breast. Another reflection springing from the narrative is—that temper is often spoiled in the years of childhood. 'The child is father to the man.' The pains and crosses of its youthful years are engrafted in its blood, and form a sullen and a violent disposition."—*Britannia.*

"We look upon 'Wuthering Heights' as the flight of an impatient fancy, fluttering in the very exultation of young wings; sometimes beating against its solitary bars, but turning rather to exhaust, in a circumscribed space, the energy and agility which it may not yet spend in the heavens. In this thought let the critic take up the book ; lay it down in what thought he will, there are some things in it he can lay down no more. Not a subordinate place or person in this novel but bears more or less the stamp of high genius. There are passages in this book of 'Wuthering Heights' of which any novelist, past or present, might be proud. We cannot praise too warmly the brave simplicity, the unaffected air of intense belief, the admirable combination of extreme likelihood with the rarest originality, the nice provision of the possible even in the highest effects of the supernatural, the easy strength and instinct of keeping with which the accessory circumstances are grouped, the exquisite but unconscious art with which the chiaro-scuro of the whole is managed ; and the ungenial frigidity of time, place, weather, and persons, is made to heighten the unspeakable pathos of one ungovernable outburst. It has been said of Shakspeare that he drew cases which the physician might study ; Ellis Bell has done no less."—*Palladium.*

"To estimate this work aright, the reader must have all the scenic accompaniment before him. He must not fancy himself in a London mansion, but in an old north-country manor-house, situated in the 'dreary, dreamy moorland,' far from the haunts of civilised men. There is, at all events, keeping in the book : the groups of figures and the scenery are in harmony with each other. There is a touch of Salvator Rosa in all."—*Atlas.*

"'Wuthering Heights' bears the stamp of a profoundly individual, strong, and passionate mind. The memoir is one of the most touching chapters in literary biography."—*Nonconformist.*

5.

POEMS. By Currer, Ellis, and Acton Bell.

Fcap. 8vo, 4s. cloth.

"A volume of poems which will not detract from the fame of the authors. The poems bearing the signature of Currer Bell exhibit the impress of a matured intellect and masterly hand."—*Morning Herald.*

"Remarkable as being the first efforts of undoubted genius to find some congenial form of expression. They are not common verses, but show many of the vigorous qualities in the prose works of the same writers : the love of nature which characterizes Currer Bell's prose works pervades the whole of the present volume."—*Christian Remembrancer.*

June, 1857.

A Catalogue

OF

NEW AND STANDARD WORKS,

PUBLISHED BY

SMITH, ELDER AND CO.,

65, CORNHILL, LONDON.

In the Press.

I.

THE ELEMENTS OF DRAWING;

In Letters to Beginners.

BY JOHN RUSKIN, M.A.,

Author of "Modern Painters," "Stones of Venice," "Seven Lamps of Architecture," &c.

Crown 8vo. With Illustrations drawn by the Author. (*Just ready.*)

II.

VICTORIA, AND THE AUSTRALIAN GOLD MINES, IN 1857.

BY WILLIAM WESTGARTH.

Post 8vo, with Maps. (*Shortly.*)

III.

THE AUTOBIOGRAPHY OF LUTFULLAH,

A MAHOMMEDAN GENTLEMAN.

EDITED BY E. B. EASTWICK, ESQ. *Post 8vo.* (*Nearly ready.*)

IV.

THE PROFESSOR. By. CURRER BELL,

Author of "Jane Eyre," "Shirley," "Villette," &c. *In Two Volumes.* (*Now ready.*)

V.

TIGER SHOOTING IN INDIA.

BY LIEUT. WILLIAM RICE, 25TH BOMBAY N. I.

Super Royal 8vo. With Twelve Plates in Chromo-lithography.

VI.

THE MILITIAMAN AT HOME AND ABROAD;

Being the History of a Militia Regiment.

With Illustrations, by JOHN LEECH. *Post 8vo. 9s. cloth.* (*Now ready.*)

VII.

FARINA: A LEGEND OF COLOGNE.

BY GEORGE MEREDITH.

Author of "The Shaving of Shagpät." *In One Volume.* (*Just ready.*)

New Works.

I.

THE LIFE OF CHARLOTTE BRONTË,

Author of "JANE EYRE," "SHIRLEY," "VILLETTE," &c.

BY MRS. GASKELL,

Author of "Mary Barton," "Ruth," "North and South."

Second Edition, Two Volumes, Post 8vo, with a Portrait of Miss Brontë and a View of Haworth Church and Parsonage. Price 24s. cloth.

"We regard the record as a monument of courage and endurance, of suffering and triumph. . . . . All the secrets of the literary workmanship of the authoress of 'Jane Eyre' are unfolded in the course of this extraordinary narrative."---*Times.*

"By all this book will be read with interest. . . . Mrs. Gaskell has produced one of the best biographies of a woman by a woman which we can recall to mind."—*Athenæum.*

"Thoroughly well and artistically has the work been accomplished; an informing method presides over the whole; every circumstance has a direct bearing on the main object of painting, vigorously and accurately, a real picture of the woman as she was."—*Daily News.*

"The profound pathos, the tragic interest of this book, lies in the terrible struggle that life was to a woman endowed with Charlotte Brontë's conscientiousness, affection for her family, and literary ambition, and continually curbed and thrown back by physical wretchedness. Its moral is, the unconquerable strength of genius and goodness."—*Spectator.*

"Mrs. Gaskell's 'Life of Charlotte Brontë' has placed her on a level with the best biographers of any country. It is a truthful and beautiful work. . . . . No one can read it without feeling strengthened and purified."—*Globe.*

"We can be sincere in our praise of this book: we have been often touched by the tone of loving sympathy in which it is written."—*Examiner.*

"This work cannot fail to be of the deepest interest; and it has a special interest for female readers."---*Economist.*

"The whole strange and pathetic story of the Brontë family is faithfully told in Mrs. Gaskell's memoir."—*Critic.*

II.

ANTIQUITIES OF KERTCH,

AND RESEARCHES IN THE CIMMERIAN BOSPHORUS.

BY DUNCAN McPHERSON, M.D., OF THE MADRAS ARMY, F.R.G.S., M.A.I., Inspector-General of Hospitals, Turkish Contingent.

Imperial Quarto, with 14 Plates and numerous Illustrations, including Eight Coloured Fac-Similes of Relics of Antique Art, Price Two Guineas.

"It is a volume which deserves the careful attention of every student of classical antiquity. No one can fail to be pleased with a volume which has so much to attract the eye and to gratify the love of beauty and elegance in design. * * * * The volume is got up with great care and taste, and forms one of the handsomest works that have recently issued from the English Press."—*Saturday Review.*

III.

THE LIFE AND CORRESPONDENCE OF SIR JOHN MALCOLM, G.C.B.

BY JOHN WILLIAM KAYE.

Two Volumes, 8vo. With Portrait. Price 36s. cloth.

"The biography is replete with interest and information, deserving to be perused by the student of Indian history, and sure to recommend itself to the general reader."—*Athenæum.*

"Mr. Kaye has used his materials well, and has written an interesting narrative, copiously illustrated with valu[illegible]e documents."—*Examiner.*

"One of the most interesting of the recent biographies of our great Indian statesmen."—*National Review.*

"This book deserves to participate in the popularity which it was the good fortune of Sir John Malcolm to enjoy."—*Edinburgh Review.*

New Works.

IV.

LIFE AND SERMONS OF DR. JOHN TAULER, OF STRASBURG (1340).

Translated from the German, with Notices of Tauler's Life and Times, including some Account of the "Friends of God,"

BY MISS SUSANNA WINKWORTH.

And a Preface by the REV. CHARLES KINGSLEY.

Small 4to, Printed on Tinted Paper, and bound in antique style, with red edges, suitable for a Present. Price 15s.

"No difference of opinion can be felt as to the intrinsic value of these sermons, or the general interest attaching to this book."—*Athenæum.*

"Miss Winkworth has done a service not only to church history and to literature, but to those who seek simple and true-hearted devotional reading, by producing a deeply-interesting life of Tauler, and giving us his sermons, tastefully and vigorously translated."—*Guardian.*

"A fragment of the best religion of the fourteenth century, most interesting in itself, and so presented as to lose none of its interest in the eyes of any reader. The Sermons have been selected with a view to their practical use, even in the present day."—*Examiner.*

"This volume has several claims to notice. It is a biography of an eloquent preacher of the fourteenth century. It gives a history of the 'Friends of God,' with which he was connected. And in the Sermons of Tauler the consideration is forced upon us how far an active pursuit of worldly concerns is compatible with devotion of the heart to God."—*Press.*

V.

SERMONS. By the late Rev. FRED. W. ROBERTSON,

A.M., Incumbent of Trinity Chapel, Brighton.

FIRST SERIES—*Third Edition, Post 8vo, price 9s. cloth.*

SECOND SERIES—*Third Edition, price 9s. cloth.*

THIRD SERIES, with Portrait—*Post 8vo, price 9s. cloth.*

(*Now ready.*)

"Mr. Robertson, of Brighton, is a name familiar to most of us, and honoured by all to whom it is familiar. A true servant of Christ, a bold and heart-stirring preacher of the Gospel, his teaching was beautified and intensified by genius. New truth, new light, streamed from each well-worn text when he handled it. The present volume is rich in evidence of his pious, manly, and soaring faith, and of his power not only to point to heaven, but to lead the way."—*Globe.*

"These sermons are full of thought and beauty. There is not a sermon in the series that does not furnish evidence of originality without extravagance, of discrimination without tediousness, and of piety without cant or conventionalism."—*British Quarterly.*

"Very beautiful in feeling and occasionally striking and forcible in conception to a remarkable degree."—*Guardian.*

"We should be glad if all preachers more united with ourselves preached such sermons as these."—*Christian Remembrancer.*

VI.

A VISIT TO SALT LAKE;

Being a Journey across the Plains to the Mormon Settlements at Utah.

BY WILLIAM CHANDLESS.

Post 8vo, with a Map. Price 9s. cloth.

"At length we have an English writer who has been to Salt Lake, and tells us all about it: he pledges his word to the accuracy of every conversation and every incident in his book. It has impressed us with the conviction that this strange heresy and schism of the nineteenth century has a stronger vitality than we had previously dreamt."—*Athenæum.*

New Works.

VII.

ANNALS OF BRITISH LEGISLATION,

A Classified Summary of Parliamentary Papers.

EDITED BY PROFESSOR LEONE LEVI.

The Yearly Issue will consist of 1000 pages super royal 8vo, the subscription for which is Two Guineas, payable in advance. The successive parts will be delivered post free, and to subscribers only.

The FOURTEENTH PART *is just issued.*

"A series that, if it be always managed as it is now by Professor Levi, will last as long as there remains a legislature in Great Britain."—*Examiner.*

"It would not be easy to over-estimate the utility of Professor Levi's serial. It has the merit of being an excellent idea zealously carried out."—*Athenæum.*

"We cannot imagine a more truly valuable and nationally important work than this. It is impossible to over-estimate its usefulness."—*Civil Service Gazette.*

"Such a work is much needed."—*Economist.*

VIII.

A RESIDENCE IN TASMANIA.

BY CAPTAIN H. BUTLER STONEY.

Demy 8vo, with Plates, Cuts, and a Map, price 14s. cloth.

"A plain and clear account of the colonies in Van Diemen's Land, which besides being very agreeable reading may be confidently consulted on all matters connected with their material resources, actual position, and social industrial aspects."—*Athenæum.*

"A perfect guide-book to Van Diemen's Land, describing simply and faithfully the country, the plants, animals, and people in it."—*Examiner.*

IX.

SIGHT-SEEING IN GERMANY AND THE TYROL, IN THE AUTUMN OF 1855.

BY SIR JOHN FORBES, Author of "A Physician's Holiday," &c.

Post 8vo, with Map and View, price 10s. 6d., cloth.

"The ground is described clearly, the things that appeared most worth seeing to a sensible, observant tourist, are set down, together with the natural impressions they produced, and the result is a work more agreeable in every way than many a book of travel."—*Examiner.*

X.

THE TREATMENT OF THE INSANE, WITHOUT MECHANICAL RESTRAINTS.

BY JOHN CONOLLY, M.D.

Demy 8vo, price 14s. cloth.

"There is not a page which will not be perused with interest, even by a non-professional reader."—*Morning Post.*

XI.

A HANDBOOK OF AVERAGE,

FOR THE USE OF MERCHANTS, SHIPOWNERS, &c.,

WITH A CHAPTER ON ARBITRATION.

BY MANLEY HOPKINS,

8vo, price 12s. 6d., cloth.

New Works.

XII.

THE POLITICAL LIFE OF SIR R. PEEL.

By THOMAS DOUBLEDAY,

Author of the "Financial History of England," "The True Law of Population," &c.

Two Volumes, 8vo, price 30s. cloth.

"Let all readers, before they take in hand the personal memoirs of Sir Robert Peel, peruse these volumes of Mr. Doubleday: in them the statesman's character and public acts are analysed in the spirit neither of a detractor nor of a panegyrist. This biography is a work of great merit, conscientiously prepared, plain, clear, and practically interesting."—*Leader.*

XIII.

THE EUROPEAN REVOLUTIONS OF 1848.

By EDWARD CAYLEY.

Two Volumes, Crown 8vo, price 18s. cloth.

"Mr. Cayley has produced a book which is in many respects good, which might have been better, but which, so far from having been yet superseded, has not at present even a competitor. As far as our examination has gone, we have found it generally accurate; and independently of its accuracy it is valuable for two qualities—the sturdy common sense and pleasant humour of the author. It is also in the main practical and sound."—*Times.*

XIV.

SIGNS OF THE TIMES: OR, THE DANGERS TO RELIGIOUS LIBERTY IN THE PRESENT DAY.

By the CHEVALIER BUNSEN.

TRANSLATED BY MISS SUSANNA WINKWORTH.

One Volume, 8vo, price 16s. cloth.

"An investigation of the religious principles at work in the Christian world; tracing, as far as modern politics extend, the action of priesthood, associations, and secular decrees enforcing spiritual dogmas. It is the most remarkable work that has appeared in modern times from the pen of a statesman."—*Leader.*

XV.

THE HISTORY, TOPOGRAPHY, AND ANTIQUITIES OF THE ISLE OF WIGHT.

By DAVENPORT ADAMS.

Quarto. 25 Steel Plates, cloth, gilt edges. Price 2l. 2s.

XVI.

STORIES AND SKETCHES.

By JAMES PAYN.

Post 8vo, price 8s. 6d. cloth.

"A volume of pleasant reading."---*Literary Gazette.*

"Mr. Payn is gay, spirited, observant; and shows no little knowledge of men and books."—*Leader.*

XVII.

ROUND THE FIRE: SIX STORIES FOR YOUNG READERS.

By the Author of "THE DAY OF A BABY BOY."

Square 16mo. With Frontispiece. Price 3s. cloth.

"These stories are supposed to be told by six little girls. The language is child-like and winning, and makes us feel that we are reading true children's stories."—*Athenæum.*

Works of Mr. Ruskin.

I.

NOTES ON THE PRINCIPAL PICTURES EXHIBITED AT THE ROYAL ACADEMY,

AND THE

SOCIETY OF PAINTERS IN WATER COLOURS, &c.

No. III.—1857.

Second Edition, with Postscript. 8*vo, price One Shilling.*

II.

NOTES ON THE TURNER COLLECTION

AT MARLBOROUGH HOUSE, PALL MALL.

BY JOHN RUSKIN, M.A.

Fourth Edition, Revised, with Preface, 8*vo, price One Shilling.*

III.

MODERN PAINTERS, Vol. IV.

ON MOUNTAIN BEAUTY.

BY JOHN RUSKIN, M.A.

Imperial 8*vo, with Thirty-five Illustrations engraved on Steel, and* 116 *Woodcuts, drawn by the Author, price* 2*l.* 10*s. cloth.*

"Considered as an illustrated volume, this is the most remarkable which Mr. Ruskin has yet issued. The plates and woodcuts are profuse, and include numerous drawings of mountain form by the author, which prove Mr. Ruskin to be essentially an artist. Keen sight, keen feeling, and keen power of expression are the qualities which go to the making of an artist, and all these Mr. Ruskin possesses. He adds to them a peculiarly subtle turn for theory, investigation and exposition. This combination makes him an unique man, both among artists and writers."—*Spectator.*

"The present volume of Mr. Ruskin's elaborate work treats chiefly of mountain scenery, and discusses at length the principles involved in the pleasure we derive from mountains and their pictorial representation. The author is more philosophical and less critical than before. Mr. Ruskin occupies a peculiar position as a writer. He compels his most vehement adversaries to admire even while they dissent. The singular beauty of his style, the hearty sympathy with all forms of natural loveliness, the profusion of his illustrations, and above all the earnest denunciation of cant, form irresistible attractions. You may quarrel with the critic, but you cannot fail to admire the writer and respect the man. High thoughts, clothed in eloquent language, are the characteristics of Mr. Ruskin's productions. * * * * * * * The present volume contains the most connected exposition of the author's theory which he has yet given to the world."—*Daily News.*

"All art is one, and Mr. Ruskin writes of painting with the ever present consciousness of poetry, sculpture and architecture, as equally implied. This it is which gives the wide and permanent charm to his writings. Interesting as they are to painters, they almost equally fascinate the general public, because in them may be read rare criticisms of natural appearances and of artistic representations. * * * We must all feel subdued by his eloquence, enlightened by his novel views, stimulated by his thoughts, instructed by his accurate observations of nature. Such a writer is really a national possession. He adds to our store of knowledge and enjoyment."—*Leader.*

Works of Mr. Ruskin.

IV.

MODERN PAINTERS, Vol. III.

OF MANY THINGS.

With Eighteen Illustrations drawn by the Author, and engraved on Steel, price 38s. cloth.

"This book may be taken up with equal pleasure whether the reader be acquainted or not with the previous volumes, and no special artistic culture is necessary in order to enjoy its excellences or profit by its suggestions. Every one who cares about nature, or poetry, or the story of human development—every one who has a tinge of literature or philosophy, will find something that is for him in this volume."—*Westminster Review.*

"Mr. Ruskin's third volume of 'Modern Painters' will be hailed with interest and curiosity, if not with submissive attention, by the Art-world of England. * * * Mr. Ruskin is in possession of a clear and penetrating mind; he is undeniably practical in his fundamental ideas; full of the deepest reverence for all that appears to him beautiful and holy, and, though owning to very strong preferences, founding those preferences on reason. * * * His style is, as usual, clear, bold, and racy. Mr. Ruskin is one of the first writers of the day."—*Economist.*

"The present volume, viewed as a literary achievement, is the highest and most striking evidence of the author's abilities that has yet been published. It shows the maturity of his powers of thought, and the perfection of his grace of style."—*Leader.*

"All, it is to be hoped, will read the book for themselves. They will find it well worth a careful perusal. This third volume fully realizes the expectations we had formed of it."—*Saturday Review.*

V.

MODERN PAINTERS.

Imperial 8vo. Vol. I. Fifth Edition, 18s. cloth.
Vol. II. Fourth Edition, 10s. 6d. cloth.

"Mr. Ruskin's work will send the painter more than ever to the study of nature; will train men who have always been delighted spectators of nature, to be also attentive observers. Our critics will learn to admire, and mere admirers will learn how to criticise: thus a public will be educated."—*Blackwood's Magazine.*

"A generous and impassioned review of the works of living painters. A hearty and earnest work, full of deep thought, and developing great and striking truths in art."—*British Quarterly Review.*

"A very extraordinary and delightful book, full of truth and goodness, of power and beauty."—*North British Review.*

VI.

THE STONES OF VENICE.

Now complete in Three Volumes, Imperial 8vo, with Fifty-three Plates and numerous Woodcuts, drawn by the Author.

Price 5l. 15s. 6d., in embossed cloth, with top edge gilt.

EACH VOLUME MAY BE HAD SEPARATELY, VIZ.—

VOL. I. THE FOUNDATIONS, *with* 21 *Plates, price* 2*l.* 2*s.*
VOL. II. THE SEA STORIES, *with* 20 *Plates, price* 2*l.* 2*s.*
VOL. III. THE FALL, *with* 12 *Plates, price* 1*l.* 11*s.* 6*d.*

"This book is one which, perhaps, no other man could have written, and one for which the world ought to be and will be thankful. It is in the highest degree eloquent, acute, stimulating to thought, and fertile in suggestion. It shows a power of practical criticism which, when fixed on a definite object, nothing absurd or evil can withstand; and a power of appreciation which has restored treasures of beauty to mankind. It will, we are convinced, elevate taste and intellect, raise the tone of moral feeling, kindle benevolence towards men, and increase the love and fear of God."—*Times.*

"The 'Stones of Venice' is the production of an earnest, religious, progressive, and informed mind. The author of this essay on architecture has condensed into it a poetic apprehension, the fruit of awe of God, and delight in nature; a knowledge, love, and just estimate of art; a holding fast to fact and repudiation of hearsay; an historic breadth, and a fearless challenge of existing social problems, whose union we know not where to find paralleled."—*Spectator.*

"No one who has visited Venice can read this book without having a richer glow thrown over his remembrances of that city, and for those who have not, Mr. Ruskin paints it with a firmness of outline and vividness of colouring that will bring it before the imagination with the force of reality."—*Literary Gazette.*

Works of Mr. Ruskin.

VII.

THE SEVEN LAMPS OF ARCHITECTURE.

Second Edition, with Fourteen Plates drawn by the Author.

Imperial 8*vo*, 1*l*. 1*s*. *cloth*.

"By the 'Seven Lamps of Architecture,' we understand Mr. Ruskin to mean the seven fundamental and cardinal laws, the observance of and obedience to which are indispensable to the architect, who would deserve the name. The politician, the moralist, the divine, will find in it ample store of instructive matter, as well as the artist. The author of this work belongs to a class of thinkers of whom we have too few among us."—*Examiner.*

"Mr. Ruskin's book bears so unmistakeably the marks of keen and accurate observation, of a true and subtle judgment and refined sense of beauty, joined with so much earnestness, so noble a sense of the purposes and business of art, and such a command of rich and glowing language, that it cannot but tell powerfully in producing a more religious view of the uses of architecture, and a deeper insight into its artistic principles."—*Guardian.*

VIII.

LECTURES ON ARCHITECTURE AND PAINTING.

With Fourteen Cuts drawn by the Author. Second Edition.

Crown 8*vo*, *price* 8*s*. 6*d*. *cloth*.

"Mr. Ruskin's Lectures—eloquent, graphic, and impassioned—exposing and ridiculing some of the vices of our present system of building, and exciting his hearers by strong motives of duty and pleasure to attend to architecture—are very successful; and, like his former works, will command public attention. His style is terse, vigorous, and sparkling, and his book is both animated and attractive."—*Economist.*

"We conceive it to be impossible that any intelligent persons could listen to the lectures, however they might differ from the judgments asserted, and from the general propositions laid down, without an elevating influence and an aroused enthusiasm, which are often more fruitful in producing true taste and correct views of art than the soundest historical generalizations and the most learned technical criticism in which the heart and the senses own no interest."—*Spectator.*

IX.

PRE-RAPHAELITISM.

8*vo*, 2*s*. *sewed*.

"We wish that this pamphlet might be largely read by our art-patrons, and studied by our art-critics. There is much to be collected from it which is very important to remember."—*Guardian.*

X.

THE OPENING OF THE CRYSTAL PALACE:

Considered in some of its relations to the Prospects of Art.

8*vo*, *price* 1*s*., *sewed*.

"An earnest and eloquent appeal for the preservation of the ancient monuments of Gothic architecture."—*English Churchman.*

"A wholesome and much needed protest."—*Leader.*

XI.

THE KING OF THE GOLDEN RIVER;

OR, THE BLACK BROTHERS.

Third Edition, with 22 *Illustrations by* Richard Doyle. 2*s*. 6*d*.

"This little fairy tale is by a master hand. The story has a charming moral, and the writing is so excellent, that it would be hard to say which it will give most pleasure to, the very wise man or the very simple child."—*Examiner.*

XII.

EXAMPLES OF THE ARCHITECTURE OF VENICE,

SELECTED AND DRAWN TO MEASUREMENT FROM THE EDIFICES.

In Parts of Folio Imperial size, each containing Five Plates, and a short Explanatory Text, price 1*l*. 1*s*. *each.*

PARTS I. TO III. ARE PUBLISHED.

Fifty India Proofs only are taken on Atlas Folio, price 2*l*. 2*s*. *each Part.*

Recent Works.

RIFLE PRACTICE.

By Lieutenant-Colonel JOHN JACOB, C.B.

With Plates. Third Edition, revised and enlarged, price 2s.

"Colonel Jacob's invention must revolutionize the whole art of war. We commend Colonel Jacob's pamphlet to the attentive perusal of every military man and every sincere lover of his country."—*Bombay Quarterly Review*

PAPERS OF THE LATE LORD METCALFE.

Selected and Edited by J. W. KAYE. *Demy 8vo, price 16s. cloth.*

"We commend this volume to all persons who like to study state papers, in which the practical sense of a man of the world is joined to the speculative sagacity of a philosophical statesman. No Indian library should be without it."—*Press.*

TWO SUMMER CRUISES WITH THE BALTIC FLEET IN 1854-5; Being the LOG of the "PET."

By R. E. HUGHES, M.A.

Second Edition, Post 8vo, with Views and Charts. 10s. 6d., cloth.

"There are few readers to whom this volume will not be welcome. It is light and pleasant reading, and conveys not a little valuable information. Few unprofessional men are so capable of forming a judgment on naval tactics as Mr. Hughes appears to be."—*Economist.*

THE COURT OF HENRY VIII.:

Being a Selection of the Despatches of Sebastian Giustinian, Venetian Ambassador, 1515-1519.

Translated by RAWDON BROWN. *Two Vols., crown 8vo, price 21s. cloth.*

"These volumes present such a portrait of the times as is nowhere else to be found. They are a most important contribution to the materials for history."—*Quarterly Review.*

A CAMPAIGN WITH THE TURKS IN ASIA.

By CHARLES DUNCAN. *Two Vols., post 8vo, price 21s. cloth.*

THE RED RIVER SETTLEMENT.

By ALEXANDER ROSS, Author of "Fur-Hunters of the Far West."

One Volume, post 8vo, price 10s. 6d. cloth.

THE FUR-HUNTERS OF THE FAR WEST.

By ALEXANDER ROSS.

Two Volumes, post 8vo. With Map and Plate. 21s. cloth.

RUSSO-TURKISH CAMPAIGNS OF 1828-9.

By COLONEL CHESNEY, R.A., D.C.L., F.R.S.

Third Edition. Post 8vo, with Maps, price 12s. cloth.

MILITARY FORCES AND INSTITUTIONS OF GREAT BRITAIN.

By H. BYERLEY THOMSON, of the Inner Temple. *8vo, 15s. cloth.*

A MANUAL OF THE MERCANTILE LAW OF GREAT BRITAIN AND IRELAND.

By PROFESSOR LEONE LEVI,

Author of "Commercial Law of the World." *8vo, price 12s. cloth.*

THE LAWS OF WAR AFFECTING COMMERCE AND SHIPPING.

By H. BYERLEY THOMSON, of the Inner Temple. *Second Edition, greatly enlarged. 8vo, price 4s. 6d. boards.*

Works of Mr. Thackeray.

LECTURES ON THE ENGLISH HUMOURISTS OF THE 18TH CENTURY.

BY W. M. THACKERAY,
Author of "Vanity Fair," "The Newcomes," &c.

Second Edition. Crown 8vo, price 10s. 6d. cloth.

"To those who attended the lectures, the book will be a pleasant reminiscence, to others an exciting novelty. The style—clear, idiomatic, forcible, familiar, but never slovenly; the searching strokes of sarcasm or irony; the occasional flashes of generous scorn; the touches of pathos, pity, and tenderness, the morality tempered but never weakened by experience and sympathy; the felicitous phrases, the striking anecdotes, the passages of wise, practical reflection; all these lose much less than we could have expected from the absence of the voice, manner, and look of the lecturer."—*Spectator.*

ESMOND. By W. M. THACKERAY.

Second Edition, 3 vols., Crown 8vo, reduced to 15s. cloth.

"Mr. Thackeray has selected for his hero a very noble type of the cavalier softening into the man of the eighteenth century, and for his heroine one of the sweetest women that ever breathed from canvas or from book, since Raffaelle painted and Shakspeare wrote. The style is manly, clear, terse, and vigorous, reflecting every mood—pathetic, graphic, or sarcastic—of the writer."—*Spectator.*

THE ROSE AND THE RING; OR, THE HISTORY OF PRINCE GIGLIO AND PRINCE BULBO.

BY MR. M. A. TITMARSH.

With 58 Cuts drawn by the Author. 3rd Edition, price 5s.

Uniform Edition of the Works of Currer Bell.

VILLETTE. By CURRER BELL.

New Edition, in One Volume, Crown 8vo, 6s. cloth.

"This novel amply sustains the fame of the author of 'Jane Eyre' and 'Shirley' as an original and powerful writer."—*Examiner.*

SHIRLEY By CURRER BELL.

Crown 8vo, 6s. cloth.

"The peculiar power which was so greatly admired in 'Jane Eyre' is not absent from this book. It possesses deep interest, and an irresistible grasp of reality. There are scenes which, for strength and delicacy of emotion, are not transcended in the range of English fiction."—*Examiner.*

JANE EYRE. By CURRER BELL.

Fifth Edition. Crown 8vo. 6s. cloth.

"'Jane Eyre' is a remarkable production. Freshness and originality, truth and passion, singular felicity in the description of natural scenery, and in the analysation of human thought, enable this tale to stand boldly out from the mass, and to assume its own place in the bright field of romantic literature."—*Times.*

WUTHERING HEIGHTS AND AGNES GREY.

BY ELLIS AND ACTON BELL.
With a Biographical Notice of both Authors, by CURRER BELL.
Crown 8vo, 6s. cloth.

New Novels.

I.

BELOW THE SURFACE: A STORY OF ENGLISH COUNTRY LIFE. 3 vols.

"This is a book which possesses the rare merit of being exactly what it claims to be. The various features of provincial life in England are well sketched. The author has gone fearlessly below the surface, and exposed much that is as true as it is terrible."—*Daily News.*

"The book is unquestionably clever and entertaining. It is a tale superior to ordinary novels in its practical application to the phases of actual life. The style is level, plain, and in good taste—felicitous epigrams flashing through the tissue here and there."—*Athenæum.*

"The novel keeps the attention fixed, and it is written in a genial, often playful tone, so that, although containing much that is romantic in its incidents, there is no strain for effect. The temper is throughout excellent."—*Examiner.*

"It is a novel worth reading, and some parts of it are worth remembering. The story offers many points of interest and dramatic power; and there is considerable humour in some of the scenes."—*Economist.*

"'Below the Surface' bears out the title well. The incidents are naturally and dramatically introduced, and all the provincial scenes are vividly represented. It is a decided success."—*Press.*

II.

THE ROUA PASS: OR, ENGLISHMEN IN THE HIGHLANDS. BY ERICK MACKENZIE. 3 vols.

"It is seldom that we have to notice so good a novel as the 'Roua Pass.' The story is well contrived and well told; the incidents are natural and varied, several of the characters are skilfully drawn, and that of the heroine is fresh, powerful, and original. The Highland scenery is described with truth and feeling."—*Saturday Review.*

"This novel we have read through with the greatest interest. It is full of life-like descriptions and finished portraits."—*Press.*

"A capital fiction. As a landscape novel it is altogether delightful."—*Globe.*

III.

THE EVE OF ST. MARK: A ROMANCE OF VENICE. BY THOMAS DOUBLEDAY. 2 vols.

"The 'Eve of St. Mark' is not only well written, but adroitly constructed, and interesting."—*Athenæum.*

IV.

FRIENDS OF BOHEMIA; OR, PHASES OF LONDON LIFE. BY E. M. WHITTY, Author of "The Governing Classes." 2 vols., post 8vo.

"Mr. Whitty is a genuine satirist, employing satire for a genuine purpose. You laugh with him very much; but the laughter is fruity and ripe in thought. His style is serious, and his cast of mind severe. The author has a merriment akin to that of Jacques and that of Timon. He works with a desire to influence rather than with a wish to amuse."—*Athenæum.*

V.

OLIVER CROMWELL: A STORY OF THE CIVIL WARS. BY CHARLES EDWARD STEWART. 2 vols.

"This novel will attract the reader by the exciting events it chronicles, and the moderation and simplicity with which it is written."—*Sun.*

VI.

FLORENCE TEMPLAR. 1 vol.

"'Florence Templar' is a tale of love, pride, and passion. There is no little power shown in the manner of presenting the high-minded Florence. The story as a whole is very good."—*Examiner.*

VII.

KATHIE BRANDE: THE FIRESIDE HISTORY OF A QUIET LIFE. BY HOLME LEE, Author of "Gilbert Massenger," "Thorney Hall," &c. 2 vols.

"The story of 'Kathie Brande' is intended to set forth the beauty of self-sacrifice."—*Athenæum.*

Recent Novels.

I.

TENDER AND TRUE.

By the Author of "Clara Morison." 2 vols.

II.

YOUNG SINGLETON. By TALBOT GWYNNE, Author of "The School for Fathers," &c. 2 vols.

III.

ERLESMERE: or, CONTRASTS OF CHARACTER. By L. S. LAVENU. 2 vols.

IV.

PERVERSION;

Or, THE CAUSES AND CONSEQUENCES OF INFIDELITY.

A Tale for the Times. In 3 vols. Second Edition.

V.

BEYMINSTRE.

By the Author of "Lena," "King's Cope," &c. 3 vols.

VI.

AFTER DARK. BY WILKIE COLLINS, Author of "Basil," "Hide and Seek," &c. 2 vols.

VII.

AMBERHILL. BY A. J. BARROWCLIFFE. 2 vols.

VIII.

LEONORA. By the Hon. Mrs. MABERLY. 3 vols.

IX.

EVELEEN. BY E. L. A. BERWICK. 3 vols.

X.

MAURICE ELVINGTON: AN AUTOBIOGRAPHY. Edited by WILFRID EAST. 3 vols.

In the Press.

I.

RIVERSTON. By GEORGIANA M. CRAIK. 3 vols. *(Just ready.)*

II.

LUCIAN PLAYFAIR. By THOMAS MACKERN. 3 vols. *(Nearly ready.)*

III.

THE MOORS AND THE FENS. By F. G. TRAFFORD. 3 vols.

IV.

GASTON BLIGH. By L. S. LAVENU, Author of "Erlesmere." 2 vols.

V.

THE NOBLE TRAYTOUR. A CHRONICLE. 3 vols.

VI.

THE THREE CHANCES.

By the Author of "The Fair Carew." 3 vols.

Oriental.

THE CHINESE AND THEIR REBELLIONS.

By THOMAS TAYLOR MEADOWS.

One Thick Volume, 8vo, with Maps, price 18s. cloth.

"Mr. Meadows appears to know China more thoroughly and comprehensively than any of its predecessors. His book is the work of a learned, conscientious, and observant person, and really important in many respects. It is the most curious book we have metwith for a long time."—*Times.*

"In this book is a vast amount of valuable information respecting China, and the sta ements it contains bear on them the face of truth. Mr. Meadows has produced a work which deserves to be studied by all who would gain a true appreciation of Chinese character. Information is sown broad-cast through every page."—*Athenæum.*

LIFE IN ANCIENT INDIA.

By MRS. SPEIR.

With Sixty Illustrations by G. Scharf. *8vo, price 15s., elegantly bound in cloth, gilt edges.*

"Whoever desires to have the best, the completest, and the most popular view of what Oriental scholars have made known to us respecting Ancient India must peruse the work of Mrs. Speir; in which he will find the story told in clear, correct, and unaffected English. The book is admirably got up."—*Examiner.*

"We should in vain seek for any other treatise which, in so short a space, gives so well-connected an account of the early period of Indian history."—*Daily News.*

THE CAUVERY, KISTNAH, AND GODAVERY:

Being a Report on the Works constructed on those Rivers for the Irrigation of Provinces in the Presidency of Madras.

By R. BAIRD SMITH, F.G.S., Lt.-Col. Bengal Engineers, &c., &c.

In demy 8vo, with 19 Plans, price 28s. cloth.

"A most curious and interesting work."—*Economist.*

THE BHILSA TOPES; or, Buddhist Monuments of Central India.

By MAJOR CUNNINGHAM.

One Volume, 8vo, with Thirty-three Plates, price 30s. cloth.

"Of the Topes opened in various parts of India none have yielded so rich a harvest of important information as those of Bhilsa, opened by Major Cunningham and Lieut. Maisey; and which are described, with an abundance of highly curious graphic illustrations, in this most interesting book."—*Examiner.*

TRAVELS AND ADVENTURES IN ASSAM.

By MAJOR JOHN BUTLER.

One Volume 8vo, with Plates, price 12s. cloth.

"This volume is unusually successful in creating an interest on an Eastern subject. It is illustrated by views of landscapes, figures and antiquities."—*Press.*

THE ENGLISH IN WESTERN INDIA;

Being the Early History of the Factory at Surat, of Bombay.

By PHILIP ANDERSON, A.M.

Second Edition, 8vo, price 14s. cloth.

"Quaint, curious, and amusing, this volume describes, from old manuscripts and obscure books, the life of English merchants in an Indian Factory. It contains fresh and amusing gossip, all bearing on events and characters of historical importance."—*Athenæum.*

"A book of permanent value."—*Guardian.*

Oriental.

DR. ROYLE ON THE FIBROUS PLANTS OF INDIA FITTED FOR CORDAGE, CLOTHING, AND PAPER. *8vo, price* 12*s. cloth.*

DR. ROYLE ON THE CULTURE AND COMMERCE OF COTTON IN INDIA. *8vo,* 18*s. cloth.*

DR. WILSON ON INFANTICIDE IN WESTERN INDIA. *Demy 8vo, price* 12*s.*

JOURNAL OF THE SUTLEJ CAMPAIGN. By JAMES COLEY, M.A. *Royal 8vo, price* 5*s. cloth.*

CRAWFURD'S GRAMMAR AND DICTIONARY OF THE MALAY LANGUAGE. 2 *vols. 8vo, price* 36*s. cloth.*

ROBERTS'S INDIAN EXCHANGE TABLES. *8vo. Second Edition, enlarged, price* 10*s.* 6*d. cloth.*

WARING ON ABSCESS IN THE LIVER. *8vo, price* 3*s.* 6*d.*

LAURIE'S PEGU. *Post 8vo, price* 14*s. cloth.*

BOYD'S TURKISH INTERPRETER: A GRAMMAR OF THE TURKISH LANGUAGE. *8vo, price* 12*s.*

BRIDGNELL'S INDIAN COMMERCIAL TABLES. *Royal 8vo, price* 21*s., half-bound.*

THE BOMBAY QUARTERLY REVIEW. Nos. 1 to 8, *price* 5*s. each.*

BAILLIE'S LAND TAX OF INDIA. According to the Moohummudan Law. *8vo, price* 6*s. cloth.*

BAILLIE'S MOOHUMMUDAN LAW OF SALE. *8vo, price* 14*s. cloth.*

IRVING'S THEORY AND PRACTICE OF CASTE. *8vo, price* 5*s. cloth.*

GINGELL'S CEREMONIAL USAGES OF THE CHINESE. *Imperial 8vo, price* 9*s. cloth.*

THE INSURRECTION IN CHINA. By Dr. YVAN and M. CALLERY. Translated by JOHN OXENFORD. *Third Edition. Post 8vo, with Chinese Map and Portrait, price* 7*s.* 6*d. cloth.*

KESSON'S CROSS AND THE DRAGON; OR, THE FORTUNES OF CHRISTIANITY IN CHINA. *Post 8vo,* 6*s. cloth.*

Miscellaneous.

ELEMENTARY WORKS ON SOCIAL ECONOMY.
Uniform in foolscap 8vo, half-bound.
I.—OUTLINES OF SOCIAL ECONOMY. 1*s.* 6*d.*
II.—PROGRESSIVE LESSONS IN SOCIAL SCIENCE. 1*s.* 6*d.*
III.—INTRODUCTION TO THE SOCIAL SCIENCES. 2*s.*
IV.—QUESTIONS AND ANSWERS ON THE ARRANGEMENTS AND RELATIONS OF SOCIAL LIFE. 2*s.* 6*d.*
V.—OUTLINES OF THE UNDERSTANDING. 2*s.*
VI.—WHAT AM I? WHERE AM I? WHAT OUGHT I TO DO? &c. 1*s.* sewed.

SWAINSON'S LECTURES ON NEW ZEALAND.
Crown 8vo, price 2s. 6d. cloth.

SWAINSON'S ACCOUNT OF AUCKLAND.
Post 8vo, with a view, price 6s. cloth.

PLAYFORD'S HINTS FOR INVESTING MONEY.
Second Edition, post 8vo, price 2s. 6d. cloth.

SIR JOHN FORBES' MEMORANDUMS IN IRELAND.
Two Vols., post 8vo, price 1l. 1s. cloth.

LEIGH HUNT'S MEN, WOMEN, AND BOOKS.
Two Vols., price 10s. cloth.
——— TABLE TALK. 3*s.* 6*d.* *cloth.*
——— WIT AND HUMOUR. 5*s.* *cloth.*
——— IMAGINATION AND FANCY. 5*s.* *cl.*
——— JAR OF HONEY. 5*s.* *cloth.*

SIR JOHN HERSCHEL'S ASTRONOMICAL OBSERVATIONS MADE AT THE CAPE OF GOOD HOPE.
4to, with plates, price 4l. 4s. cloth.

DARWIN'S GEOLOGICAL OBSERVATIONS ON CORAL REEFS, VOLCANIC ISLANDS, AND ON SOUTH AMERICA.
With maps, plates, and woodcuts, 10s. 6d. cloth.

LEVI'S COMMERCIAL LAW OF THE WORLD.
2 Vols., royal 4to, price 6l. cloth.

JUVENILE DELINQUENCY. By M. HILL and C. F. CORNWALLIS. *Post 8vo, price 6s. cloth.*

DOUBLEDAY'S TRUE LAW OF POPULATION.
Third Edition, 8vo, 10s. cloth.

McCANN'S ARGENTINE PROVINCES, &c.
Two vols., post 8vo, with illustrations, price 24s. cloth.

ROWCROFT'S TALES OF THE COLONIES.
Fifth Edition. 6s. cloth.

GOETHE'S CONVERSATIONS WITH ECKERMANN.
Translated by JOHN OXENFORD. *2 vols. post 8vo, 10s. cloth.*

KAVANAGH'S WOMEN OF CHRISTIANITY EXEMPLARY FOR PIETY AND CHARITY. *Post 8vo, with Portraits, price 12s., in embossed cloth, gilt edges.*

KAVANAGH'S WOMAN IN FRANCE DURING THE 18th Century. 2 *vols. Post 8vo, with 8 Portraits, 12s., in embossed cloth.*

Poetry.

ENGLAND IN TIME OF WAR. By SYDNEY DOBELL, Author of "Balder," "The Roman," &c. *Crown 8vo, price 5s. cloth.*

"'England in Time of War' is a series of lyrics representing the emotions of those who are left at home to bear the passive sorrows of war, and of those who go out to brave its perils."—*Westminster Review.*

"That Mr. Dobell is a poet, 'England in time of War' bears witness in many single lines, and in two or three short poems."—*Athenæum.*

THE CRUEL SISTER, AND OTHER POEMS. *Fcap. 8vo, 4s. cloth*

POEMS. By MRS. FRANK P. FELLOWS. *Fcap. 8vo, 3s. cloth.*

"There is much easy simplicity in the diction, and elegant naturalness in the thought."—*Spectator.*

LOTA, AND OTHER POEMS. By DEVON HARRIS. *Fcap. 8vo, 4s. cloth.*

"Displaying high poetic genius and power."—*Eclectic Review.*

POEMS OF PAST YEARS. By SIR ARTHUR HALLAM ELTON, Bart., M.P. *Foolscap 8vo, price 3s. cloth.*

POETRY FROM LIFE. By C. M. K. *Fcap. 8vo, cloth gilt, 5s.*

"Elegant verses. The author has a good ear, a pleasing fancy, and a refined mind."—*Economist.*

"In some of the pieces of this genial and pleasant volume we are reminded of good old George Herbert."—*Literary Gazette.*

"The characteristics of these verses are grace, tenderness, and earnestness."—*Brighton Herald.*

"Very readable and pleasant."—*Examiner.*

POEMS. By WALTER R. CASSELS. *Foolscap 8vo, price 3s. 6d. cloth.*

"Mr. Cassels has deep poetical feeling, and gives promise of real excellence. His poems are written sometimes with a strength of expression by no means common. In quiet narrative and the description of a particular state of feeling, and the presentation of a single thought or image, he shows great power."—*Guardian.*

GARLANDS OF VERSE. By THOMAS LEIGH. *Fcap. 8vo, 5s. cl.*

"One of the best things in the 'Garlands of Verse' is an Ode to Toil. There, as elsewhere, there is excellent feeling."—*Examiner.*

"Pleasing verses, sketching nature well, and displaying force which promises further development."—*Athenæum.*

BALDER. By SYDNEY DOBELL. *Crown 8vo, 7s. 6d. cloth.*

"This drama exhibits the growth of a morbid and immense ambition, its struggles, its misery, and its sin. A most legitimate subject for tragic presentation, this descent of the moral being in proportion to the proposed ascent of the intellectual, and duly fit to 'purge the soul with pity and terror.'"—*British Quarterly Review.*

"The writer has fine qualities; his level of thought is lofty, and his passion for the beautiful has the truth of instinct."—*Athenæum.*

POEMS. By WILLIAM BELL SCOTT. *Foolscap 8vo, with Three Etchings, price 5s. cloth.*

"Mr. Scott has poetical feeling, keen observation, deep thought, and command of language."—*Spectator.*

"These poems, by a Painter, are stamped with the impress of a masculine and vigorous intellect, full of thought and with great force of expression."—*Guardian.*

POEMS. By MARY MAYNARD. *Foolscap 8vo, 4s. cloth.*

"We have rarely met with a volume of poems displaying so large an amount of power, blended with so much delicacy of feeling and grace of expression."—*Church of England Quarterly.*

POEMS. By CURRER, ELLIS, and ACTON BELL. *Fcp. 8vo, 4s. cloth.*

DOINE; or, NATIONAL LEGENDS OF ROUMANIA. Translated by E. C. GRENVILLE MURRAY, Esq. With Music. *Crown 8vo, price 7s. 6d. cl.*